The Sleepwalker's Introduction to Flight

SIÔN SCOTT–WILSON

The Sleepwalker's Introduction to Flight

Macmillan New Writing

First published 2008 by Macmillan New Writing
an imprint of Pan Macmillan Ltd
Pan Macmillan, 20 New Wharf Road, London N1 9RR
Basingstoke and Oxford
Associated companies throughout the world
www.panmacmillan.com

ISBN 978-0-230-70544-9

1 3 5 7 9 8 6 4 2

A CIP catalogue record for this book is available
from the British Library.

Typeset by Intype Libra, London
Printed and bound in Great Britain by
MPG Books Ltd, Bodmin, Cornwall

For my father, Hugh.

We miss you.

Acknowledgements

I'd like to thank all those people who made this novel a reality:

The entire team at Macmillan, especially Will Atkins, my editor, for his faith, insight, patience and all-round brilliance. It's been a wonderful experience.

I'd also like to thank Sian, my incomparable wife, for helping me through the writing process. You've always been my greatest supporter in all things. And thanks for dealing with all the upturned 2CVs.

For any writer encouragement is the fuel that keeps us going. I've been fortunate to receive regular top-ups from: Audrie and Simon Clarke, Nigel Hinshelwood and Lizzie, Heather Manners, David Thackray, Richard Manners, Victoria Helstrip, Rick and Susie Burridge, Malcolm Pryce, my mum Yvonne, Tanya Morel, Fiona Benn, Jean and Stan Lewis, Fiona and Rupert Lewis, Mark and Nikki Sayer-Wade, Siobhan, Bill, Sharon, Harry, Nell, Shay, Dee, Elspeth, Dave.

Thanks also to David and Sue for the medical bit.

Finally, thanks to my boys, Cameron and Rory, for providing the PS2 soundtrack.

Prologue

The figure on the precipice is a distant sketch, lacking all detail. There is nothing to show what has brought him to this. He's a man literally on the edge, perhaps even the brink of madness.

He stands motionless, arms outstretched like a sleep-walker, and yet is surely more awake and alive at this moment than most of us will ever be.

For an instant he hangs, leaning into nothing before exploding in a blur of motion, a human pyrotechnic; whirling, spinning, fizzing as gravity takes him.

At the last possible second he unfurls, comes to a point and plunges, like a perfect dagger, into the waves below.

One

I'm in the tub, one of those massive ancient things with curly feet; cast iron overlaid with a whitish skin of enamel. Despite my mother's Vim and vigour, the enamel appears to have contracted some kind of geriatric disease over the years; the areas of most frequent contact have become brown and scabby and are beginning to flake, like tiny liver spots. The good news is that I can gently scratch my back as I lie here, immersed in the oily, opalescent distillation of Wright's Coal Tar soap.

I like to pretend that my willy is a little man on a desert island, which, for complicated geophysical reasons, is sinking into the sea. I waggle him about, frantically searching for rescue. The island continues to descend, slowly and inexorably, into the warm grey water, taking the castaway with it. Then up he pops once again, revitalized and wearing an inflatable life jacket. Obviously, you can't keep a good man down. But I have to exercise caution here, as I'm forbidden to lock the door. My mother has already caught me at this game once before. She went cross-eyed and all sort of gaspy: 'Bernard, he's playing with himself again,' she shrieked, like I was drowning. I'm an only child and very unlikely to be getting a brother or sister any day now, so frankly, who the hell else would I be playing with? But there's no point having that kind of conversation with my mother.

For this, my father rewarded me with a good talking-to – a rambling stream of euphemism and bluster featuring a variety of improbable musical instruments. These occasional lectures are more or less his only form of communication with me and invariably leave us both disappointed and resentful.

Bernard Hough is perhaps ten years older than my mother; a short, pugnacious man with a comb-over who seems to have gone through life with a perpetually surprised expression on his face – like the world just twanged his braces. His favourite expression is 'Oh really?' but he can deliver it with such a variety of subtle inflections that he can make it mean almost anything he wants it to. My father's 'Oh really?'s contain a veritable cornucopia of meaning if you know how to decipher them. He was a bank manager back in the seventies, one of the first to catch the property boom on the back of a one-per cent preferential staff mortgage, which has left him a very wealthy man. His last regional manager was a man by the name of O'Reilly and, from time to time, I amuse myself by imagining my father's conversations with his ex-boss.

I also amuse myself by farting, though rarely in front of my parents. My mother always looks so disappointed, as though this perfectly normal bodily function was some kind of wretched and devastating moral lapse: 'Has someone left the gas tap on?' She sniffs sanctimoniously. So I tend to restrict this activity to the bathroom. There's only me to offend for one thing, and I am never offended by my own farts; although I am occasionally surprised. On especially flatulent days I pretend to be a Clavadista, one of the brotherhood of Acapulcan high-divers, luxuriating in the jacuzzi after a breathtaking, clifftop performance.

I decide that 'castaway' is too risky today. My mother is under the weather again and has taken to her bed, which is only two rooms away from the bathroom. Instead, I decide to resume training. I've been refining this technique for a couple of years now, ever since I stumbled across Miguel Sanchez Domingo on Youtube. Miguel is the Clavadista Loco, greatest of all cliff-divers; he even has his own website.

I clamber up on to the slippery edge of the tub and balance by curling my toes over the rim. Unlike Miguel and the genuine Clavadistas of La Quebrada, who employ an absolutely perpendicular entry, I use the flat-dive method, in order to dissipate kinetic energy. I launch myself at the steaming surface in a bellyflop.

Almost immediately I can sense that something is wrong. I recall reading somewhere that it is possible to kill a person by driving the nasal bone into the brain and, for a ghastly moment, I fear that this is what I have done to myself.

I'm underwater now, floaty. The scary thing is that I know that the warm creamy water surrounding me is gradually turning red. But really, I'm too tired and comfortable to care.

Two

It seems that my mother has saved my life, but only because she urgently needed the bathroom. I think she was more relieved to find me drowning than playing 'castaway'. Nevertheless, the sight of my naked buttocks bobbing up and down in that blood soup appears to have delayed her recuperation by a week or two.

I'm in the spare room, assessing the damage in the dressing-table mirror. It's one of those chintzy, fussy antiques with a triptych mirror designed for four-foot-something Victorian ladies, so it's ideal for my father to adjust his comb-over.

I crouch to inspect my face and profile. No surprises there. I was never the most gorgeous of specimens, but at fifteen, I do have youth on my side. I'm slim, clean-limbed, olive-complexioned, but my nose has been horribly bent and now points emphatically to the left. In later life I might have attained a certain swarthy, brooding appeal, but that's out of the question now. I have become Eddie Munster's elder brother.

I console myself with my hair. I've got great hair, incredibly thick, black and luxuriant hair, which is why I now spend so much time with my back bent, locked inside these three angled mirrors, admiring the back of my head. From behind,

I'm a great advertisement for shampoo, from the front, seat belts.

Our GP, Dr Hemstock, tells me that my nose bone is now frangible and can no longer be relied upon to protect my face or brain. This strikes me as odd. I have never found my nose to be much good for protecting my brain – usually the other way round.

I consider the words of Miguel for the millionth time: 'You cannot begin to live unless you take yourself to the edge.' He's right of course, total immersion is what I need; absolute commitment. To a Clavadista a broken nose means nothing, a minor setback – although in the case of my nose, it's a setback of some forty-five degrees from the perpendicular.

It's pretty clear I've outgrown the bathtub.

I'm startled by the creak of a floorboard. In the doorway is my father, puce in the face, as always, waving an ancient wooden Slazenger tennis racquet. I drop to a protective crouch, using both hands to cover my privates. From his expression, I realize that he now suspects me of playing with myself in front of the mirror. For one horrible moment I think he might actually be about to swat me with the racquet and engrave a grid of strings across my pink behind, like some kind of surreal *Financial Times* crossword puzzle. Instead, he simply holds out the racquet. 'Tennis,' he barks. 'You're playing tennis with Coombs and, for God's sake, put some bloody clothes on first.'

'But . . . but I hate tennis,' I stutter.

He arches an eyebrow. 'Oh really?' What this tells me is that he thinks I'm spending far too much time indoors, onanizing; I don't get nearly enough fresh air or exercise; and that today, and probably every day for the rest of the long

7

summer holiday, I'm playing tennis with sodding Coombs whether I like it or not.

I dress quickly in a mixture of old sportswear and find the smirking Coombs in the driveway, leaning against his black Range Rover. Barry Coombs owns the detached turreted red-brick Victorian house which overlooks our back garden; a great bearded lout of a man who's something or other on the borough council. He's also involved in property and captain of the Caversham Lawn Tennis Club. In short, a pillock of the community.

Coombs wears a pristine white Aertex tennis shirt and a pair of shorts at least three sizes too tight, extruding plump hairy legs like a couple of parboiled Weisswursts. As if he wasn't a grotesque enough caricature of a middle-aged plonker, he's also sporting stripy wristbands and matching towelling headband.

'There he is, the young Henman. Come to show us how it's done, eh, Michael?'

Coombs only talks to me like this when he thinks there's a chance of being overheard by my father. The rest of the time he snarls like a publican's pitbull.

I climb into the Range Rover and buckle up. 'All right, Mr Coombs?' I mumble, in a tone that I hope will discourage further conversation. Some hope. It turns out that Coombs is trying to inveigle my father into certain dubious local property speculations, which is why he's sucking up and doing him this favour today. Coombs spends the journey pumping me for information as to the likelihood of my father 'filling his boots'. As if I would know. I grunt a few mono-syllables and jiggle the electronic windows until Coombs cuts me off with the master switch.

*

Out on the hallowed turf of the Caversham Lawn Tennis Club, Coombs unzips a gigantic racquet bag and selects one of perhaps half a dozen state-of-the-art graphite racquets from its depths. 'Right, Mikey, your dad wants me to play you in. But – and it is a big but, as the bishop said to the actress – even though I'd like to do your dad a solid, you need to be of a certain standard to become a full-time card-carrying member of the Caversham Lawn Tennis Association. No exceptions. You've got to be good. I can't make allowances. Got it?'

I nod dumbly and try not to grin, caper, or leap the net for joy. Game, set and match to me. Coombs doesn't realize it, but with those words he's just enabled me to ace my father and utterly scuttle his plans for getting me out of the house this summer. I'm going to play so awfully and with such potty-mouthed bad grace it'll make Greg Rusedski sound like a Mormon choirboy.

'Oh, yeah, and Mikey, your dad wants me to let him know whether I think you've been really trying. If not, he'll want to know the reason why. You're not to muck about, basically.' With that, Coombs throws the ball high and does a corkscrewy thing with his arm.

I'm not ready, for one thing; I'm still in shock from the way my father has vicariously smash-returned my best efforts at scuppering him straight down the tramlines; and for another, this wooden Slazenger racquet is completely wonky; warped from having sat in our damp garage for twenty years without the benefit of a press. I give Coombs's serve a half-hearted swat but it spins away from me like a googly from Shane Warne.

In truth, I'm not that bad at tennis. At any rate, I know I can do better than this. Although I loathe sports, the school games master, Evans-the-Physical, tells me I do have unusually good balance and hand to eye coordination.

'Right, warm-up over,' barks Coombs.

I stand on the baseline and watch Coombs's bizarre wind-up. This time I'm prepared: I step back and take a pace to the right, allowing the off-spinning ball to bounce and begin its downward arc. When it does, I catch it with a stunning top-spin from the Slazenger's sweet spot. Only there is no sweet spot, just sour rotten catgut mesh, which emits a loud cartoon-like twang as the bright yellow ball pings off and sails over the fence into the trees beyond. I can feel the painful vibrations all the way up to my elbow.

'Right, Michael, you can owe me for that ball.'

Coombs continues to paste me into the beautifully trimmed lawns with his oversized racquet head. But – and it is a fairly big but, as the young athlete said to the fat bearded lout – as the match continues odd members of the club begin to cluster around the court and, for some reason, begin to cheer me on.

Coombs enjoys a crowd. He makes an 'aggahhh' sound when he serves, as though the effort is devastating his trapezoids; he preens and prances athletically, huffing and spluttering like there was a championship at stake. Each time I take a point, though, I'm applauded wildly and I can see it's getting to him.

Coombs swishes ineffectively at one of my rare passing shots. 'Bad luck,' he bellows, without troubling to see where the ball lands.

'Actually, I think it was in.'

'Don't think so, Michael.'

'I'm sure it was.'

Coombs approaches the net and beckons me over. He keeps his voice low, mindful of the crowd.

'It can be in if you like,' he hisses, 'in which case, you're out. Or it can be out, in which case I might still decide to play you in. Up to you.'

It's a good point and I concede it.

'Forty, love,' he announces, to murmurs of disapproval from the sidelines.

He winds up again and sends down a rocket.

'In,' he exults, punching the air.

It's not, of course. Not even close.

We change ends. I manage to serve a fizzer which, due to the idiosyncrasies of my antique wooden racquet, swerves through the air like a pretzel and bounces straight up into Coombs's tightly sheathed nuts. I am given what can only be described as a standing ovation by the spectators.

Inevitably though, and despite the urging of the crowd, I lose in three straight sets: six-love, six-love, six-one.

Coombs leaps the net. Happily, he catches a trailing foot and down he goes, the back of his head crashing into the lawn. He picks himself up, feigning indifference, and trots over, all smiles and bonhomie. He grips my hand, hard. Too hard.

'Did I . . . am I played in?'

Coombs smirks, applying more pressure.

The members begin to disperse but two bright-eyed, sprightly old ladies wander over – identical twins by the looks of it.

Coombs releases my hand.

'The boy played well, Coombs, and with a busted old racquet too.'

'What are you thinking of, letting the boy play with a broken racquet?'

Coombs recoils and raises his eyebrows. As he does so, the tight, sopping headband crawls up his slimy forehead before suddenly contracting at the top of his head, flipping his thick salt-and-pepper hair into a sumo wrestler topknot. 'Look, I didn't force him to . . .'

The ladies shriek with mirth, which instantly endears

them to me. I want to howl with laughter too as he snatches away the offending headband. But I keep a straight face since Coombs currently holds my fate in his sweaty paws. 'I did try though, Mr Coombs.'

'Of course you tried, love,' replies one of the old dears.

'Not much you can do with a racquet like that though. Shame that Coombs didn't think to lend you one of his,' sniffs her sibling.

'He's got some lovely racquets.'

'A great sackful.'

Coombs bristles and looms over the twins. 'Look, you two, I can cancel your memberships right now, and then what are you going to do all day, collect old plastic bags in a shopping trolley and talk to your cats?'

The sisters stand their ground for a second before scuttling away. 'The boy was good. He played his heart out,' one of them gets in a Parthian shot.

'The Pond sisters,' spits Coombs. 'Pain in the arse. Always late with their subs.'

I look down at the grass and try not to smile. 'Well, I tried, Mr Coombs,' I say with a touch of unctuousness, 'but I just wasn't good enough.'

'No. You weren't good enough.'

'But I did try.'

'You tried to make me look a prat.'

'But you'll tell my father I tried?'

'I'll think on it.'

Coombs spins on his heel. He packs his racquets and I observe with satisfaction a great indelible emerald and brown grass stain smeared down the back of his white shorts. I'm still gloating about this when I realize that the bastard has gone and driven off without me.

Three

I've spent the morning at Edmund Kerr's.

Edmund is my only friend and, indeed, only my friend because I pay him: I pay him to use his laptop – Bernard believes that the internet is a corrupting influence, so I don't have a connection at home, or even a computer for that matter – and I pay him so that my father can see me hanging out with him. My father generally approves of Edmund and the Kerrs.

I hate Edmund with a passion.

Alison Kerr, his mother, is a grumpy old heifer from Morningside. Although I've never been to Edinburgh, I've done a bit of internet research on Edmund's computer and one of the jokes about Morningside ladies is that they're so tight they greet you at the door with the words: 'You'll have had your tea then?' I can vouch for this. Even though I've known Edmund nearly all my life I've yet to be offered so much as a beaker of bath-water by Mrs Kerr.

She thinks the sun shines out of her son's fundament. It doesn't. It shines down from a clear blue sky through the lens of Edmund's merciless magnifying glass on to the fur or skull of whichever luckless rodent Edmund has in his power. Like most classic fledgling psychopaths, Edmund has graduated from ants and spiders and likes to bind small rodents in Sellotape before griddling their brains.

He also enjoys downloading Japanese bondage pornography on to his computer – I've checked his internet Favourites file.

The arrangement is that he leaves me alone to surf the net. For the past few weeks I've been conducting an online investigation into the history of the Clavadistas in the blissful solitude of his bedroom. Edmund only puts in an appearance when Mrs Kerr brings the lunch tray.

Naturally, I'm forbidden to touch it.

I detest watching Edmund eat but it's hard not to, given that he regards lunch as some kind of spectator sport.

'I'm having one of my ham sarnies now,' he announces.

I keep my back to him while I click away. 'You realize that the Clavadistas of La Quebrada dive from a height of a hundred and twenty feet into just eleven feet of water? And that's if they're lucky. It's a shallow inlet, so the trick is to synchronize your dive with the incoming waves. You can't pull out if your timing's off. And then there's the wind to consider. It's pretty amazing really. Get one tiny thing wrong and . . .'

'. . . You're a jam sandwich. A great soggy jam sandwich,' slobbers Edmund. 'This one's ham, though, soda bread and wholegrain mustard with honey-glazed ham.'

I'm trying to shut him out but my stomach is growling like a junkyard dog.

'It says here that there's been cliff-diving in La Quebrada since the eighteenth century and that it may have had a religious, or at least, spiritual significance. Even today Clavadistas still say a prayer at the shrine of Our Lady of Guadalupe at the top of the cliff. The dive is an act of faith. I find that very inspiring.'

'I'm going to have a biscuit now. Will it be the milk chocolate Hob-Nob, the Ginger Nut, or the Jammy Dodger? Hmm, I wonder, I wonder, wonder, wonder . . .'

I don't wonder at all. He's going to eat all three of them along with everything else on the congested tray.

'In Matzelan, this old guy, Mario Gonzales Aguilar, is still diving at sixty-seven. How cool is that?'

'Perhaps I should offer Mikey one today?'

I know it's a trap, but I can't help myself: I spin in the chair, eyes wide. I should have known better. Edmund has only forced me to turn so that I can watch him take a bite from the enormous wedge of Black Forest gateau in his chubby fist.

In my own back garden I pace the lawn, assessing our trees, finally fixing on the large oak by the hedge. It's climbable and there's a good, solid, overhanging branch about twenty feet high.

'What's up with you then, silly-arse?' In a clatter of loose metal parts Gerry hauls out the old Punch mower. I'm always pleased to see Gerry, so I grin; the kind of smile that actually stretches my face and makes the cheek muscles ache. They're not used to the exercise.

Gerry's a true mate.

Not a friend exactly, because I'm only fifteen and he's about seven or eight years older, but he's a lovely man. That sounds a bit gay but I don't think I am gay. I'm fond of Gerry because he treats me like what I say matters, like an adult. And he lets me read his comics.

Gerry drives a battered Toyota pick-up with an exhaust like a Swiss cheese and comes about once a fortnight to mow our lawn – we never quite know when. My father employs Gerry because he's the only person capable of breathing life into the antique Punch mower in the garage. For some reason, my father believes that a lawn should have stripes, and proper stripes can only be achieved with an old-fashioned motor-mower.

Gerry adores plants and dreams of becoming a botanist, but to the world at large he's just a greasy-haired, oily-fingered layabout with no future and an antisocial car. My mother hates Gerry for almost exactly the same reasons that I adore him. She thinks he's a man with tattoos; she doesn't know the half of it. Gerry is *the* tattooed man – an entirely different thing. In the garden, Gerry wears a black T-shirt and cut-away black jeans, but I've seen Gerry's body in all its glory. Sometimes when it's hot and my parents are out, he strips off down to his grey undercrackers and sunbathes. Every inch of Gerry's body other than his face, neck, and possibly the groin area, is covered in virulent green, red and blue ink. I'm not sure about 'down there' because Gerry has never offered to show me. I'm curious of course, but don't like to ask.

The thing about Gerry is that he's a work of literature as well as being a work of art. I'm not talking D. H. Lawrence here, more DC Comics. Some of Gerry's vignettes are every bit as exquisitely rendered as Art Kane's finest. I know, because over the past few years Gerry has been smuggling all the latest issues in to me.

I adore Marvel's Iron Man because he's physically knack-ered but I especially like DC's new version of Batman, the Dark Knight, because he's so . . . well, dark and psycho-logically flawed.

Gerry is himself, a cartoon character. If you care, or can bear, to inspect the miniscule but lovingly rendered frames adorning his torso you'll begin to understand him. You can see imprinted across his skin the chronicles of Gerry, a potted history as it were. There's a four-frame sequence radiating from his right shoulder in which he qualifies from the world's top universities and receives doctorates from Oxford, Stamford, Harvard and, oddly, Hull. Elsewhere, Gerry is depicted discovering a new species of orchid in the jungles of South America. In another ten-frame sequence across the small of his back you can see how Gerry's cultivar-breaking viruses have become the wonder of the tulip world. Gerry later develops a new strain of green rye-grass which is found to have anti-oxidant and anti-ageing properties. After a great many floralogical adventures Gerry establishes a botanical academy before retiring, aged thirty, to a Bruce-Wayne-style mansion, complete with rose gardens and a fabulous collection of souped-up ride-on motor-mowers. The curious thing about these comic-book fantasies is that they all, without exception, depict Gerry sans tattoos.

Gerry knows everything about plants and horticulture but what prevents him getting the first foot on the ladder to success are the very tattoos he sports. Gerry is a contradiction in his own skin.

'Hey Gerry,' I shout, 'know anything about Clavadistas?'

Gerry silently rolls a thin squirt of tobacco in a Rizla sheath, licks it shut and lights up. He takes a puff and exhales a sad sigh of smoke. 'Aspidistras, I know everything about aspidistras. Clavadistas, I've never heard of.' He sucks away, decimating the slim roll-up like the fuse of a cartoon bomb.

'It's a brotherhood of high-divers and I'm going to be one.'

'Good for you,' he says, tweezing the burning ember between blackened finger and thumb, pocketing the remainder. 'How can I help?'

I point up at the thick oak branch high above our heads. 'We're gonna need a stack of planking to build a stable platform off there,' I announce, 'and a kid's paddling pool.'

Gerry considers this for a moment. 'That shouldn't be a problem, Mikey,' he says.

Honestly, you've just got to love someone like that.

Four

Unlike my father, I'm not good with money. On Friday mornings he gives me the princely sum of five pounds, which I have to sign for in a scary-looking leather-bound ledger. I suspect this is a bit under the odds. I only have Edmund Kerr to go by and it's about a quarter of what he gets. I supplement it by doing little jobs that are too small for Gerry, like weeding for the Postlethwaites (but I suspect they're ripping me off).

I'm not sure I understand the principle of pocket money – what does it actually represent? If it's remuneration for all the work I do around the house like washing and drying, taking out the rubbish, polishing the shoes, etc., then I'm earning considerably less than the minimum hourly rate and may need to alert the European Court of Human Rights. If, on the other hand, it's simply a token of the pride and joy I bring my parents then I'm on to a bit of a winner here.

Two or three pounds of the bounty usually goes straight to Edmund for letting me mooch around his house and use his computer. The rest I spend on myself.

I'm in a kind of halfway house at the moment; a moist, watery shed between the states of childhood and manhood. I spend my money on a combination of sweets, chewing gum, Airfix models and, occasionally, fags. I bought a six-pack of Stella Artois once but didn't much like the taste and nearly threw up. I gave the remaining cans to Gerry with the words, 'Here, have a Stella . . . or trois.' I don't think he got it.

I've been avoiding Edmund for a couple of weeks, so I can save up for lumber and nails, which are surprisingly expensive – even the two-by-four offcuts.

'What? You thought this stuff grew on trees or something?' said Len, the old yardman in the green coat as we loaded up Gerry's Toyota – really, he's wasted on Jewsons.

Gerry's up in the oak with a saw while I direct operations from below. I haven't supplied him with specs or a plan or anything but I'm confident that Gerry knows exactly what he's doing.

'And what exactly do you think you're doing up there in my bloody tree?' My father stands at the top of the lawn, quivering like a rabid mastiff.

'I have no idea, Mr Hough, it's a project of Mikey's.'

Thanks, Gerry, I think, shuddering at the 'H' word – Hough. It's my surname too but I loathe it. I don't mind my first name at all; it's classical, biblical and capable of contraction to Mike or Mikey without being harnessed to some disagreeable rhyming couplet, unlike, say, Hank, Billy or Enus. But Hough – pronounced 'Hoff' – sounds like a punch in the stomach, or an elderly asthmatic, hawking up in the morning.

Hough. Hough. Hough. Even though my father has been able to trace our ancestry back to the Doomsday Book, I wish it could have been something cool, like Blaze, or Bond, or Flint. My mother was a Cooper, which is not so bad. They say that most Anglo-Saxon surnames reflect an occupation of some sort; you can find millions of Smiths in the phone book and you know exactly what their ancestors did in the medieval villages. The same is true of Bakers, Butchers,

Farmers, Brewers, Fowlers and Farriers. You have to wonder what the Houghs got up to though. Personally, I think they just sat there coughing up sputum and passing on disease: *'You need a barrel made, Aelfric? Go thou and see Cooper, second wattle-and-daub lean-to on the right. Arrows? Speak with Fletcher there. Ah, Wulfsten, you want the bloody flux? Get a couple of days off work? Go and talk to Ethelred Hough, he'll sort you out.'*

The twentieth-century Hough is still standing at the top of the lawn, waiting for a response, tapping a brown brogue, huffing.

'Gerry's helping me build a tree house.'

My father's eyes narrow.

'It's okay, I bought the stuff with my own money, from Jewsons. I've got receipts.'

He clicks his fingers. I retrieve the crumpled papers from my pockets and hand them over. My father pockets them, no doubt for his accountant as a tax write-off, and purses his lips before gazing up at Gerry again. I can tell that he thinks Gerry sitting on a high branch armed with a hammer and saw is a recipe for disaster. 'I hope you know that I'm not paying you for this, Gerry.'

'I do know that, Mr H.'

'Good. And if you saw that branch off while you're sitting on the wrong end, you'll break your neck. And I'm not insured against cretinism.'

'I'm aware of that too, Mr H. I was just fixing up a two-by-four platform for the lad – on my own time.'

'Good. Well, on your own time then.' With that, my father disappears back into the house through the French windows.

*

Our positions are reversed: I'm now the one twenty-foot up the oak, standing gingerly on Gerry's cobbled-together platform. The overlapping timbers creak and shift under my feet as I inch towards the edge, shivering in my trunks. 'Now I know why they call things Gerry-built,' I say. It's not a good joke, not even close; I only say it because I'm shit-scared and gibbering.

'Shut the fuck up and do your dive,' wheezes Gerry from the lawn below. He's out of breath from inflating the paddling pool; he takes a quick drag on a skeletal Rizla to open up the bronchials. 'Get on with it, Mikey. I've got somewhere else to be this afternoon.'

Gerry's got the garden hose pumping away in the plastic pool, the two-and-a-half-foot-high walls are overflowing with crystal-clear water. At this altitude it resembles a stray contact lens. I suddenly realize what a ballsy little bastard the Great Miguel actually is, given that he's spent his career flinging himself from twice this height on a daily basis.

'Do it or don't do it,' orders Gerry. 'Just make it quick.'

From this height I can look right into the second-floor windows of Coombs's Victorian Gothic monstrosity over the hedge. I gaze up a floor to the window of the nearest turret – blank like all the rest. I'm just wasting time here, trying to delay the inevitable. I labour to control my breathing and try to visualize a perfectly pancake-flat entry into the pool. My heart is beating furiously now; I focus on the shingled turret next door instead of the target below. Suddenly the spectral figure of a young girl in flowing white appears at the grey-green window. She looks me dead in the eyes, pleading, mouthing a message; pounding at the pane as though trying to escape.

I blink and she's gone.

The platform creaks ominously as I shift my weight. 'Ah . . . Gerry, I think I just saw a ghost.'

'Was it yours?'

'Uh . . . no. I don't think so.'

'Then you got nothing to worry about. Just fucking dive, will you?'

I curl my toes over the edge. 'Ah . . . I definitely saw something weird next door.'

Gerry cranes his head, peering up like a worker-ant on the sniff of sugar. 'You're panicking, Mikey, hyperventilating. I can hear it from down here. You know what? I think this is a really bad idea. Just stay where you are and I'll come and get you, okay?' Gerry begins to ascend the little wooden batons that we've nailed to the trunk.

There's no way I'm going to let Gerry coax me down from the oak like a stranded kitten, or worse, carry me down. So I push off from the platform, launching myself in a flat-dive out into space.

Five

I'm conscious and can sense that time has passed but it's not like waking from a dream where there are random memories, fractured impressions and snatches of thought. A nano-second ago there was nothing: no sense of self. In an instant I'm here and aware. I think therefore I am.

There's no fuzziness, either, no blurry, confused after-effects – I'm not God or Napoleon, I know with crystal clarity that I'm Mikey Hough, apprentice Clavadista.

I also know that I didn't land right, which is why I'm keeping my eyes shut. I didn't entirely miss the paddling pool: I remember my lower torso slapping water even as my face hit the lawn with a sickening thump. Here's something else Miguel should tell the kids – apart from 'Don't try this at home' – 'In this business, a miss is as good as a mile.' I can't feel anything below my neck and don't want to open my eyes, in case I'm just a head on the pillow.

'Hello, Michael.' A voice I don't recognize; nice warm voice with the kind of accent I've only ever heard in films.

'It's Mikey,' I reply, but the words are distorted.

Oh Christ – they've amputated my body at the Adam's apple and given me a cyborg voicebox.

'Mikey, is it? And here we are, all this time, been calling you Michael.'

'How bad am I?' I croak.

I can hear a sharp intake of breath. 'Oh, you bad, Mikey. I'm waiting to find out what your daddy going to do when he sees you awake.'

Thanks for reminding me, whoever you are. Perhaps he'll just clout me around the head with a rolled-up newspaper and leave it at that.

'Come on now, Mikey, open them eyes. We been taking bets on what colour your eyes are.'

'I don't want to,' replies the cyborg in a weird tremolo. 'I think I might have bits missing.'

'Oh, no. You all there, boy. Believe me, you are definitely all there.'

Whoever this person is, she's not taking this conversation that seriously. No decent person would do that to a para-plegic, or a mere head on a pillow. Maybe, just maybe, I got away with it after all. I flutter my eyes and am instantly blinded by the glare.

'Ah shit, they green. I lost five pounds on you, Mikey. Here, boy, put these on and I'll chase the sun away.' I hear the swoosh of curtains being drawn and the unmistakable sounds of a woman rummaging in a handbag. She gently hooks a pair of sunglasses over my ears.

It takes me a while but by blinking and squinting through the dark lenses I can make out the shape of my bed and, thank God, the outline of my own unabbreviated body beneath the sheet. I can make out colours too. It's a hospital room but not brilliant white as I first imagined: the walls and curtains are a glossy utilitarian mint-green, same as my sheets. The only additional splashes of colour come from the tubes emanating from my body: bright reds and a lurid yellow.

'Oh, don't you look fine.'

I can move my head a little, so I gaze up into the enormous, shining face of my nurse.

'I'm Aggie – Nurse Koroma to you, boy, and don't be thinking about giving me any trouble just because you're awake now.' She reaches for my limp hand and takes it in her own. I can just feel her dry touch, like the ghost of a handshake. I can't see her face though, because amazingly, my eyes are filled with tears. I don't remember anyone looking quite so pleased to see me before.

'Aggie!' I shout. 'I need Nurse Aggie.' I've been drinking plenty of water but the voice is all wrong, not quite as metallic, but still strange to my ears.

Eventually Aggie trundles into my room, all sixteen stone of her, and she's not happy. 'I told you, Mikey, it's Nurse Koroma.'

A while ago, as I winced in agony, Aggie removed the catheter tube from my urethra, so I feel I have every right to be on first-name terms here. I'm still as weak as a kitten and, although I'm slowly getting feeling and movement back in my limbs, I'm not yet capable of hauling myself out of bed. I must pee, and since Aggie's already seen my willy on more than one occasion, she draws the short straw, so to speak.

Aggie brings a bedpan, pulls back the sheet and I scream in terror. Forget about the voice, they've amputated my modest little castaway and given me, in return, a great clumsy truncheon of a thing wearing a fright-wig; a terrible, God-forsaken donkey's knob of a transplant.

'What *is* this place? What have you people done to me, Aggie?' I sob as I writhe around the bed.

Aggie gives up on the bedpan and holds her head in her hands. 'Oh boy,' she sighs, 'they don't pay me enough for this.'

*

I'm dead.

In Hell.

Forget the lake of fire. Hell is trudging on jelly-legs, going nowhere for all eternity. Satan's minions wear lime-green nylon and whoop at me. Motivational phrases, mostly. My thoughts are jumbled but I try to shut them up by dropping one trembling foot in front of the other. It only makes them worse.

Occasionally they let me lie down. This is when Aggie appears and makes it all go away.

Aggie always wears white. I think she might be an angel.

'Your father has promised to come tomorrow. I spoke with him on the phone this afternoon and he's delighted to hear that you're recovering your strength. He's given me permission to chat with you now,' Dr Darrow explains in a gentle, mellifluous middle-class voice.

I like Dr Darrow very much, but then I'm fond of everyone right now: Dr Darrow has given me some kind of tranquillizer which enables me to take on information without getting hysterical and deliberately missing the bedpan.

'The thing is, Mikey, you've been lucky. Other than shattering your cheekbones and nose, the accident has done no major . . . uh . . . *physical* damage. I'm afraid we've been keeping you in a semi-comatose state since you came round a fortnight ago; our physios have been working you on the treadmill and it's given us time to do a few tests. Naturally you are somewhat weak through muscle wastage, which is quite normal. Although I would advise against entering a marathon at this time, physically you are as fit and healthy as can be expected, but . . .'

Darrow produces a hand-mirror from behind his back.

It's lucky that I'm pretty well out of my head on the happy pills because I'm able to laugh and cry at the same time. The damage was bad enough after I dived into the bath, but now my face is something else. My hair is Rip Van Winkle long, and luxuriant as ever, but my cheekbones have no contours whatsoever and my nose has been almost completely recessed into my face. No wonder I was feeling bunged up. I look like Tom the cat after he's been spanged in the face with a frying pan. I'm doubly mortified to discover that I've got one of those wispy little Fu Man Chu moustaches and pathetic bum-fluff beards.

Darrow presses on. 'The thing is, you see, the thing is, you've been in a coma for quite some time. You're eighteen now, Michael.'

Fucking great. I've missed acne and all that adolescent angst. Nothing can prick my happy-bubble right now. 'I see. Well . . . can I have a shave then?'

'I see no reason why not.'

'And a large whisky?' I grin at Aggie. For some reason she's not smiling back.

'Uh . . . there is one other thing,' says Darrow.

Even through the blissed-out haze this doesn't bode well.

'CAT scans have revealed some damage to the brain, although of a very limited and localized nature.'

'Ah.'

'It seems that the trauma to your face may have impacted on the hypothalamus, more specifically a tiny, tiny area known as the suprachiasmatic nucleus.'

'What exactly does that mean?'

'It might mean a great deal or it might mean nothing. The human brain is very resilient. You're not going to be a moron, Mikey, we can see that already.'

'But what might it mean, potentially?'

'Well . . . uh . . . let's discuss that once you're up and about. We've decreased the sedative-hypnotic dosage now, so you should be feeling more yourself. In the meantime, get some rest.'

Six

'In the meantime get some rest.' I mean, really, what kind of advice is that? I've been flat out on this bed for the past two years. My mind is clear and I don't feel remotely like sleeping. I want to run and leap about. I want to make up for the past two years and devour life like Edmund eats lunch. I want to stuff myself with ice cream and Twiglets; feel the wind in my hair, climb trees and drink Stella Artois. Christ, I wouldn't even object to a quick set of tennis with Coombs.

The curtains are drawn and I can tell by the relative silence that it's night. I don't need the sunglasses now, but they're lurid pink and studded with diamanté and I feel more optimistic with them on. Besides, Aggie has fixed them to the flat bridge of my nose with a flesh-wrenching strip of medical sticking plaster.

There's a stack of dog-eared *Reader's Digests* on my locker. I open one at random: 'Laughter, the best medicine.' That's nonsense for a start, the stuff Darrow's been giving me is the best medicine and I'm already planning a hissy-fit tomorrow so I can score another massive dose before my father arrives.

I flick through the curling pages and skim a biographical piece by someone called Chip Burroughs. 'Clubhouse in the Elm' turns out to be a Proustian tale of American childhood and lost love centred around the rickety tree-house at the bottom of Chip's garden. Chip and his saccharine buddies enjoy cook-outs, sleepovers and play interesting games of 'truth or dare' up there in the old elm. At no point do any of them take a running header off the platform into the lawn below – more's the pity.

I don't think I can bear to read about 'Old Smudger – The Dog Who Wouldn't Die', so I roll myself off the bed and go looking for company. Actually, the first thing that happens is that my pipe-cleaner legs collapse beneath me. I don't give up easily though, and crawl away, inching towards the door.

Like Old Smudger.

In the corridor a glinting tubular-steel structure looms over me, an abandoned Zimmer frame. From down here, at ground-zero, it resembles the scaffolding for a Wendy house. I briefly consider the fate of its previous owner and, although I do feel a bit mean about this, I'm going to have to hijack – or more precisely, lojack – the thing. Through a combination of grim determination, locked elbows and some quite astonishing limbo moves I manage to haul myself, hand-over-hand, up the structure. I wait for a brief spell of dizziness to pass before taking my first step. Through the sullen hum of neon lighting, the ubiquitous backbeat of cardiograph, and the squeal of Zimmer wheels on lino, I detect hushed human voices and the occasional stifled laugh.

I shuffle towards the sound and find myself at the threshold of a four-man ward. While the occupants of the two furthest beds sleep soundly, dead to the world, or perhaps just dead, the other two are very much alive and kicking, and playing cards with Nurse Aggie.

'Oh my God, it's Dame Edna's illegitimate son,' chuckles an elderly man with a bruised and puffy face.

Aggie glances up at me before continuing to deal. 'You

better watch your mouth there, Roger. Those be my glasses the boy got taped to his head.'

The three of them inspect their cards. I take this as a tacit approval of my presence and shuffle in. Aggie looks grimly up again in my direction. 'What you doing here, boy, looking like Liberace's ghost?' It seems that only Aggie is allowed to take the piss out of the diamanté glasses.

'I can't sleep.'

'You get yourself back to bed. It's late and there's no decent people awake at this time of night.'

'You're all awake.'

'These ain't decent people. These be two desperate hustlers trying to cheat Aggie out of her rightful fruit.' There's a huge mound of plums, tangerines and black grapes on the table between them.

'You're gambling for grapes?'

'What the hell else would we be playing poker for in a hospital – colostomy bags, used needles, enemas? What do you think, boy?'

'Raise you, Aggie,' says the man with the swollen face.

'Shit,' replies Aggie. Even though I've only read about poker on the internet, her reaction tells us all that she's been bluffing for sure.

'I'm raisin too,' announces the man on Aggie's right, rolling out a pile of purple globes with tightly bandaged fingers. It must be an old joke, no one smiles.

Aggie abruptly folds, leaving the two men to psych each other out. 'You should be in bed.'

'I've been in bed for two years now.'

'Then another night ain't gonna hurt you.'

'Oh, come on, Aggie. And anyway, why aren't you in bed?'

'Aggie's doing double shifts,' explains the man with the bandaged fingers as he hauls in the pot. 'She needs the money.'

I'm glad he's won, he looks like he needs the fruit or indeed, any form of nutrition; he's got that malnourished, pallid skin, stretched tight over angular cheekbones like a storm-rigged tent. He must be fifty or so; red-grey hair sticks upright from his head in a way that suggests a fiery energy, but the stick-thin wrists and ankles protruding from orange cotton pyjamas give the lie to that. I notice that, like his fingers, his toes are also tightly bandaged.

Aggie is still cross about losing but remembers her manners: 'Mr Truffles, this be Mikey. Mikey, this card-sharp be Mr Truffles. Don't never trust his ass where grapes are concerned.'

I shake the mummified hand, thinking: haemorrhoids.

'And this other hustler cheat is Roger.'

'Ah yes, nice to meet you there, Mikey.'

I cop Roger's hand; a strong handshake for an elderly man. Roger has to be eighty, if he's a day, but if there's such a thing as a life-force, he has it in spades. Roger has a battered, bruised black grape for a head and I wonder if he's allowed to slap it down on to the table and break the bank.

'Now, go back to bed, boy,' says Aggie.

'Really, Aggie, I'm just not sleepy.'

'Go to bed, Mikey.'

'Oh come on, Nurse Karoma, does the young man have fruit?' Roger has pitifully few tangerines left to bet with. I suspect his intervention might not be entirely philanthropic.

'That boy got nothing. His folks give him Jack-shit in two years here.'

Nice. Thanks for breaking the news gently, Aggie. But since I've got nothing to bet with, I shrug and prepare to about-Zimmer.

'What about the glasses? I'll have those glasses. I'll trade you a couple of tangerines for them.'

'Them glasses be mine,' Aggie objects but is shouted

down by Mr Truffles, who correctly points out that possession is nine-tenths of the law.

By five thirty a.m. I know almost everything about my opponents: I know that Mr Truffles's real name is Richard Babcock. A celebrity chef back in the eighties, with a string of London restaurants based on the signs of the Zodiac. Ironically, a venture that turned out to have no future – first to founder were Scorpio in Notting Hill and Virgo in South Kensington, bringing the entire celestial empire crashing down with them. Pretty soon Mr Truffles was using the cognac to flambé his own despair. Personal decline followed swiftly and for the past five years he's been living hand-to-mouth, using his old press cuttings to line the walls of the cardboard structure he now calls home. It's been an unseasonably severe spring and massive quantities of brandy have failed to prevent the onset of frostbite in his toes and fingers. I can certainly vouch for his cackhandedness, as I've been able to see all his cards for the last sixteen deals.

Aggie says she comes from a fly-speck town in Louisiana, called Poverty, and claims to have been blown here by Hurricane Juan back in 1985. A gigantic Dorothy in pink diamanté glasses. To be fair, a hurricane *is* about the only force that could uproot someone like Aggie.

I also know that Roger, more precisely retired Squadron Leader Roger Williams, is a genuine World War Two Hurricane pilot. In aerial combat he shot down six aircraft. Now he's stuck here in this ward with a plum for a head. Roger's home was broken into last week; there wasn't much of value other than a Distinguished Flying Cross medal, which the burglars swiped before beating him senseless.

'Right, that's two hundred, give or take, from you, Mr Truffles; three hundred odd from you, Roger; and Aggie . . .

I've given up counting.' Not only have I won the diamanté glasses back, but I'm owed well over a thousand grapes, twenty-seven tangerines, thirty-five kiwi fruit and a bunch of bananas. I'm a gracious victor though, happy to accept signed and witnessed IOUs. It's been a great night and I feel like doing back flips. I prance about the ward – so far as that's possible on a Zimmer frame – celebrating my success.

The game of poker hinges on maintaining a deadpan expression at all times; having a face like a skillet is a distinct advantage.

Seven

'You got a licence for that thing, then?'

I'm in the middle of a slow pirouette on the Zimmer but manage to squeak to a halt.

Two men stand in the doorway. 'My name is Detective Sergeant Davis and this is DC Wenner. We're looking for a Roger Anthony Williams. Ward seven is it?'

'That's me. Good morning to you, officers,' says Roger.

The plainclothes coppers step into the ward. The taller and paler of the two inspects his notebook with pink-rimmed gecko eyes, unconsciously finger-combing the tufts of his ginger moustache. 'DC Wenner and myself have come to speak to you about the burglary of last Friday, July fifteen.'

'I was advised that someone might be along to interview me. I was beginning to give up on you.'

An almost imperceptible swallowtail of irritation appears on Davis's brow. 'The law moves in mysterious ways, Mr Williams. It may surprise you to know that there is a considerable amount of serious crime in the Thames Valley region.'

'I'm quite well aware of that, believe me,' replies Roger.

'You're on our list, Mr Williams, same as everyone else. It's long list and we get to you when we get to you. Now, I realize that it is quite early in the morning but I'd just like to point out that DC Wenner and I have been on since midnight and we were hoping to get this done before we go off shift. Of course if this is a bad time, or . . .' Davis pauses, glancing meaningfully at the fruit and card-laden table '. . . in any way inconvenient for you, we can always come back another day.'

'No, no. Forgive me, but it has been eight days since the burglary and so far nobody's—'

'If you have any complaints about the handling of this case, you're quite welcome to write to the Chief Constable.' Davis delivers this information with the kind of indulgent smile usually reserved for small children or lunatics. His companion, a lumpish individual with a head like a badly crafted slab of plasticine, nods in agreement.

'I hardly think that will be necessary. But, can I ask, do you have any promising leads; any hunches as yet?'

'Hunches might be all very well for Nostradamus,' pronounces Davis, 'but they're no use to us.'

Roger looks blank.

'The Hunchback of Nostradamus . . . the bells, and all that,' explains Davis. Wenner helpfully mimes Quasimodo hauling on a rope and, fair play to him, it is a remarkably accurate impression. I'm not sure who, but either Truffles or Aggie stifles a guffaw while Roger maintains an impressively dignified expression.

'Hunches have no place in the contemporary crime-fighting armoury. We look for information, sir – hard facts. They may not seem like much to the man in the street but when all of these tiny facts are collected and reassembled by the right kind of deductive mind, that's when you get the full picture. That's modern police work for you.'

Wenner nods gravely.

'I see,' says Roger, although he plainly doesn't. 'And how many of these facts do you possess . . . ah, at this time?'

Davis makes a show of consulting his notebook. 'So far, we have your name, and let's see . . . your address: 3B, The Cascades, Caversham Bridge.'

Somehow I don't think we'll be seeing Roger's precious DFC any day soon now.

Davis smirks expansively and surveys the ward. Aggie's gone uncharacteristically quiet and fusses with a drip feed on the far side of the room. I notice that Mr Truffles has shrunk back into his chair and is feigning sleep. Davis's roaming, reptilian gaze now settles on me. 'Oy, whatcha wearing them silly glasses for? The sun's not even properly up yet.'

'I'm blind.'

I have no idea why I said that. Some weird compulsion to give authority the finger, probably.

'I see,' Davis replies, unconscious of the irony. 'Well, I think someone's been having a laugh at your expense.'

Wenner smirks, like a clumsy toddler just took the dull blade of a modelling knife to his blob of a head.

I can't believe that these two are prepared to take the piss out of a poor crippled blind boy in drag-queen sunglasses – they'll be kicking the Zimmer frame out from under me next. For a couple of coppers, they're not exactly what I'd call PC, so I decide to give Davis a bit of pay-back. 'Sergeant Davis, can I ask you a question?' I roll my head and direct my enquiry at the ceiling in the accepted Stevie Wonder manner.

'Course you can.'

'Do you think I could have a career in the force . . . you know, as a detective sergeant or something?'

Bull's-eye. It's plain that Davis is some kind of Poirot wannabe and he's torn between irritation at my presumption and downright hysteria. He sucks his teeth, inhaling a few coconut-fibre moustache hairs. 'Sorry, young man, but I'm afraid the answer is no. As far as I'm aware it's not possible for the visually challenged to join the force. Not my decision of course.'

'What about Harry Norris on dispatch?' offers Wenner.

'He's a bit Magoo. Not completely blind though, is he?'

'Might as well be . . . huge milk bottle specs on him. Like telescopes.'

'Short-sighted is not the same as being a mole-man, Wenner.' Davis rolls his own pale-blue, pink-rimmed orbs and returns his gaze to me. 'I know it's disappointing.'

'It is a bit,' I say, addressing the far wall. 'How about the dog-handlers?'

A brief but transparent look passes between the two policemen, a long-suffering look that says: the sooner this is over the better. Davis grimaces, 'Uh . . . the thing is, in the dog-handling division you're supposed to be handling the dogs, not the other way round. Your highly trained attack-dog would end up spending his whole time trying to stop you falling arse-over-tit down manholes or running into hedges and things. No, I think you'd better forget about the force. But we do appreciate your interest and that.'

I hang my head in defeat but out of the corner of my glasses I can see Aggie crouching behind the furthest bed, convulsed with silent laughter.

I pretend to crash into a locker as Davis riffles his note-book, red biro hovering over the lined pages expectantly. 'Right then, Mr Williams, is there anything else you can tell us about the night in question?'

'Yes, absolutely, one of the—'

'We understand that the break-in occurred some time between midnight and five a.m. – is that correct?'

'Not "some time" – they broke in at four twelve a.m. precisely. I checked my watch, which they subsequently took from me. Omega Dateline with a black leather strap.'

'Very good,' says Davis, 'I admire precision. Which is why

I myself favour the Tag Heuer.' He treats us to a quick flash of his watch. 'So, at four twelve precisely they stole your watch.'

'Actually, four seventeen and twenty-three seconds was the last time I saw it.'

Davis laboriously scores out the previous rubric.

'And then they beat me up. After which they took a bit of cash; about three hundred pounds; then they found my DFC in the tea caddy, which, really, is the only thing I value.'

'One Omega Dateline – black leather strap, three hundred quid and one DFC.' Davis laboriously scrawls all this in his notebook. Wenner nods reassuringly. Finally Davis looks up. 'Excellent. You know, Mr Williams, you'd be surprised what this actually tells us. To you, it means nothing. A collection of random occurrences, as utterly unconnected as Her Majesty the Queen is to . . . to the King of the Krauts. But to us – to the trained mind – it's a collection of facts that piece by tiny piece is already beginning to pay dividends. You'd be surprised how much this little collection of clues has already told us about the perpetrators; how they look, how they sound, how they even dress.'

'But I already know all that.'

There's one of those fabulous cartoon-pauses, like when Wiley Coyote realizes that he's just stepped off the cliff and is now hanging in mid-air.

'What?' says Davis.

'Nobody's actually asked me for a description of the burglars. Or anything else for that matter,' explains Roger diffidently.

'All right,' says Davis slowly, as though speaking to a child, 'so you got a good look at your assailants?'

'They were masked, well, one of them was. The other one was wearing tights.'

'Tights?'

'Over his head.'

'Ah, I see.' Davis's red biro flutters across the page like a dragonfly in heat. 'Any distinguishing marks?'

'The one with the tights on his head was tallish, dark and had a great many tattoos.'

My heart lurches. I know that description well enough.

'The masked one was wearing a kind of black silk pyjama-suit with a hood. He was carrying an old fashioned toilet-chain thing. That's what he hit me with as a matter of fact.'

'Sounds a bit like nunchucks,' observes Wenner.

'Unquestionably,' Davis nods sagely. 'Definitely, those, ah, nanny wassnames, just spell that for me . . .'

'Oh Mikey, there you are. For crying out loud, we've been looking all over the hospital for you.' A furious young nurse stands at the doorway, hands on crisp green hips. I don't know her but she sure as hell knows me. Doubtless she's been giving me bed-baths every day for the past two years and so is entitled to any kind of liberty really – that's just one of the many drawbacks of the comatose state: you don't know who's seen what, done what and when to you. 'Mikey, you better get back to your room now. Your father's arrived. He's come to take you home.'

I rush in headlong panic from the room at the rate of six inches a minute on the Zimmer. Aggie bustles over and kisses me. This is brave of her; I can tell she's not comfortable around the policemen. I hand her the wonderful glasses. 'No, you keep 'em, boy,' she says, 'to remind you of old Aggie.'

Actually, she's the one who really needs them now; I can see tears in the corner of her eyes, but I put them in my pyjama pocket anyway and trundle away, waving at Roger and Truffles.

'Oy,' shouts Davis, 'you lying toe-rag, you're never blind.'

He's smiling, but those red-rimmed eyes of his refuse to participate. 'Congratulations on your miraculous recovery . . . sir.'

I've barely been out of bed for seven hours and I'm already on this copper's shit-list.

Eight

Bernard Hough pulls on tight black leather driving-gloves before placing his hands on the Volvo's wheel at the prescribed position of ten-to-two. They're surprisingly racy, these gloves, with Velcro straps and perforations. He flexes his fingers and I notice that one or two tiny but coarse black hairs have escaped and are poking through the holes. For some reason I find this shocking, like something you're not supposed to see, something deviant. It gives me the shivers.

My father puts on a flat cap before easing out of the hospital car park at a sensible eight miles an hour. I wonder why it is that motorists with the least élan or hair feel the need to accessorize like this.

'Did you sleep?' he asks.

A strange question given the circumstances. 'Yes, thanks. For about two years, I think.'

My father takes his eyes off the road for a split second to glance at me. 'I meant the last couple of nights.'

I decide not to tell him that I've been up all night playing no limit Texas Hold 'em for grapes and assorted soft fruits with a bunch of hustler sharpies. 'Little bit. Obviously I was very excited about coming home.'

'You got *some* sleep though?'

I nod, wondering where this odd line of questioning is

leading. Perhaps he's planning to keep me up nights for the next week, working on a two-year backlog of household chores.

'Only Dr Darrow told me you weren't in your room when he checked on you last night.'

Sod it. Not only did I miss the chance of scoring more of those happy pills but Doc Darrow's gone and dropped me in it too. Surprisingly my father doesn't press the point. He seems uneasy, chewing his lip. There's something not quite right here.

'Michael,' he drums the wheel with those perforated black puddings of his, 'how long did you actually sleep for last night?'

'Not very long really.'

Behind us an ancient Mini honks twice – some poor soul, late for work and no doubt irritated beyond reason at our preposterous speed. My father glares briefly in the rear-view mirror and curls his upper lip. He's not going to give them the satisfaction of a response other than to lift his foot a centimetre or two off the accelerator. Our speed dips from a stately twenty-three miles per hour to a sedate eighteen. The Mini honks again, but it's a futile gesture. The streets of Caversham are narrow and busy at this time of the morning so there's absolutely no chance of overtaking and my father's not about to pull over.

'These racing demons must learn that some of us will not be rushed. Slow and steady wins the race, Michael.'

I'm grateful for the distraction. I was beginning to find the interrogation distinctly unnerving. There's a break in the oncoming traffic and my father increases his speed a touch. As we turn up St Peter's Hill, the Mini pulls out and attempts to pass. But the old banger lacks acceleration. In my wing mirror I can see black smoke belching from its overtaxed exhaust.

My father taps his accelerator. 'If these speed-obsessed lunatics end up a smoking mess of tangled metal then I can scarcely be held accountable.'

I get the impression that he's mentally preparing his defence for when he's quite rightly charged with manslaughter and dickless driving.

We're almost neck-and-neck now: a twenty-six-mile-an-hour Grand Prix – Bernard Hough being one of the Grandest Prix on the road. In his favour, my father not only has the gloves, but horse-power to spare under the hood of this late-model Volvo.

The speedo hovers just under the thirty mark but at the critical moment Bernard's nerve fails him and rather than risk a ticket he concedes defeat and falls back.

The ancient Mini wheezes past. It's the Pond twins. From my perspective, it seems I met them only yesterday, so I give them a friendly wave. Even though there's no sign of recognition, they toot back anyway.

'Don't encourage them, bloody reprobates in their souped-up muscle-cars,' grouches my father. 'Hooligans everywhere these days. Short, sharp shock is what they need.'

Getting the wrong kind of teacake from Waitrose would probably constitute a short, sharp shock for the Pond twins but I keep my own council.

At least there are no further questions for the remainder of the journey.

Bernard strides into the house with a manila folder tucked under one arm. I limp slowly behind, hospital-issue crutches supporting my withered limbs. There's no 'Welcome Home' banner draped across the driveway; no ticker-tape or balloons; not even a yellow ribbon tied around the oak in the back garden – just a platter of pilchard sandwiches.

'You've grown.' My mother emerges from the kitchen.

She gives me a peck on the cheek and offers the plate. 'Did you have a . . .?' She trails off. We both know she was about to say 'a good time'.

We stand in the hallway unable to disguise the uncomfortable fact that we're struggling to find anything to say to one another.

I decide to put her out of her misery. 'Ah, well . . . it's nice to be home.'

She extends an uncertain hand and gently squeezes my arm. 'You got thin.'

Bernard nods in grave approval at this observation.

I can see a tiny blue vein pulsing under the translucent skin of her temple and I want to speak to her, apologize, or at least reassure her in some way. But we're like backpackers without a common language, clumsily wishing one another well with smiles, nods and encouraging sounds.

'Well, I should just . . .' my mother points uncertainly back towards the kitchen, looking to my father for help.

Bernard clears his throat. 'Right then, no point standing around here all day.'

I take the opportunity to sneak a quick look at the manila folder under his arm, and by reading upside down, I see that it contains my hospital notes. Typical of my father not to want to discuss them with me.

'If it's okay, I think I'd like to go upstairs now. To my room.'

'Don't worry, Mikey, we've kept it for you just as you left it.'

There's a bit of a kerfuffle as I try to take the plate while managing my crutches.

My mother picks the sandwiches off the floor, blows the fluff off them and puts them in my hand. We're all relieved. She retreats to the kitchen with the empty plate while my father escapes to his study. I'm left alone in the hallway, sandwiches squashed in one hand, crutches in the other and a flight of stairs ahead of me, which seem about as climbable as the north face of the Eiger without ropes.

I reach the summit about ten minutes later and, like one of those heroic but disastrous expeditions, it's possible to track my ascent route from all the equipment I've been forced to abandon in my wake. Crutches, cucumber slices and pilchards, mostly.

My mother wasn't kidding about my bedroom; it hasn't been touched. Everything is shrouded in a thick layer of dust, like Miss Haversham's wedding breakfast. There's even an old pair of pants still lurking under the bed. The fish tank is empty and dry, with a greenish tint to the glass. At one time I had a couple of tropical fish in there: Loh Hung, a sort of Chinese carp reputed to bring good fortune – not to themselves though, obviously. There's no trace of my Loh Hung so I drop in a few of the fragile pilchard skeletons and am quite pleased with the effect; a sort of aquarium of horror.

It's good to see my collection of meticulously crafted model airplanes still hanging from the ceiling: Stukas, ME109s, Spitfires and Hurricanes, frozen in a perpetual dogfight. When he's discharged, I'll see if Roger would like to come over and take a look.

I run my hand across the ammonites and trilobites on the windowsill before reaching for my amber. I've always loved this object: a smooth yellow lump of prehistoric sap containing a minute mayfly. My touchstone. Mayflies are the most ephemeral of creatures and yet this one is already over a million years old and will probably outlast us all. I hold it up to my eye and inspect the delicate filaments of its tiny wings. In the soft golden aura it resembles a tiny angel, small enough to jitterbug on the head of a pin.

I can't say it's wonderful to be back in this room; it's not

45

exactly crammed with happy memories, but it's comfortable and it's familiar, like slipping into an old shoe. There is an odd feeling of displacement, though. I've been away for two years, but to me it feels like I've only been gone a day.

On the dresser are some unfamiliar items: half-a-dozen wrapped presents representing two years' worth of missed Christmases and birthdays. I'm far too mature now to get excited by a few presents – for at least thirty seconds anyway, which is all the time it takes me to totter over there and begin shredding festive paper with trembling claws.

First to emerge is a thousand-piece jigsaw puzzle, depicting the Cotswold stone bridge at Bourton-on-the-Water. Next, a white shirt a size too small with a clip-on tie. There's a sweater, gloves and, unbelievably, a balaclava. There's also a set of chest expanders and a solitaire board with pink glass playing pieces.

The cards aren't much better. The most heinous of the four features a tinted photo of a grinning twerp in a fifties race-car with a large metal badge affixed, proclaiming: 'It's my birthday.' If it had said 'I am a moron' instead, I could have worn it, along with my tight white shirt, clip-on tie, sweater and balaclava, while playing solitaire or puzzling over the bridge at Bourton-on-the-Water.

In a funny kind of way, I'm impressed. Some of this merchandise must have been out of stock since the war years.

I've left the heavy book-shaped one till last. I'm not optimistic. I slowly peel back the paper and there it is; the unmistakable shape of a bat wing. It's a pile of comics from Gerry: every single issue of the Dark Knight from the past two years.

It's night when the knock comes; I hadn't even noticed it getting dark. My mother is silhouetted in the doorway with another plate of sandwiches and a mug of something. She wrinkles her nose. 'Are you in here, Mikey?'

'Yes.'

'I can't come in, you know what the dust is like on my allergies.'

I slip the Dark Knight, issue number 53, under my pillow just as she flips the light switch.

'Did you like your presents then?' she says from the doorway. 'I see you're wearing your badge. Although . . . it's not actually your birthday today. You do know that, don't you, Mikey?' She seems confused.

'I'm okay, Mum. It's just ironic.'

'I see,' she says, sniffing again. 'Well, I'll just leave this here then. Tongue and sliced egg, is that all right?' She lays the plate and glass at the threshold like a prison warder. 'There's some hot milk . . . to help Mr Sandman on his way.'

My father's head appears at her shoulder like a glove puppet. 'Did you sleep, Michael?' he asks abruptly.

'Just a little lie-down. A nap.'

'He had the lights off when I came in, Bernard,' advises my mother helpfully, 'but I think he was awake and reading a magazine.' At this, my father's face creases into a suspicious frown.

'Looking at a magazine, with the lights off . . . oh really?' Thankfully he decides not to pursue this line of enquiry and gazes around the room with distaste. 'It's like a bloody badger's sett in here already.'

I fake a yawn and stretch so that I can shove an incriminating corner of the Dark Knight further under the pillow. The yawn seems to do the trick on my parents too.

'Well, we'll say goodnight then,' says my father.

'Goodnight.'

'Sleep tight, Mikey.'

I don't sleep tight, though. I don't sleep at all.

It's three o'clock in the morning; I'm standing in my father's study holding the manila folder. And it's a bloody nightmare.

Nine

There's a lot of stuff in the notes about pre-frontal cortexes and parietal lobes but none of that's a problem. There's a tiny structure, no larger than a pimple, the suprachiasmatic nucleus mentioned by Dr Darrow, and this is the nub of the issue, so to speak. I have, as they say in the medical profession, gone and totally smashed the granny out of it, crushed it like a bug on a windscreen. On the lined page, Doc Darrow's penmanship lurches from a mildly untidy sprawl to seismic frenzy in the space of two short sentences: 'In conclusion,' he writes, 'we suspect that the patient may have *permanently impaired his ability to sleep.*'

Drugs, of course, are being prescribed, specifically powerful sedative-hypnotics. For the past two weeks they've managed to keep me in a semi-comatose state with elephantine quantities of these things. The problem is, I've developed a tolerance. Any higher dosage now and they risk suppressing my respiratory functions.

Darrow and the specialists are not certain, but they suspect that the hypnotics are causing my unhinged hypothalamus to trigger a rush of adrenaline and a 'compensatory adenylatcyclase cascade'. In simple terms, when they try to put me to sleep, my brain fights even harder to stay awake. I can see how this is all going to play out from Darrow's ancillary papers – photocopied pages from the *Lancet* and other medical journals referring to a rare but similar condition known as Fatal Familial Insomnia. The inescapable fact is, no human being has ever gone for more than a few weeks without any form of sleep – fragile organisms that we are. Soon, my speech will begin to slur, I'll become delusional before slipping into psychosis and then finally, in a fortnight, my exhausted nervous system will begin shutting itself down. The experts are in the dark here and there's no time to figure out a solution. In his concluding paragraph Darrow blithely advises that we continue with the sedative-hypnotics and inform him of any change or improvement. It sounds like a forlorn hope. Effectively, he's washing his hands of me and my dreams.

I close the folder, aware that my parents have adulterated the warm milk tonight, which is the only reason I'm not screaming.

Then again, I'm not sleeping either.

In a way, I suppose this is all very liberating. For the next fortnight I'm free from the stifling constraints of this house: I can run away to the circus, become a high-diver, drink lager, smoke fags and read comics to my heart's content. I'm free from all responsibility. In a couple of weeks' time it won't really matter what I've done; I'll be a foaming lunatic on the verge of a cerebral meltdown. And this is something I've often wondered about: are we fundamentally moral creatures or is it just the fear of the consequences that prevents us from doing exactly as we please? I'll be sure to have this one out with God, Buddha and the lads when I catch up with them.

I slap the folder back down on my father's desk; a few of the loose papers float down on to the carpet. I couldn't care less; I'm beyond Bernard's law now, beyond any laws other than those of biology, which is why I need to pee.

The downstairs loo has a cistern that clanks like a ship-yard in a gale, so I open the kitchen door and hobble out on one crutch into the back garden. I quietly relieve myself in the shadows of the old oak.

A fox emerges from a clump of bushes at the bottom of the garden. The creature sniffs the air in a way that reminds me of my mother, before trotting across the lawn. I watch as he makes straight for the bin and nudges off the lid and begins to excavate.

The moon casts an odd, frenzied light. Amoebic shadows gather and ooze across the lawn, like Satan's lava lamp. There's a freakish quality to the night air, or perhaps it's within me; I can't be sure. It might be the drugs or the onset of delusion but I'm definitely not feeling myself. Then I notice that's exactly what I am doing; standing there jaw ajar, this ruddy great cock still in my hand, hanging out like the neck of a freshly killed turkey. I quickly stuff it away. Don't want that fox getting ideas.

The creature glances furtively about, then, amazingly, belches. I had no idea they could do that, sly buggers. I remain perfectly still as he melts back into the shadow of our privet.

There's a smooth trough in the soft earth at the base of the hedge, which explains how he's been getting in. I widen the gap with the end of my crutch before inching my emaci-ated frame through the tangle of roots and dead vegetation. I emerge on the other side in Coombs's back garden.

Although I'm still wobbly on my pins it's gratifying to feel a little of my old strength and balance beginning to return. I've lived in this place all my life, yet this is the very first time I've set foot on Coombs's property. I've never even been allowed across to retrieve a ball.

There's a single light in one of the downstairs windows giving out a soft yellow glow; no more than a twenty-watt bulb's worth. I once read about an African dictator who had the country's power supply switched off whenever he went abroad – the tight-fisted Coombs is like that: he never knowingly leaves a light on. I'm curious, so I hobble over to the little window, push up on my toes and peer inside. It's a storage cupboard, full of accumulated junk and sporting paraphernalia. I can see Coombs's bag of racquets on one of the shelves, old golf clubs and, interestingly, one or two of my own long-lost soccer balls. If I'm karking it in a week or two, I'm buggered if I'm going to let bastard Coombs keep my footballs. Over my dead body.

Flakes of paint curling away from the warped frame reveal that the wood underneath is rotting. The window itself is secured from the inside by a rusty ironware latch. I take off my ludicrous badge, bend back the pin, wiggle it through the gap in the soft, cheesy wood and flip the catch. The window opens with the merest tug. I'm just figuring out how the hell I'm going to find the strength to haul myself up over the ledge when my heart stops.

A deathly white face floats before my eyes, green-black mouth open in a silent scream.

This is not real. I'm certain of that. Like the fox belching, it's a product of my drug-addled, sleep-deprived cortex. But it's still given me a hell of shock.

And it's screeching at me.

I ignore it and scan Coombs's garden for something lightweight, something I can use to stand on.

'Who the fuck are you?' it screams in a shrill falsetto.

I spot a plastic wheelie-bin which might do the trick.

'Don't ignore me and walk away, you flat-faced fucking snedger. I asked you a question.'

It's a pretty foul-mouthed figment of my imagination, to be sure.

I close my eyes and wait for the delirium to pass, like the dizzy spells on the ward. But the nightmare persists, inside my head now: 'Is there something wrong with you?'

'Yes, I can't sleep. Now, be gone.'

I half open one eye: the head is still there, only this time not so terrifying. There's a hint of a smile and the features seem familiar in some way. 'That's no reason to go sneaking around like some kind of pervert, breaking into other people's houses.'

I concentrate hard, willing the apparition to dissolve.

'Are you constipated? What do you want?'

'I want you to be gone. You're not real. Go away.'

'You go away. Go on, piss off.'

Great. Now I'm arguing with myself, shouting at my own fantasy creatures, like a mad bag lady.

'I'm not going anywhere until I've got my balls out.'

'Oh, for fuck's sake!' it snarls, slamming the window and locking it.

I put my hands to the window to see whether it really is closed. I give the glass a gentle tap with my badge to make certain and the face reappears, squishing itself against the pane. 'I'm serious, fuck off now, or I'm calling the police.'

In theory my condition may have put me beyond the law but I still don't fancy spending the last two weeks of my life getting truncheon-stroked by Wenner and Davis for breaking and entering, or worse. Even in this woozy, bewildered state it's evident that I'm having a conversation with something flesh and blood and female, especially when this person opens the window again and leans out, giving me an uninterrupted view down the happy tunnel of her white cotton nightie.

She's scrutinizing me too. Thankfully my trembling,

wasted physique and Tiny Tim crutch seem to be inspiring more sympathy than fear.

'I'm sorry,' I plead. 'I didn't mean to scare you. Actually, you scared the hell out of me. I thought you might be an hallucination or a ghost or something . . . I'm on very strong drugs.'

The girl tosses her Goth-black hair and smiles grimly. 'I am a ghost, but only of my former self. Where's your shit then?'

It takes me a moment to realize what she means.

'They're just sedatives, sleeping stuff . . . I'm Mikey, from next door.'

She frowns suspiciously before the penny drops. 'Ah . . . I know you . . . you're the idiot who fell out of the tree. I thought you were supposed to be dead.' She stares a moment longer before coming to a decision. 'All right, give me a hand, I'm coming out.'

We wriggled back through the fox-run easily enough, but I had to ditch my crutch at the foot of the old oak and she was forced to half drag, half carry me up the batons as we ascended.

It took a good ten minutes to get up here but we settle ourselves on the rickety platform and catch our breath.

'Here,' she says, handing me a cigarette. 'You busted me sneaking a crafty one in the junk cupboard. Coombs hates me smoking in the house.'

'Sorry about that.'

'Yeah well, Coombs hates a lot of things I do.'

'No, I meant sorry about scaring you. Like I said, I can't sleep.'

'Join the club.' She takes a deep first puff of her own ciggie, leaving a green-black lipstick smear on the filter. 'Sleep is just wasted life anyway.'

*

I've never been good with the opposite sex. My only real experience up till now has been end-of-year school discos where the genders glare at each other from each end of the room, like Korean border guards. Only the coolest kids ever made it across that minefield unscathed. I tried it once: summoning all my courage to ask the gorgeous, sophisticated, wise-cracking, fourteen-year-old Natalie Corbett to dance, holding out my arm in what I imagined was a chivalrous gesture. She looked me up and down, cracked her gum a couple of times and said, simply: 'Eff off, Hough,' leaving me standing there, marooned on the wrong side of room, like a novelty teapot.

The girl shifts on the rickety boards and peers across at the neighbouring faux-Gothic turrets with a grim expression. 'I'm Livia, Coombs's so-called god-daughter.'

I take a nervous little drag. 'If you're his god-daughter why haven't I seen you before?' It's an abysmal line, on a par with 'Do you come here often?', but she doesn't seem bothered. The burning tip of my cigarette glows like a Red Dwarf, briefly illuminating Livia's kabuki-white face.

'Don't see him much, thank Christ. Never even visited before last month. Coombs and my mum have some kind of history from way back before I was born. Mum's sick. She's been ill with something for years, in and out of remission, turns out to be fucking leukaemia. Now she's in one of those waddyacall'ems – places where people go to die?'

'Hospice?'

'That's it. Sounds like horse-piss and smells like it too.' She pouts, shrugs. 'That's life. A few months back I got myself expelled from boarding school and so here I am, God help me, stuck with that man Coombs. Nowhere else to go.'

Despite all the Hallowe'en make-up, there's something

appealingly vulnerable about this girl. I don't want her thinking I'm a teapot or a snedger, but there is something I must know: 'Livia, about two years ago I was standing on this platform and I swear I saw you, or someone very like you, up there in the turret window . . .'

Livia's face turns to alabaster. 'I told you, I've never been here before.'

'You're sure?'

'Of course I'm sure.'

I've inadvertently crossed some kind of a line here. Livia brusquely stubs out her cigarette on the warped planks and gets to her feet, smoothing creases in her white cotton nightie. 'I've gotta go. You should too, Mikey. Try to get some sleep.'

'I can't do that.'

'Why not?'

'For one thing, I doubt if I can get down from here on my own. And secondly, I can't sleep.'

She laughs. In the weird half light, her lipstick glows cadaver-green. 'Take a pill, Mikey.'

'I'm serious. I can't sleep and they say it's going to kill me.'

'Nobody dies from not sleeping. You feel like death sometimes, but you don't actually die . . .'

'There's something wrong with my brain. They think I'll be dead or a drooling idiot within a fortnight,' I reply.

She looks at me with new respect. 'Wow. Bummer.'

I wish I'd used that line on Natalie Corbett. Livia sits down again, all trace of that strange reserve replaced by an ill-concealed curiosity. 'Are you serious?'

'Really. You can check my medical notes if you want.'

'The Great Adventure, Mikey,' says Livia breathlessly. 'How do you feel about it?'

'How do you think I feel?'

'You seem pretty ho-hum about the whole thing, if you don't mind me saying.'

'I'm sedated up to the eyeballs, Livia. I've been seeing weird things all night. I'm only just holding it together.'

'So what are your plans?'

'Just getting down from this tree, I suppose, without killing myself a fortnight early. I dunno.'

For some reason this irritates her enormously. 'That is just so short term. You need to think bigger, Mikey. My mum's dying too, but she's stuck in bed, wasting away in some horse-piss dump, too weak to do anything but puke.' She leans over, grips my arms and shakes me so hard I nearly topple out of the tree again. 'For Christ's sake, use the time you've got left. For the next two weeks, you can do anything you like. And you're on double-time because you can work nights. You can do anything. No repercussions, Mikey. Don't you see? For the next two weeks you're a god; a pretty weedy-looking god, but a god nevertheless.'

She's right of course. I'm feeling mellow enough not to mind this kind of talk; it's like we're discussing someone else. And, in any case, there is something I'd really like to do: 'I want to get all my old footballs back from Coombs.'

Livia tries to conceal her disappointment.

The weedy-looking god has spoken . . . and asks, can he have his ball back?

I'll have to do better than that: clearly, my novelty value is wearing pretty thin. I need a better mission, something cool and daring; something impressive involving the combined forces of injustice and oppression. Trouble is, I've never had that much contact with the combined forces of I and O and wouldn't have a clue where to find them.

'Well,' yawns Livia, 'it's been . . .'

'No, wait,' I say. I've just remembered twinkly old Roger and his brush with the underworld. 'If you must know, I'm planning to find a missing medal, for a friend of mine – a fighter pilot.' Livia's eyebrows leap, a microsecond or so out of synch, like a pair of performing dolphins.

'A war hero, in actual fact,' I add.

'Wow,' she says. 'Which war? The Gulf?'

'The Second.'

'The second what?'

'Uh . . . World War.'

'Christ, how old is he?'

'Ancient. But he's sort of like everyone's idea of their favourite grandfather: he's witty, cheats at cards, he's full of life and hardly smells at all. Only at the moment his head's all purple and swollen because he got burgled and badly beaten up and the only thing he really values got stolen.'

'I wouldn't know about grandparents, Mikey. Never had any,' mutters Livia sourly.

'As a matter of fact, nor did I. But that's why I like him. He's sort of like the grandfather I didn't have, but wish I did, if that makes sense. Anyway, he's a hero and he's old and needs my help. I've sworn to get his medal back for him. That's my mission. I didn't want to tell you because it's going to be dangerous. The people who stole it are quite violent criminals.'

Livia peers at me with new-found respect, or deep suspicion. I can't say for sure in the dark.

'So what's the plan, Stan?'

I take a deep breath and try to inject a little steel into my tinny voice. 'My plan is to get the medal back, come hell or high water.'

'That's a mission, Mikey, not a plan. What's the plan?'

'To . . . ah . . . track the burglars, hunt them down and get the medal back.'

'Yeah . . . okay. Still more of a mission than a plan, though.'

'To . . . move through the night streets like a shadow, following every lead, missing nothing, taking nothing at face value . . .' I trail off.

Livia is deeply underwhelmed.

'That is just juvenile drivel, like something out of a comic. You haven't actually got a plan, have you?'

She's right, of course, but what the hell did she expect? Two minutes ago I didn't even have a mission.

She gazes at me, oddly, shyly. 'I can help, if you like.'

I'd like that very much.

'I wouldn't mind a partner. And I do need a strategic brain. But you're going to have to leave the dangerous part to me. That has to be the arrangement.'

Livia cackles, teeth gleaming blue-white in the moonlight. 'Ah, that goes without saying, Mikey. Any physical stuff, like martial arts and climbing trees, obviously we leave entirely to you.'

We shake hands self-consciously, at which point Livia appears to remember something. 'Oh yeah, and in return for my help, I'd like you to do one little thing for me.'

'Which is?'

'I want you to kill Coombs.'

It's hard to read that face in the eerie half-light, with its thick layer of white foundation and brutal mascara. But I'm pretty sure she's not joking.

Ten

I watch the sun rising spectacularly over the playing fields, investing the panorama with a liquid quality and the tones of molten Welsh gold. Dandelions punctuate the landscape like scattered coins. In a copse of trees behind me, a wood-pigeon coos. My sentiments exactly.

I've never been out here at dawn before, I wonder why. All this beauty so close to hand and it takes the prospect of numbered days to force me to see it.

I left Livia a few hours ago with a promise to meet later tonight. I prefer to be on my own now that the sedatives are wearing off. I need to get my head straight, although in a way I suppose it already is – you could lay a spirit level across my face without tipping the bubble.

I've made a list on a pocket pad of all the things I should do before the mentis becomes compost. In no particular order they are:

1 Retrieve footballs from Coombs. Mission complete.

2 Donate footballs and old comics to Gerry.

3 Donate model aircraft collection to Roger.

4 Donate amber to Aggie.

5 Think of something to give Mr Truffles – my ski gloves perhaps? Or my mum's copper pans?

6 Donate balaclava, jigsaw puzzle and clip-on tie to Edmund.

7 Find Roger's medal.

8 Kill Coombs.

Not much of a legacy. Apart from numbers seven and eight (both entirely down to Livia) I'm disappointed to see how mundane it all is.

I'll start the day with an easy one.

'Oh my God, it's alive,' bellows Edmund from the hallway. Mrs Kerr holds the door, looking faintly alarmed. She doesn't invite me in.

Not surprisingly, Edmund has grown; he stands on the threshold, hands on hips, in a viyella shirt and grey slacks, bloated with blustering self-confidence and cake. Great clumps of him hang suspended over his waistband like melted candle-wax. He peers into my face, not bothering to hide his disgust.

'Trick or Treat, is it, Mikey? You know it's not Hallowe'en for another four months?'

Mrs Kerr attempts to suppress a smile at her son's wit. 'What is it, Michael Hough?' she asks, in her insincere Morningside lilt. 'Of course, we're happy to see you alive and well – only, should you not be home, in bed?'

I shrug, holding out the bundle of stuff. 'I brought some things for Edmund. I won't be needing them any more.'

Mrs Kerr's smile tightens, compressing her red lips; she is mortally offended. 'That is kind of you, Michael. But as you can plainly see, the Kerr family is not in need of assistance. When we require charitable donations your parents will be the first to know.'

Despite the sarcasm I can see her avaricious eyes scanning the pile in my hands. Even she can tell that it's all crap.

'Off you go now, Michael Hough.' She ushers her son back inside and begins to close the door.

'Hang on,' orders Edmund, shoving the door back open with his bulk. 'I'll have the balaclava, if Pancakes doesn't want it.'

To my amazement he whips it off the pile and tries it on. A black-eyed pea on a kettle drum.

'Perfect,' he announces.

Mrs Kerr gives an almost inaudible 'tut', turns on her heel and leaves us to it.

Edmund's chubby face beams out at me from that awful helmet. 'So, Pancakes, you know you've got a new neighbour since you've been away?'

'I'd prefer it if you called me Mikey.'

'Pancakes is better,' he insists. 'You look like one of Genghis Khan's mongoloids, with your face all flattened in.'

'Mongols.'

'Same difference. You can't smart-arse me any more, not with your brain all smashed to bits. I got five GCSEs and two 'A' levels, and a place at the University of Western England to study agriculture next year. How many did you get of anything, Pancakes?'

This is the first time I've seen Edmund in two years and he's getting to me already. Age does not seem to have mellowed him. He's worse, if anything.

I'm surprised at Edmund's bitterness.

'Yeah, Coombs has got some little Lolita stashed over there. I've seen her around the place. Supposed to be his god-daughter, but the word at the CYC is she's his bastard from some junkie slag he once shagged. The old druggie's about to peg it and now he's got to look after the girl. Otherwise they spill the beans.'

'CYC?'

'Caversham Young Conservatives,' he explains, preening.

Which explains everything about the new Edmund; especially the shirt and the slacks.

'Her name's Livia.'

Edmund winks. 'Livia, is it? You don't hang about, do you, Mikey? Nice little diddies on her too.' He begins to rub his own mammoth tits. 'You may be first off the blocks there, but that face isn't going to do you any favours with the ladies.' He grabs his groin with both hands and thrusts out his hips. 'I'm going to go and see if young Livia wants to play with my dolly. She can watch it being sick if she likes.' He nudges me hard with a pudgy elbow to underline the innuendo, only it's me who feels like being sick here. Livia may be completely barking and homicidal, but for some reason I feel strangely protective of her.

'Clarice . . .' sighs Edmund, 'Clarice . . .' He sucks in air, slobbering wetly in what he imagines is a fine impression of Hannibal Lecter.

'Liviaaaaa, I can smell your—'

'You got fat,' I say, abruptly.

Edmund's smile fades. He stops licking and swivelling and I can see that I've scored an easy bull's-eye. 'Oy, Pancakes, it's my glands,' he blusters.

'Yeah, your saliva glands.' I totter away on my crutch.

A Dickensian bell hanging over the door tinkles gently as it opens. Sylvester's on Oxford Road is one of those jumbled, timeless places with a scuffed wooden floor and a central counter that might be a repository for anything from humbugs to haberdashery. In fact the glass cases are full of Roman denarii, sixteenth-century sixpences and assorted stamps. You'd expect the owner to be an elderly, tweedy, home-counties type, but this Sylvester is a middle-aged pony-tailed American hippy in a leather waistcoat. A Celtic pendant dangles over his sparse grey chest.

63

'I got your address from the *Yellow Pages*,' I say.

The eponymous Sylvester eyes me without interest. 'So, whaddya you want, Slim, a medal?'

'I do, as a matter of fact.'

Sylvester considers this for a while, sniffs, leans down and produces a trayful of bronze and silver discs from under his counter. 'I got medals.'

It's a collection of mostly American Temperance Society medallions nestled in pink satin.

'I'm looking for something World War Two and British: a DFC.'

Sylvester rubs his nose and considers me for a second or two. 'You want to start a collection? Try stamps. I got Papua New Guinea ones. They have, you know, like, real tits on their stamps, okay?'

He pushes a small semi-transparent envelope across the counter. I'm not going to be fobbed off with some National Geographic micro-porn. I shove it straight back. 'I want a DFC. It says in your ad that you sell medals.'

'Sure. Sometimes I sell medals.'

'I want a DFC. How much?'

Sylvester rests both elbows on the counter and cradles his head, holding my gaze. He speaks slowly and deliberately. 'You know what pisses me off? People coming in here chasing the big war medals: the VCs, MCs, DFCs, Silver Stars. Greedy jerks read somewhere that military decorations are a great investment, so they think they can just go out and buy 'em. Well, they can't. Not from me at any rate. Let me tell you this: even if I had a DFC, which I don't, I would never sell it to someone like you. These things ain't used cars or two-bit fucking stock market shares, they cost blood. You don't just get to buy and sell courage, you gotta earn it.'

He pushes the package of stamps back across the counter. 'Here, take this for nothin' and fuck off.'

I'm going to die soon anyway, so I drop my crutch and snatch at his forearm and hold it with both hands and all my strength. There's an eagle's head and the word 'Airborne', tattooed across the stringy tendons.

'I know what medals are and I know what they mean. So, thanks for the lecture. I just want a DFC and if you won't sell me one, you better just tell me where I can find someone who will.' I can feel my eyes begin to bulge with the effort.

Sylvester whips his arm from my grip in a deft and surprisingly painful twisty manoeuvre.

'Ow, shit.' I retreat a pace, nursing skeletal wrists. 'It was earned,' I insist, 'by a friend of mine. It was taken from him.'

Sylvester's expression softens; his deep-set lacklustre eyes regard me now with something less than outright hostility. 'You're a gutsy streak of piss, ain'tcha?' He gives me an odd smile before sliding open another drawer.

A tray of American military awards.

'These are mine.'

'Good. You can keep them.'

'My very own. I earned 'em.'

There are three purple hearts, a bronze star and a silver star in the collection, each engraved with the same girl's name. '"Awarded to Silvia Francolino . . ."' I intone.

'Silvia, that's me,' explains Sylvester. 'It's not easy growing up with a faggy name. Like in the Johnny Cash song: "A Boy Named Sue". I guess that's what made me do all those dumb things.' He chuckles. 'In the jungle I only ever wore a flak jacket so they got to calling me "The Vester". I just put the two parts together.'

I silently finger the medals, waiting for Silvia-Vester to pick up the threads of the conversation.

'Listen, Slim, if you got a friend who earned a DFC, then he's probably a bigger fool than I am, but I salute him. I'd like to help. Trouble is, those things are almost like VCs now. They're worth something. You got the provenance – you name the price. The market's small and select but it's sucking them up. Way out of my league.'

'So you can't help?'

'I didn't say that.'

Sylvester peers deep into my eyes. It's not easy to hold his gaze but I have nothing left to lose.

'You really want to get this thing back?'

'I do.'

He's the first to break the eye-lock. 'I believe you, Slim. I don't know how and I don't know why, but you got a genuine thousand-yard-stare on you, my friend: like you don't give a fuck any more. Believe me, I know that look.'

It seems I just passed some kind of bizarre 'Nam test.

Chelt-Nam, in my case.

'You gonna tell me what happened to your face?'

'No.'

Sylvester chuckles. 'I like you, Slim. So, this medal was stolen, yeah?'

'Yeah.'

'Okay, then you could do worse than start at the Tank Engine, it's a nightclub under the railway arches. A lot of stuff that goes "missing" finds its way there sooner or later, if you know what I mean. Ask for the Fat Controller. Tell him I sent you.'

'Silvia sent me?'

'No, fucker – not Silvia – *Sylvester*. You ever tell anyone my name is Silvia, I'll kill you. Speaking of which . . .' He reaches under the counter and brings out a glossy pistol, expertly pulling back the slider before releasing.

'That's . . . my God, that's a gun.'

'Yeah, it's a gun. And it's what I carry when I do business with those people. You understand?'

'Wow.'

'Nickel-plated, Colt 45 automatic. The American dream.' Sylvester's eyebrows cavort like caterpillars in heat above deranged blue eyes.

'I've never seen a real one before . . . how do you . . .?' I find myself caressing the slick barrel.

'No big deal. You're supposed to keep the end with the hole well away from you. All the shit in the world comes out of there.'

'Cool,' I say, mesmerized.

'You want one? A hundred fifty.'

'Quid?'

'Nah, jelly beans . . .'

'I don't have that kind of cash.'

'Ah, it's only a replica anyways.' Sylvester shrugs, the gun disappears back under the counter. 'Well, just watch yourself with those people, okay? And don't make me regret this conversation.'

'Don't worry, Silvia . . . and thanks.'

'*Sylvester*, fucker!' he bellows after me.

Eleven

I'm ashamed to admit that after getting the bus back from Oxford Road I did nothing more constructive than sprawl across my bed reading DC comics, stuffing myself with a quarter of Barker & Dobson's Mint Humbugs. These are easily the best and we're lucky there's a little newsagent at the bottom of St Peter's Hill which sells them loose from those nice big glass jars. I have six missions to go and, even though time is short, I do think I'm entitled to a bit of R&R, as we 'Nam vets like to say.

I wait patiently for the sun to set: like the Dark Knight, I prefer to do my work while the city sleeps.

It's late. I'm fizzing with energy and entirely focused. I shave for the first time with Imperial Leather soap and one of the disposable hospital-issue razors, leaving my face tingling and raw.

A plate of curling potted-meat sandwiches and a mug of hot milk was left outside my door an hour or two ago. I want to stay sharp tonight so I limit myself to a few sips. The potted-meat sandwiches I simply flush down the loo, cutting out the middle man.

It's time.

I admit I've never actually been to a nightclub before, but

I've seen pictures in the magazines and people go smartly dressed, otherwise they're not allowed in. And I know that jeans are absolutely forbidden.

None of my old clothes fit. My pastel-blue, smart-casual slacks are, if anything, a little looser around the waist but now woefully short in the leg – I must have grown at least six inches since I last wore them. Luckily I've got a pair of ankle socks in almost exactly the same shade, so they won't look too ridiculous.

I've advanced a couple of shoe sizes too. Apart from my cheap hospital slippers there's only one pair in my closet that come even remotely close to fitting: a pair of brand-new ox-blood loafers that my mother bought years ago in a sale on the basis that I'd grow into them. They resemble house-bricks, but at least they've retained their shop window shine.

I pull a paisley sweater over the tight white shirt and inspect my reflection in the full-length mirror on the wardrobe door.

I may not be completely up to speed with current trends, but even I can tell that this not exactly hip – more hip replacement. I look like a Florida geriatric. I'm a screaming nightmare in polyester. There's nothing for it, though: I'll just have to brazen it out and keep well away from any naked flames.

I have another squiz in the mirror. It's not a repulsive face. Gaunt, of course; flat and almost featureless; scary at first, daunting to the untrained eye. But like a prairie, or the Nullarbor Plain to the Aborigines, once you get to know it, you become accustomed to the emptiness and might even find something in that barren wasteland to love. And there are other advantages, apart from poker – it's impossible to put an age to. I could be anything from sixteen to sixty. If I was to live on past my sell-by date, I'm pretty sure that I'd look the same in my nineties as I do now. I'm not unhappy with this. Why would I be? My life expectancy is entirely too short for vanity. That's what I tell myself at any rate.

I run a comb through my shoulder-length Prince Valiant hair before emptying my piggy bank. I fill my pockets with handfuls of loose change – the weight helps to pull the trousers down a couple of inches, covering a little more of the exposed sockage. I'm well aware that the classier disco-theques like the Tank Engine are likely to be expensive, and my only concern is that after paying for a couple of drinks these elasticated trousers will start to ride back up again.

TINK . . .

TINK . . .

TINK . . .

At first I ignore it. Must be some kind of aural hallucination. I fasten the top button of my shirt in the mirror.

Suddenly my world explodes. There's a rock the size of my best ammonite on the carpet along with a million shards of glass. I stand, frozen for a second, before lurching to the shattered window.

On the lawn below is a young girl in a raincoat. Someone I've never seen before.

'Did you throw that?'

'What the fuck are you doing up there? I've been chucking pebbles for about twenty minutes.'

I have no idea how to answer this.

The girl twitches with frustration. 'You can't hide, Mikey. Get down here, right now.'

I recognize the voice now and the stroppy intonation. It *is* Livia. But the make-over fairy must have been busy today.

'Shhh . . .' I hiss. Livia's bellowing is surely loud enough to wake the dead. Mercifully there's still no response from my parents' end of the house, which leads me to suspect that they may have been helping themselves to my sedatives.

No need to tempt fate though. My limbs are beginning to feel as though they might actually belong to me now; on a single crutch I make my way downstairs at the speed of a sprightly octogenarian and I'm out through the kitchen door in a matter of minutes.

Livia is achingly beautiful without all that Kabuki muck; just a lick of mascara and a streak of lipstick. She's one of those lucky women who look better without a ton of make-up, which is probably why she lays it on in geological stratas.

'Go away, Livia. I'm busy tonight. I have a lead; I might be on to something.' It breaks my heart to say it, but I worry that she'll be a liability.

'I'm all set. Come on, Mikey, what have you found out and where are we going in the filthy white underbelly of Reading's netherworld?'

'As a matter of fact, *I'm* going to a discotheque,' I announce urbanely.

Without warning Livia shrieks with laughter. I have to clamp my hand over her mouth to shut her up, terrified that she'll manage to rouse my parents after all.

I release her but she continues to shake in silent mirth. 'Say that again,' she says.

'What?'

'"Discotheque". That's so funny, the way you said it.'

I don't see what's so amusing here. 'Discotheque. What?'

'They call them clubs these days, Mikey. Which one?'

I'm not answering. I fold my arms.

'Oh, come on, Mikey. Stop being a baby.'

'The Tank Engine if you must know. But you're not invited.'

Livia grins, then her face morphs into an expression of genuine concern. 'Mikey, the Tank Engine is an edgy, happening place, not some school dance. Dressed like that, you're not even going to get through the doors of the local Rotary.'

'I don't think you're anyone to tell people how they should dress,' I snip.

Livia simply opens her raincoat. 'Well, I'm coming with you,' she says.

Christ. It's Vampirella.

'Do you like?' she asks, twirling.

'Absolutely not. It's indecent.'

I'm not big on super heroines but Vampirella would have to be my favourite. Strictly speaking she's not a real 'super' and her adventures are a bit tedious, but I've always been a great fan of her costume. And here it is, in the flesh, as it were.

Under the raincoat, Livia is wearing nothing more than a cutaway crimson corset-type-thing, sheer white tights and a pair of red leather, thigh-high boots. I'm shocked yet thrilled at the same time, and to my horror I can feel the much neglected, bearded old castaway in my trousers beginning to exhibit alarmingly twitchy signs of life.

My gimlet-eyed companion notices instantly. 'Uh-oh, Pinocchio's telling fibs again.'

I sputter, dropping my hospital-issue crutch, scrabbling in my bulging pockets for the stack of loose change. 'I'm . . . it's not . . . it's all this cash in my pockets.'

Livia rolls her eyes. 'God, you are such a liability.'

I funnel the cascade of loose change back into my pockets, anchoring my wayward trousers, and make one last attempt to claw back my self-respect. 'Look, things could get a bit heavy tonight, which is why I can't let you come with me. Besides, you just can't go out dressed like that.'

'No, Mikey. *You* can't go out dressed like *that*.'

'Livia . . .'

'I'm coming, whether you like it or not.'

I already know that there's not much point arguing with Livia. Life's too short.

As it turns out we were both wrong. One flash of that costume to the steroidal doormen outside the Tank Engine and we are both ushered in ahead of the queue. For aesthetic reasons I decide to leave my crutch at home, and although I'm still a bit unsteady on my feet, so is everyone else at this time of night.

The security men are quite complimentary about my duds too: 'Ironic-retro. Nice one, mate,' chuckles the huge baldy-bouncer, as he stamps the back of my hand with a tiny ultra-violet picture of a steam train.

We weave our way through the thudding back-beat and flickering gusts of laser-blasted smoke. At the bar my height gets me served quickly. It seems that Reading clubland is full of stunted runts in hoodies and baggy jeans.

So much for a dress code.

The drinks have a steam-railway theme. I order two Stokers-Cokes which I suspect might have rum in them and am utterly shocked by the price. Even after I've unloaded a double cascade of silver and coppers on to the bar top I still have to ask Livia to help out with the tab. God knows where she's keeping her cash now that she's removed her coat, but she hands me a wedge of fivers and is quickly surrounded by a pack of drug-ravaged lounge lizards. They gaze at her with that familiar Edmund-sex-monster leer, but she doesn't seem offended. Quite the opposite actually. She's obviously going to be pumping these guys for information, so I leave her to it.

I glance back through the strobing crush of gyrating bodies, limbs undulating like the shadowy fronds of anemones in a waist-high sea of dry-ice vapour, and I'm amazed to spot someone I actually know. It's Gerry: Gerry – but not Gerry.

The sun-faded old black T-shirt has been superseded by a tight crew-neck, his extravagant pompadour is now a short spiky statement of upward mobility, and, as he shimmies through the room, beautiful people raise their hands to him like plants groping for the sun.

I wave like mad, but Gerry fails to notice, or perhaps doesn't recognize me. Instead a red-Lycra-suited bartender on roller skates skids to a flashy halt and cocks his head. 'What can I do for you, sir?'

'You know someone called the Fat Controller?' I have to shout over the music but I'm certain he can hear. Yet he spins abruptly on his wheels, turning his attention instead to one of Livia's lizards. 'Sylv sent me . . . to see the Fat Controller,' I bawl.

The flunkey one-eighties so fast he lays track marks. 'I'll fetch the Ginger Ninja,' he blusters, wiping his hands on his candy-striped apron before scooting away.

Minutes later a stocky ginger-nut in black silk pyjamas taps me on the shoulder. With a brief flick of his head he wordlessly indicates a shadowy stairway to the rear of the club. We climb two short flights and the Ginger Ninja throws open the door to a huge attic room the size of Paddington concourse. A massive, waist-high trestle affair fills the space, every inch of which is covered in miniature-gauge railway track and scaled-down countryside.

By the far wall is a man in his fifties with a slick, black, slicked-back, silver-winged hairstyle. His fingers flicker across a control panel studded with buttons and sliders. The Fat Controller. Only he's not fat and he wears a shiny charcoal silk suit over a yellow silk shirt. Disappointingly, there's no top hat.

To his left is a diminutive, nervous-looking thing, covered in tattoos, not Gerry-style tats, though, rough-edged prison tats made with crushed charcoal which, according to Gerry,

74

are jabbed into the skin like multiple snakebites – even the ones that have been professionally rendered are plain ugly or indecent. He smokes the dregs of a roll-up which he cups in his hand between puffs as though someone might want to snatch it off him. On his right is the massive baldy-bouncer who liked my outfit. I flash him a smile of recognition which is not returned.

I wait in silence. Countless tiny diesel engines flit around the tracks at hyper-speed until the Fat Controller has had enough. He flicks a master switch leaving thirty or so trains high and dry, stranded between stations.

The tattooed one passes his boss a hand-towel.

'Cheers, Herbal.' The Controller grins, and wipes sweat from his pallid forehead, like Elvis after a Vegas performance. He throws the towel back to Herbal and waves me over. 'So, what can I do for you?'

'You're the Fat Controller?'

'Yeah, I'm the Fat Controller. I did used to be an enormously fat bastard.'

The baldy-bouncer nods in affirmation, like his personal trainer just ordered a swift fifty reps of that bullneck.

'These days, my controlling is mostly confined to my trains and my calories.' The Fat Controller shrugs. 'So I probably can't help you, whatever it is you're after. You'd be surprised how much psychic energy it takes to run a night-club as well as a fully operational railway network.' He nods at the massive model layout before him. 'Even on a one-to-one-fifty scale.'

'From what I've seen, you do it very well.'

The Controller looks at my face without bothering to hide his revulsion, irritated by the transparent toadying. 'What do they call you?'

'Mikey.'

'What is it that you want with me, Mikey?'

I have to say, the Controller seems perfectly pleasant, if a bit nerdy. I get straight to the point. 'A good friend of mine got burgled and beaten up a while ago and he lost something that means a lot to him. I'd like to get it back.'

The tiny crease of irritation on the Fat Controller's pallid forehead expands into a gorge. 'Why me?'

'Because Sylvester said you might know how to find things.'

The Fat Controller inspects the undercarriage of one of his engines. 'I'm not guaranteeing anything, but go on.'

'It's a small thing and I'm sorry to bother you, but I'm looking for a stolen medal – Royal Air Force.'

His eyes light up. 'Ah, you just mentioned the other great passion in my life, Mikey. I myself am an enthusiast for the skies, being part-way through my PPL. I have recently come into possession of a Cessna Skyhawk. I love it up there – me, two wings and the clouds. Closest you can get to God, without playing a harp.'

'Or being an astronaut,' rumbles the baldy-bouncer.

'Or a Shaolin monk,' offers Ginger Ninja.

'Or fucked off your face,' suggests Herbal.

The irritable crease reappears. 'Oy, shut it. I'm doing business here.' The Controller dabs a stray droplet from his upper lip. 'Give me a description.'

'It's a Second World War DFC, that's a Distinguished Flying Cross. Sort of a—'

'I know what a DFC is.'

'It belongs to an ex-pilot called Roger Williams. He doesn't have much else. It's very precious to him.'

The Controller considers me for a moment. 'I understand that, Michael. I come from a very modest background. I'm not especially proud of it. Let me tell you, there's no dignity in being skint all the time. My personal possessions mean everything to me. You got brothers or sisters?'

'No. Only child.'

The Controller grins. It might just as easily be a grimace. 'I was the runt, the youngest out of nine kids, always got the short end of the stick in a huge family with fuck all. You learn to fight to the death for everything: food, money, clothes, a bit of quality time with your mum – the works. I spent half my life with too little, the other half with – some would say – too much. Acquisitiveness and greed become very hard habits to break. As you can see, I still enjoy my little toys.' The Controller shrugs. 'It's what comes of a horrible fucking childhood.'

I'm not quite sure how to respond here. I think I've just been warned not to mess with this man's train-set – or his sarnies. I decide to try a little empathy. 'I did have an imaginary friend once,' I say.

'So?'

'I think my parents loved him more than me.'

The Controller goggles. Without warning, he laughs. A sharp series of 'ack's, like a cat coughing furballs. It ceases as abruptly as it began.

'That's good, Mikey. But you'll never really know what it's like to live at the arse-end of hand-me-downs unless you've been there.'

'I'm sure.'

The Controller scrutinizes my outfit. His private agony is almost tangible.

'Mikey, this DFC, I'm not saying I've got it, or can even get it, but out of interest, how much are you prepared to pay?' He taps his front teeth with the engine's brass coupler.

I pat my pockets for the reassuring bulge of Livia's bank-roll. Obviously I'm going to have to haggle a bit. 'I'll go up to nine.'

'Nine big ones? You really want this gewgaw?'

'I do.'

His eyes are flat, dead and grey, like a shark's. 'Maybe I can help, but I'd want cash up front.'

'No problem,' I slap two of Livia's fivers on to the roof of a small country station – Tilehurst, I think – and wait for change.

The Controller doesn't miss a beat. 'Did anyone check this cunt out?'

The Ginger Ninja is quick to disassociate. 'Never seen him before. Came in tonight, slinging the Vester's name about.'

The Controller shakes his head in disbelief. 'Chuck him out, Eugene, and kick his arse in the alley, for good measure.'

I find myself instantly immobilized by the baldy-bouncer, my pipe-cleaner arms wrenched agonizingly up behind my back.

The Ginger Ninja executes a couple of wild spins before throwing a spectacular punch. His fist quivers an inch or so from my face. I can't be sure if this vibrating thing is genuine Kung Fu or just the early onset of Parkinson's. 'Wooah-ah-cha-chaaa, Eagle-claw strike,' he screeches.

'Just get him out of here,' orders the Controller. 'Don't do serious damage though. I think this one might be a couple of vouchers short of the pop-up toaster.'

Evidently I've disappointed him in some way.

I'm hoping Livia doesn't spot me as I'm frog-marched across the club by these toughs. For one thing, I don't want her to know that I've messed it up. For another, I suspect she's mad enough to try to take them on.

In the smelly old alley, the Ninja doesn't seem to want to stick to the arrangement: instead of kicking me up the arse, he rabbit-punches me in the stomach. I flail at him. It's a feeble effort of course, but I manage to catch him on the bridge of the nose and it makes his eyes water. There's a disagreeable tussle and I'm forced to curl up into a ball until I hear what sounds like Gerry's voice. 'Come on, Ninja-boy, he's had enough now,' he says and the kicking stops.

I pop my head out like a tortoise and see that I'm not mistaken: it is Gerry. He gazes balefully down at me, shaking his head. 'Nice to see you up and about again, Mikey,' he says, with just a trace of irony.

Eugene, the baldy-bouncer and Herbal seem happy to back off but the Ginger Ninja steps into Gerry's space. For a moment the two of them stand nose-to-nose, like a pair of rutting stags.

The side door bursts open and Livia emerges from the club, furious. 'What the fucking hell are you doing, you bloody oaf-bastards?'

Livia crouches and cradles my bleeding face in her arms. I milk the moment for all it's worth. 'Oh, Livia, thank God . . .'

She lets my head fall back on to the scabby concrete. 'Yes, all right, Mikey. Let's not overdo it.'

I get to my feet, massaging the bump. 'Thanks.'

Gerry and the Ninja continue to circle one another. Gerry's a good head taller and despite the Ninja's flashy 'woo cha-cha' shenanigans, I know who I'll be putting Livia's money on here.

'This is the Controller's business you're messing with, Gerry,' warns the Ninja.

'I'm aware of that,' agrees Gerry, 'but I know this lad. You've given him a little slap and that's fine, but you want to give him some more and you'll have to come through me first.'

Wow. Gerry's been reading way too many comics but it seems to have the desired effect. There's a sort of unspoken truce; the baldy-bouncer, Gerry and the Ninja disappear back inside the club, no doubt to explain themselves to the Fat Controller.

Herbal hangs about in the alley with us, looking shifty, before coming to a decision of some kind. 'Medals is it?' he hisses like some Dickensian villain, and gestures for us to follow.

Despite the glass frontage it's impossible to see inside the Sunnyside-Up Café from the pavement: the pane is so yellow and misted with dinosaur breath. Herbal shoves open the door and hustles us over to the nearest unoccupied green leather-look bench. He offers up a long-fingered, grimy hand. 'They call me Verbal Herbal,' he murmurs, nervously. 'They call me that for three reasons: one, because my given name is Herbert, hence Herb, hence Herbal. Two, because I am quite partial to a smoke of the jazzier, herbolic substances. And three, because I do tend to bang on a bit once I get going – that's the Verbal bit. And, come to think of it, there is a fourth . . .'

'We get the idea,' says Livia, absently scratching at a petrified lump of organic matter welded to the pink Formica surface. 'So, what do you want? What are we doing in this dump?'

Herbal taps his nose with a stained yellow forefinger. 'It's not what I want, Sweet-Cheeks. It's what you want.' He gazes around the café suspiciously and lowers his voice to a con-spiratorial whisper – entirely unnecessary, since every other table in the place appears to be hosting the same huddled, muted conversation. Neat, tiny packets pass swiftly from hand to hand, like a miniature mail room. 'You want to know about a DFC? There was a DFC, an old war medal that got lifted a few weeks back . . .'

I nod enthusiastically.

'If you don't mind me saying, offering the Fat Controller

nine quid for it might not have been the sharpest move, given that a medal of this nature might be worth as much as four large on the open market. That's four thousand squid, my friend.'

No wonder the Fat Controller was a bit testy. 'Well, that's that then,' I sigh. 'I'll never be able to buy it back at that price.'

'Who said anything about buying?' replies Herbal, grinning.

I can see that Livia's getting impatient with all this tap-dancing. 'You work for the Fat Controller, you're with his crew, why would you want to help us?'

Herbal gives her a wry smile. 'Very astute, *ma petite* Crème Brûlée, but there's no real loyalty in this game, just loose affiliations based around two classic and distinct behaviour modifiers: carrot and stick, cash and fear. In this particular instance I am motivated by cash. It's a calculated risk of course: on the upside I'm reasonably certain that I will emerge financially better off; on the downside, there's a chance of getting my kneecaps smashed. But it is a very small chance, since what I might let slip to you every other fucking scallywag in the Thames Valley knows anyway.'

Livia's left leg is vibrating with frustration. 'Fine, Herbal, you obviously know where our DFC is, how much for the information?'

Herbal recoils like she just kicked him in the testicles. 'For Christ's sake, keep your voice down. You want to get me topped?' He eyes dart around the room. 'I may ramble on a bit, Dolly-Drops, but I do not actually *sell* information.'

Livia pulls her raincoat tight and jumps to her feet. 'What the bloody hell is the point of you then?' she snaps.

'Calm down, girly.'

'And don't call me "girly".'

'Steady on, Honey-Cakes. Naturally, I do have *something*

to sell.' Herbal seems to be digging himself in deeper with every response.

Livia controls herself and sits nicely – little Dolly-Drop that she is.

Herbal opens his mouth to continue but snaps it shut again with the arrival of our waitress, a huge woman in a grubby pink nylon uniform who slaps down menus like Nurse Koroma dumps a bum poker hand. Her name, Brenda, is scrawled in black marker on a piece of sticking-plaster stuck over the top of an oblong badge. It speaks volumes about staff turnover at the Sunnyside-Up.

'Help you?'

'What's the coffee like here?' I ask.

Brenda tips her head to one side and stares up at the ceiling for a moment, blinking through spider-leg lashes. Some artistically inclined toddler has done her make-up tonight, with a packet of extra-large crayons. 'That's a tough one. Let me think. Uh . . . it's not really like anything I can describe. Sewage, I suppose, would be the closest thing.'

'That good?'

'It doesn't have to be good when you're still open at four-thirty in the morning.'

'How about the tea?'

She sucks her teeth with a pained expression and dolefully shakes her head. I drop the menu. 'Just a glass of tap water then, for me.'

'Excellent choice, sir. We have it specially piped in by the Thames Valley Water Authority. I think you'll enjoy its gritty texture.'

'I'll give the tea a go,' announces Herbal.

'Diet Coke,' orders Livia.

'And I'll have a fried egg on toast,' I add, in deference to the café's name and the fact that even I can cook an egg without poisoning myself.

We wait in silence while Brenda waddles back to the counter with our order. Over the till is a dog-eared sign which says in large type: 'The Management can accept no responsibility.' Just that – it's not clear whether this is meant to be a warning or a terrible admission of failure.

'I'm no snout,' hisses Herbal, huddling us again, 'but I am a dealer in fascinating, educational and self-improving herbolic and pharmacological experiences. Were you, and your tasty young bit of cheesecake, interested in availing yourself of my exciting portfolio, I might let slip a couple of facts which would interest you.' Herbal hunches and glares at Livia for a second like a trodden-on snake.

'Right,' says Livia, 'I'll take some whiz. Five grams, if the price is right.'

Herbal rummages in a small black bag and produces a small polythene pouch which he passes under the table. Livia licks her finger and dips it into the powder before rubbing it across her upper gums. I've seen people do this before on the telly but could never figure out why. I imagine it's the drug-buyer's equivalent of kicking the tyres on a used car.

Livia runs her tongue around and smacks her lips. She nods. 'How much?'

Herbal grins, and though snaggled, his teeth are surprisingly delicate-looking, almost transparent. 'I'm robbing myself here, Pineapple Chunks, and it's only because you're such a reasonable young lady and I like his face . . .'

'Don't be ridiculous,' snaps Livia. I'm not sure whether to be offended. At any rate Herbal abandons the charm and gets to the point. 'Seventy.'

'Not for that crap. Thirty-five, tops.'

A sly expression drifts across Herbal's ratty countenance. 'Funny thing. I never feel much like nattering after haggling; squeezes all the sociability out of me, like an old toothpaste tube.'

'Fifty.'

'I'm as quiet as a church-mouse saying his prayers.'

'Sixty-five then,' spits Livia.

'Done.'

I count thirteen of Livia's crisp fivers into Herbal's grubby hand. 'Now, funnily enough, I do feel a bit chatty. You know what? If you and your delightful slice of Pavlova here were to take a little drive down Wallingford way, you would not consider it a wasted journey.'

My delightful slice of Pavlova quietly fumes while Brenda returns with the order.

I notice that my egg is runny; the yolk appears to have been garnished with something black and springy, possibly pubic. I consider complaining but daren't risk it in case Brenda smart-arses me with one of her ferocious put-downs. Besides, I'm absolutely ravenous.

Herbal dips his head in the direction of the steamy window where a thread of sun is beginning to erase the night sky. 'Looks like a fine one too. As I was saying, if you were to drive down Wallingford way, you would certainly be warm today. You'd be getting very warm indeed if you went in that direction.' Herbal shovels seven teaspoons of sugar into his stewed tea and gives it a quick stir. The word 'War' is crudely emblazoned across the knotted knuckles of his left hand. 'And if you were keen on aviation, there's a small airfield down there that might interest you. Pilots can be superstitious folk and like to mount things in the cockpit for good luck – photos, jewellery, medallions, crosses and such religious iconography.' He takes a sip from the mug, looking immensely pleased with himself. 'All that's happened here is that we've done a perfectly legitimate piece of pharmaceutical business and then chatted about the weather for a while. Am I right?'

I nod. 'Herbal, why do you have "War" tattooed on one hand and "Peas" on the other?'

'It's a long story,' he says, grinning through glassy teeth.

Twelve

'We're going to what?'

'Nick it back, of course,' says Livia, sitting on the foot of my bed, blithely inspecting her polythene package. There are panda-rings round her eyes; she looks exhausted and suddenly quite fragile.

'That's it?'

'It's a simple plan, Mikey. They're always much better than the complicated ones.'

'You can't just waltz into an airport and start pinching things. They have security guards in those places; and dogs, and machine guns.'

'I'm not talking about hijacking the plane. Besides, it's just an airfield, not an airport – completely different thing. "Security" is probably just one dozy pensioner in a gatehouse, with a cat or a hamster. There are no dogs with machine guns.' Livia chops up a little heap of white powder with my Swiss Army penknife on the glossy box lid of my Cotswold jigsaw, where it sits, festively, like a ridge of fresh snow along the parapet of the bridge. 'You've become quite negative for some reason. It's very depressing. Considering you've only got two weeks left, you should at least try to enjoy them. Live a little.' She plays with a couple of stripy plastic straws from the Sunnyside-Up Café, linking them together to make one long one. She wags it at me for emphasis.

Livia's right: I am a little down – mainly because she's just reminded me of my sell-by date. I have no idea what kind of strange hormonal cocktail is being shaken and stirred in my head; even though I haven't slept, it feels like I got out of bed the wrong side this morning.

There's a hesitant tap on the door. 'Mikey . . . are you decent?'

Livia instantly disappears under my bed like a terrier down a rat hole, leaving the incriminating box lid on the carpet.

My mother stands at the door, breakfast tray in one hand, vacuum hose in the other. She places the tray on my chest of drawers. 'Your father has decided that this room needs a good going-over. He asks that you try to be a little more hygienic and not leave your soiled old tissues piled up under the bed.'

There's a stifled squeal from that very location, which I mask with a fit of coughing.

'The dust can't be good for you, Mikey.' My mother steps on the button and the machine takes a slow emphysemic breath. 'Just look at that,' she says, referring to the coating of powder on the jigsaw lid. The hose hovers over the box for a moment and, to my horror, Livia's outsized stripy straw appears from under my bed like the questing proboscis of some weird insect and begins a frenzied pre-emptive vacuuming action of its own.

'You know that most house dust, about ninety per cent, is actually *dead human skin*?' I have to shout over the din of the machine.

Fortunately my mother's heart is not in the task and she's easily sidetracked. 'Oh dear,' she warbles. 'Is that true?'

87

'The remaining ten per cent is mostly dust mite droppings and other faecal matt—'

My mother regards the hose with horror, drops it as if it were an angry anaconda and dry retches, obliterating Livia's manic snuffling.

The door slams and I hear urgent footsteps in the direction of the bathroom.

Livia's nostrils resemble two Polo mints as she rolls out from under the bed. The panda shadows have disappeared and her eyes are startlingly bright; she looks enormously pleased with herself, like she just got back from a camping holiday in an oxygen tent. 'Fuck, that is excellent toot.'

I'm furious with her. But it's hard to stay cross with Livia, especially after I down the glass of milk on my breakfast tray. I can tell from the lovely mellow warmth spreading up from my toes that there's a heap of Darrow's sedatives in there. As usual, they don't make me sleepy, just well-disposed. 'Livia,' I say, 'you should take it easy on the drugs. I don't think they can be good for you.'

Livia grins, like someone inserted a vice between her cheeks. She checks her watch. 'It's past nine already, Coombs has gone to work, daylight's burning. Wait for me in the driveway.'

A racing-green open-top MG appears outside the house, revving wildly. In jeans, crisp white shirt and sunglasses, the driver has a wholesome, just-stepped-out-of-the-shower, girl-next-door look. Dark hair cascades down her back in loose wet trails. I sprint down the drive, hoping that my mother isn't watching from an upstairs window, and dive into the passenger seat.

'Suck exhaust, fucker,' bellows the girl next door, as we screech away, cutting up Mrs Postlethwaite's Metro. Livia's jaws are working hard, grinding her teeth like she's grinding the gears. She turns to give me another piano-key grin and narrowly avoids the postman. 'Coombs's MG, his pride and joy, which I've . . . ah . . . borrowed for the day. The business, *n'est pas?*'

I buckle up.

Livia is still manic and dangerously heavy-footed by the time we hit the outskirts of Wallingford, although I have to admit that she is an excellent driver – but only because she's been repeating that Dustin Hoffman *Rain Man* phrase for the past fifteen miles and it's driving me mad.

'. . . course, I'm an excellent driver,' she announces, for the hundredth time.

'Yes, Livia,' I sigh, 'you *are* an excellent driver.'

'Ha, I knew I'd get it out of you in the end.'

'Watch out for the bloody ditch.'

'Ha.'

Mercifully I catch sight of a bright orange windsock fluttering away to our right.

'Take the next turning there,' I shout over the howl of the wind, the bellow of the engine and the pounding of my own heart.

At the end of a narrow country lane we pull up at a barrier in a cloud of dust. From a squat-looking concrete kennel, a pack of dogs sets up a hoarse clamour. Three security guards emerge from the gatehouse, clutching hamburgers, not one of them a doddery old pensioner. They wear professional-looking bomber-jackets with 'Ard-Corp Security' stencilled across the back. Each of them has a walkie-talkie at his belt.

'You members?' snaps the leader, a brutal-looking man with an iron-grey flat-top.

Livia airily dismisses the question with a flick of her wrist.

'We were just passing and wondered if we could sign up for lessons . . .'

'There's no flying school here, love.'

I can see a tiny cabin at the edge of the field. 'Perhaps I could just check at the clubhouse over there.'

The flat-top wipes a gob of mayonnaise from his chin with his sleeve. 'Unfortunately, you can't come past this barrier unless you're a member.'

'How do I get to be a member, if you won't let me in?' I object.

The man smiles, tiny black eyes refusing to participate. 'Tell you what, mate,' he says kindly, 'why don't *I* give you a quick flying lesson . . . on the toe end of this boot?'

'Oh that's nice, that's charming,' says Livia, gunning the MG into reverse. 'Well, I'll be writing a letter to the Flying Association . . . Group . . . Authority . . . about you.' She does at least manage to spatter their burgers with gravel as we spin away.

We're parked up in a beautiful spot just outside Wallingford, sprawled across a Hunting Stewart car rug on the grassy bank of the Thames. And, as Herbal predicted, it's turned out to be a beautiful day. Livia rummages through a couple of hastily packed Tesco bags, producing packets of salami, ham, assorted cheeses and French baguettes, like a magician delving into a hat. There's even a tin of anchovies, a jar of artichokes and one of pickled onions.

'I cleaned out Coombs's fridge this morning,' she explains. 'I'll get it in the neck tonight, but what the hell, our need is greater.'

Livia has forgotten to pack a knife so I smear a wedge of Port Salut across the bread with my thumb – a nice soft cheese with an orange skin and a mild flavour, like Dairylea only chewier.

Livia kicks off her loafers before producing a wooden disc which she sniffs. 'Now this, Mikey, is the dog's nuts.' Actually, it smells like the dog's bum. I watch in disbelief as she slathers reeking grey slime across her baguette. 'Camembert. A bit overripe, but that's its charm.'

This is all new to me. Cuisine-wise, the Hough family is firmly locked in the fifties with our lamb stews, roasts, potted meats and pilchards. Exotic is a jar of redcurrant jelly and a fruits of the forest yoghurt; anything more racy is 'Dago muck'. When I was younger I made the occasional attempt to steer our trolley towards the free samples on the deli counter in Tesco's but my father always overruled me. 'Mikey, where do you imagine the expression "Deli-belly" comes from?' he'd ask, with a withering look.

I feel I might be on safer ground when Livia peels open a tin of anchovies. Although they resemble stunted sardines, they smell so awful I decide not to risk it. 'Maybe just some ham and a pickled onion for me,' I say.

'Oh God, I knew it. I loathe pickled onions but I had a feeling you might like them.'

I'm touched that Livia decided to bring the pickled onions for me. 'I've always liked pickled onions. I'm only allowed to have them with cold cuts on Saturday. And I'm only allowed two.'

Livia passes me the jar. 'Here, have the lot. Eat them all. We'll keep the roof off.'

I tweeze a couple out between finger and thumb and pop them into my mouth. Haywards – the absolute best. Livia looks on in fascinated horror, like someone watching a car accident. Suddenly I want to make her think well of me, impress her in some way; demonstrate how much these pickled onions mean to me. 'Sometimes I used to sneak downstairs at night and drink most of the juice out of the jar.

I think I could probably still do it. It's almost pure vinegar.' I raise the container to my lips.

Livia smiles and puts a hand on my arm. 'Don't do that, Mikey. You don't need to. I just brought them because I thought you might like them. They're not pearls, you know.'

Indeed they are not. Pearls are quite different: smaller, softer and much less piquant. Inferior in every respect. I would only eat a pearl onion at a party or in an emergency.

Livia lies on the rug and stares at me for a while. 'It's funny, Mikey, sometimes I look at you and I see six foot, long hair: average dude. And then I realize I'm looking at a child.'

'You're a year younger than me,' I retort, putting her in her place.

'You've lost so much time and you have so little left. I get sad for you, Mikey.'

I have no idea what's going on here, but it seems that pity is at the heart of it. I don't want to be pitied. So far, no one has pitied me. Not even my parents. 'I'm very fine, for your information. My father says that we all have our numbered accounts and when we overdraw in the bank of life, we go and explain ourselves to the area-manager-in-the-sky.'

Livia jerks and her eyes contract to pillbox slits. She's almost spitting now. 'That's the problem. Your parents are so ghastly middle class that even when their son is dying they don't want a fuss; they don't want to draw attention to themselves – no net curtains twitching, no hushed voices over the garden fence. They communicate with you through dishonest innuendo and platitude. They want a quiet departure: "Regrettable, but . . . hem hum . . ." and so on. Fuck them, and fuck their hypocrisy. How dare you sit here, drinking vinegar, and tell me that this is very fine?'

I slowly screw the lid back on the jar and lie back on the rug, head to head with Livia, so close I can smell her breath. I was hoping it might be sweet but of course it smells of rancid cheese. The breeze caresses our cheeks through the shifting branches of a nearby elm. Livia slowly relaxes, puts her arms behind her head and closes her eyes. 'How do you know all this stuff, Livia? How do you know so much more about everything than me?'

'Everything what?'

'Food, for a start. You can eat food that smells like dog shit without batting an eyelid.'

Livia's smile broadens. 'It's not about how much time you've had or how long you have left. It's about what you do with it and what you learn from it.'

I peer down the length of my skinny body through the gun-sight of my pale blue socks. A swan cruises past on the greenish river below.

'I despise your family, Mikey.'

'You don't know my family.'

'Oh, there are no secrets in suburbia: I know all about the neighbours. I know, for example, that Jenny Postlethwaite has a disabled sticker which she uses in the Waitrose car park, and even though Dennis Postlethwaite fancies himself as Berkshire's greatest horticulturist, he's not checking out seed catalogues in his shed at nights. I also know that while your mother thinks she's been going through a weirdly prolonged menopause, the only thing actually wrong with her is that she's a snivelling, self-absorbed hypochondriac. Meanwhile your pompous stuffed-shirt of a father is down at the golf club, burying his head in the nineteenth hole, or he's polishing that Volvo of his. You know, he won't even let your mother adjust the seat settings when she drives, in case he can't get it back to precisely the way that suits his bum? That's got to be the textbook definition of anally retentive.'

'You're very . . . judgemental,' I say.

'They're very easy to judge. But, I suppose in their own way, they have looked after you. You've been protected in that cocoon of theirs. And now look at you, you've got no time left and you won't even try an anchovy.'

'I don't want to get ill.'

'You are ill. You're dying.'

'Thanks for reminding me.'

'Mikey, a lot of things have happened to me. Actually, a lot of bad things. But sometimes, bad things can be good things, do you see that?'

'No.'

'It's like inoculations, sometimes you have to have a bit of the bad stuff in your life to give you strength, immunity. So you can go out and enjoy other stuff.'

'I don't see how eating an anchovy is going to make me a better person.'

Livia's head falls back on to the rug. She lies there for a while, blinking moistly into the sun. At length she says, 'What have you heard about me? What's the goss?'

I shrug. 'You're Coombs's god-daughter, you've been at some posh boarding-school, your mum's not well, you got expelled or something and now you're here for a while, living with Coombs. That's it.' I sit up and tear off a lean strip of ham and decide not to confuse things by introducing Edmund's Lolita theory.

Livia pulls herself upright and hugs her knees. 'I didn't go to boarding-school.'

I open the jar, fish for another pickled onion and catch a whopper.

'I've been in a young offenders institution since I was fifteen. Bad things, Mikey.'

The gigantic onion remains frozen before my lips.

'Go on, say something then. Speak into the microphone,' orders Livia, shoving the glistening orb into my slack mouth. 'Good things, too,' she says. 'I learnt a lot. I can tell the difference between a decent Chablis and a bad Chardonnay;

94

gut-rot brandy from a fine cognac; I can tell a truffle from a chanterelle – my bunkie was an Anglo-French girl – and I can tell whether a gram of toot's been stepped on. I can pick a lock and make a respectable shank out of a plastic comb and a nail file.' Livia's head drops abruptly, thick dark tresses falling about her face creating a line of shadows in a strange, visual echo of her incarceration. 'Now you know,' she murmurs.

If I was cool, I'd gently lift her chin and kiss the grief from her face. But I'm not, and I can't.

'Truffles?' I say. 'I know someone called Mr Truffles.' Livia peers up, her eyes are red-rimmed, but, thank God, she's not actually crying. 'Mr Truffles is a friend of mine, who is also a friend of Roger, the man who lost the medal. We should go and see them both. I think Roger will be really chuffed to know that we're on the trail of his DFC.'

Livia's eyes go small again as she turns to face me. 'You mean . . . you haven't even told this person that we're trying to *find* his medal?'

'Ah, well, not as such. No.'

Thirteen

The south block cafeteria is clean and functional enough for a place where eating is done more for distraction than for pleasure or nutrition. Now that his ribs are healing and he's fully mobile, Roger spends most of his time here with Truffles, or in the TV room. Anywhere but on the ward.

'I can't bear all that farting, groaning and snoring. It's no way to go, you know. There's no dignity in it.' The bruising across his face has subsided, livid purple fading to a blotchy magenta-flecked yellow. His eyes are no longer bloodshot and swollen, but lido-blue and constantly on the move, as though still scanning the skies for enemy fighters. He wears a quilted satin dressing gown, which reminds me of a smoking-jacket. Mr Truffles sits placidly by in orange pyjamas, a pair of surgical gloves encasing his blackened, crabbed hands. Livia sits next to me, smiling and sipping tea as though butter wouldn't melt. There's a mound of petits-fours on the table and, but for the PJs and the nondescript tubular furniture, we might be taking tea at the Ritz with a couple of dotty old uncles. I can tell that Mr Truffles is desperate for us to try a pastry. I'm still full of pickles and ham so I go for a small one, a tiny diamond-shaped confection with an almond on top.

Roger scrutinizes us with those fast-roving eyes. I get the impression that they don't miss much. 'I'm very flattered that you'd want to go to all this trouble for me but at your age the two of you don't want to be wasting your time chasing around after some silly old duffer's bauble. You should be out, having fun, burning the candle at both ends, getting up to no good.'

'We're doing a bit of that too, Roger,' says Livia, scanning the plate. 'Wooh, madeleines! I've never been able to resist a madeleine.' She nibbles a delicate icing-sugar-covered tower. 'Proper Genoese pastry too . . .'

Mr Truffles perks up. 'You know the difference?'

'I do and this is exquisite, unlike the so-called English madeleine, that coconut-covered piece of crap with a glacé cherry on top – 'scuse my French. Now, you're not going to tell me that these are NHS prescription?'

A flush of pleasure illuminates Truffles's haggard face. He gazes modestly down at his handiwork. 'I've made an informal arrangement with the catering staff here. In return for a little light prep work they let me loose amongst the pots and pans for an hour or two every day. I'm a bit rusty but it's like riding a bike, really, you never completely lose the knack.'

'I have to report that I've put on almost a kilo since Mr Truffles has been back in action,' announces Roger happily.

'And very well you look on it too,' replies Livia, opening up a second front in this charm offensive. 'Very natty, if you don't mind me saying.'

Roger preens in his scarlet gown like a music-hall Lothario. 'Ah, if only I were a few years younger.'

'And if only I were a few years older.'

'This is nice,' I say of my diamond-shaped thing. 'Sort of pastry flavoured, with a nut.' I'm completely ignored. My ex poker buddies are far too busy beaming and twinkling at the irascible, foul-mouthed, car-stealing, drug-crazed madeleine expert next to me.

Roger chuckles and smoothes his surprisingly thick white

hair. 'You're very kind to an old man, but it grieves me to say that I am, more or less, spoken for.'

'All the best ones are,' retorts Livia.

'As it happens, there are lady friends calling on me this afternoon. So if you wouldn't mind going easy on the pastries, Mikey . . .'

I brush crumbs from my shirt and fold my arms emphatically.

'Lady friends, plural?' Livia tuts in mock disapproval and waves a finger at him.

'Identical twins. Charming, and quite impossible to tell apart. So much so that I have no idea which one I'm supposed to have . . . an understanding with. But then that's half the fun, you see.'

'Mikey . . . Mikey Hough, is that you, boy?' a voice bellows. I turn to see Aggie's grinning face across the room. She bustles over, parting the crowds like an ocean liner. I jump to my feet and extend my hand.

'What the hell you doing back here, boy? You missing the enemas? Or old Aggie's sponge baths?' Aggie inspects my outstretched hand with disapproval before batting it away. 'Don't you be getting all formal on Aggie, now. You get here and give me a proper hug before I tell all these people I seen your winkle.'

There may be one or two exceptionally hard of hearing or comatose patients in the furthest reaches of the hospital who miss this nugget, but I doubt it. Livia screeches with delight. I don't mind though. Aggie enfolds me in a bear-hug. She's so wide that my arms don't meet, not even close. Like Roger, I suspect she has managed to put on an extra pound or two from Truffles' cooking. She settles herself in my chair while I locate a spare.

'Roger, push them cakes up this way. Can't you see

Aggie's wasting away over here?' To Roger's consternation, Aggie makes short work of the remaining pastries. 'Come on now, what you doing back here, Mikey?' she demands, hosing me with crumbs.

'I came for my fruit. You still owe me three thousand grapes, some tangerines and a few hundred kiwis.'

'You get nothing from me, boy. Gambling debts don't mean nothing to Aggie.'

'Aggie's a welsher,' sighs Roger. 'Never pays up.'

'Do I look Welsh to you, Mikey?' she asks, commandeering my tea.

'Aggie, if you're not going to pay up nicely I may have to send someone round to collect my fruit.'

'You send who you like, boy. Send the Man from Del Monte, I'll kick his ass. The Man from Del Monte be saying, "No – No more please, Aggie. Stop kicking my ass."' Aggie seems especially pleased with this idea and beams at her audience before licking the icing sugar from her fingers. 'Who you be, child?' she asks Livia.

'Livia . . .'

'Olivia. That's a beautiful name, sweetheart.'

'No, Livia. Livia Knox.'

'Say again?'

'Livia Knox.'

Aggie stops dead, the smile draining from her face. She stares at Livia for a while before turning to me with a strange expression, not anger exactly but something approaching it, mixed with a kind of resigned sadness. 'Of all the girls in the world, Mikey,' she sighs.

'Hello? And what is your problem, exactly?' snaps Livia.

I'm having trouble keeping up here, Aggie's gone all *Casablanca* on me. She hauls herself to her feet, shaking her head. 'Now, you two just would have to go find each other, wouldn't you?'

'What is it, Aggie?' I plead. 'We haven't done anything wrong.'

'It's not what you think you done, Mikey; nor you, child. It's who you be . . .' We watch, dumbfounded, as Aggie stalks away, muttering to herself.

'Well, what the hell was that all about?' Livia asks.

None of us have the answer.

For a minute or two there's a grim, uncomfortable silence around the table, which Roger breaks with a cheerful grin and the words: 'There is some good news: if Mr Truffles is judged to be fit and sound of wind and limb, he is to be released tomorrow. And, sleeping in the next bed as I do, I can vouch for the fact that he is perfectly sound of wind.'

We offer congratulations; mine are somewhat reserved given what I know about Truffles' previous accommodation, but Roger puts me straight: 'My humble little place on the river is ideal in many respects but too much for one old man on his own. The spare room, for example, can easily accommodate an additional cardboard box, and so . . .'

'So, Roger has kindly offered me the use of that room,' confirms Truffles.

'It's not exactly the presidential suite at the Hilton but it will at least keep him sheltered from the weather and such.'

'Better than Piss Alley, any day,' affirms Mr Truffles, 'and there's enough cardboard in the kitchens here for me to make myself a decent bed.'

Roger nods enthusiastically but I can see that Livia is horrified. 'You're giving Mr Truffles space in your spare room but he's still going to have to live in a cardboard box? Well, aren't you Mother-bloody-Theresa?'

'Oh, Heavens-to-Betsy, I'm no saint and this is by no means a charitable arrangement,' says Roger. 'Mr Truffles will pay his way by cooking for me.'

Livia is now livid. 'That is just shocking, Roger."

All that twinkling disappears in, well, a twinkling. Roger fixes us with a stare, like he's trying to tell us something, almost pleading. I'm something of an illiterate when it comes to reading expressions but the sudden pain in my shin is unequivocal. I glance down to see that Roger is wearing heavy-duty black leather brogues under the satin dressing-gown. I'm reasonably certain that he wants us to shut up. Of course he'd do a lot better to kick Livia – in the teeth.

'I can't believe that you're taking advantage of someone's predicament to make them slave for you while they live in an old grocery box.'

'No, please. It's not up to Roger. This is my decision,' intercedes Truffles. 'I set the conditions, not Roger. I'm not worthy to sleep in a bed yet.' Truffles has never been one to put himself forward but now he speaks with a passion. 'I've done . . . I've done some terrible things, made bad choices, let many things slide in my life, including myself. I have to earn the right to sleep in a bed again. Roger has offered me a way back in but I need to do it on my terms. When I'm ready, I'll ask Roger for a bed and I'm sure he'll deliver, but first I must come to terms with what I've done to myself and . . . others.' Truffles smiles weakly.

'Mr T., I wonder if I could prevail on you to conjure up another round of those miraculous dainties, since Mikey has proved so incapable of controlling himself?' prompts Roger, holding up the empty plate.

Truffles nods gratefully and scuttles away to the kitchen.

Roger shrugs. 'A lovely man who made some unlovely choices . . . then again, who hasn't?'

'I'm sorry,' says Livia, 'it wasn't my place to speak to you like that.'

Roger inhales the thick cafeteria air. 'His son was seven, but well used to a hot stove. Well trained in hot-pan disci-pline. And here's the irony: Mr T. was only cooking chips.

The simplest, most basic of all British cuisine. But he was drunk and fell asleep, and the chip-pan caught fire. His son tried to put it out. Not before the little boy lost his hands and most of his face. Mr T. dealt with it in a manner you and I might not have. But it was his choice. Now, he must find his own way to forgive himself.'

Livia has never been slow on the uptake. The penny has dropped, along with her head, which now hangs in shame, framed by those long chestnut strands. 'I'm sorry, I didn't think . . .'

Roger reaches over and pats her hand. 'You have a finely developed sense of right and wrong, of black and white. But alas, so much of what we do sits in those hard to distinguish grey areas. You're still very young and penetrating the grey is about the only ability that does improve with age. It comes with the hair colour.'

'I could still kick myself.'

Roger resumes twinkling; with double-string, fairy-light incandescence. 'I kicked Mikey instead. So, all's well.'

Livia's head shoots back up, forgiven.

Dignity and self-respect are fundamental to the human condition, unless of course your name happens to be Mikey Hough. I rub my ankle and note with some degree of satisfaction that Roger has a rather undignified bogey lodged up his left nostril. I decide not to tell him.

'Of course a bargain has two sides. If Mr Truffles falls back on his old ways he'll have me to answer to,' advises Roger, with mock strictness.

Livia does a kind of coy wriggly thing in her seat which I wish she would do for me but I doubt she ever will. She's staring at him like someone just rubbed her eyeballs with a chamois leather and I suddenly realize I might be jealous of a man almost four times my age. But I can't really dislike Roger. He may be old but he's not an arse, unlike Coombs or my dad. And I know that Truffles is in good hands; whatever demons he is wrestling with, he won't be alone now. And if they're the flying kind, with leathery wings and stuff, Roger will shoot them down. He's an air-ace and he's got a medal to prove it. Except, of course, he hasn't any more.

Despite the boot in the shin, I find I want to prove myself to Roger. For some reason I need his approval. The medal search has metamorphosed from a task to a quest. 'Roger, I promise you, one way or another, we're going to get your medal back.'

'Oh, goodness me, no. I don't want you two to risk yourselves any further than you have done already. All you've really discovered is that a private aircraft exists that may or may not have a DFC attached to the cockpit; a DFC without provenance. It won't do, you know.'

'It's your DFC, Roger,' I squeak.

'You don't know that for sure, so why don't we let the specialists have a go first, eh?'

'The specialists?'

'The police.'

'The people who came here to talk to you?'

'The very same. They are quite experienced at solving crimes, Mikey.'

'They had no idea what a DFC even is for a start, and could care even less. They couldn't even detect that I wasn't blind.'

'Well, they're detectives whether you like it or not. I agree that they weren't necessarily the sharpest knives in the drawer, but it's not all like the films you know, when it comes to detective work, I expect it's slow and steady wins the race.' Roger pulls a card from his pocket. 'DS Davis and . . . let's see, Wenner. If you think your information is sound, go and see them.' He hands the card to Livia and makes an appeal. 'Please, you're a sensible young lady. I won't thank you for exposing yourself to any further danger on my account. I insist on this.'

Livia nods gravely. 'Don't worry, Roger. Case closed.'

Now it's my turn to stare at the table. I pick up my mug to find that somehow Aggie managed to finish my tea before she left. I swallow disappointment instead and rise with all the dignity I still possess. 'Bogies at six o'clock, Roger,' I mutter, before stalking across the room.

Fourteen

'Tell him I'll be there in twenty,' bellows Davis as he barges into the tiny sterile interview room, followed by the lumbering Wenner. He stops short at the sight of me. 'Well, look who it isn't, our young friend from the hospital. No white stick then, Mr . . .?'

I shake my head sheepishly. 'Hough, it's Michael Hough,' I say.

Davis grabs a seat and peers across the table, chewing gum. Wenner nods, producing a pristine notebook and a new black biro. Livia introduces herself and there's a flurry of noncommittal handshakes.

I'm relieved to find that Thames Valley's finest are reasonably brisk today, almost affable. 'So, what's up? What can we do you for?' Davis tips back the chair and puts his arms behind his head to reveal Rorschach-blot armpits.

'I . . . we – that is to say, Livia and I, might have some important information regarding one of your investigations.'

'I'm all ears,' announces Davis. 'Fire away.'

'It's about Roger Williams's missing DFC – there's been a development . . .'

Thankfully the arms come back down. 'That is good news, Mr Huff. Absolutely excellent. There's nothing we like more than members of the public running off in all directions, trying to do our job for us, especially when they have no idea what they're doing and end up muddying the waters of a painstaking, orderly investigation run by professionals.'

Maybe not that affable, I decide. 'We just came across this piece of information by accident really and I'm just passing it on. We're honestly not trying to do your job or play detective or anything.'

Davis places his hands flat on the table and leans in. 'That's just as well now, isn't it, seeing as how you're blind?'

'Ah, well, I think you might have detected that I wasn't really blind last time we met.'

'Bloody right, and we don't take kindly to people taking the piss.'

'No, we bloody don't,' confirms Wenner, writing this all down, including, I hope, his own critical contribution here.

'I apologize if we have muddied the waters in any way but can I ask how far you've got in the Roger Williams investigation?'

'No offence, Mr Huff, but we don't, as a rule, discuss ongoing cases with members of the public, or anyone else who just happens to wander in off the street.'

I have to bite my lip. 'Of course, I understand perfectly. And no offence taken.'

'Some people, especially the members of the press, do get quite arsey about these things, without really understanding the length of time, the sheer grinding nut-work, the hours and the sweat that goes into solving every case.'

If the state of those armpits is anything to go by, the Thames Valley region should be a crime-free zone by early evening. 'Well, you might be pleased to hear that we've short-circuited all that sweat and ah, nut-work . . .' I was going to leave the 'case closed' explanation to Livia but she's gone uncharacteristically quiet; jaw slack, head drooping, so I give them the good news myself: 'I'm pretty certain that we've located the whereabouts of the stolen DFC . . .'

Wenner scribbles something in his book. Davis beams. 'That is just ace.' He leans across the table and actually shakes my hand. 'We've been so worried about that one.'

'Been keeping me awake at nights,' adds Wenner.

'We're thrilled that you've gone out and cracked it for us.' The smile disappears. 'D'you read the local papers, Mr Huff?'

'Not for a while.'

'If you did, you'd know that right now Reading is awash with class-A drugs, a sea of cocaine and speed, driving a crime-wave of epic proportions. In the last month alone we've had list of felonies that would make your hair curl: arson, muggings, aggravated assaults, multiple burglaries. Just last night some poor old pensioner had a heart attack and pegged it after receiving a threatening phone call. What was a minor bloody nuisance may now be a homicide investigation. And somewhere out there, floating on that ocean of shit, is a speck, a tiny bit of flotsam which is your mate's missing DVD. Not exactly a priority for us at this time.'

'DFC,' I say.

'Whatever.' Davis shrugs.

Livia's head has sagged almost to the level of the table top, where she emits a low rhythmic sound like a tiny buzz-saw. She snorts suddenly, catching herself; her head jerks back up and her eyes flicker for a moment before closing again.

'That's a nice little bird you've got there,' points out Wenner. 'You and Nancy Drew on the case of the missing DVD? Up all night, on the trail, were you?'

'On the tail, more like.' Wenner smirks.

'She does look a bit shagged out,' agrees Davis, throwing me an envious glance.

Livia opens bloodshot eyes, blinking fast. 'I have to go and powder my nose now,' she announces groggily.

'Down the corridor, second on the right, young lady,' advises Davis, 'and thank your lucky stars you don't have to be accompanied by a WPC – bunch of lezzers, the lot of them,' he bawls at the self-closing door.

I have to cut this futile conversation short before Livia reappears, wired as a junction box, with a nose on her like one of Mr T's powdered madeleines. 'Well, thanks very much, you've been a tremendous help,' I say, getting to my feet.

'It's what we're here for,' replies Davis cheerfully.

Thankfully, that little sarcasm is one of the many things these two are utterly incapable of detecting.

It's early evening as we screech back down the Oxford Road towards the Royal Berkshire. Livia is now completely revived, and revving like our overworked engine. Under the urine-tinted haze of a sodium streetlight I watch as a forlorn figure in an off-white shirt and threadbare cords struggles with an old shopping trolley, tilting and shoving against the raised kerb. I just have time to catch sight of his crabbed, rubbery hands as we fly past. 'Stop,' I shout. 'I think I just saw Mr Truffles.'

'Don't be ridiculous,' says Livia, fighting to control the fish-tailing vehicle. 'He's not due out till tomorrow.'

'I swear it was Truffles.'

Livia eyes me sceptically for a moment before shooting a glance in the rear-view mirror. 'You sure?'

'I recognized the hands.'

Livia slows and makes a controlled and surprisingly considerate U-turn. We drive back and pull over. On the pavement the hunched figure shuffles past, head down, pushing a trolleyload of cardboard, battling the wonky front wheel.

I'm not wrong, it is Truffles.

Livia toots the horn. 'I like your new wheels, Mr T.,' she bellows.

Truffles peers up and grins broadly. 'Second-hand, but a good runner, only one previous owner – Tesco's, as it happens.' He taps the handlebar fondly. 'I've been discharged, a bit earlier than I expected – they needed the bed. Clean bill of health, I've just got to be a bit careful with these hands of mine for a while.' He waggles fingers; a bunch of condom-sheathed, blackened bananas.

'Didn't anyone come to pick you up or anything?'

Truffles seems puzzled. 'Who?'

'I don't know, family or someone?'

Truffles stares down at his tatty baseball boots. 'No. They're . . . not . . . they don't know about any of this.' He perks up. 'Anyhow, I'm off to Roger's place now, The Cascades, down by Caversham Bridge. Got a roof over my head. Can't complain about that.'

'And you're planning to walk all the way?'

'I don't have two pennies to rub together, not even bus fare. Roger's busy entertaining his lady friends and Aggie went off duty at four. I didn't like to ask. In any case, it's really not that far.'

'Get in this car, right now,' orders Livia.

Livia can be pretty intimidating when she's like this. Even so, Truffles is amused. 'I appreciate the thought, young lady, but you do realize it's a two-seater you've got there and what with all this matching luggage . . .' Truffles indicates the old cardboard boxes and unused pizza cartons stacked in the trolley.

'Two and a bit.' Livia jerks her thumb at the tiny compartment behind us.

Truffles and I flatten out the cardboard and manage to shove most of it into the boot. Other than that there's just a washbag and a few slim packs of surgical gloves. In deference to his frailty and former celebrity, I relinquish the passenger seat and contort myself into the cramped space in the back, hanging on for dear life as Livia negotiates the narrow roads to Caversham Bridge.

I feel a bit sick by the time we pull up at The Cascades, a compact development of low-rise apartments overlooking the river. They've got that boxy, seventies look about them, all straight lines and flat roofs. The Cascades appears to be a genteel retirement community but it's almost too quiet and there's an air of recent dereliction about the place; one or two of the apartments have newly boarded-up windows. As we unload, a net curtain twitches and a frightened, elderly face appears briefly at the window before disappearing again.

Roger's front door has been sealed with bright yellow plastic tape, giving it a bizarrely festive appearance. Truffles rips the stuff away and turns the key, and we're instantly assailed by a foul miasma, like something died. In the hallway are signs of a violent struggle; spatters of dried blood fleck the walls and floor. We switch on the lights and crowd into the sitting room. There we locate the source of the terrible smell, in the centre of the carpet. 'Shit,' says Livia, correctly identifying the disgusting heap. I take a deep breath and rush to the sash window; the catch has been forced and it slides open easily. Cool evening air rushes in.

In the kitchen, the fridge is almost as horrifying; the contents have erupted in a layer of grey-green mould an inch or so thick, like a carpet of reeking volcanic ash.

'I should probably make some tea or something,' says Mr Truffles.

'Tea would be nice.' We're avoiding the subject. Nobody

wants to talk about the object on the living-room carpet but we all know that one of us is going to have to get rid of it.

'*I'm* not doing it,' announces Livia.

'No, leave it to me,' says Mr Truffles. 'I'll just put the kettle on then pop next door and see if one of the neighbours can spare some fresh milk.'

'Go on, Mikey, you deal with it,' says Livia.

'I'm not touching that thing. It's inhuman. It's like a monster.'

'It won't do you any harm. Don't be such a baby.'

'I'll throw up. I'm already queasy from your driving.'

'All right. We'll play "stone, paper, scissors" for it. Agreed?'

'Fine with me,' says Truffles, who has finally cottoned on.

'Agreed,' I say, with some relief, knowing that Mr Truffles's twisted fingers will force him into making a fist – the symbol for stone. So I'm going to do paper and I'm in the clear, no matter what Livia chooses.

'Ready?' says Livia. 'One, two, three . . .'

Of course it wasn't Livia. She set about the fridge and the hallway with a couple of Brillo Pads, half a litre of Cleen-O-Pine and a few hundred milligrams of chemically induced energy. Between us we've got the place looking pretty respectable and smelling like a Scandinavian wood – albeit one in which the bear already took a shit.

In the meantime Truffles has managed to charm a neighbour into bringing fresh milk for our tea. Although he's explained our presence here, the formidable Mrs Hodges seems ill at ease, the cup trembling in her pudgy fingers. 'My late husband, Lawrence, was an hotelier, you know. We had the Blue Boar in Chertsey for many years and after that, the White Swan over at Pewsey. We'd always imagined we'd end our days here, with a view of the river. It was a wonderful place when we first moved in ten years ago – still is, but it's not safe. Nowhere's safe now, of course. It's like we're under siege. Time was, Lawrence wouldn't serve anyone in the saloon bar unless they were wearing a jacket and tie. These days, you're lucky if they're wearing a shirt. And if they are, it's usually a hideous glistening nylon thing with a great number on the front and "Beckenham" or "Revolto", or some such, across the back. The lunatics have taken over the asylum. And as for the police . . .' Mrs Hodges gives a derisive snort.

Out of respect for Mrs Hodges, Livia uses an elegant little pair of silver tongs to launch a couple of sugar cubes into her cup. 'Well, I think it's a lovely spot, Mrs Hodges.'

Mrs Hodges smiles sweetly. 'Oh, it would be if it weren't for . . .' and without warning she suddenly roars at the top of her voice, 'Them!'

I don't know about the asylum, it seems to me that the lunatics may have taken over The Cascades. The woman is literally barking.

'Yes – *them*. They want us all out of here. They've had a go at poor Mr Williams and Mr Shippham; the Emmetts have packed up and moved out; and they got old Teddy Parslow last night. Bang – dropped down dead of a heart attack.' Mrs Hodges turns and bellows at the open kitchen window. 'But they'll not do it to me; they'll not drive me out. I'm staying put.'

She's on her feet now, rummaging in her handbag.

I'd have made a terrible psychiatrist. My response to any kind of abnormal behaviour in public places is to put my head down and find something infinitely fascinating about my knees or my shoelaces. I do this now, stirring tea with stony resolution. Out of the corner of my eye I can see that Livia is twisted in half with suppressed laughter.

'They'll have to pry this taser from my cold, dead hand

before that happens,' announces Mrs Hodges in deadly earnest.

'A taser,' chirrups Livia. 'How exciting, aren't they illegal?'

Mrs Hodges holds up a small black electronic device, like a Dictaphone, with two tiny spikes on the end, and, even though she seems perfectly composed now, she passes the object to Livia, which proves that she is definitely certifiable. 'Lawrence and I brought it back from one of our trips to Florida, smuggled back inside a transistor radio. Lawrence's view was that what most young thugs today needed was a short, sharp shock.'

'How does it work?' asks Livia.

'It delivers a hundred thousand volts to whichever part of the body you shove it up against. Very low amperage, so there's no lasting damage. It disorientates yobbos for several minutes, as poor Lawrence would tell you, were he still with us.'

Livia aims the device in my direction. 'Ah, so you'd better watch out, Mikey,' she warns.

Truffles interjects, 'Don't point that thing at people, even in jest, Livia.'

I wag my teaspoon at Livia, to emphasize the point – that's her told.

Mrs Hodges laughs; a weird high-pitched trill from such a formidable lady. 'There's absolutely nothing to worry about, the Stun King 600-S has a safety catch that is—' At which point I can only assume that she karate-kicks me in the chest. With a judder of excruciating pain I'm hurled backwards, still in my chair. My head hits the lino with a percussive crack.

I'm paralysed and for a second or two I lie there staring up at the stained ceiling, counting perforated plasterboard panels. I smell ozone.

'Oh, Mikey, I'm so sorry.' Livia's voice.

For the second time in forty-eight hours Livia cradles my head in her hands. This time she's genuinely upset; fat tears carve shiny tracks down her cheekbones.

'I pressed the trigger. I thought the safety was on.'

My limbs tingle as control returns. I leap to my feet feeling oddly energized, surprisingly chipper in fact.

'I thought you were supposed to shove those taser-things into people for them to work?'

'You are,' sniffs Livia. 'It must be the damp in here, but I got an arc, like a tiny lightning bolt. It jumped straight up through the end of your teaspoon.'

Sure enough my teaspoon lies on the floor nearby, a twisted, mangled lump of scrap. 'Apart from the bump on my head, I don't actually feel too bad.'

'I should think not,' bellows Mrs H., brandishing the weapon. 'These items are perfectly safe. Almost a hundred per cent non-lethal. Can't see why the government makes such a fuss.'

She turns briskly to Mr T., all business. 'Now, what are you planning to live on here? You're going to need more than just a pint of milk, you know. You must have provisions. I have plenty of eggs, bread, spaghetti, sugar, a few tins, that kind of thing.'

'I couldn't, really . . .'

'Don't be ridiculous. It's what neighbours are for. There's nothing edible in this house. And there are too few of us left in The Cascades as it is. Come along.'

'Well, if you insist, Mrs Hodges.'

'Deirdre.' She actually simpers.

'Deirdre,' concedes Mr T., giving us a doubtful, apologetic grin before allowing himself to be dragged away.

Livia dabs her eyes with an old tea towel while I retrieve my chair.

'Poor Mikey. You didn't need that on top of everything else.'

Alone now, we scrutinize one another over willow-pattern teacups.

'Mikey, are you doing what you want to be doing? I mean, with the time you have left . . . and all that? Would you rather go to DisneyWorld or something, because I'm sure I—'

'I'm fine, Livia,' I say. 'I couldn't be having more fun: going on picnics, buying drugs, getting kicked around by coppers, beaten up in discotheques, electrocuted . . .'

'I'm glad to hear that.' Livia gives me a wobbly smile. 'You know, there's something *I'd* like, Mikey.'

'What's that?'

'It's stupid. I'm embarrassed.'

'Tell me.'

'A photograph. I'd really like a photo before . . . oh God, that sounds . . .'

'Of me?'

'No, of Coombs, who'd you think? Of course of you.'

There's a major blockage in my throat and my eyes have gone all blurry. 'But I'm . . .'

'You're you, Mikey. You're . . . sort of . . . my best friend and you're going away. And I don't want . . .' Livia's lips form a tiny delicate ring as she prepares to sip. Even as I watch, this perfect structure collapses into a messy pout. Her lower lip begins to tremble. 'I . . . I don't think I want you to go, Mikey.'

I reach out to touch her hand just as the Trimphone sounds. We leave it to trill for a while in the hope that Truffles might answer on an upstairs line, but he doesn't. It could be Roger, so I pick-up the wall-mounted handset. 'Hello?'

'Who the fuck is this?'

'Mikey. Who's this?'

'A friend.'

'What do you want?'

'Bit of advice for you. Get out while you can, or face the consequences.'

The phone goes dead. I replace the handset and join Livia back at the table. 'Wrong number,' I tell her.

Composed now, Livia finishes her tea. 'We should get going,' she says.

'You know what I'd really like?'

'What?'

'I'd just like to be able to finish my tea in my own time for once.'

Livia shrugs. 'Why not? Coombs will be back home by now anyway. He'll know I've cleaned out his fridge and the pantry and he'll have discovered his precious MG is missing. So I suppose I can hardly drop myself any further into the shit.' She pours herself another cup and tweezes in a couple of lumps with the tongs.

'Go on then,' she says, smiling, 'how did you deal with that disgusting turd on the carpet in the end?'

I shrug. 'I got a little pair of silver tongs from the kitchen here . . .'

Livia thumps me pretty hard.

Fifteen

It's late by the time we pull in to our quiet little avenue. Livia seems distracted; I can't tell whether it's because she's just tired or because she's mentally preparing herself to face the wrath of Coombs. I offer to give her moral support but she insists on dropping me off first before turning into Coombs's driveway.

I creep down the hallway, where there's a chest full of my father's old electrical detritus. Bernard has yet to come to terms with the digital age, but he hates to throw anything out if it's even vaguely functional and I do know that there's one of those weirdly ancient but serviceable Polaroid cameras in there somewhere. If memory serves, I think it even has a timer for self-portraits. I rummage and find it under a tangle of shattered fairy lights, shove in a couple of AA batteries and check the dial. I'm in luck, there are still eight exposures left in the cartridge. Since the flash seems to be working too, I decide that the treehouse would make a good location for my upcoming shoot.

I'm heading for the kitchen when my father barks at me from his study, 'Mikey, is that you? A moment of your time, if you please.'

The last thing I need right now is my father and his

circumlocution, but I'm trapped. I ditch the camera on the carpet outside before entering.

'Come in, Mikey, come in. Sit ye down, sit ye down.' He gestures at the unoccupied chair facing his desk, an antique nursing chair which gives him the height advantage. I sit with my knees almost up to my chin and try to avoid eye contact. There's a large trout on the wall above his head which I'm convinced is bogus. I've never known my father to go fishing – he doesn't have the patience, or the rod, for that matter.

My father also keeps a variety of executive toys on his desk; a tiny metal stick-figure on a magnetic disc; one of those racks full of moveable pins which shape themselves to the contours of your face; and a Newton's cradle. I reach up and set the chrome balls in motion: clack, clack, clack . . .

'I'd rather you didn't do that, Michael,' says my father, trapping the spheres in his outstretched palm. 'They're not for playing with.' He reaches down into a drawer for something. Meanwhile, I scoop up the pin-rack and push my face into it and leave an impression that's as flat as the Utah Salt Flats.

'Put that down, now,' orders my father, brandishing the manila folder. 'I need you to be focused for a second. It's time we talked about things. You're sleeping all right, are you?'

'Up and down really.'

'I see. Well, it says here, Michael . . . it says here that the doctors believe you may be suffering from a sleep disorder of some sort.' He fingers his moustache. 'I should tell you that I don't approve of sleep disorders. In the Corps . . .' My father flicks his head to indicate the little military plaque on the wall '. . . we didn't have sleep disorders, just lazy bastards and shirkers. And we made short work of them.' He's referring to his National Service stint in the Pay Corps back in the fifties. 'You didn't find me lounging in my pit every morning. I was out there, every day, rain or shine, handing out pay-packets, getting them damn well signed for, despite adversity.'

'I'm sure you were very conscientious.'

'I remember one time during the Suez Crisis, in just a few short hours between elevenses and lunchtime, Corporal Bernard Hough single-handedly dispatched over three thousand little brown—'

'Chaps?'

'Envelopes, Michael.'

Recalling Livia's words about my parents looking after me in their own way, I bite my tongue and try to appear attentive.

'The thing is, I'm not sure that I subscribe to the whole notion of sleep disorders at all. Get yourself to bed at a decent hour, close your eyes and that's all there is to it. And try not to think unhygienic thoughts, Michael.' My father sets the stick-figure twirling on its magnetic disc. 'There was a fellow in my squad; insomniac . . . name of Brigstock, wouldn't get up in the mornings. So one morning I had the bugler blow Reveille into his ear. I didn't hear much about sleep disorders after that – and *he* didn't hear much of anything at all. The man was discharged a month later with an ear-drum disorder. But at least that was genuine. He wasn't swinging the lead on my watch. D'you get my drift here?'

He taps the manila folder. 'No matter what it says in here, this is *not* an excuse to lie there abusing yourself till the small hours like some kind of drug-addled popular singer. Academically you've got a lot of catching up to do. And while we're on the subject, may I ask where you've been all day and what you've been doing?'

'Studying over at Edmund's.' I lie without a moment's hesitation.

'Oh really?'

For a second, I think he's on to me and that this is one of

his suspicious 'Oh really?'s. But he smiles thinly and I realize that it's an 'Oh really?' of approval – I'm a bit out of practice at judging.

'I'm glad to hear it, Michael.'

'Edmund's got computers and all the books and things, so that's where I'm planning to be most days and . . . ah, evenings too.'

'Very wise,' agrees my father. 'Have you eaten tonight? Your mother has a kidney and sweetbread thing keeping warm for you in the oven.'

I get to my feet, rubbing the cramp from my knees. 'I'm fine, thanks, I had something at the Kerrs.'

'You're sure?'

'No, really . . .' I insist, closing the door behind me.

I retrieve the camera and tuck it under my jersey as I hurry through the kitchen, where I catch the acrid aroma of tonight's feast. A mug of tepid, sedative-enhanced milk sits waiting for me on the table, thick white skin floating on the surface. I knock it back on my way out.

By the time I stagger to the base of the oak I can already hear the row from next door. Coombs is bellowing like a wounded elephant but I can't see a thing through the overgrown hedge. This is more than anger. Coombs sounds completely out of control; I'm becoming seriously concerned for Livia's safety. Instead of climbing the tree, I locate the fox-run and scramble through. I must have filled out a little over the past few days because I have to use elbows and knees to shove and wriggle my way through the dense undergrowth. The voices are louder now; Livia seems to be giving as good as she gets until she's abruptly silenced. My heart pounds with fear. Wasted muscles tremble with exertion as I arch my back and pop my head up on the other side. I haul myself into a crouch, hunched low in the shadow of the hedge, and am instantly aware of another presence in the garden.

Not ten yards away is a grotesque figure sheathed in skin-tight black, silhouetted against the house; its gut shockingly distended out of all human proportion. There's no face, just a weird proboscis; a gigantic blowfly on two legs. Like something from a Bosch painting.

I catch sight of Livia at one of the unlit upper windows, mercifully unharmed. Downstairs, a savage Coombs paces the living room.

At this moment I'm far more concerned about the demon in the garden than Coombs – at least Coombs is vaguely human.

The creature watches intently as Livia slowly unbuttons her white shirt. I catch a glimpse of her breasts, perfectly white in the moonlight like those English madeleines she claims to despise.

The thing on the lawn stands transfixed, panting; a harsh abrasive hiss. I wonder if this is it: the beginning of psychosis, a manifestation of my disintegrating mental state. It's not the Devil. I'm certain of that.

I'm no eschatologist, but as far as I'm aware, when Satan comes for you he doesn't usually stop for a quick wank first.

Either way, I'm getting a souvenir. I flick open the flash block. Check that I'm charged up. Don't want to miss this one.

'Hey you, say "cheese".'

The creature spins. I pop the flash, bringing light to Lucifer.

'Jesus. I can't fucking see.' The thing squeals like a gelded hog and claws at its eyes. The proboscis slides away to reveal a sweating disc of fleshy white face.

It's Edmund. Wearing my old balaclava.

'My *eyes*,' he howls, staggering away. 'My eyes are burning.'

I look down to inspect the proboscis lying discarded on the grass, a black rubber mask housing a powerful-looking lens – a night-vision scope. These things work by intensifying light; no wonder the big pervert's eyes were smarting.

Mrs Kerr should have warned her son about the dangers of masturbation. It can make you go blind.

I pocket the photo for posterity. Still a bit flash-blind myself, but manage to retreat through the fox-run and find my way to the old oak. I run my fingers over the thick trunk, find the lower baton and climb, camera dangling from the loop on my wrist.

With difficulty I manage to haul myself up on to the creaky platform and crawl over to the edge. Edmund's long gone, there's no further sign of Livia or Coombs through the windows.

A brilliant flash illuminates the oak. For a moment I wonder if the Polaroid has misfired. A jet of orange flame settles, hovering in the air a few feet from my eyes. In the shadows behind I can see the silhouette of a man, sitting with his back against the trunk. The flame drifts slowly towards his face before it disappears, leaving only the bright red tip of a cigarette tracing arcs in the night air.

'You're an idiot, Mikey. D'you know that?'

'Gerry? Christ, you scared the shit out of me. What the hell are you doing?'

'Waiting for you.'

'Why can't you come to the house like a normal person?'

'I haven't been back for two years. Your dad fired me after your little stunt; said he'd get the law on me if he ever saw me round here again.'

'I'm sorry to hear that. If it's any consolation, the garden looks like shit and the hedge is overgrown.'

'Thanks for that.' I can hear a smile in the voice. The tip of his roll-up glows fiercely like a miniature volcano. 'It's been busy out here tonight. Better than watching TV. You know your girlfriend's got a bit of a Peeping Tom problem, don't you?'

'It was Edmund Kerr; he's gone now,' I growl, 'and he won't be back either.'

'How's that then?'

'I took a picture of him, wanking.'

'Whatever turns you on, Mikey. Your young lady was in a bit of strife earlier.'

'She pinched Coombs's MG and cleaned out his fridge.'

There's a low chuckle from the shadows. 'Bit of advice, Mikey. You might think old Barry Coombs over there is a buffoon. Let me tell you – he's not. Steer clear of him.'

'He's just a bully.'

'I'm serious about Coombs. Keep out of his way. What I really want to know is what the hell you were playing at down at the Tank Engine last night? Big mistake, Mikey. You think *Coombs* is a bully? You get on the wrong side of those people at the Tank Engine and they'll really fuck up your train.'

'Gerry, the Fat Controller has something I want.'

'The Fat Controller has plenty of things that people want, but they don't usually go about getting them by strolling into his club and taking the piss.'

'He stole it, or at least his people did.'

'Oh my goodness. Did he? Well that changes everything. That is just scandalous. I hope you've reported it to the police.'

'I have.'

'Big mistake Number Two. Who'd you speak to?'

'Someone called Davis and . . .'

'Wenner . . .' Gerry sounds relieved. 'Look, I had to do a lot of fast-talking last night to get you off the hook. It cost me, but everything's cool now.'

'How did you manage to do that then, Gerry? How come if these people are so scary you can talk to them and suddenly everything's cool?'

'I told them you were a retard.'

'Fuck off, Gerry.'

'No, I'm serious. You know, what with your face and all, the Fat Controller was inclined to be benevolent. He thinks you're not the full shilling.'

'He thinks what?'

'That's a result, Mikey. Don't get funny on me.'

The retard has temporarily lost the power to speak.

'I knew you'd be up here.' Livia's face appears at the edge of the platform. I can see from her wet hair that she's changed and showered. She hauls herself up, revealing a lacy black top.

'Ah, your sidekick,' announces Gerry approvingly, constructing another roll-up.

Even in the weak glare of Gerry's lighter there's no hiding Livia's split lip. There's a tiny trickle of blood still oozing from her left nostril. As a result, she's not her usual charming self. 'If you like, I'd be more than happy to sidekick you right off this platform,' she snarls.

Gerry wheezes with suppressed mirth. He takes another drag. 'Grab a pew, young lady, and listen up. I'm trying to tell the Dark Knight here that real life isn't like the comics. You of all people should know that, Livia Knox.'

Livia deflates like a whoopee cushion. 'Who are you and how do you know my name?'

'I'm Gerry. Mikey will vouch for me.'

Actually I'm not at all sure that I want to vouch for Gerry now. I don't know whether he's one of the good guys or what any more.

'I remember you,' mutters Livia, 'you were with those scumbags at the Tank Engine.'

Gerry expertly rolls a couple of slim white tubes in the dark. He lights them, passing one to Livia, the other to me. 'As I was saying, you two have stirred up a hornet's nest and my advice is that you walk away. You're in the clear now, but just leave well alone. Stay out of the Controller's business, don't mess with Coombs, and for fuck's sake, keep well away from the Tank Engine, if either of you want to live to see nineteen.'

'Mikey's not even going to live to see September,' says Livia, 'so why should he worry?'

Gerry peers at me from the shadows, genuinely shocked. 'Mikey . . .?'

'It's true, Gerry. I'm not sleeping. I got some kind of brain injury from the dive.' I shrug. 'There's no hope.'

Gerry takes a long drag. 'Jesus Christ, kid. They didn't tell me that. I'm sorry.'

The sedatives are kicking in, that familiar mellow heat works its way upwards from my toes, merging with the nicotine rush like a riverine confluence at the tip of my skull.

'What do you care, what difference does it make to you?' scoffs Livia.

'I do care,' insists Gerry quietly. 'I looked out for you once, Mikey.'

Livia rolls her head. 'Oh, well done, Gerry. We'll be sure to give you a spot in church when we do the eulogies: "I looked out for him once . . . before I became a drug dealer."'

Gerry sighs, the sound of infinite patience. 'Yeah, I do a little work for the Fat Controller these days, in the club, but not dealing. I lost all my gardening jobs around here, thanks to Mikey's gracious and forgiving father.' Gerry takes a final pull at his roll-up and stubs it on the old boards in a shower of sparks. 'Funny thing about life, you start out as a kid with huge, exciting dreams and the bigger you get, the smaller your dreams become. Finally, they're not even dreams any more, just faint hopes. Right now, in a way, I'd settle for a job weeding for the council . . .'

'Oh, boo-hoo . . . serves you right for making yourself look like a walking doodle-pad,' snaps Livia, a trifle unkindly.

'I can see why you like this one,' says Gerry, 'she's very amusing.'

'You're lucky you *can* still dream, Gerry,' I point out. 'I don't dream at all.'

'No, I don't suppose you do.'

There's a silence in the old oak until Gerry rummages in his jacket pocket and produces a handkerchief, a white flag of truce, which he offers up to Livia. She dabs the clotted blood from her nose and lip.

'I always wanted to be a Clavadista, a high-diver, Gerry. Do you remember?'

Gerry chuckles. 'How could I forget?'

'Well it's too late for that now. The big dreams have gone, so I'll just have to settle for finding an old man's medal. It's all I have left.'

Gerry takes a deep breath, he sits quite still for a moment in the shadows before exhaling. 'Dammit, Mikey,' he says, 'you really know how to put the screws on . . . I just know I'm going to regret this.'

'You'll help then?'

'If I can.'

'The medal is a Distinguished Flying Cross and it's at a private airfield out near Wallingford, in the cockpit of—'

'How the hell do you know that? No, don't tell me. But do me a favour, both of you, whatever else you do, do not go anywhere near that airfield.'

'I thought you were going to help?' protests Livia.

'I will, but I'm not about to commit suicide with you.'

'Well, that's where the medal is. I can't afford to buy it back, even if the Controller was still willing to sell it, so our only option is to steal it back. And to do that we have to go the airfield.'

'Steady on,' says Gerry, 'what's all this "we"?'

'If you haven't got the balls . . .' taunts Livia.

Gerry is too wily to rise to such a kindergarten ploy. 'I've got the brains, Livia,' he replies evenly. 'You're the one with the balls.'

This has the effect of instantly silencing her. I can almost hear the fizzing of her synapses as she attempts to figure out whether she's just been subtly complimented or sneakily insulted.

'There is another, better option,' announces Gerry.

'We hijack his train-set?'

'Actually that's pretty close. Get your hands on something really precious to the Controller, something to bargain with.'

'Such as?'

'Any idea why the Fat Controller is actually called the Fat Controller?'

'He used to be an enormously fat bastard.'

'He was too. Vegas-years Elvis? Forget about it. A featherweight. This was a colossal, twelve-quarter-pounder-munching carb-monster. He'd have had Livia and me for breakfast and afterwards used you for a toothpick, Mikey.'

'He seems pretty normal now.'

'Yeah, you wanna know how he did it?'

'A diet, I expect.'

'Weight Watchers.' With that, Gerry leans back against the trunk, a smug little grin on his face.

'And?'

'And what?"

'And what's the big deal about Weight Watchers?'

Gerry leans forward once again, excited. 'National Slimmer of the Year, 2002.'

'Uh . . . I may have missed something here, Gerry.'

'Accolades – medals, ribbons, certificates. If there's one thing the Fat Controller's really proud of, it's those Slimmer of the Year trophies. Probably loves them even more than his train-set, or his plane. He keeps them in a specially made cabinet at home. And here's the irony of the thing: while the Tank Engine is tight as a drum, the Fat Controller's home is wide open to a little nocturnal larceny. He's over at the Engine every night until dawn, so the house is empty. He can afford to be relaxed about security because nobody in their right mind would ever think of burgling the place. Until now, that is.'

'What about his wife?'

'There is no Mrs Controller. He lives alone.'

'Right then,' Livia announces, jumping to her feet, hyper again. 'Good plan. Let's get to it.'

The platform sways ominously.

'Hang on a second,' says Gerry. 'I'll give you the address but there's no way I'm gonna be a part of this.'

'We've got no transport, so unless you think we should take a cab to a burglary, you're just going to have to be our wheelsman, Mr Doodles,' insists Livia.

'Shit,' sighs Gerry, 'I know I'm going to regret this. I'll drop you off and I'll wait for you, but I'm not going inside. The B and E is down to you.'

I have no idea what this means, but Livia does. 'Ha, piece

of cake,' she announces, producing a small leather wallet from her jeans.

Gerry nimbly lowers himself from the platform. 'The pick-up's parked a couple of streets away. Wait for me at the end of the drive.' With that, he's off, shimmying down the trunk like a macaque.

By contrast, I descend with the speed of a glacier.

'Mikey?' Livia asks, once we're on the ground.

'What is it?'

'Can I ask you something personal?'

'What?'

'Do I come across as a bit . . . sort of . . . *mannish* to you?'

'No, Livia. To me, you're . . . I think you're . . . well, you've got bosoms.'

That didn't come out right.

Sixteen

Gerry kills the engine of his smart new black-and-chrome pick-up but keeps the headlights on full beam while we scope out the target: a large mock-Georgian house at the end of a secluded tree-lined cul-de-sac.

He reaches behind him for a black holdall, hauls it on to his lap and empties out the contents with a metallic clatter. Rusting tools cascade to the floor at my feet, including a claw-type implement which rakes a hepatital furrow down my shin.

'Ow. What the bloody hell are you playing at, Gerry?'

'Mikey, you two are about to go and burglarize the home of an individual who, on the soiled-undergarment scale, rates a medium-to-heavy wash. You are not exactly well prepared. You have no alibi, no disguise and, more importantly, no means of carrying away the proceeds. This is an empty bag for the loot. That's the best I can do for you.'

'I thought you said this place would be easy,' objects Livia.

'I never said that. The Casa Controller is a softer target than the Tank Engine, certainly, but I never said it would be a doddle. You should be aware that there are CCTV cameras mounted front, rear and side.'

'Oh, great,' grumbles Livia, unbuttoning her jeans. 'Right . . . don't look.'

We're puzzled, but Gerry and I turn away to stare fastidiously out through our respective side windows. My senses are on full alert now; I hear the sibilant swish of cotton on nylon, unmistakable undressing sounds. For reasons best known to herself, Livia is about to strip off and go in naked. It's not exactly what I would call an ingenious disguise, but who am I to question her methods?

'Okay,' she announces.

We turn to find her still fully dressed, jeans buttoned. She's gnawing away on something in her right fist – something emphemeral and softly black, like a puff of papal-chimney smoke. With a gentle rip she hands me one ragged leg of her sheer black tights. 'Now get that over your head.'

The nylon slips smoothly over my face like a cobweb. There's a wonderful warm sweet yeasty smell, the aroma of freshly baked bread with a dash of cider vinegar: Livia's secret scent. This is, without doubt, the most wonderfully intimate moment I have ever shared with a woman.

I'm first out. I exit the vehicle in a staggering crouch. There's only one street light in this cul-de-sac, so I keep well within the shadows of the trees on the opposite side of the road. In a series of well-timed scuttles I bring myself hard up against the low picket fence, the border of the Controller's property. I topple over the creaky barrier in a kind of geriatric commando-roll and land on my back on the front lawn, almost certainly in full view of the wall-mounted camera. Speed is crucial here.

I pick myself up and hobble across to the columned porch.

'What kept you?' Livia is already at the massive door, fiddling with the lock.

'Where the hell did you come from?'

'Is that a philosophical question, Mikey?' Like mine, Livia's head is encased in a ragged black nylon sheath. Only she's a small black bullet: sleek, lethal and undeniably sexy; whereas I resemble something from one of Edmund's weirder Japanese internet sites. I know this because Livia's shoulders start to heave. 'You look like a gigantic black dildo.'

'This wasn't my idea, if you remember. How'd you get here so quick?'

'I came in through the front gate.'

'You didn't try to evade the cameras?'

'You can't evade the cameras. They're crap – fixed positions, not servo-controlled. The Fat Controller has now got me on some grainy black-and-white video walking through his front gate . . . for about a tenth of a second.'

'He'll be able to see you're a girl when he freezes the image.'

'Then he'll have me narrowed down to about three billion possible suspects.'

I'm irritated because she's right as usual but also because she doesn't seem to realize that I'm genuinely concerned for her.

'Quiet now, I need to concentrate here.' Livia puts her ear to the lock.

'What are you listening to?'

'Shhh.' She pushes a little screwdriver into the aperture and twists.

'That's just a screwdriver, you're never going to—'

'Mikey, either be quiet or shut the fuck up.' She takes an object from her leather wallet: an angular needle, slim and gunmetal blue – like a piece of kit from the Delta Force Tapestry Squad. She deftly slides this wondrous tool over the top of the screwdriver and begins to probe, her entire body quivering like a red setter. A tiny click. 'One down,' she announces, pushing further.

'One down, what?'

'I've got the second pin.' She prods, there's another audible click. 'Ah, ha.' She twists the stubby screwdriver and continues to poke around. Click. 'Number three.'

'Number three what?'

'Another pin. It takes a bit of time and skill and . . . bingo, that's number four.'

'Surely there must be a quicker way?'

'Mmmh . . . there it is – number five. And thank you very much, you've been a great audience.'

The stubby screwdriver turns freely now and the huge white-panelled front door glides open. Livia flashes me a Tic-Tac grin through the black nylon mesh. 'Of course there's a quicker way. It's called a sledgehammer. But there's no finesse in that. I don't approve. It shows a great deal of disrespect for your victim. Anyhow, we're in now. Come on, let's go wipe your bum with the bastard's toothbrush.'

If it's true that the Esquimaux, or whatever they call themselves these days, have fifty-odd words for the various colours of snow, then they'd have no problems describing the Fat Controller's place – there's no hallway as such, just an expanse of blinding white shag-pile, at the far end of which is a pearlescent baby grand. There's a massive curved leather sofa centrepiece, which Nanook of the North might recognize as a precise and popular shade of polar-bear-pissed-on katabatic ice-crust. The blueish bubble-glass tops of the surrounding coffee tables lend an appropriately glacial glare. To prove that he has nothing against primary colours, the Controller has studded the room with a variety of garish fripperies: red and gilt Asian art, and an oddly endearing antique carousel horse with an expression hovering somewhere between indignant and astonished. Exactly the look I'd have if someone came along and shoved a candy-striped pole right through the middle of my back.

I give his mane a sympathetic pat.

Livia makes straight for the sound system; an ultra-slim state-of-the-art Bang & Olufsen, and begins flinging the Controller's CDs around. 'Tony Bennett, for Christ's sake.'

'What did you expect?'

'He's a club owner.'

'It's his private stuff, Livia. Leave them alone.'

'Barbara Streisand? He's got to be kidding.'

'We're not here to take the piss – just the awards. Don't mess with his private things.'

'Neil Sedaka?' Livia sends the offending silver disc skittering across the room, and inspects the walls.

There are no certificates in this room; this must be where he does business – drug business, given the glass-topped tables and the leather sofa-thing. This is the exoskeleton. We'll find the inner man in a smaller room – a place he keeps the things he really values.

Livia cocks her head; there's cynicism under the fifteen-denier and a sneer in the voice. 'Jesus, this place, soulless – utterly tragic.'

Livia is entitled to her opinion, but the truth is, if I were to live long enough to afford a seven-bedroom house, it would look pretty much like this, wall-to-wall white shag-pile carpet and a Bang & Olufsen stereo and probably Neil Sedaka. I'd have a place for my trophies of course; my chunk of amber, a few fossils – and the left leg of Livia's black tights. But this is probably not the time or the place to make such an admission. 'You look upstairs, I'll look down here.'

Livia nods and sprints up the beautifully carpeted stairs.

Just outside the kitchen is a pale blue cellar door. I open it and descend. The tiny room is the soul of the Fat Controller – or perhaps just his large intestine. Unlike the rest of the house it's overwhelmingly, shockingly pink. There's a gigantic home-theatre entertainment system, a pinball table and a life-size bucking bronco machine. Framed gold records and lacy women's underwear festoon the walls. Curiously, there's the odd framed pair of Y-fronts up there too. The centrepiece is a recent photo of a grinning Controller in leather flying helmet about to climb into the cockpit of a gleaming white Cessna.

On a table there's also a collection of beautiful little steam engines like the Flying Scotsman, and turn of the century, Orient Express chuffers. A perspex case houses what I take to be a model railway station, until I look closer. The Caversham riverside location is instantly recognizable, but in this architect's version The Cascades has been supplanted by a gigantic concrete-mall-type development with multi-storey parking.

Two miniature grinning figures shake hands in front of the structure like some kind of surreal wedding-cake couple. There's also a sheaf of plans, which I quickly unroll. It's a draughtsman's plan of The Cascades as it is now; most of the blocks have been shaded in: the vacant ones that the developers already own or control. A pitiful few remain occupied; these are marked with black crosses.

The room suddenly feels claustrophobic and creepy. That's when I notice it. In the far corner is a gilded trophy cabinet.

A weird high-pitched sound from upstairs spurs me into a frenzy of activity.

Three minutes later Gerry's black gardening bag is crammed full of framed Slimmer of the Year certificates, before and after photos and a clutch of small golden trophies. The roly-poly version of the Controller is bloated and sweaty and looks like Elvis's mum. In every 'before' shot he wears a brightly coloured polo shirt and grey tracksuit bottoms. Odd how the morbidly obese always plump for sports clothes.

I clank back up the stairs and find Livia in the hallway, looking strangely guilty. I give her the thumbs-up. 'Mission accomplished.'

She's already at the door, checking to see if the coast is clear. 'Good work, Mikey,' she hisses, sprinting down the path towards the car.

Hoping she hasn't done any lasting damage to the Controller's music collection, I take one last look at the den before making my own escape. To my relief, the remaining CDs are intact.

I give the nice little carousel horse a farewell wink, which is when I notice what Livia has done.

Seventeen

'Pure, unadulterated evil,' breathes Livia. 'I swear to you –
Clayderman, Sedaka, Streisand . . .'

'Worse than anyone ever imagined,' agrees Gerry, awe-
struck.

I sit, arms folded, in stony silence while these two giggle
and toast one another with mugs of sweet tea like a couple
of intoxicated schoolgirls.

'Mikey, don't just sit there with a face like a bag-lady's
bra, you must want a cuppa after your ordeal? And well
done, by the way,' whispers Mr Truffles. 'I have Darjeeling
or pure Ceylon, or if you'd prefer, PG Tips.'

Good old Mr Truffles, he may not have much sensitivity
in those fingers any more but he still has plenty to spare in
his heart. I should be happy; content that my friends are
getting on so well. But there's something subtle that I'm
missing here. A few hours ago Livia and Gerry couldn't agree
on anything, now they're simpering, batting eyelashes across
Roger's pine kitchen table.

I make a quick objective assessment of Gerry and have to
admit that he is a handsome specimen, with his thick, spiky
hair and those wide, sensitive brown eyes. He chuckles for a
moment over his Earl Grey and I realize how easy it is to be
fooled into thinking that he's a nice guy when, in fact, he's

just a bloody tattooed Lothario with a lame pick-up truck and even lamer pick-up lines.

'I'm fine thanks,' I say to Mr Truffles, a little louder than necessary. 'Very happy.'

Instantly Livia's piercing gaze settles on me. 'You're not fine, Mikey, you're in a grump again. We've done what we set out to do tonight, what is wrong with you now?'

'Nothing.'

'Nothing?'

'Nothing that you can do anything about.'

'We haven't known each other for long, but you know what? I've never known you to be happy, Mikey. Perhaps it's a permanent state?'

'If you were in my situation . . .'

'I know your situation. We all know about your situation. We all have a limited time. Nobody knows where the end of the line is, not even you. I've told you, it's about how you use the time.'

I do a pantomime-grin face. 'Says Miss Laugh-A-Minute? When were you ever happy . . . without artificial stimulants?'

Fantastic. That nasty little barb seems to have penetrated all right. Livia's face folds like a crumpled snot-rag, and for an evil moment I think I've actually made her cry. But then her cheeks blossom, bright red with anger. 'Mikey. You are not now and will never be entitled to talk to me about that stuff. You think you have a monopoly on unhappy because your crappy, uptight parents didn't love you? Well, fuck off and get over yourself. You ain't seen nothing.'

With the perfect timing of an ex-chef, Mr T. slaps a plateful of steaming pancakes on to the table and pours authentic maple syrup over troubled waters. 'Eat. All of you,' he insists.

We're the classic gang. We've done the job and got away

with it. We're back in our safe-house and now, true to stereotype, we're beginning to fall apart.

'Who's grumpy?' challenges Mr T., brandishing his blackened skillet. 'Who can be unhappy with a mouthful of one of my pancakes and maple syrup? Not possible.'

I take a bite at my pancake and it's bloody marvellous. Fluffy. And real maple syrup. My God. Something else I've never tried before; something else I'm really going to miss.

'Just to start you off, I was happy, very happy once,' announces Mr T. as he refills Livia's mug. 'Some years ago, when I had a chain of restaurants in London based on the signs of the Zodiac, my flagship was a seafood place in South Ken – 'Cancer'. One night Her Highness, the late Princess of Di, popped in for a lobster bisque. No fuss, no rigmarole – just a swift lobster bisque and a walnut roll. You could have knocked me down with a breadstick, because not ten minutes later, who do you think?'

Mr T. has the floor unopposed because we're all too busy stuffing ourselves with these miraculous pancakes.

'It was Boy George. Can you imagine? Double icons. Boy George had the seared tuna with a ginger glaze . . . or was it the wasabi cream? No matter. So, not only did I get two major personalities on a soft Tuesday night, but – and I know this is hard to believe – then, bugger me, I get Simon Le Bon.' Mr T. waves his skillet about like a Chinese table-tennis champ – I've never seen him so animated. 'All three sent compliments to the chef, which was of course, me. I've never been so ecstatic, before or after.' Mr T. glances up to see if we're listening.

We are.

Half-chewed pancake remains frozen in three sets of jaws.

'It was all more or less downhill afterwards, but, blimey O'Reilly, I was happy for a while there.' Mr. T. turns, gently

lays the pan back on the hob, and takes a sip of his Darjeeling.

Livia breaks the silence with the question I think we all
want answering: 'Uh, who the *fuck* is Simon Le Bon?'

'More pancakes?'

Gerry stops preening for a second and puts on his serious
face. 'I know what you mean, Mr T., I once took a lemon tree
and brought it back to life.' He sneaks a glance at Livia, who
is rapt.

'Ah . . .' says Mr T.

'Life gives you lemons, you make lemonade,' I retort,
hoping to pre-empt the punchline of this tedious homily.

'It was a little tree in the back garden of one of those big
Upper Warren Avenue houses. But it was in a terracotta
pot. Too small for it, you see? They tried to give all the sun
they could but the poor thing didn't exactly have the best
start in life.' Gerry chuckles, and amazingly, so do Livia and
Mr T. 'The owners finally gave up on it and asked me to take
it away . . . to the dump.' Gerry pauses for breath. 'When I
took it the thing was nine parts dead, for sure. But I replanted
it in my hydroponics studio, which, by the way, is a grand
name for what is just a top-floor flat with a skylight and a
few patented nutrition and hydration systems of my own
design. I keep a few selected plants there.'

'What *kind* of plants, mostly?' asks Livia, archly.

The two of them chuckle. I don't get it.

'So, to cut a long story short, I looked after this ailing
plant for a year, repotted it, tended the leaves and made
sure it was getting the right soil, the right amounts of water,
nutrients and sun, and then finally one day, a bud. The bud
flowered and then, a single tiny lemon. Like a diamond.'

'Diamonds aren't yellow,' I point out.

'Oh, they can be. Any colour they can be,' insists Gerry.

'I'm telling you, I've never been happier than when I saw this one tiny diamond of a lemon – truly happy.'

Livia's eyes shine as she looks at him. 'Like nursing a sick child back to life.'

'Life is the breath of the Almighty. For me cultivating that lemon was like doing cosmic CPR.'

'That is so wonderful,' breathes Livia.

I don't think it's wonderful in the least. 'I can buy half a dozen huge lemons at Sainsbury's for about one pound fifty,' I announce.

Livia emerges from her glittery eyed trance. 'Mikey, we keep thinking that you're a grown-up, because you resemble one. But it may be that you lost so much time that you missed out on some fundamental things, like learning to listen and having a bit of respect for other people and their thoughts.'

I look at Gerry, who furrows his brow and nods. I feel a heavy hand on my shoulder. It's Mr T.'s banana-fingered grip. 'It's time to grow up, boy. So what about it, Mikey? Why don't you tell us something about yourself?'

I take a deep breath. 'I've never been happy,' I say. 'I have no memories which I would describe as happy.'

'Liar,' says Livia.

'It's true. I have never enjoyed my life.'

'Which is why you are embracing death with such good grace?'

'Diamonds can't be any colour, they're colour*less*,' I mutter. Unbelievably, I'm clipped around the ear. It's an expert clip, not hard enough to render me deaf, but professional enough to hurt like the bugger, coming as it does right on top of the bump after my tasering. I know that Mr T. is responsible, but I turn anyway to register disappointment.

'Tell us something about your life, Mikey,' he advises.

'I don't know what to say.'

Perhaps the memory can be jogged by a smack on the

head, in any case an odd, ancient story does pop into my head, something I haven't thought about in years; a moment which, at a pinch, could be described as happy. 'Okay,' I sigh, 'this one time, my father took me with him on a business trip to the Highlands of Scotland, just me and him – he was looking over some property up there – and we stayed in a place called Glen Clova, just bed and breakfast rooms over a pub. It was nice being up there. Cold and clean.

'I slipped out very early one morning and walked up this sort of mountain overlooking the valley. I didn't have any proper gear, just wellies and a coat, so I didn't get to the top, just to the snow-line, which was high enough. I stopped in a clearing to look back at the view just as dawn was breaking. It was beautiful. And then suddenly there it was, a squirrel.'

My audience is underwhelmed. I even suspect I might even be about to get skilleted.

'What a great story,' sniffs Gerry.

'Ah, this was no ordinary squirrel. It was a red one.'

Gerry nods sagely, without irony. 'Well, not too many of those left,' he acknowledges. 'That must have been a sight.'

'It was. Just me all alone on a rock, in my coat and wellies, pine trees all around and the sun coming up, making the snow sparkle. And this little rare squirrel gazing at me from the edge of the clearing. Of course, red squirrels aren't like these grey rat-things we get down here. They're about half the size, like miniature mountain lions, with ginger tails. This thing didn't seem to have any fear, like it had never seen a human before. So I dug in my coat pockets and came up with a few stale pieces of Cadbury's Fruit & Nut which I held out. It's just sitting there looking at me and I'm looking at it. And those few moments were pure magic.'

I'm gratified to see that Livia's mouth is at half mast here.

'That's more like it,' says Gerry.

'Bravo,' chuckles Mr T.

'Beautiful,' whispers Livia.

'I'm keeping still as a statue and I wait. I've got all the time in the world. This dainty little squirrel trots up through the snow and comes up to my hand. I'm thrilled. It's dawn and I'm up in the mountains covered in snow and this wild thing, this rare beast, has been tamed by my offering of chocolate.'

'And you claim you have no happy memories,' says Livia.

'The thing went for me. It had no interest in the chocolate whatsoever, despite the embedded nuts. It savaged me. I staggered back down to the B and B trailing blood and had to have about twelve stitches, which is very painful right in the web of your hand, let me tell you.' I show them the livid scars in the strip of flesh between thumb and forefinger of my right hand.

'But yes, for a moment or so I was happy. Thank you so much for asking.'

Eighteen

Livia is the only one at the table who isn't bent double with laughter. That chestnut head merely bobs up and down like a velour doggie in the rear window of a Ford Sierra. 'Livia?'

'Whass?'

'You should get some shut-eye now.'

'No, s'okay.'

'It's time for you to go to bed, Liv.' I put my hand on her arm.

She reacts like I just cattle-prodded her. 'I'm not missing the fun.'

'There's nothing to miss, honestly. Nothing will happen for hours, we'll wait. Everything can wait. Just get some sleep.'

She glares at me with eyes rimmed-red from fatigue or grief or both. 'Mikey, we both know there isn't the time for sleep. *You* can't wait. It's another day already. We're on a clock here.'

Suddenly, it's *my* Livia again. She's looking out for me. And I can't resist. 'Okay, so what do you want to do?'

'We go straight to the Tank Engine and do the deal, of course.'

'Bad idea,' warns Gerry.

'Nervous?' retorts Livia.

Gerry takes this juvenile jibe in his stride. 'It's not that.'

'What then?'

'The club has been closed for the past hour and a half.'

Livia checks her watch. A few minutes past seven thirty a.m. 'Shit.'

'So, what now?'

I can tell by his expression that Gerry already has the answer. 'You need to find a middle man, a negotiator, someone who can talk to the Controller and get some kind of a deal done.'

Livia runs her hand across Gerry's shoulder. 'So, Gerry . . .'

'Christ, not me. I wasn't suggesting me. Let me make this very clear to you: I am not now and have never been involved in anything you've done tonight. If the Controller got wind of the fact that I've helped you, he'd have the skin off me.'

'Might make an interesting conversation piece for his living room,' points out Livia, coyly assessing the tats on his arms.

'Missy, you ain't seen nothing yet.' Gerry lifts his tight black T-shirt.

Livia giggles, pretending to be shocked.

Gerry drops the shirt and coughs. 'You've got his Weight Watchers stuff now and that's a powerful bargaining chip. But first you've got to get to the poker table in one piece. As I said, you need an intermediary.'

'Someone who's part of the Fat Controller's circle, but who won't kill or maim us on sight,' adds Livia.

'Exactly,' sighs Gerry.

I pick up the clanking bag. Gerry tuts and sighs as though I'm beyond redemption. 'Never take your actual hostages to a ransom negotiation, Mikey. That bunch of thieving bastards will have the gear off you quicker than you can say "knife" and then where will you be? No. What we need are a couple of photos of the merchandise.'

Gerry insists on waiting in the truck outside; Livia and I enter the Sunnyside-Up Café to find Verbal Herbal at our old table. He's not surprised to see us. 'You hear the news? The grapevine's been fizzing big-time.'

'We don't give a fuck about the grapevine, Herbal. We want to do some business here,' snaps Livia.

Herbal grins. 'The Controller got B & E'd last night. Nobody burglarizes the Controller. Right now the only business in this town is information – hard facts. Hard facts are worth more than hard drugs today, my little Strawberry Chupa-Chup.'

Herbal's phone shrills, he listens intently for a few moments. 'Yeah, yeah . . . yeah. I'll get back to you.' He cuts the call and gestures to the banquette seat opposite. 'Take a weight off.' We sit down opposite him. 'Now, what can I do you for?'

'First off, I need a gram of whiz that's not been stepped on with a ton of icing sugar,' demands Livia.

'No can do at this time.' Herbal shrugs, as the phone shrills again. He raises a restraining hand as he speaks. 'The Turks? What have they said? Nah, fuck 'em, they're bull-shitting . . . not interested.' Herbal cuts the call and returns his attention to Livia. 'You may be a Scrumdiddlyumptious Toot-Sweet, my love, and it breaks my heart, but right now I can't give you the personal service you deserve. Last night the Fat Controller was deprived of some very valuable property. There's a lot of people out there claiming the inside track right now. Whoever can reconcile him with that precious gear is the big winner. A couple of grams or so of whiz is nothing by comparison. So take this half G, on the house . . .' Herbal slides a small baggy of white powder across the table, 'and fuck off. I'll see you soon, okay?'

Livia palms the bag with the speed of a Las Vegas card-sharp. Herbal's phone shrieks again. He waves us away but we sit tight. 'Yeah, yeah . . . that might help, yeah . . . got that. I'll pass that on. I'll let you know if it's worth anything.'

Herbal cuts the call and treats us to a deeply aggrieved expression. 'What?' he says.

I slap down my pile of Polaroids.

Herbal gasps. 'Holy Christ, that's a gigantic blowfly, whacking off.'

'Ignore that,' I say, sweeping the shot of Edmund off the table. 'Take a good look at the rest.'

Seven slightly out of focus Polaroids of the Controller's awards and certificates, sitting on Roger's kitchen table.

Herbal gazes at us like we have an incurable contagious strain of black spot. 'Have you any idea what you just stepped into?'

'We certainly do,' replies Livia, calmly slicing up a thick line of Herbal's powder on the filthy table with the edge of a laminated milk shake menu. 'Hard facts, like you said, Herbal.'

'Shit, you burgled him; I hear you fucking chopped his horse's head off and stuck it in his bed. The Controller thinks it's a fucking gang war.'

'It is.' Livia selects a plastic straw from the dispenser before snooting up a huge amount of the white powder along with a bunch of ancient toast crumbs and fried egg detritus. I'm glad to see that she's getting a good breakfast along with the pharmaceuticals. 'My gang versus his. It was a bloody carousel horse. I sawed its head off. What's the big deal?'

'What goes around, comes around,' I point out. Nobody gets it.

Herbal shrinks into his seat, brandishing his phone at us like a crucifix keeping vampires at bay. 'I only flog a few drugs . . . and a bit of tittle-tattle here and there. That's it. I'm a middle man.'

Livia tosses her head. 'God, where have I heard that before?'

Herbal's eyes bulge like someone connected his ear to a foot-pump. 'You are dead people walking. I'll give you a ten-minute head start before I ring the Controller. Can't say fairer than that.'

Livia launches herself across the table and grabs his windcheater. 'First off, Herbal – you can't fuck us off, because *your* information put us on to the Fat Controller in the first place. Second, we don't crumble under threats . . .'

Herbal gazes down at Livia's balled fist mushing the flimsy nylon of his jacket. To his credit, he does have a certain savoir faire for a small-time hustler in a cheap anorak. Livia looks as grim as I've ever seen her.

'Thirdly, we are in possession of the stuff the Controller most values.'

'That's not in question,' concedes Herbal as Livia releases him. 'The issue is, why should I get directly involved? What's in it for me?'

'We don't tell the Controller who put us on to the medal in the first place.'

Herbal scratches his thinning hair. 'All this, just for a stupid medal?' He laughs, a strange repeated guttural bark, revealing those glassy teeth. 'Have you any idea what this fucking medal's worth?'

'You told us about four grand,' I say, 'but it's priceless to the guy who lost it.'

Herbal nods encouragingly in the way that people do when they think you're an idiot. 'Yeah, about four large –

max. Not worth getting dead over. But it's your funeral, my friends.' He shrugs and swivels. 'Sylv,' he bellows.

In moments my old friend the Vester appears at our table. 'What's up, Herb?'

'These two reckon that there's a medal out there worth dying for.'

'Most serious medals are worth dying for, Herb. That is the point.'

Herbal scowls. 'Well, how would you like to negotiate an exchange – a bunch of shitty certificates for a tin-pot medal?'

'These things are all relative, dude.'

'It should be a straightforward handover. Do you want to do it or not?'

Sylv gazes at Livia. I know he recognizes me when he raises an eyebrow a millimetre or two in my direction. 'Yeah, I can do this, Herbal. What's my end?'

'You negotiate a straight swap. I get my percentage for arranging the return of the goods and you get a grand for getting it sorted. You want it?'

'I want it,' says Sylv.

'Okay with me.' I nod. 'Sylv's good.'

'It wasn't ever your choice,' snaps Herbal as he punches numbers into his mobile. He speaks for a few moments before passing it over to Sylv, who embarks on a brusque, whispered conversation.

Livia sniffs.

'You're in luck,' announces Sylv eventually, covering the mouthpiece. 'Turns out the Controller wants to negotiate, instead of killing you immediately in the most painful manner possible. It might involve a few broken teeth.'

'I don't know about that.'

'Shut it, Mikey,' snaps Livia. 'Tell him we want a straight exchange, no violence – all his shit in return for the DFC. Or nothing. Simple.'

Sylv mutters into his phone for a moment. 'That sounds agreeable to the Controller.'

Livia grins.

Sylv nods, phone to his ear, before announcing that the exchange will take place at the Tank Engine tomorrow night.

'Absolutely not,' I interject. I have nothing to lose, so I reach over and grab the mobile out of Sylv's hand. 'Controller?' I say. 'This is Mikey Hough. We've met before.'

'Yes, Mikey Hough. I am the Controller,' he replies. An even, baritone voice.

'You want your stuff back? Intact?' I ask.

'Of course I do,' he replies, very much in control.

'Well then, you have to meet us in a public place.'

'What are you playing at here, Michael?'

'If you think I'm just strolling into your club you must take me for an idiot.'

There's a silence on the other end. 'Look, we'll give you your stuff back in exchange for the DFC. You know this is fair.'

'I agree. Where did you have in mind, Michael?'

I'm thinking fast. Then it hits me.

'The Thames Valley Indoor Lido. Twelve sharp.'

'I don't visit swimming pools, Michael, kids piss in them. And I'm not a swimmy kind of person.'

'Well, put some trunks on, Controller, because that's where we're going to do it.'

'It's not what I do, Mikey.'

'Then there's no deal.'

I cut him off.

The phone shrills into life again almost immediately. Sylv answers. 'Thames Valley Indoor Lido,' he confirms.

'Tell him I'll see him there at twelve.'

'In trunks?'

'Everyone has to wear trunks.' I grin. 'That's the beauty of it.'

Nineteen

'Well,' says Gerry, cutting the engine of his pick-up. He turns and gently takes Livia's hands between his. 'This is it, I reckon. When this is all over I don't suppose you'd like to . . .?'

'Go to the pictures? Hold hands in the back row? Have a bit of a snog?' I heckle from the back seat.

'For God's sake, Mikey,' snaps Livia.

'When what's over? When Mikey's over? Is that what you mean?' I can't stop myself.

'When the medal thing is over. When this is done. Perhaps . . .' continues Gerry.

'Don't mind me, the spare wheel.' I shrug. 'Pretend I'm not here.'

'Well, you are here,' says Livia. 'And while you're still here you can behave like a civilized human being. Gerry's put himself at risk to help us. You could at least be grateful to him instead of behaving like a spoiled brat.'

'What's he done? Apart from driving us around a bit? He didn't help with the burglary. He's not even coming to the handover. Thanks for driving us around a bit, Gerry.'

'My pleasure, Mikey.' Gerry grins at Livia. 'Don't worry, Mikey and I are old friends,' he says. 'I've known him since he was knee-high. He is an acquired taste.'

Livia gazes at him for a moment before kissing him softly on the cheek. 'You're one of the good guys, Gerry. I wasn't certain at first but I'm pretty sure you are on the side of the angels, with your lemon trees and all.'

'You don't fancy a tour of my hydroponics studio then?'

Livia smiles slowly. 'No, I have my own lemon tree to contend with right now.'

Gerry turns in the driver's seat to look at me. 'I'm so proud of you, Mikey. You're doing a good thing here. A strange thing, but a good thing. Now get out and look after yourselves.'

I climb out of the old pick-up, puzzled. Livia emerges from the front passenger side with the holdall and gives me a lopsided smile.

I'm still trying to work this out when Gerry leans across and winds down the passenger window. 'The Hope Diamond,' he shouts.

'What about the Hope Diamond?'

'It's blue. Sky blue. And flawless.'

With that, Gerry is gone in a cloud of exhaust fumes, leaving the two of us outside the Thames Valley Indoor Lido.

Neither of us have trunks or towels so we're forced to buy them at the Lido shop at vastly inflated prices. That is to say, Livia does, with Coombs's cash. As some kind of punishment I am presented with the tightest, briefest pair of red and yellow Speedos available anywhere other than an Action Man Scuba set.

I lug the holdall full of the Controller's awards into the men's changing room, where I quickly slip into my motley wisp of nylon and string. I decide to wrap the towel around my waist to avoid traumatizing elderly ladies and children before stashing the holdall in locker 101. The key comes with a thick rubber band which is meant to go over your wrist but fits snugly round my upper arm.

When we meet outside the changing rooms I'm gratified to find that the skin-tight motif also applies to Livia's own bright green one-piece.

At the ticket booth a young Indian girl is attempting to deal with a group of three unusual-looking men trying to shove their way through the turnstiles with brute force.

'Do you have a concession, sir?'

'A concession to what?'

'A concessionary pass for age, or income, or a family discount perhaps . . .'

'I don't fucking think so.'

'Then that would be three adults?'

'Yes, that would be three adults.'

'Without discount? You don't have a Thames Valley Leisure Card? You can use it here, you know, to get a five per cent discount.'

'No, I think it's safe to say that none of us have a Thames Valley Leisure Card.'

'Would you like a Thames Valley Leisure Card? You can purchase one here and so get up to twenty per cent off at the Butterfly Farm, the Model Village and . . .?'

'No, I don't think that will be necessary.'

'If you enjoy the pool and feel that you would like to join the gym there is a concessionary card. The concessionary card might represent a big saving . . .?'

The big baldy leans in close to the glass and slaps down a twenty-pound note. 'Just fucking let us in. Three adults, no concessions, no discounts, no fucking about. All right?'

The Indian girl hands over the change as the trio muscle their way through the turnstile, but fair play to her, she doesn't give up. 'If you're in business together, and I think you might be, there is a corporate rate. Feel free to ask me about a corporate card after your aqua-experience.'

Livia and I skitter behind a coke machine and observe as the Controller, the baldy-bouncer and the Ginger Ninja stand before the men's changing rooms. The baldy-bouncer holds a small bag which contains their swimming gear and, I hope, our medal. We scuttle through the side door, splashing through the verruca-busting footbath into the pool area.

I'm worried. There's no sign of Sylv. And the big clock on the wall tells us that it's already five to twelve.

At precisely midday, three figures emerge from the male changing rooms, like a trio of great white sharks: the baldy-bouncer wears a lurid pair of Bermuda shorts which flap about his ankles, the Ginger Ninja sports slick black budgie-smugglers along with a tight black rubber bathing cap, and the Controller has opted for an Edwardian-style bathing costume designed to cover as much of his body as possible. Now I can understand his reluctance to appear in swimmers; clearly his sagging flesh has never come to terms with that gigantic weight loss; it hangs like blobs of grease to a cold kebab.

The three of them scan the pool and quickly clock us on the far side. The Controller mutters something to his two employees. They split, approaching from both ends of the pool. Livia and I stand our ground. In any event there's nowhere else for us to go.

The Controller joins us, in his Edwardian trunks, nodding affably. 'I assume you've brought the gear?'

'We have,' I agree. 'It's in a locker.'

'The key to which is currently flapping around on that nasty little chicken wing of yours?' he says, nodding at my arm.

'That's correct.'

The Controller turns on his heel. 'Well, there's no more to be said then, is there? Take it, lads.'

Eugene lurches for my arm. I turn to run and am instantly caught in Sylvester's wet and stringy embrace. He's wearing washed-out green shorts and a bright orange life vest; a pair of dripping flippers dangles from one hand.

'Easy there, buddy. There's no running poolside. You could slip and have a very nasty accident.'

In one quick movement, with his free hand, Sylvester rips the key from my arm, easily snapping the cheesy old rubber.

'Nice one, Sylv.' The Controller grins. 'Let's have the key and we'll all be on our way.'

'Very good; I believe this is the key to your property, Controller. Now I'd like to see you follow through on the handover, if you don't mind,' says Sylvester, with an odd formality.

The Controller inspects Sylvester like he's flyshit. Sylvester returns his gaze. The whole reason I chose a public swimming pool in the first place was precisely so that it would be impossible to produce a weapon. Nevertheless, we're outgunned here in terms of sheer physicality. The Vester doesn't lack courage or principles but he's not exactly a spring chicken.

'Get fucked, Sylv. Just give us the key, it's done.'

Sylvester shrugs. He seems disappointed. 'Be fair, Controller,' he sighs without conviction.

'Fuck off, Sylv. You're getting paid here.'

'Herbal set this up. I'm being paid by the middle man to see fair play.'

'It's my money that's paying you, you twat.'

'That's as may be. But I'm my own man. I take jobs on my own terms. I do what I'm paid for.'

The baldy-bouncer takes a step forward, whips away the

towel from my waist and drapes it round his own sweaty neck.

The Controller nods with approval. 'My crew and I take what we like when we like. You better come to terms with that, or you are going to have a problem, Sylvia . . . Mr Vesty . . .'

'Just Vester,' Sylv corrects him softly, 'or the Vester, which is equally fine.'

'Just give me the key and piss off . . . Mister the Vester.'

'Sometimes an issue isn't really about power or about money, Controller. Sometimes it's just about something as simple as a towel.'

I couldn't agree more. 'They've got my medal and now they've got my towel as well,' I object.

The Controller stops and looks me up and down for a second. 'You're Michael. I remember you.'

'I'm Mikey.'

'You were supposed to be a retard.'

'I'm not.'

'No. Anyway you can fuck off now. I'm taking my property and I don't ever want to see you again.' The Controller fixes me with those shark eyes.

'I want my medal.'

'Don't annoy me, Michael Hough. You're lucky I don't kill you here and now for my fucking carousel horse.'

'I didn't actually do that, but I apologize anyway. If it's any consolation, I really liked your carousel horse. I must have my medal, though.'

'All Mikey wants is the medal; it would make him so happy,' says Livia, in a way that would persuade me to oil-wrestle the baldy-bouncer dressed in the world's tightest swimsuit, but the Controller is immune, doesn't even bat an eyelid.

Instead, the baldy-bouncer flicks my arse with the towel.

'Last chance, Vesty.' The Controller grins. 'Hand over the key, or we'll just have to take it.'

With that the Ginger Ninja adopts an impressively threatening martial posture, fingers curled, one leg raised. 'Whoo cha chaa . . . Eagle claw strike,' he warns.

Sylvester takes half a pace to the side and in a blur of movement slaps the Ninja twice across the face with his flipper. The twin reports seem to lag half a second or so behind the action. There's a moment of stunned silence; we all watch as two livid red blotches appear on either side of the Ninja's pasty face. Blood seeps from his nose; he begins to cry. Alarmed mothers create a clear space around us, nervously ushering their children away.

'Frog-flipper bitch-slap,' pronounces Sylvester evenly.

Wow. I can't believe my luck in getting this old Viet-nutter as my referee.

The Controller shakes his head. 'Christ on a bike, Vesty, was that really called for?' He gestures to the wounded Ninja, whose nose is now leaking blood and snot in equal quantities. 'Go and get that seen to, you prat.'

Sylvester raises the flipper, more as an object of curiosity than a weapon. 'That was a love-tap, Controller. I could have given him a blow with the edge of the flipper, which would have crushed his windwipe. Doesn't have to be a flipper of course, could just as easily be a floaty board.'

'All right, Vesty, we get the message.'

'So, you see, Eugene,' continues Sylvester, 'the whole towel thing back there was an abuse of your power. A trivial thing, but exactly the kind of behaviour which sets off major conflicts: wars, police actions, hostage crises and such,' he explains reasonably. 'I'd like you to hand back the towel.'

The Controller rolls his eyes impatiently. 'Give him back his fucking towel, Eugene. You happy now, Vesty?'

Eugene flings the towel at me with bad grace.

The Controller shakes his head, exasperated. 'You've always been outside my organization, Sylv – outside any fucking thing actually, including the boundaries of sanity. What do you want? More money, is it?'

'I'm happy with my end. I don't take sides, Controller, I do my job without fear or favour, I just want what's fair here. That's what I'm paid for. Even-Stevens. Give the other party their article.'

'The medal?'

'Yes, the medal.'

The Controller grimaces before nodding abruptly to Eugene. 'Give them the bloody medal and we'll all be on our way, if that's all right with Grambo here.'

Eugene produces a silver cross from the back pocket of his voluminous Bermuda shorts. He skims it across the surface of the pool. It bounces a few times before sinking in the deep end.

'That's it, that was the medal,' says the Controller.

'That was *the* medal?' queries Sylvester.

'That's it,' confirms Eugene.

'My work here is done then,' confirms Sylvester. He chucks the key to Eugene before bending to pull his flippers back on.

Eugene and the Controller hurry to the changing rooms while Sylvester gently lowers his scrawny arse back into the water.

'Thanks, Sylv, thanks a lot,' I shout, but he's already off, floating away on his back, flippering gently, eyes blissfully closed. I have no idea whether he hears me or not.

I look at Livia and grin. 'We did it. We finally got the DFC.'

Livia inclines her head towards the far end of the pool. 'Before you start patting yourself on the back too hard, there's a bunch of thieving little knackers bottom-diving over there. You don't want to lose that medal again after what we've been through.'

Sure enough, there's a bunch of emaciated, acne-spattered kids ducking for pennies. Fortunately, most of them don't appear to have the lung capacity to descend to the real depths – too much glue, too many fags, most likely. Still, no point tempting fate . . .

I want to do this right, with a flourish and a bit of ritual to mark the moment. I climb to the topmost board and stand, gripping the edge with my toes. There's no springboard at the top – no need for one – just a fixed concrete platform.

Tiny faces tilt upwards, echoing shrieks and laughter subside to an expectant hush.

I can be beautiful up here. Nobody sniggers at my flat, devastated face from this altitude. I hold my arms out straight before me like a sleepwalker, slowly bend my knees. My wasted calves and thighs explode with what little power they have and catapult my frail body into an abbreviated arcing tumble from the platform. For a second, I can see myself pancaking on to the water, belly smacked redder than the Ninja's face. But somehow at the last moment my body finds its own equilibrium; I straighten to a perfect point, breaking the surface, sharp, clean and precise.

At any rate adequately enough not to have busted my back, arse or hips, or lost my trunks in the process.

I arrive, questing fingers outstretched, at the blue-tiled depths and scoop the glittering cross. Mission number seven complete. I breathe a sigh of relief. This turns out to be a bad move fifteen feet under water.

'Well, it is a medal.'

   'Good. We've finally got the bloody thing,' sighs Livia. '*A* medal.'

'*A* medal? Not *the* medal?'

'A Salvation Army Medal.'

'A Salvation Army Medal?'

'Quite a nice one, to be fair. For "long and faithful service"'

'Not the . . . ?'

'No, not the DFC.'

'The sneaky rotten bastards. You should never have trusted them.'

'So, what do we do now?'

'We backtrack. We go to the last known location of the DFC.'

'You're not seriously suggesting that scary airfield with all those attack-dogs and the lunatics in black bomber-jackets?'

'Well, we're not going to let them get away with this. Besides, there were only a couple of dogs,' sniffs Livia. 'Puppies, really.'

Twenty

'Can I ask you a question, Mikey? Be honest with me.'

I've shared a great deal with Livia over the past week or so, including her undergarments, so I'm wondering why she's being so coy now. 'Fire away.'

'How'd you learn to dive like that?'

I'm sitting in the sideways seat on the bus, with chlorine eyes and a worthless alloy cross in my hands. 'I didn't learn. It's already there, in my head.'

'So how did you know when to straighten up before you hit the water?'

I shrug. 'I don't know, when it kind of felt right. I can't explain it.'

'It was dumb luck, wasn't it?' Livia grins. 'Or, maybe, you've been secretly practising?'

'When? When was I supposed to practise? It's something I feel . . . an instinct, like ballet.'

'Ballet's not an instinct.'

'Truly, I don't know. But a guy I really admire once said this: "You cannot begin to live unless you take yourself to the edge."'

'That's just drivel, Mikey.'

'It means something to me. It's a profound statement about risk and reward; it's about utterly committing yourself to the dive and trusting your natural abilities. At least I think it is.'

Livia snorts with laughter. An unnatural sound on this glum, chuntering bus. Passengers crane their necks to stare. Finally, Livia takes a breath and makes her eyes go wide. 'Well, Mikey, however you did it, it was . . . it was something else.'

'You know when I was up there, on the board, I felt totally at home. I was a bit nervous until I stepped off, then about halfway some kind of intuition just took over and I saw exactly how I was going to hit the water before it happened. It sounds weird but it was the most natural thing in the world. It must be the way a chess master can scope the board and instantly see all the moves.'

Livia gazes at me with an expression I'm not familiar with. 'Don't undersell yourself. You're nothing like a chess master, Mikey. Those chess freaks all have milk-bottle glasses and keep their shirts tucked into their underpants.'

'Indeed they do not,' objects the middle-aged woman to Livia's right.

'I beg your pardon, were we speaking to you?' sputters Livia.

I take the opportunity to slip a hand down the back of my shirt and untuck the tail.

'Grand masters like my son are neither dull nor visually challenged. I find the stereotype tiresome. They have an extraordinary outlook on life. Ask him something, you'll find him quite the chatterbox.' She indicates the genetically perfect eight-or nine-year-old blond boy on the seat beside her.

'No, that's quite all right, he looks a nice, normal boy; you must be very proud,' smiles Livia. 'I apologize for the generalization.' She returns her attention to me, but infuriatingly, that excitingly unidentifiable expression has been replaced by one of plain irritation. 'Anyway, as I was saying, before we were bloody interrupted . . .'

'If you think profanity offends either myself or my son, you'd be wrong. We find third-world debt, poverty, pollution and stereotyping far more offensive,' interjects the woman.

The little boy nods sagely.

I can tell that Livia has had a little top-up of Herbal's toot in the changing rooms, which means she's a tad less tolerant than usual. She swivels her head one hundred and eighty degrees, Linda Blair-style, to address the woman. 'I'm not talking to you, okay? When did I ever give you the impression that I wanted to have a conversation with you?'

The woman is middle-aged with frizzy dyed red hair and has a pair of tinted glasses suspended on a beaded necklace. She ought to be in some kind of tie-died kaftan, but instead wears a trim beige two-piece and seems sublimely unfazed by Livia's aggression. 'That's quite all right, young lady. We don't need permission for a dialogue; communication is a human birthright.'

'Fucking right,' pipes up the little blond boy.

The woman smiles thinly. 'He's only nine but he already understands the superficial shock value of profanity. Like you, he uses this infantile mechanism for attention and control. We encourage it.'

'If you don't mind,' says Livia, 'we're having a private conversation here.'

'If you don't mind, we'll listen in,' insists the woman. 'My son is like a sponge at this stage, he very much enjoys adult debate.'

Livia grimaces, but the fact is I'm really enjoying the exchange and in any case, I'm on a bit of a high. 'I think I might have what it takes, Livia. I might actually be a natural-born Clavadista.'

'Mikey, don't . . .' sighs Livia.

'Clavadistas – brotherhood of Mexican high-divers. Famed for their clannishness and fearless demeanour. Much to be admired,' intones the blond kid.

'Hey, right,' I say, 'that's amazing. How d'you know all that? Nobody else I know knows that.'

'I read,' replies the blond kid impassively.

'Wow.'

'Are you seriously expecting to become a Clavadista?' he asks.

I peer round the middle-aged woman to take a closer look at her son. 'Well, yeah. I thought I might give it a go. Why not?'

The blond boy considers this for a moment. 'You live in the Thames Valley. That might be a problem for an aspiring Acapulcan cliff-diver. And you don't look like much of a diver to me. You appear to have missed a couple of times.' He shrugs. 'But then I suppose anything's possible if you put your mind to it.'

'Do you think so?'

I'm enjoying the little genius but, clearly, Livia isn't. She shoves me back into my seat and shouts into Blondy's face. 'Don't . . . don't encourage him. Don't make Mikey hanker for something he's never going to have, you . . . you bloody mutant. Oh Christ, listen to me . . . I'm having a rational conversation with a nine-year-old.'

The boy's mother nods sympathetically. 'He's getting some of his aggression out and he's getting some back from adults.'

Unbelievably Livia stamps her feet. 'Just stop talking to us, okay? Go and overdose on Smarties or something.'

The boy considers this for a moment before producing a sticky packet of Fruit Polos from his pocket. 'Smarties are for morons. I prefer these, they don't make me hyper.' He pops a red one into his mouth. 'Is he your boyfriend then?' he asks, slyly.

For the first time Livia appears to lose her composure. She gulps air. 'That's none of your business.'

'He's a boy and he's obviously a friend,' insists the prodigy.

'All right, Brainiac, why don't I ask you a question?' says Livia. 'What's heavier, a ton of feathers or a ton of lead?'

Blondy doesn't miss a beat. 'Don't be so bloody juvenile,' he replies. 'Ask me a proper question.'

Much as I adore this sweary blond boy, I love Livia more. She's out of her depth here, so I leap to her defence. 'Okay, answer this: what happens when an unstoppable force meets an immovable object?'

The boy-genius considers. 'Is either party prepared to compromise?' he asks. 'That's the thing, isn't it? Who backs down first? That's what it comes down to, isn't it? A most interesting conundrum.'

The bus pulls up at our stop, twenty yards or so from The Cascades.

Livia and I get to our feet. 'Think about it,' I say.

As she passes, Livia bends over the young boy with a smile. I'm surprised to see that she's softened enough to embrace him before giving him a valedictory peck on the cheek. His mother beams.

There's a sudden ear-slicing pre-pubescent shriek and Livia hustles me through the hissing doors. 'What it comes down to,' she bellows, 'is who strikes first and who strikes fastest. End of lesson, kid.'

'Oh my God, it's Roger. They've let you out.' Livia squeals and flies into the older man's dressing-gowned embrace.

'Ah, therapy, at last,' sighs Roger at his own kitchen table as he gives Livia a reciprocal squeeze. I'm not too happy about the position of his hands. It's her bum though, so I keep my thoughts to myself.

Eventually Roger releases her and notices me. I clasp his hand. As always, I'm astonished by the strength in that grip and the power in those blue eyes. 'Mikey, from what I hear, you've been doing all sorts of things I don't entirely approve of.'

'We got a medal for our trouble, Roger,' insists Livia, loyally.

'Did you? Did you really?' gasps Roger.

'We did get *a* medal,' I say quietly, 'just not yours.' I hand over the cheap alloy Salvation Army cross with enamelled centrepiece.

Roger takes it reverently between his long-fingered hands and inspects it for some moments. When he looks up his blue eyes are clear. 'Well, as you already know, this is not my medal. Clearly, this is not a DFC. But if medals have any value whatsoever it's to recognize the kind of actions that we, as decent people, aspire to.' He holds the object up to the light. 'This is better than the DFC – I'm holding the Order of Mikey and Livia. You've put yourselves in harm's way for an idea; something you think is right. Nobody can ask more than that. I accept this medal and I think I got the better end of the deal.'

'But we didn't get your DFC for you, Roger,' says Livia with tears in her eyes.

'No matter, my dear,' he says, stroking her hair.

Mr T. deposits a pile of steak and onions in the centre of the table and I'm reminded of the fact that I'm ravenous. Livia catches his disfigured hand and gives it a brief, grateful squeeze. He responds with an understanding wink before returning with the mashed potatoes. 'Get stuck in, then,' he orders just as the doorbell rings. He trots off to answer it.

I don't need a second invitation to fork a steak off the top of the pile. I'm still trying to manoeuvre the bloody slab to my plate without anyone noticing that it's the largest by some ounces when Mrs Hodges stomps in like a force of nature. 'Last night Miss Simkins had something shoved up her,' she bellows, waving her horrible taser.

Roger is instantly on his feet, giving me a steely prod in my bony upper arm. 'Mikey, for goodness sake, a lady has just walked in,' he hisses. 'Where are your manners? Get yourself up, boy.'

I shove my chair back and leap up, feeling like the worst kind of yobbo.

'Mrs Hodges, how marvellous to see you,' he drawls urbanely, moving round the table and sliding back a chair for her. 'You find us slumming it as always, but please, if you can bear it, take a seat and join us for a light, late luncheon.'

Mrs Hodges transforms from hysterical neighbour to stately dowager in a nano-second. The taser disappears and she actually simpers as she settles herself. 'They never said you were home, Air Commodore.'

'Ex-Squadron Leader. I was only discharged this afternoon. You will, of course, excuse the mufti,' he says, gesturing to his attire.

Livia sniggers.

'I'm sure we'll all feel a great deal safer now that you're back, Air Commodore.' Mrs Hodges's takes the vacant seat at the head of the table.

My gorgeous steak sits atop the platter, fork ready, sticking out of the dripping pink flesh, and so is fair game for Roger. He scoops it and deposits it on Mrs Hodges' plate before slathering on a thick layer of onions. 'Dig in, don't stand on ceremony now,' he proclaims. 'Deirdre and I are old friends, eh, Deeds?'

'Indeed we are, Air Commodore.'

Livia, Mr T. and Roger steam into the platter leaving a residue of fatty scraps. I scoop the remnants and go big on mashed potatoes with gravy.

Somehow Mrs Hodges manages to ingest my dinosaur-size steak and still doesn't leave anyone else room to get a word in edgeways. 'You know of course about the abusive phone calls, we can deal with those, but there have been physical assaults on Derek Williams, Arthur Shippham, the Emmetts of course and poor old Teddy Parslow; and then there was the burglary on this very premises, Air Commodore. Since then there's been an assault on myself, repulsed with a taser. The latest is Miss Simpkins. She was targeted last night. I don't like her, I have an issue with all her cats and their toilet habits, but that doesn't mean I want to see her hounded out of The Cascades. We're sitting ducks here, unless you band us together. I may be a little paranoid, Roger, but I'm not entirely witless.'

Roger finishes chewing a mouthful of prime fillet. Roger never rushes into any kind of decision. Mrs Hodges waits with baited breath. Actually we all wait with bated breath.

'Deirdre, our time has come and gone. We're old, we have nothing left to change the world with. We fight about small things, imagined injustices. I'm not some superannuated Spartacus. There's nothing I can do. Speak to the police, if you must.'

'The police?' Mrs Hodges laughs without mirth. 'I've called the police and they are either powerless, inept, or simply not interested. Either way . . .' She shrugs.

'I'm tired, Deirdre. I've spent my whole life fighting for big ideals, now I just want to be a curmudgeon; to bicker about my neighbour's cats' toilet habits.'

'Well, whether you want to face it or not, The Cascades have been under siege for some time now. Too many things have happened: muggings, actual bodily harm, your burglary.

It's no coincidence and you know it. Miss Simpkins was brutally attacked and had a foreign object shoved up her.'

'The lady with the cats.'

'That's the one. She was set upon on her own doorstep. In the mêlée her Vick's inhaler was punched right up one of her nostrils. This is only the latest in a long line of attacks on the residents. Surely you can see that this is a sustained, well-considered campaign to get us all out.'

Roger shakes his head, unconvinced.

'It's true,' I interject. 'They do want you out.'

'Heavens-to-Betsy, Mikey,' sighs Roger, 'not you as well? What would anyone have to gain? No, I'm sorry, it won't do you know. The world is unquestionably a dangerous place but I don't want to hear any more about this "conspiracy". And Mikey, I expected better from you. It won't do, you know.'

'And I expected better from you. You were a hero once, the DFC. is testimony to that. But since I've known you all I've seen is some kind of ostrich – a man who shoves his head in the sand and hopes for the best. You don't care whether we find your medal or not.'

'Mikey, you can't talk like that,' objects Livia, horrified.

'I can say anything I like,' I retort. 'I've got nothing to lose, unlike Roger here, who is only interested in himself and his own comfort in his declining years. You don't deserve the medal we gave you, Roger; what I've learned about medals from all this is that they're not really about a single act of courage, I think they're awarded for a way of life: a set of principles. You don't just get one, and then turn your back on everything they stand for. I learned that from my friend Sylvester. So give me that medal back, you don't deserve it.' I hold my hand out.

Roger's pale blue eyes hold mine across the table for a moment. He takes the Salvation Army cross from his dressing-gown pocket and examines it for a moment. 'No,' he says, 'I don't believe I will.'

He gazes at me with something approaching sympathy. 'I'm not angry with you, Mikey. I would not allow many people to speak to me like this in my own home; certainly very few of your generation. But, regrettably, you are one of a few of your age whose remaining days can be numbered in single figures. As such you have an inkling of what it might have been like to be a pilot back in nineteen forty. That entitles you to talk about the meaning of courage. And you're absolutely right when you say that the medal doesn't belong to me. It doesn't. I got it only because I was the flight leader. Really it belongs to four other, braver men. It was given, I think, for a great many courageous acts, not just one, and certainly not just mine. This is not vanity, Mikey. It's why my DFC was . . . is, so precious.'

I'm touched but I've lost patience with his excuses. 'That's all very well, Roger, but it doesn't alter the fact that Mrs Hodges is not paranoid, she's right. This *is* happening. There *is* a co-ordinated conspiracy to get you all out of The Cascades. Livia and I were in the Fat Controller's house last night. I saw an architect's model for a mall-type thing with multi-storey parking, right slap-bang in the middle of where your nice Cascades is now. And there's a set of plans, which shows that these people already own all of the vacant property here. They've marked big black crosses over the blocks that are still occupied, including this one. The Fat Controller is working with a wealthy and powerful property developer named Barry Coombs and they have a very vested interest in driving you out all of here.'

'Is that true, Mikey? You are absolutely certain of this?'

'I swear it. I was in his den. They think you're a pushover, Roger.'

'I see.' Roger leans across the table, his face hardens. 'Very well, Michael, exactly who is this Fat Controller rotter, where is he . . . and what the bloody hell does he think he's doing with my DFC?'

Twenty-One

We're on the move again, only this time it's Roger at the wheel, and we're piled into an elderly Hillman Hunter. He drives like Livia, only faster.

'Out of the way, sloths,' he bellows at the Postlethwaites before screeching to a halt right outside my driveway. 'Off you go, lads and lasses. You know the drill.'

It's all happening at hyper-speed now that Roger has taken command. My job is to sneak into the house and return quick-smart with a pile of Doc Darrow's sedatives. Livia is charged with retrieving Edmund's abandoned night-vision equipment from Coombs's back garden. The difference between the two missions is that while all the lights are off in Coombs's house, the evidence suggests that my parents are very much at home. I tentatively unlock the front door and take a furtive step into the hallway.

'Oh yes, would that be you then, Mikey?' Predictably, my father squats, a hyper-alert toad, in his study.

'No, it's a cat-burglar,' I reply.

'Very amusing, as always,' Bernard's brisk voice echoes off the walls. 'You'll come in and see me, won't you?'

Damn.

I walk the corridor like a condemned man and enter Bernard's lair.

'Mikey, Mikey, Mikey,' he sighs.

I make a point of looking around for my two namesakes.

'You can be as jocular as you like, Mikey. But where will that get you, in the scheme of things? You've already missed out on the most critical two and a half years of education, your entire GCSEs, and I don't want any son of mine ending up an amusing loiterer. Do you understand? There are very few positions for comedians in this world of ours. You claimed to be spending these long summer days studying over at the Kerrs with young Edmund. However . . .'

He's checked up on me. I don't believe it – game over: I've finally goaded Roger out of his inertia and I'm having the time of my life with Livia; provided I don't suddenly spiral into the slack-jawed neural shut-down phase or get killed by the Fat Controller over the next couple of days I might actually end up getting a snog. But I just know that Bernard is about to order me to spend my last few precious days of sentient life closeted away with a doughnut-scarfing, hamster-murdering, Peeping-Tom-ing Young Conservative.

'In case you were wondering, I haven't checked up on you, Michael. I'm still prepared to take you at your word here, but, really, you need to convince me that my trust has not been misplaced. In short, what exactly have you been doing with your time?'

I'm appalled to find myself close to tears. The protective sedative veneer has sloughed away over the past few hours, forcing me to face the chest-thumping reality of my condition. I'm brittle, punchy and I've had enough of all this pussyfooting. If I'm not permitted to be in denial, I don't fucking well see why Bernard and my mother should be.

'You want to know what I've been doing, Mr Hough? I've been dying actually. And you bloody know it. What the hell does studying matter now?'

I detect a momentary flash of panic in his eyes. 'Don't be

absurd, Mikey. We've been through this before,' he blusters. 'You're perfectly healthy. And I won't have you using some quack doctor's quack diagnosis to shirk work.' He appears momentarily flustered at the unintentional rhyme. Here,' he pushes a plain white mug towards me, 'your mother left this for you, over an hour ago now. She's concerned. We both are. We'd like you to have an early night for a change. Go and get a good night's sleep.'

Naturally, the milk is stone cold and comes complete with the usual repulsive skin on top but, by God, I need it. I knock it back without a breath. I can feel the slimy skin dangling from my upper lip as I replace the mug.

'And for Christ's sake, wipe that ridiculous moustache off. You look like bloody Stalin.'

The blessed narcotic instantly envelopes my jangled nerve endings like warm treacle. I find myself reasonably content to resemble bloody Stalin.

'I am ill though,' I insist, as the milk film begins to droop.

'You are not ill.'

I watch cross-eyed as the milk skin stretches and dangles under my nose like a loop of toddler's snot. 'I have this bloody awful cold, you see . . .'

My father sighs before picking up the phone. 'That's it, Michael. I'm ringing Mrs Kerr. I regret this; I had expected to be able to treat you like an adult. I had hoped to indulge you with the liberty to act on your honour, but I find you incapable of taking anything seriously. Clearly we must treat you as though you are still at the age you were before the . . . ah . . . thing – the occurrence. Michael, if I do discover that you have been engaged in academic pursuit at the Kerrs, as you claim, then I will certainly apologize. But if I find that you have been bunking off, as I suspect, then you will be utterly forbidden to leave this house from now until I have found a suitable crammer college for you in London in September.'

'*Esse potius quam videri.*'

'Christ almighty.' Bernard nearly falls out of his leather button-backed chair.

'I do apologize,' explains Roger. 'I'm most terribly sorry for barging in to your beautiful house like this, but I dropped Mikey off earlier. And then it occurred to me that I really ought to come and introduce myself. The front door was wide open, so . . .'

Bernard still has the phone in his hand, frantically jabbing nines. 'I'm calling the police, unless you leave right now.'

'No, you don't have to do that. This is Roger.' I grin, enjoying the drama.

'Roger who?'

'Roger . . . ah . . . Rab . . . Rabbett,' I blurt. The best I can do at short notice.

Roger flicks me an irritable glance before extending a long-fingered hand. 'I'm a private tutor, semi-retired of course. I've been educating your son.'

Bernard slowly lowers the telephone back into the cradle. 'How . . .?'

'Strictly speaking I've been engaged to bang some sense into the other young man, the . . . ah . . .'

'The Edmund,' I prompt.

'The Edmund,' agrees Roger smoothly. 'I've been employed to give the young Edmund a little extra tuition over the summer and as your son has been "in situ" it seemed churlish not to include him in my tutorials, especially since young Michael, unlike the other oaf, has demonstrated such a facility for the lingua Latinus: *Non solum nobis, tenax propositi, per ardua et astra, aut disce aut discede*, et cetera, et cetera . . .'

'Et cetera . . .' echoes Bernard, warming to the white-haired twinkler standing humbly before him in an old but well-tailored tweed jacket. He nods approvingly. 'You're tutoring my son in the classics?'

'Amongst other subjects. But I'm not here to dun you for money. I have already been well recompensed for my efforts by young Edwin's parents.'

'You're sure I don't have to pay?'

'Indeed. From you, I ask for nix, nada . . . zerox.'

'Xerox?' Bernard raises a sceptical eyebrow. 'What did you say your name was?'

'Rabbett. Not to be confused with the aurally over-endowed pest. No relation.' Roger glares at me. 'That's not to say that some of my young charges don't regard me as a pest of sorts, but that's only because I badger them to extend their intellects, particularly in regard to classical studies. I have even been known to . . .'

Bernard considers this for a second before smiling. 'Yes, yes, I get the picture.'

'Well, there it is then,' says Roger with his 'well there it is, then' kind of smile. 'I'm here to assure you that your young chap is having his intellect stretched by a professional. And once again, I can only apologize for barging in unannounced like this. What must you think of me?'

Bernard smirks. 'Don't mention it, Mr Rabbett, I appreciate what you're doing for my son. Clearly, it would be inappropriate and insulting for me to offer anything by way of hard cash, given that the Kerrs have the matter well covered. I dabble in property, so perhaps you won't be offended if I offer you a tip: if you do happen to have anything put aside for a rainy day, might I recommend that you invest it in a prime chunk of riverine real estate – that stretch from Caversham Bridge down to The Cascades? Anything you can get your hands on should do the trick, even a short lease. I don't pretend to be able to predict the future, but I have a number of influential friends who are about to develop thereabouts.'

Roger nods sagely. 'As it happens, I already have an investment, in that general area.'

Bernard taps his nose. 'Canny, sir, very canny.'

Roger clenches his jaw by way of reply, but manages to turn the grimace into a grim smile.

It looks like we're home and dry when, true to form, Bernard decides to push it.

'Mr Rabbett. Roger. There's something I've always wanted to ask a person with a firm grip of the classics.'

'Indeed?'

'I've tried a few people but never had a satisfactory answer. I wonder if you could precisely translate the words "*fide et fiducia*"'.

It's the motto on his stupid Pay Corps shield. Nobody cares how it translates. And now we're fucked. I'm certain that Roger the Rabbit-Badger hasn't a clue what it means. He gazes coolly at my father without missing a beat.

'There is no exact translation. What it loosely means is: "Do your job . . . faithfully . . . no matter how unpopular."'

Bernard almost swoons. He loves this. He jots the phrase down on his desk pad.

'It's not strictly word for word . . .' warns Roger, 'but close enough, I feel. Well, goodnight then, Mr Hough.'

'Goodnight to you, sir,' replies Bernard, all bonhomie, as he rises to shake Roger's hand once more.

'I'll show Mr Rabbit out then,' I say, sniggering, as Roger hustles me back down the corridor.

'Now, stop buggering about and get the ruddy drugs,' hisses my personal tutor and Latin dominus.

*

177

I make straight for the roll-top desk in the living room. Because my father is still up and about, it's unlocked, and of course it's crammed with Dr Darrow's wonderful product. I grab a few paper bags filled with what appear to be Darrow's strongest capsules and scuttle back down the corridor.

I pop my head into my father's study as I pass with a pantomime yawn. 'Good night, I'm off upstairs. For an early one.'

Bernard peers up from his desk pad where he's been laboriously lettering Roger's translation with an italic nib. 'So you should, Mikey, so you should,' he says. 'I know you laugh at me sometimes, but I try to do what's best, on the whole. The things I tell you are the things that I think will be good for you.'

'I do . . . I do know that . . . Dad.'

'You're a strange young man, Michael; not at all like your mother or myself. Even before the . . . ah . . . incident you were always an enigma to us. Nevertheless, we always took the trouble to ensure you kept to the right path. My best advice is that if you follow my corps motto you won't go far wrong – "do your job, faithfully, no matter how unpopular", which in your case, means getting your head down, getting a good night's sleep and getting back to the books and your tutor, bright and early tomorrow.'

I'm touched. If it wasn't for the hot milk I'd probably be a weeping mess on the floor. As it is, even through the warm fuzz of the sedatives, I can see that Bernard is attempting to connect in some way here.

'I'm sorry for all the worry I've caused you,' I say. 'And all the trouble and the expense . . . and all that sort of thing.'

'That's quite all right, Michael. Speaking of which, I want you to know that your mother and I haven't forgotten about your weekly allowance. You've accrued quite a tidy sum while you've been . . . away.' Bernard reaches for the old ledger on the shelf behind him. 'Somewhere in the region of four hundred pounds.'

'Dad, I don't know what to say . . .'

'Don't mention it, Michael. I'm delighted that you're keeping busy under the auspices of the erudite Mr Rabbett, but I do understand that a young man needs to blow off some steam from time to time. I was once your age too, you know. So I've decided to let you have a little something on account. This is for you to have some fun with, paint the town red and such. Live a little. I don't expect to see receipts. Shall we say, ten pounds?'

'Ten . . . pounds?'

'No, we'll make it a round fifteen. Sign here, Michael.'

'Christ!' I scream as Roger flips us round the pitch-black backroads of Wallingford.

'Oh, do pipe down, you're not the first young man whose father doesn't understand him.'

'I was objecting to your driving, Roger, for Christ's sake, slow down.'

'Oh.'

'You're going to kill us or get us stopped by the cops before we even get close to the airfield unless you start driving like a normal person.'

'The pizzas are getting cold.' Roger has metamorphosed from an old relic in a dressing-gown to Bruce Willis in the space of four hours. 'You've been boring the bejeebers out of us for the past twenty minutes, mewling about your parents, so just shut up now. Your father may be beyond redemption, but you are not. You have standards and principles, which is why you are in this vehicle, on this mission. Come to think of it, it's because of your principles, and those of Livia, that I'm here.'

'You're not concerned about stretching my intellect then, Mr Rabbit?'

'No. I'm here to live up to whatever ridiculous standard entitles me to wear that medal of yours. The medal you haven't actually awarded me yet. And to let that ruddy Controller know exactly who the hell he's dealing with here.'

'And the Latin?'

'Utter balls, mostly: a couple were old World War Two squadron mottos, along with the actual RAF motto. The rest was more or less gibberish.' Roger smiles almost imperceptibly, as though remembering something. 'Actually, one bit was pretty sound – *aut disce, aut discede*. Learn or shove off – while we live, we learn. A genuine truth, Mikey.' He takes his eyes off the road to wink at me. 'How are the pizzas doing?'

On the scabby leather back seat beside Livia is a leaning tower of assorted, twelve-inch boxed pizzas. Mr T., with the aid of Mrs H., crafted and baked these toothsome objects back at The Cascades before inserting them into a dozen reasonably clean branded pizza cartons from his hoarded stack of cardboard. They look and smell authentic enough.

'Dunno,' burbles Livia from inside Edmund's night-vision mask. 'But woah, this is sooo weird.' Livia waves her hands in front of the protruding lens, undulating palms like a stoned hippy. 'This is trippy, looking at the road in the headlights, it's kind of all green and spacey, like a vortex. Ah . . . I think I'm going to puke now. Stop the car.'

'Quiet,' snaps Roger. 'I'm not stopping for anything other than a major collision. Those pizzas on the back seat are getting less appetizing by the minute. Take that mask off and don't touch it again till we get there.'

Livia peels away the black rubber face-piece with a sucking sound to reveal a sweaty, white face. 'Fascist,' she mutters audibly.

'I'm not even going to bother explaining why that is an

utterly inappropriate comment,' drawls Roger, whisking gears.

We pull up at the airfield gatehouse in a cloud of dust and a clatter of gravel.

'What d'you want?' challenges a hulking guard in an Ard-Corps Security bomber-jacket.

I'm glad to see that it's not the guy who offered me flying lessons, but then this one is a lot bigger and, if possible, even less friendly.

Roger winds down his window. 'We brought the pizzas,' he announces.

'For who, from whom?' growls the monster.

'For youm,' replies Roger.

The black-jacketed giant briefly examines the car before making a decision. 'We didn't order any pizzas. You've got the wrong place. This is private property. Go on now, piss off. Get out of here, you silly old sod.'

'Smell that,' says Roger, snatching a pizza box from the back seat and wafting it out of his window.

'Sniff that,' replies the guard, waving a shiny, black-gloved fist under Roger's nose, like a mamba preparing to strike.

I wind down my own window. 'We brought freshly baked gourmet pizzas from the Fat Controller. Just so we know, who is it that's sending them back?' I ask with an exaggerated designer-lisp.

The black-jacket walks slowly round the front of the car, shoves his head into my window, invading my space, spittling my face. 'Who the fuck might you be?'

I recoil, at the hostility and the breath. 'I am the chef, I created these pizzas, but if you don't want them, that's fine. We'll take them back to the club.' I turn to Roger, lisping blithely, 'The Controller will give them to his boys at the

Tank Engine and then, hopefully, fire these ungrateful ogres in the morning. Drive on, Roger.'

Without missing a beat, Roger engages reverse and drops the handbrake.

'Hold up, hold up, hold up there . . .' the black-jacketed monster considers the situation. 'You're saying that those pizzas have been sent out to us by the Fat Controller?'

'No, they're a freebie from the Jobcentre – to encourage moonlighting.'

A couple of the junior-jackets behind him chuckle at my little sarcasm.

I wave airily out of the window as I expand on the nature of our mission: 'They're a kind of business-efficiency tool as well as a little perk because the Controller recognizes the fact that you have to sit here, in the middle of nowhere, all night. He knows it's not a whole bunch of laughs and he knows that from time to time you lot bunk off to get kebabs and burgers and stuff. It's better for him if you didn't do that. So, he sent us over here with our gourmet pizzas for you. *You* get primo scoff, *he* gets alert guards. Win – win.'

The Ard-Corps spokesman is warming to the idea, but the pizzas are cooling fast and he's still not entirely convinced by our nondescript motor. 'So how come you're not in a proper delivery van or something?'

'I chef for a well-known restaurant.' I brandish one of the boxes, to convince him of my credentials. 'I'm between shifts here and I have created twenty, beautiful, scrummy pizzas in my break. I only make them – I don't give a flying fuck who eats them. It's not my job to force you to have them. I get paid either way. I'm not insulted . . . *Rojer, andiamo.*'

Roger guns the engine and puts the old Hillman into reverse again.

'Hold up, I said.' Black-jacket looks shame-faced. 'All

right, I'm pretty chuffed that the Controller sent you down here. Usually the lads and me get treated like the dregs.'

'Right . . . yeah . . . fuggin ay,' chime in the two lads behind him.

'We're certified security operatives but we get all the shit work. We'd love to do the doors on the clubs with all the tips and tail, but I suppose we're not pretty enough like them Flash-Harry-glamour-boys he's got down at the Tank Engine, or maybe we don't have the right haircuts or wear the right trousers. Maybe it's just that we're too serious and dedicated.' The guard slaps the front offside of the Hillman Hunter with his left palm, emphasizing the word 'dedicated'. The old motor takes a dent for the team.

'Or maybe it's because I might have overdone it once or twice. But if someone's asking for a clump, then they're going to get a clump.' The giant is now pounding away at the off-side wing. 'So is it fair that just because I lost my temper one time I end up stuck out here in the middle of nowhere? Is that any fucking way to treat loyal staff?'

We wind windows and lock doors as the monster moves round the side, grips the roof and begins rocking with both hands. 'It's very fucking demotivating.'

In theory we're completely secure inside this testament to good old-fashioned British engineering, but we're still getting slammed around, bashing our heads against the windows and door-sills. It's like being in an earthquake. I can hear the ancient suspension squealing like an hysterical schoolgirl before I realize it's me.

'Fuck, sorry . . .' grimaces our assailant, taking a step back, breathing heavily, 'I get a bit carried away sometimes.'

Despite having been duffed up by this psycho while locked inside a stationary vehicle, I unwind my window a sliver and make one final plea through the inch-wide aperture. 'So, just to be clear about this, before they get any colder . . . do you think a slice of gourmet pizza would be nice, or not nice?'

I'm so banged about I forget to lisp.

'Nice, I reckon,' he concedes. ''Bout fucking time the Controller remembered us. Least he could do. And you lot are all right, an' all,' he nods at Roger, 'with your grandad making deliveries. Good to keep the oldies busy; I like it.' He nods at the two minor apes behind him. 'You go for it, lads.'

Mr T.'s pizzas quickly disappear into the kind of jaws I've only ever seen in cartoons or paleontology documentaries.

Twenty-Two

Given that I take a couple of heroic daily doses of the very same drug, I'm amazed and appalled to see what a light dusting of Darrow's sedative does to the Morlocks. Within minutes the two junior-jackets simply melt on to the asphalt before passing out. The big man takes a little longer to go down.

'I'm somewhat fatigued,' he announces, before wagging an unsteady black-gloved finger at us. 'And I believe it might have something to do with your hooky pizzas.' With that, he folds at the knees, crumbling like a condemned tower block.

'Phase one, accomplished,' declares Roger. 'Phase two: locate the aircraft. Mikey . . . Mikey?'

I should be elated, but my ability to consume vast quantities of these potent drugs without even yawning makes me realize just how seriously damaged I am. I should be feeling like Superman but instead I feel like a freak.

It's been nine days now and I'm reminded that I'm on borrowed time. By now I should be exhibiting at least some of the symptoms of sleep deprivation; in theory perhaps even entering psychosis phase. So why hasn't anything happened? With a thrill of fear I realise that I may have the answer: none of this stuff is real. I'm having a kind of Boy's Own adventure in my own mind. 'Ah . . . Roger?'

'Quiet now and give me a hand with this great lummox.'

'I've just had a nasty thought.'

'Mikey, I can't shift these oxen by myself. Help me get them back inside the guardhouse.'

I don't trust anything now, I'm not even certain that Roger is real. He's a sprightly old man with twinkly blue eyes, a war hero in a tweed jacket with leather-patched elbows. I can easily imagine my subconscious throwing him up as a major character in my self-created fantasy hallucination; a sort of amalgam of a surrogate father-grandfather-figure. But then that would only be the case if I am who I imagine myself to be. But what if I'm not? What if I'm not Mikey Hough at all?

'Mikey, a hand here, please.'

'I'm having a bit of an existential crisis right now.'

The man who may, or may not, be Roger Williams speaks slowly and precisely: 'By all means have your crisis after you help me shift this fat man out of the road.' Roger hooks his hands under the guard's armpits and heaves. 'We don't have a lot of time. Take his legs.'

'I'm having weird thoughts.'

'This is a bad time for delayed adolescence. I need you focused now.'

'I can't tell whether I am who I think I am. I mean, how can I say for sure that any of this is really happening?'

Roger sighs, releasing his burden. 'Generally speaking the great philosophers argue that the reality of the human condition can be defined by pain and suffering. Do you agree?'

I nod vaguely in the dark.

Roger cuffs me incredibly hard across the side of the head. 'Well, *that's* reality. You'll notice it's quite different to illusion. So, shut up, stop getting hysterical and help me shift Billy Bunter here.'

My left ear is now ringing like a Trimphone but at least it confirms that I'm not delusional.

It takes a while, but we finally get all the Ard-Corps Security boys out of sight. As I return to the Hillman, I know for sure that something is not right with the universe: I got clumped pretty hard around the head and didn't hear a corresponding peal of laughter from the back of the car. I open the passenger door to find Livia breathing shallowly and sweating white. She surrenders the mask and gives me a weak grin as she climbs out. I feel her swaying gently, steadying herself against my arm.

'What's up, Livia?'

She manages a weak smile but remains uncharacteristically silent. We wait by the guardhouse while Roger reverses the Hillman into a small copse fifty yards back down the road, concealing the vehicle under the protective shadows.

'What kind of aircraft are we talking about here, Mikey?' bellows Roger on his return in what he imagines is a whisper.

'Just a normal Cessna, so far as I know.'

I hand Roger the night vision mask; he scans the airfield.

'There's a couple of Cessnas out there on the apron. A 150 basic trainer and a Skyhawk 172. Which?'

'How should I know? The best one. The Controller likes his toys. Oh, wait, there was a photo at his house. It's got really big flared arches over the wheels.'

'The Skyhawk.' Roger throws me the mask and strides ahead into the darkness, past the hanger, shoes tip-tapping purposefully against the concrete.

Livia sags, a dead weight on my arm, until finally she stops altogether and gazes up at me like a sick puppy. 'I think I have to sit down for a moment.'

'Roger,' I shout, 'there's something up with Livia. I think she might have eaten some of the pizza.'

'Christ, Mikey, did you not explain what was going on here?'

'Of course I did. So did you. She knew the plan.'

Roger shakes his head. 'Great, that's all we need. Remind me never, ever, ever to do anything like this with you two again.' He trots over to the nearest of the Cessnas and pops open the compact aluminium pilot's door.

'Where should I look?'

'The medal should be right there in the cockpit, fixed to the dashboard.'

'Control panel.'

'Control panel, whatever.' I shrug.

'Good, because I'm not hunting around all night for the bloody thing. I'm going to take a quick shufti at the control panel and if it's not here I'm going to check out the trainer. If I don't find it in that one, all bets are off, we're going straight back to the car and home. That's it. You and Livia make a solemn promise to give up this quest here and now. Is that understood? I don't want to hear another word about it. Is that a deal?'

'Deal.' I nod.

'Oh, and I get to keep the Sally Army medal.'

'I'm unlikely to challenge that, Roger, I'm on borrowed time already.'

'Try to be a little more positive, Mikey.'

'You try being positive when your life expectancy is measured in days.'

'I did that, back in the summer of nineteen forty, as I have to keep reminding you.' Roger hoists a glittering black brogue on to the footplate above the wheel arch and hauls himself up into the cockpit.

I bite my lip in the dark before crossing my fingers.

'My God, I take it all back. There *is* a ruddy DFC here.'

I'm stunned. There's something poleaxing about being

right when you spend your life being wrong in everyone else's opinion. I feel like the tramp who just won the lottery.

'It looks like mine but I can't be sure. The problem,' he bellows from the cockpit, 'is that your thieving rotter has had some kind of a bracket made; it's bolted on to the control panel. I'll need tools. Give me a minute and I'll try to find something on board.'

To keep myself occupied I slip the rubbery night-vision sight over my head and cast around, checking to see if the coast is still clear. It takes a few moments to orient myself to this brand-new landscape of dark green fuzz. As I get the hang of it I can distinguish the avian profile of the Cessna above me, I can even make out Roger's head, bobbing about in the cockpit window.

Livia is down on the cold hard runway at my feet, slumped against my legs, more or less unconscious. We all know that Livia would snort Mont Blanc if anyone so much as mentioned good powder, but what she's done tonight suggests that she was never really that interested in the outcome of our mission.

I turn my head and gaze idly over at the prefab clubhouse hut, expecting to see a tranquil horizon of light green static. Instead half a dozen dark figures and compact silent vehicles are moving silently and inexorably towards us in a disciplined fanning formation. 'Roger, do you have a whole bunch of friends who own electric golf carts and keep attack-dogs?' I ask.

'This is a bad time to get silly again,' says Roger.

'I don't think I'm imagining this.'

'You're being melodramatic, as usual, Michael.'

I rip the night-vision mask off and throw it up into the cockpit. 'If you don't believe me, look for yourself, there's an army heading this way.'

The masked Roger peers out of the cockpit door, like a

shrew, sniffing the air from its burrow. The good news is I'm not delusional; it's also the bad news: 'Michael, you're absolutely right and, alas, they have our only exit covered.'

'What are we going to do?' I wail.

'Clearly we can't get back to the automobile,' he pronounces, fiddling with the control panel.

I'm not sure that legging it is an option either, given Roger's age, my health and Livia's drug-addled condition. All I can think to do is fling myself across Livia's prone body and start kicking away like a mad cyclist. I doubt if that'll keep a battalion of Dobermans at bay for long, though.

The propeller suddenly roars into life unnervingly close to my head.

'If you don't want to get battered, killed or arrested, you'd better come right now,' bawls Roger over the engines. 'I just gave the game away.'

'Must get Livia,' I bellow into the gale. I haul her off the concrete in a clumsy fireman's lift and totter towards the taxiing aircraft. My heart is pounding, but a surge of adrenaline gives me the strength for another few yards.

'Sling her up here,' orders Roger. The plane is only travelling at the speed of a brisk stroll but I can hear him throttling up the engines. I shove Livia across the passenger seat, Roger grabs her by the scruff of the lacy neck with his left hand and hauls her up through the door. The plane begins to pick up speed.

'Quick as you can now, Mikey,' shouts Roger. 'I can't slow down or we'll undercook and run out of yardage.'

What Roger fails to take into account is the fact that I've been in a coma for two years and although I've put on a bit of bulk and regained some semblance of mobility in the past fortnight, I'm still fundamentally as weak as a kitten. Lugging Livia on my shoulder for a few yards has done for me. My knees are jelly, I've got nothing left.

I clutch my sides and gasp for breath as I watch the little Cessna pull away and gather speed. I can hear Roger gunning the engines, just as I can hear from behind me that the Ard-Corps reinforcements have discarded any attempts at stealth and are approaching mob-handed, and worse, they've almost certainly released the dogs.

The white shape of the Cessna is soon lost in the darkness and within seconds even the comforting buzz of the engines has faded to nothing. For a moment I'm left in a weird state of sensory deprivation – pitch black and stony silent.

The dogs whine, catching my scent.

I wonder if the Dobermans will tear me apart before the Ard-Corps team use my head for a football, or vice versa. I don't mind, I'm ready to go.

I wait for the hounds to finish it.

The drone of the Cessna rises in the background, increasing in volume over the yelping of the dogs. The white outline of the little aircraft reappears from the gloom, heading back towards me. For a moment I'm baffled. Roger should have had no difficulty taking off: he's a decorated pilot wearing night-vision equipment. Tears prickle the corner of my eyes when I realize that he must have turned round to pick me up.

The machine throttles down; Roger pops his head out of the tiny plastic side window. 'Mikey, if you're still out there, grab the stanchion and hang on. I promise I'll have you down in ten minutes or so.'

I totter faster than I've tottered before and manage to grab the wing strut as it passes, almost wrenching my shoulders from their sockets. My feet kick wildly for purchase and somehow find the solid wheel fairing below. We take to the air just as some kind of dog-monster snaps at the space I occupied a second ago. In the dark I give it the finger and am very nearly blown off my perch.

Twenty-Three

I've always wanted to visit a water themepark, one of those places where they have all the slides and convoluted flumes, but of course I never managed to convince Bernard.

'Those bloody things are like outsized intestines, why on earth should I pay good money to ride in a gigantic bowel?'

Because you might feel at home there, Bernard. You big selfish shit . . .

By all accounts the steepest flumes are actually pitch-black inside. You just have this absolutely intense sensation of speed as you ride the cascading water. If this night flight is anything to go by, I'd have loved it.

It's wonderful, hanging out here, feet on the wheel arch, body angled into the wind; an extraordinary rush, an intoxicating cocktail of velocity, excess adrenalin and sensory overload. The sheer joy of being snatched from the jaws of death, or in this case a Doberman.

'Ah, Mikey?'

My eyes are shut tight against the breeze.

'Hello out there, Mikey . . . are you . . . ?'

I don't want to, but I open my eyes. Turbulence instantly whisks my vision into lachrymose mousse.

I turn my head to face the cockpit side window, where I can detect the blur of Roger's grey head above me.

'. . . You still . . . hanging on . . . there, Mikey?'

'I'm great. I love it. It's an incredible rush,' I bellow against the wind.

Roger shakes his head and cups an ear.

'A rush,' I scream, grinning to myself in the dark.

'. . . Don't like . . . go any faster or you'll . . . blown off . . . hang on . . . whatever you . . . don't panic.' Roger opens the pilot door and hangs out, supported by his harness. Every other word is lost, snatched away by the shrieking headwind.

'I love this,' I yell, shaking out my ridiculously long tresses behind me like a Lalique car-hood ornament.

'I'll have you . . . ground . . . about thirty seconds . . . try not . . . hysterical.'

'I'm not hysterical, I'm having a fantastic time.'

'Try . . . think . . . something else. Don't . . . whatever you do . . . and don't look down. I . . . you're terrified . . . God's sake, Mikey . . . don't . . . the strut.'

'I'm having the time of my life. Just shut up, Roger and fly,' I bawl against the oncoming gale.

'I've talked . . . frightened people . . . and . . . do this with you . . . both feet on . . . hands . . . linked . . . around the strut . . . perfectly strong . . . okay?'

'For God's sake, look at me. I don't have any fear of heights. Do I look scared?' I release one hand and perform a bouncy little jig on the wheel fairing.

'. . . Michael . . . losing it now. Calm down . . . absolutely still and just . . . just hang on . . . half a minute longer . . . get you down if it it's the last thing . . . just . . . calm.'

'Don't be ridiculous,' I bellow, but Roger's head and shoulders have already disappeared back inside the cabin.

I wrap both arms around the wing strut and close my eyes. The breeze slices and dices my tresses, vigorously massaging my scalp. I am the avian Garbo. And I want to be alone.

It's impossible to gauge height with any real precision in the dark, but perhaps a hundred feet below us is a small farmhouse surrounded by a few illuminated outbuildings. We circle slowly, losing height. More lights flick on as we lose altitude, investing the house with a cosy, yellow aura. I'm still enjoying myself but the headwind has begun to chill my bones; my hands are seizing up. It's clear that Roger has picked this remote farm as a landing spot and, much as I'm enjoying the ride, I'm looking forward to getting indoors. The engine chunters; overhead I hear the creak of servos as Roger engages the flaps. The Cessna bleeds speed and seems to hang in the air. Of course it's an illusion. I sense the ground rushing up to meet us, Roger's side window slides open again, he sticks his head out. 'Hang on tight, old boy . . . might . . . a bit lumpy.'

Something clatters against the wheels as we drop. I twist my body to present my back to whatever is below. My lower legs and buttocks are thrashed raw by waist-high whippy stalks as we jounce along a pitch-black field. My arms are numb. I'm wondering how much longer I can hang on when we hit a rut and I am catapulted head-first into the night. I grimace, anticipating the impact. This turns out to be a bad move, since I more or less break the fall with my teeth. Fortunately, the field has been well irrigated and I haul myself out from a forgiving porridge of mud and stubble.

The sadistic stalks appear to be some kind of cereal crop, wheat probably. There are tufts in my hair and I'm still spitting husks and grit long after I've picked myself up and tested all my limbs.

Some way ahead I can see the Cessna safe and in one piece, taxiing to a halt in the soft yellow light of the farmhouse windows. In all the time that I've known him, it's never once occurred to me to question Roger's flying credentials. Now of course, I never will.

There's no one to greet me when I arrive at the farmhouse, so I let myself in, tripping over uneven flagstones in the pitch-black hallway. My questing fingers search the darkness and find a handle, something curved and wooden at any rate, which comes away in my hand with a worrying clatter. Ahead is a thin strip of light.

The door at the end of the hallway is flung open by a silver-haired lady in blue slacks and a canvas shirt to reveal a shabby yet comfortable kitchen reeking of cats and woodsmoke. Roger stands in the centre of the room by the open Aga, frantically fiddling with a large rubber torch. He looks up and blinks rapidly. 'Good God, Michael. We thought . . .' his voice cracks. It takes him a moment to regain his composure before he's suddenly all squadron-leaderish again. 'Scrambled the search party, couldn't find any batteries for this bloody thing though. Livia's been preparing flaming torches.'

I'm relieved to see Livia upright at the pine table, more or less repatriated to the land of the living. There's an outsized box of matches and half-a-dozen thick twists of newspaper set before her. She gives me a tired smile.

'Knew you'd be fine, of course. Anyone under twenty-five who can't bale out of a moving aircraft without pitching up in the mess for a nightcap is either dead of a broken neck, shot by the Nazis, or a creampuff.'

I take a deep breath. 'I think your nineteen forties standards may not be entirely applicable to modern youth, Roger.'

'And we're all so much the worse for it. But you may be

right. Marvellous to see you in one piece though. I think I will have that whisky, now, girls.' Roger slumps into the dilapidated armchair by the stove.

A substantial tumbler of whisky and a thick hunk of fruit-cake are deposited on the arm of his chair by a second, identical silver-haired biddy in identical slacks and canvas shirt. She places another in front of Livia.

Roger raises his glass to me before taking a gigantic swig.

'Well, I'm very grateful to you for coming back for me at any rate.'

'Oh, goodness me, Mikey, is that what you thought? Had to turn into the wind. Couldn't take off otherwise.'

I'm still trying to process the implications of this piece of news when the silver-haired bat holding the door snaps at me. 'What are you doing with my umbrella? Roger, why does this young man have my umbrella? It's not raining out there, is it?'

'I have no idea.'

I find that I'm clutching a green umbrella by the smooth wooden handle, which I happily relinquish. The woman snatches it away, suspiciously.

'Have you eaten, young Creampuff?' enquires the second of the identical silver-haired harpies. 'Not for a while,' I mumble, eyeing Roger's fruitcake.

'You look as though you consumed a good portion of our wheatfield.'

'Do all these modern young men have such awful teeth, Roger? Is this the future, do you suppose?' asks the silver-hair at the door.

'I think you should give the lad a whisky and allow him to speak up for himself,' says Roger.

The last time I spoke to these twin lunatics they were on my side. I'm not enjoying the Pond twins now that they're ganging up on me.

Livia sniggers and takes a sip at her whisky.

'You don't have any right to snigger,' I hiss at Livia. 'I'm so cross with you. You went fucking tonto on us.'

'Oh, that's rather charming; you come, unannounced, into our house with your bad teeth, steal our umbrellas and swear at our guests,' chides the twin at the door. 'I'm not at all sure you deserve any cake.'

'I'm sorry, but that's how I feel.'

'Or lemonade.'

'Sit. There.' The twin at the door gestures at a straight-backed chair by a gigantic Welsh dresser.

I obey, cakeless and furthest from the Aga, while the twins return to their own seats on either side of Roger and resume fawning. They may be mad but they're right about my teeth: disgusting, still coated in slime and scraps of wheat.

Livia throws me the box of matches with a grin. I use the long thin sticks to surreptitiously pick out the worst of the muck while they blather.

'Of course, Roger, we weren't . . .' begins one of the sisters.

'Frightened,' finishes the other.

'Asleep, I was going to say,' corrects her sibling.

'We knew that a light aircraft landing out of the blue in our wheatfield at the dead of night would simply have to be Squadron-Leader Williams. It's just . . .'

'Kismet,' interjects her sibling.

'Common sense,' corrects her twin.

'We had a slight emergency,' explains Roger, 'nothing serious.'

'Well, I must say, you look very . . .'

'Dashing, as always.'

'Calm and collected, I was going to say,' corrects her sister peevishly, 'as well as dashing,' she adds, flourishing a huge old-fashioned decanter.

'Perhaps young Michael would care for a little drop first,' suggests Roger kindly.

'The young fellow who's done nothing but swear and pick his teeth since he arrived?'

'Precisely. Now where are my manners? Georgia and Georgina, may I formally introduce Michael? Michael, these two lovely young girls are the Pond twins.'

Unbelievably, the two bickering old lunatics actually simper.

'I'm Georgia and that's Georgina. I don't say so myself of course, but if you have trouble telling us apart, they do say that I'm the one with the eyes.'

'And I'm the one with the complexion,' Georgina informs me.

'I see.' But I'm none the wiser. As far as I'm concerned they both have identical swimming-goggle eyes and Dead Sea scroll complexions. 'We met once before,' I say in an attempt to appease the old bullies.

'Did we, indeed?' muses Georgina.

'I lost an umbrella last May. Was that you?'

'Yes, was that you? Did you pilfer it?'

Livia snorts.

'No.'

'I can vouch for the fact that Michael was in a coma at that time,' confirms Roger evenly.

Georgia's mouth compresses to the size and shape of a paper cut. Unconvinced.

'And so where exactly did we meet, young man?' asks Georgina.

'A few years ago now. You won't remember.'

'Indeed we will. We're not entirely . . .'

'Gaga,' finishes Georgina.

'Unobservant, I was going to say.'

'At the Caversham Lawn Tennis Club. I was playing Councillor Coombs.'

'Don't tell me? Hough's boy. You're the chappie who had to use a decrepit old Slazenger and still fetched Coombs a good one right in the . . .'

'Goolagongs?' suggests Georgina.

For once, her sister agrees: 'The goolagongs, exactly. You beat me to it.' Georgia smiles at me. 'As you can see, my sister and I have this uncanny telepathic connection. It's to do with being identical twins.'

'Well . . . yes, I was the one who got him in the, ah . . . goolagongs . . . that was me.'

'You look different. But that settles it. You must, you absolutely must, have a slice of cake and some whisky.'

'Some champagne, if we had any.'

'And after that we'll make up a couple of beds in the spare room. And Roger, you'll take the sofa, as usual.'

I raise a questioning eyebrow at Roger, who pointedly ignores me while levering himself to his feet. The sisters rise at the same time.

'Tempting, but alas, there is too much to be done. The new day is almost upon us and there is a very white and very obvious aircraft sitting in your front paddock which also happens not to belong to us. No doubt the owners will have their stooges airborne at first light to recce the entire surrounding area and I simply cannot expose you ladies to unnecessary risk.'

'You are not seriously considering flying off in the dark again, Roger?'

'What choice do I have? I don't want to sound melodramatic but these are rather disagreeable people we're dealing with here.'

'Where will you go?'

'I have no idea. But I can't leave it here. I'm sorry I even got you involved. Shouldn't have touched down at all, only I could see that Michael was panicking.'

'I was not.'

'Michael, you were hysterical and gibbering with fear, you almost let go of the wing-strut.'

'There's no shame in that. I don't much like flying either.' Georgina strides over and pats my hand. 'Did you soil yourself?' she asks with concern.

'I . . .'

Livia's shoulders are now shaking so violently that whisky sloshes from her tumbler.

Mercifully, I see a way to change the subject, recalling the outbuildings which I saw from the air. 'Wait, I've had a thought. Do you have a barn of some sort?'

'Oh, that won't be necessary, young man. If you hose yourself down properly you can still sleep in the spare room. You might want to get up from that chair though,' advises Georgia.

'Not for me,' I say. 'To hide the plane.'

'The barn.' Roger snaps his fingers. 'Good thought, lad.'

Georgina is slightly quicker on the uptake than her sister. 'It's got roller-doors, I think it might do.'

Roger turns to gaze out of the window, where we can all see the first pink thread of dawn flickering in the distance.

'It's later than I thought,' announces Roger grimly.

Terrified farm cats flee in all directions as Roger taxis right up to the wide roller-doors and cuts the engine. The prop slowly winds down, leaving a residual drone hanging in the air. It's going to be a tight fit but looks feasible. Roger jumps from the cockpit and joins the rest of us as we take hold of the wings and push, manhandling the Cessna through the gap. The nose is through but the wing tips clang against the doorposts. We're too wide by at least a foot.

In the watery light, Roger's face is now plainly visible, anxiously scanning the heavens. I realize that what I thought was the residual drone from our engine is nothing of the sort – there's another aircraft up there somewhere and it's hunting us. Bandits at six o'clock. Quarter to, in fact.

'It's not going to go in straight. We'll have to back up and try for an angle,' announces Roger.

All five of us push until our faces are puce, even Livia. The plane trundles backwards a few inches, but it's harder this way, there's a slight incline towards the barn; we're pushing uphill and the wheels keep getting bogged down in the sucking farmyard ooze.

'That'll do.' Roger orders, 'Now, everyone push forward on the right wing.'

The wing swings around. If we can just clear the doorpost on this side we can get the aircraft safely inside at the angle.

Clang.

The wing still overlaps the doorpost by a measly two inches. We're going to have to back up again for another attempt.

We're not exactly a gang of navvies here. The drone is getting louder by the second and we're panting away like telephone sex pests but we're going to have to summon up the strength from somewhere.

'Bugger this,' shouts Livia, relinquishing her handhold on the fuselage. She stomps off into the barn.

I gaze across at Roger. There's no sign of judgement there; his face is impassive as he continues to heave.

The drone increases in volume, segueing into a full-throated machine roar. Curiously the sound now seems to surround us, echoing through the half empty expanse of barn. I look around expecting to see a helicopter or something, but all I see is Livia in goggles, standing at the wing tip. For a surreal moment I think she might be about to take the Cessna up into the air for a dogfight. Instead, she raises her arms above her head and brings down a huge, industrial-looking chainsaw which bites through the wing tip in a shower of sparks. Livia swiftly cuts the power, discards the saw and takes her place once again at the fuselage. 'Come on then, you old cripples. Put your backs into it.'

The truncated right wing now clears the doorpost by a good three inches. With an astonishing burst of energy from us the rest of the plane slips neatly through the gap.

Roger and I race to the roller-doors and pull them to, just as a small white object appears through a break in the clouds above the farm. It circles the property a couple of times before losing interest and moving on.

Livia sprawls on her back over a hay bale, breathing heavily. I trail Roger as he advances towards her. Even from behind, I can tell by the rigid set of his body that he's not best pleased.

'Do you realize what you've just done, young lady?'

'I think so,' chuckles Livia.

'You just mutilated a hundred thousand pounds' worth of aircraft.'

'I did, didn't I?' Livia grins.

'I'm speechless.'

'Good, then don't give us a speech. What I did is make the bloody thing fit into this barn. And just in time too, by the looks of it.'

'You took a chainsaw to an object of great beauty.'

'I got the job done, Roger.'

'You pretty well destroyed a wonderful machine.'

'And what about those shmeshy things the Germans flew in the war, how are they any different?'

'I have no idea what you're talking about.'

'The smeshermitts . . . aeroplanes. The German ones. Oh, come on, you know perfectly well.'

'Livia, I'm so disappointed in you, especially after tonight's performance. And so is Mikey.'

I hate the way Roger has suddenly dragged me into this; besides, although I am still a bit disappointed with Livia's performance tonight, I think Roger is being unfair here. 'Messerschmitts,' I prompt.

'Exactly. Weren't they supposed to be beautiful aircraft or whatever? Mikey still has a bunch of plastic models dangling from his bedroom ceiling, so they must have been quite something.'

'I just haven't got around to taking them down yet—'

'Shut up, Mikey,'

'I don't see how that is relevant,' snaps Roger.

'You shot them out of the air, didn't you? Drilled them full of little holes? Destroyed them? Knights of the sky and all that?'

'That was different. I had to. It was a question of exigency.' Roger's tone is still sharp but he's losing the moral high ground here and knows it. 'There was no chivalry up there and very little glory: it was exhausting and squalid, if you must know, and most of the time we tried to shoot the other man in the back, before he even knew we were there. That's the plain truth of it.'

The Pond twins contribute nothing either way but their silence is eloquent testimony.

There's a stand-off in the huge barn while Roger weighs up Livia's argument. Livia sits upright now on the hay bale and observes him through narrowed eyes as she sucks on a piece of straw.

Finally, Roger capitulates. 'You're right, Livia, I'm grateful to you for reminding me of a lesson I learned years ago and should never have forgotten: machines can always be replaced, people can't be.'

Livia smiles and leaps to her feet. 'Gi' us a kiss then, you cantankerous old bugger.'

For all sorts of reasons the Pond twins and I are relieved when Roger only busses her chastely on the forehead.

Along with the chainsaw the Ponds' barn is an Aladdin's cave of interesting power tools; Roger makes short work of the bracket around his medal with a Black and Decker power-saw. Livia and I sit together on the hay bale and applaud as Roger emerges from the cockpit with that elusive silver cross cupped safely in both hands.

We're expecting a speech but Roger is silent and intro-spective. After the recent run-in with Livia I imagine that he's taking a moment to remember past comrades. It's still a bit of an anticlimax though, given all we've been through.

I nudge Livia and whisper, 'You might be square with Roger, but you're not right with me yet.'

Livia nudges me back right in the ribs, 'I know what you're thinking, Mikey, but I wanted to talk to you about that.'

'I bet you did,' I say, smugly.

'I don't know what happened last night and I'm scared.'

'Oh, ha, ha.'

Livia nudges me again, this time a lot harder, her voice hoarse: 'I swear I have no idea what happened. I was wear-ing the night-vision mask one minute – and it was pretty trippy, watching the road – then my heart started jumping around, I felt a bit sick and faint, then I don't remember any-thing after until I woke up, just before we landed here.'

'You ate some of the doped pizza, Livia.'

'Mikey, I swear to you, I didn't eat any of the pizza. I think there might be something wrong with me.'

'Livia, how much sleep have you had since we met? A few hours. You've been awake almost as long as I have. And you're doing it with amphetamines. I think your body's just telling you to slow down. It's had enough. That's all it is. You're exhausted. Stop putting all that awful stuff up your nose and go to sleep for a night. Just get a good night's rest and you'll be fine.'

Livia turns to me and smiles. Like a waxwork in a blaze, her expression melts into something alien and unreadable. 'Oh, Mikey, I can't sleep now. If I do, I might miss what's left of you. I'd sleep for days and you'd be gone when I woke up and I couldn't handle that.'

My own features have betrayed me too; I want to smile but can't force the ends of my mouth upwards. My lower lip is beginning to tremble like a springboard and somehow my face has drifted closer to hers than I ever thought possible.

She inches towards me – without having to incline her head, since I have no nose to speak of.

Our lips brush.

'Everybody, look what I've found. There's a cargo,' shrieks bloody Georgia or Georgina.

Livia and I part; clamshells dropped in vinegar.

The Pond twins gleefully haul packages from under the passenger seats and drop them to the concrete floor of the barn. These things are vacuum-packed in heavy-duty green PVC and are about the size and shape of an average house-brick.

'Do you think it might be cattle-feed?' asks one of the Pond twins hopefully.

'I doubt it.'

'I'm sure it won't do any harm to check one,' chirps Livia disingenuously.

Before I can stop her, she approaches the nearest package,

armed with a screwdriver; she stabs down on the tight plastic wrapping in a Norman Bates frenzy.

There's a puff of white powder and I know this is very bad news.

Livia shoves her face into the slit and inhales.

Twenty-Four

'What is your problem?' objects Livia, as I steer her away from the bricks.

'I thought we just agreed you've done enough of that stuff?' I hiss.

'That was before a hundred kilos of grade-A Charlie suddenly landed in my lap. I've been slumming it with Herbal's crummy, stepped-on whiz, now all my white Christmases have come at once. Look at the way it's shimmering, almost pearlescent, that's how you can tell it's totally uncut. This stuff is primo yayo. You think I'm going to pretend it's not here? Nobody has that much willpower.'

'It doesn't belong to us. You're not entitled to a single pinch of this stuff, primo yoyo or not. We've got to find a way to get every bit of it back to the owners or they're going to completely kill us.'

'As opposed to semi-killing us? Anyway, why should you worry?' Livia bites her knuckles. 'Oh, my God, I'm sorry, Mikey, that just slipped out. I didn't mean it.'

'No, you're right.' I slump on to a hay bale. 'Why should I worry? None of this is my business. We found the medal. I've done my bit. Game over. Really I should just go home . . . and wait.'

'Don't say that. It's not over. You're not walking out on

me, I won't allow it.' Livia gazes down at me, her voice softening. 'Mikey, you're right to be worried, about Roger and me and Mr T., Mrs Hodges, Gerry, the Pond twins. We're all part of this thing now and it's a long way from over.' Dark brown eyes narrow, a foxy expression flits across her face. 'Besides, we had a deal, remember?'

It seems so long ago now that it takes me a moment to recall the Devil's pact I made on that first strange night up in the treehouse. 'You can't be serious?'

'How about a minor concussion?'

'No.'

'One good smash in the face, requiring low-level medical attention?'

'Look at me, Livia, Coombs would snap me in half.'

'You could clout him with a shovel.'

'He could hit me back, with his fists.'

'Okay, new deal.'

I'm instantly on my guard. 'What now?'

'You don't give up on us and we'll call it quits.'

I let out a long-suffering sigh, but it's only for effect; so that Livia doesn't think I'm a complete pushover. She's right of course: I can't walk away now, not while they're all sitting on this hundred-kilogram keg of lethal white powder. 'I'll finish what we started, Livia, but I'm not damaging Coombs for you. I hope that's understood?'

Livia drops to a crouch, her face, once again, only inches from mine. She peers deep into my eyes without flinching. 'Mikey, I adore you. You are easily the best person on the planet. The best person with a willy, anyway.'

I have no idea whether I'm being damned with faint praise or if this is a genuine compliment. With a profile like mine, you take what you can get.

Livia remains in the crouch, steadying herself by resting her hands on my thighs. 'Mikey . . . before we give the

Controller, or whoever, this stuff back do you think I might just take the teensiest-weensiest smidgen for myself? Something they won't miss. Say, about the size of a small Cadbury's Fruit & Nut bar?'

I can feel the warmth of her hands; I imagine I can even feel the soft undulations of her palms through the fabric of my jeans. She's so close now I can smell whisky and cake on her breath; blood drains from my head and thunders towards my loins. 'Uh . . . well . . . uh . . . okay then.'

'Thank you, Mikey,' she responds bouncing to her feet. 'And by the way . . .'

'What?'

'You may not be very good-looking or anything, but I do love you to bits.'

Much as I enjoy hearing that she loves me to bits, I can't shake the feeling that I've just been manipulated in some way.

'I don't know, perhaps we should feed it to the cattle,' suggests Georgia.

Georgina considers this. 'Might increase the yield a bit.'

'There's no way you can keep any of this stuff,' I say.

'I think we should pour petrol on it and just burn the lot,' announces Roger. 'It's drugs.'

'Cocaine, to be precise,' says Livia.

'You can't do anything with it, other than return it as intact as possible and as fast as possible,' I insist.

'It's ruddy drugs,' objects Roger.

'Primo drugs,' pronounces Livia.

'Burn the lot,' orders Roger. 'These substances are a blight. We'll be doing the world a favour.'

'We'll have to shift the lot all the way over to the compost heap then,' says Georgia.

'Which will take a—'

'Big sweaty man with his shirt off,' interjects Georgia.

'I was going to say, "an hour or two",' advises Georgina. 'But then I was going to say "by a couple of big, sweaty men with their—"'

'Trousers off?' suggests Georgia.

'Yes, exactly. It'd take an hour or two, if done by two big sweaty men with their shirts and trousers off.'

'I'm sorry,' I announce. 'You cannot burn this stuff, you cannot move it, you cannot even touch this stuff for the moment.'

'Why?'

'I was going to ask exactly that,' says Georgina.

I attempt to give the sisters some perspective. 'Do you know how much this white powder is actually—'

'About five to eight million pounds sterling is what this white powder is worth to a distributor,' finishes Livia.

This shuts them up. And gives them some perspective.

Roger clears his throat. 'Ah . . . that is a great deal of money.'

'It's a conservative estimate. By the time the street dealers step on our bags of snow, it'll probably make about twelve mill.'

'So it's like wine, is it? They step on it to squeeze out the best?'

'No, it kind of works the other way round to wine, Roger,' Livia murmurs.

'Oh, my goodness,' breathes Georgia.

'Yes,' I shout. 'Now can you see why I was going on about the plane?'

'No,' says Georgia.

'Me neither,' says Georgina. 'I thought we agreed that the plane wasn't important.'

'The Cessna is like an ice-cream cone.' Livia smiles. 'It doesn't really matter; it's a comparatively cheap and disposable delivery system for the ice-cream scoop. If you want to burn something, burn the plane, nobody cares. But Mikey's right, the scary thing here is the white powder. That's what everyone wants. That's really what they're hunting for. The aircraft that flew over us earlier didn't spend too much time looking around but that doesn't mean your farm isn't on some kind of list.'

'We need to get all these green plastic bricks back to whoever owns them as fast as possible before they come after you and kill you. And they will come after you. They'll come after you like a ten-million pound nemesis. Is that understood, ladies?' I say.

The ladies are not impressed. 'There's something wrong with him.'

'Oh, well done,' I say.

'Shut up, you two.' Livia narrows her eyes as she speaks. 'Mikey's right. This is serious. They will kill you and once they've killed you, they'll come back and kill you again, and all your relatives. Believe me, I know what certain people are capable of for only five grand's worth of this stuff. So, nobody touch it. Mikey and I will go back to Caversham, get a reliable decent-sized vehicle – a Volvo Estate – then we'll come back, pick up the entire consignment, and figure out a way to get it back to the owners without any repercussions. And that'll be the end of that. In the meantime, leave it well alone.'

The only person I know of with a Volvo Estate is Bernard. Clearly, Livia and I need to talk.

Georgia Pond draws the short straw and chauffeurs us back to Caversham in the old Mini. She takes corners in a straight line and treats the amber traffic lights like they owe her money. She sits, hunched over the wheel, muttering under her breath the entire time about how her sister is so patently unworthy of Roger.

*

Georgia executes a messy hand-brake turn in Coombs's pristine gravel driveway just as the man explodes from the garage at the wheel of his open-top MG. He skids to a halt as Livia and I clamber out.

Coombs inspects us with thin-lipped disapproval as Georgia's Mini departs in a dense cloud of stone chips. 'Where you been all night, girly? As if I didn't fucking know.' He smirks in my direction. 'What's this, Root-a-Retard-Week? You couldn't do any better than that?'

Livia makes for the front door in silence, head down, shielded by those long tresses.

There's a shrill blast from the horn, 'Oy, you, get back here. I haven't finished with you yet.'

Livia stops and slowly turns. 'What is it, Coombs? I'm tired.'

The man gazes up from the car with an odd smile on his face. 'You're not going to call me Daddy, then?'

'Fuck off, Coombs, you're just *in loco parentis*. Being a reptile, you're not even a related species, thank God.'

'Oh, that's nice, I give you a roof over your head and you call me a reptile: you steal my money, nick my car and stay out all night snorting drugs. You give me nothing but disrespect, girly, but you're quite happy to jump into bed with the spanner from next door, first chance you get. You want to sharpen up your act, love, lest I chuck you out on to the streets.'

'Do what you like, Coombs. I could care.'

The man's expression softens; he may even be grinning now. It's not easy to tell under all that face-fuzz. 'You know I'd never chuck you out, Liv, I'm your guardian, I've promised to look after you.'

'You're Coombs, you're a twat and I hate you.' Livia stands on the gravel transmitting all the hate in her heart through her eyes. 'I don't care who you think you are or what you think you can do. I'll be out of here soon. Away from you.'

'Is that what you think? You'll be going home, back to old Mum's?'

Livia makes no response but I can see that Coombs's abrupt tone-shifts are beginning to unnerve her.

'Your mum, of course!' He chuckles, slapping his forehead theatrically. 'Got a memory like a sieve. There was a message on the answerphone last night. From Huntly Hall Hospice.' Coombs reclines in his MG. 'I erased it though.'

'What?' spits Livia.

'Well, let me see if I can remember what they said . . .' The MG begins to trundle slowly down the drive.

Livia crumbles; she runs to the dawdling vehicle and seizes the door like a castaway gripping a lifeboat. 'Please?' she begs.

Coombs smiles and applies the brakes. 'Ah, so you're going to be civil now?'

'Please, Barry.'

'That's nice.' Coombs grins; wet pink lips emerge, splitting apart the dense black fuzz around his face. 'So, what's with the moron, Liv?'

Livia looks around, unsure.

I can see that for some strange reason my presence is bothering Coombs, so I make this easy on Livia and let my shoulders slump and my jaw go slack.

'He's from next door, Barry. It's not what you think.'

'I know he's from next door,' he whispers. 'What's it doing here, with you?'

'He just tags along. Doesn't bother me. He's very amiable really.'

I smile stupidly, on cue. It does the trick.

'What a colossal fucking idiot. Shame really, he was a bright lad before he went and nutted the daisies from twenty feet up.' Coombs shrugs. '*Caveat emptor*,' he mutters curiously, like an incantation.

'He's away with the fairies now.'

'Oh, Jesus,' Coombs looks like he's just bitten a raw onion. He swallows convulsively. 'Turned him nancy as well, did it?'

'No, I mean he's just not with us any more.'

'I see.' Coombs sniffs. 'With a face like that he's not likely to get much joy from either side of the fence. I still don't like him hanging about with you though.' He pops the MG into first gear and gives the accelerator a warning rev. 'Anyway, young lady, much as I've enjoyed this little chat, I've got business to see and people to do.'

'Please, Barry, the message.'

'Oh yeah, the message. I'll give you the message. You're entitled to that since you've been so nice and polite.'

Livia releases the door and smiles with relief. 'Thanks, Barry. I do appreciate it.'

Coombs licks his lips and composes his heavy features. 'The thing is, Livia, the news is not all that wonderful.' He pouts, arching fleshy lips in a parody of misery. 'The thing is, your old junkie-slapper of a mum is about to kark it. And guess what? She'd like to see you before she pops her clogs.' He grins hugely, before pouting again. 'But of course, by now it might already be too late. Oh dear, maybe you shouldn't have been such a dirty little stop-out all night. What d'you think?'

'I . . . I . . . how am I going to get there, Barry?'

Coombs shrugs. 'Fucked if I know. It's only thirty miles or so to Huntly Hall. Get a taxi. Oh, I forgot, you've got no money. You'd be wasting your time poking through my stuff again because there's no cash in the house.' Coombs grins happily. 'Oh dear, and you can't nick the MG again either, since I'm driving it.'

'Barry, please. Can't you . . .?'

'The Range Rover? No luck there. It's in for a service. So, I'd put your thinking-cap on if I were you, Livia. But don't take too long. If she hasn't already checked out permanently, she soon will do.'

The MG squirts gravel and slithers down the end of the driveway, where it stops for a moment. 'Hey, I just had an idea,' shouts Coombs, 'why don't you ask Mongo there, to carry you on his back?' With a grin, Coombs screeches out on to the road and is gone.

Livia turns to me. 'Where does your dad keep the keys to his Volvo, Mikey?'

'Ah . . . now I wanted to talk to you about that.'

'No time,' she declares, banishing objections.

Twenty-Five

I'm still wondering about *caveat emptor*, Coombs's curious Latin epithet, as I let myself in through the front door and slip silently along the hallway into my father's study. I'm just sliding open his desk drawer when, with a shock, I'm aware of another person in the room. My mother sits, stock-still, huddled in the low chair at the roll-top desk, my medical notes in her lap. Her presence here is very nearly as taboo as mine. 'Your father's out golfing,' she explains softly.

'You were reading my notes.'

'I was.' My mother reaches down and retrieves a couple of stray sheets from the carpet.

'Bernard thinks it's all nonsense.'

'He's like that with me too.' She sighs.

'He reckons it's all in the mind, which I suppose, in a way, it is.'

My mother smiles weakly. There's a distance between us, too wide and too late to bridge now and, to her credit, she doesn't try.

'Mikey, you mustn't think so badly of him. There's no manual. No instruction book. We wrapped you in cotton wool, I see that now.' She puts the last few pages back in order. 'The problem is, we just sort of left you there and forgot to unwrap you.' She rises and stows the manila folder in my father's roll-top desk. 'You were wanted, which is a lot more than you can say for some.' She gazes sadly out of the window before turning to me. 'What are you after, Michael?'

There's no point dissembling. 'I need the spare keys to the Estate. Livia's mum's . . .'

'Then you must have them.' My mother fishes the spare Volvo keys from the roll-top and throws them across to me without another word.

I must have my touchstone before I leave. I slip upstairs to fetch my lump of amber. We could all use some luck right now.

In spite of the urgency, or perhaps because of it, Livia pilots the Volvo with uncharacteristic care and courtesy through towns and villages, getting us to Huntly Hall without incident some forty minutes later.

From the driveway, Huntly Hall fails to live up to the promise of its title. It is, or at least, was, a handsome Palladian building, surrendered to the public sector some time in the mid-seventies by a cash-strapped, tax-crippled family. The current owners have done their level best to destroy any residual aesthetic value, as the jagged row of grey Portakabins scattered wantonly in front of the crumbling façade testifies.

I doubt if Livia has time to register any of this. We pull up at the nearest and smallest of the Portakabins; she hauls on the handbrake and sprints inside without pausing to lock up.

'My mum, where is she? Her name's Jane Knox, Mrs Jane Knox, and she's dying,' she gabbles breathlessly at the reception desk.

'I'll thank you to calm down, young lady,' the receptionist scolds, glossy crimson mouth forming an almost perfect

'O' of theatrical disapproval. She's on the wrong side of plump middle age, and over-compensates with excessively delicate, girlish gestures. The computer at her desk bristles with small brightly coloured hairy things and amusing stickers. 'I can see that you're concerned.' The woman tweezes a biscuit from the half-empty pack beside her and clamps off a perfect semi-circle with that O-shaped orifice. 'But you'll need to fill in some forms first if you want to visit. Surname, please.' She begins pecking away at the keyboard with a single plump forefinger.

'This is an emergency, my mother is dying, she might already be—'

'You're obviously upset, young lady.' The woman stops typing and sips from a mug emblazoned with the slogan 'Hot 'n' Steamy, just like me'.

'I am upset.'

'I can see that but we all have to—'

'We all have to *what*? Wait while smug functionaries like you stuff themselves with Hob-Nobs and tea and suck away the last seconds we have with our loved ones?'

'I really don't think . . .'

'Precisely,' says Livia, 'you don't think, and worse, you don't feel. Do you behave like this to everyone who comes in here? The elderly? The confused? The grief-stricken?'

She's glaring now. 'I do my job, Miss . . .?'

Livia sniffs contemptuously before pelting through the prefab corridor towards the main building.

As we race up the circular stairway I'm able to see how Huntly Hall has metamorphosed from a place of wealth and privilege to a sad shell of dispossession and hopelessness: plush carpets have been replaced with grey lino, wallpaper obliterated by hospital-green gloss. And it smells, my God, it smells: sweat, rot, death, shit. Livia wasn't wrong when she mentioned horse-piss; that too.

'Where's my mum?' shrieks Livia, standing at the nexus of yet another nightmarish, underlit corridor. 'I want to see my mum. I want to see Jane Knox, *nowww*!' she howls.

A young, startlingly tall Indian in a white coat appears as though by magic. He looms over us, beckoning with a finger before placing it to his lips.

'What?' sniffs Livia, suspiciously.

The doctor ushers Livia and me into one of the many identical rooms branching off from the upper wing. Livia races to her mother's bedside; the doctor intercepts me, gently taking me by the arm. 'Are you related to Mrs Knox?' he whispers.

I peer up into his unlined brown face and realize that we might actually be the same age. He's not only taller than me but he's done a hell of a lot more with his life. 'I'm a friend of Mrs Knox's daughter.'

'Mrs Knox is very ill – *in extremis*. If you'd prefer, you're welcome to wait downstairs.'

'I promised to stay with her daughter.'

'This will not be pleasant,' he advises. 'You may not want to stay.'

'Why?'

'Mrs Knox is dying.'

'So am I.'

He accepts this without comment as a glib scrap of juvenile faux-philosophical smart-arsery. 'She's dying and fighting it.'

'Surely everyone should fight it.'

The man gazes down at me. 'Sometimes it's better to go peacefully. Two days ago Mrs Knox insisted that we take her off the medication. She's weak and in terrible pain. We thought she might go last night.' The doctor's voice drops to a whisper. 'I'd like to get permission from the daughter to put her back on the morphine, at least let her pass in comfort.'

I know he's doing his best but he's making it sound like Livia's mum is constipated. 'Why did she come off the medication?'

'It happens from time to time. Sometimes, at the end, people think they need to be clear-headed.' The doctor sighs and glances over at the bed where Livia now sits, clasping her mother's hand. 'There are no cures in this place. The only thing we *can* do here is manage pain: we're here to spare people the agony; the living as well as the dying. Believe me, this way will be far more painful for both of them.'

'Why?'

The doctor stands there, pensive, chewing his lower lip. 'Mrs Knox thinks she has something to tell her daughter.' He shakes his head dismissively. 'It's a story your friend doesn't need to hear. I'd like you to convince her to give me permission to resume the morphine and let her poor mother pass in peace.'

The doctor is undoubtedly a man of compassion. A frustrated man. And if he were having this conversation with anyone else they'd probably agree with him. It just so happens that he's speaking with someone who is also in the process of dying, and I don't need anyone else telling me how I should or shouldn't go about it, so why should Jane Knox?

The doctor grimaces and stalks from the room.

I grab one of the light tubular chairs and move it into place beside Livia, where she clasps her mother's frail hand. My presence seems to revitalize Mrs Knox in some way. 'That you, Ivvy?' she mutters through cracked lips.

'I'm right here.'

'Thought you might be. Hoped you might be. How you doing, my girl?'

'Ah, well, you know . . . surviving.'

'You were always good at that, not like your old mum, eh?'

'You did all right, Mum, you did your best . . . I brought someone to see you. Mum, this is Mikey.'

'Bring him over, I can't see him.'

'He's here, Mum, sitting next to me.'

'Let me feel his hands then.' Livia gently places my right hand in her mother's skeletal grip.

'He's got good hands – dry and strong. Say a lot about a man, hands do. You must be a good man, with hands like these. Look after her, will you? Someone has to look after her. Coombs won't.'

Mrs Knox releases me from her feather-light grip. Livia retrieves the withered claw and draws it up to her cheek. The doctor was right: I don't want to be here.

'I know that, Mum.'

'You don't know. You don't know anything. Coombs won't do a thing for you, not when I'm gone. The instant he knows I'm dead, he'll put you out onto the streets, or worse. Expect no help from that man.'

'Like I said, Mum, I'm a survivor.'

Jane Knox's face collapses in a wave of pain. I can see nothing of Livia there: the hair across the pillow is long and nicotine-blonde, her skin is fragile, almost transparent, and crisscrossed with a network of tiny wrinkles, like a crumpled sheet of tracing paper. There's a zinc pail under the bed, containing an inch or two of some foul glistening liquid.

'There's something you need to know. About me.'

Livia runs her palm across the woman's forehead. 'Mum, I didn't come here for any deathbed confessions, you are what you are and there's no need to torture yourself about any mistakes you may have made; I don't hold anything against you. I'm here because you're my mum: I wanted to see you, that's all.'

Jane Knox licks parched lips. Her daughter trickles a tiny stream from the plastic bedside jug into that awful chasm.

The woman continues in a flat monotone as though reciting the catechism: 'I had a habit, you knew that. I kicked it. Hardest thing I ever did, but I did it because you were on the way, for the love of you. You coming along was the best thing that ever happened to me for all sorts of reasons.'

'I know all this.'

Jane Knox flounders, struggling for breath. Livia grabs the transparent plastic mask at the bedside and holds it over her mother's nose and mouth. A few desperate breaths, after which her mother signals for its removal. 'I want to talk, love.'

'You can't talk if you can't breathe, you silly cow.'

Livia's mum smiles grimly. 'The trouble is, Ivvy, the junk. It's a two-headed snake: it doesn't just poison you with the craving, the fangs stay in you. You get straightened out, then you find out what you owe. It's a deep dark hole. That was me: no job; no man; and a bub on the way, in a squalid little flat in Reading.'

'I know all this stuff, Mum. I know someone came along and gave you a leg-up, a loan. But you never told me who. I know how hard it was. Don't relive it, not now, not for me.'

Jane Knox grins horribly. 'Yeah, someone came along all right. Don't know whether you'd call it a leg-up exactly, more of a leg-over. Coombs.'

'Oh, for fuck's sake, Mum.'

'Hard to believe, but he was good-looking in those days, nice dresser too, big curly sideburns. He owned the leases on a few of our bed-sits at first. Then he bought the freeholds on the whole building. Then a few more. He was my landlord. I couldn't pay him in cash, so I paid him the best way I knew how. I was trying to get myself straight, but I just owed and owed. Couldn't see a way to get out of the spiral, my darling. So, when he offered his deal . . .' Jane Knox falls back on the pillow, exhausted and sweaty. 'I took it, my love.'

Livia and I flick a glance at one another. Like a cracked radiator, the life is trickling and sputtering out of Jane Knox even as we watch.

'What deal, Mum?'

'Mrs Knox, you left a bit out.'

Livia smacks her old mum around the face, which seems to do the trick.

'Mum? What was it, Mum? What was the deal you did with Coombs?'

Jane Knox's eyes flutter open. 'I just told you. I don't want to go through it all again.'

'That's the bit you didn't tell me.'

Livia's mum rolls her eyes. For a moment, I think she's gone. Then: 'Oh, fucking hell, Ivvy, why d'you make me tell you all this again?'

'Just the deal bit, Mum. Just so I can get it straight.'

'Coombs bought you, Liv. He bought you as a bub. He bought you before you were even born, in exchange for your mum's debts. Not for him – I'd never have done that – for some other people, some spunkless middle-class couple he had lined up. They wanted a newborn baby. So I sold you.' Her voice takes on a junkie's wheedling tone, 'To give you a better life, Ivvy, a chance. You can see that, can't you?' The woman is so dehydrated that she's unable to raise a tear.

Livia is torn between grief and anger at this baffling, illogical confession. 'I don't get it, Mum. *You* brought me up, not some middle-class couple.'

Jane Knox actually grins, for the first time, at the memory. 'In the hospital they did some kind of tests. Turns out you had a heart-rumour. That snotty couple didn't want damaged goods, see.'

'What?'

'I got the cash and I still got to keep my lovely Livia.'

'They paid you for nothing?'

'Not the full whack but enough to get me out from under.'

'What's a heart-rumour, Mum?'

'I don't know, my love. Nothing. At the hospital they told me it was nothing. The couple sent you back because they're the kind who send back a good bottle of wine if the cork hasn't come out just right or the label's on skewy.'

With a barely discernible head-pivot Livia gives me permission to leave, and by Christ, I want to. I shove back the chair with a tiny scraping sound, which rouses Jane Knox, she gazes up and twists her neck towards the light, like an ivy stem. 'I warned Coombs that I'd grass him if he didn't look after you.'

'You blackmailed him?'

'When I got ill, I didn't know what else to do. I would have done it, too, if I had to. I'd have given evidence to a court of law. He did sell a child, Livia. He went ahead with the deal. Some other kid, a toddler. Probably one of his own little bastards from another poor junkie he'd knocked up.' Jane Knox wheezes horribly at the irony.

Livia rakes fingers through the flesh of her own face.

'And now?' asks Livia.

'Now, you're on your own. I won't be around to give evidence. Coombs has no reason to worry about you. Get away from him now, Ivvy.'

I can detect the first traces of panic in Livia's voice as she grips her mother's shoulders: 'And what about my dad? Who was he? What was his name?'

Jane Knox sighs. It's a weird sigh and it goes on for far too long.

Twenty-Six

Livia remains bleakly silent as she steers the Volvo into our driveway. Her face has been oddly slack for the past hour, like an ill-fitting rubber mask. Although I have an inkling of what must be going through her head, I have no real sense of her mood. I attempt to assemble my features into an expression of support and concern.

She switches off. Mercifully there's no sign of Bernard, so I assume he's still out with his Rotarian pals, getting squiffy at the nineteenth hole, boring the slacks off them with his *Fide et Fiducia*.

We sneak around to the rear of Coombs's Victorian Gothic pile, and Livia unlocks the back door and cocks her head, listening, sniffing, straining the senses for Coombs's presence. Satisfied, she leads me into the kitchen. 'Wait here,' she orders mechanically. 'I'm going upstairs to get my stuff together.'

Mr Truffles would love it here; it's a chef's wet-dream: long stainless-steel galley, multiple gas hobs and a central island-cum-workstation, the whole place festooned with glistening copper pans, complicated wire colanders and shiny, Inquisition-style devices bristling with blades and cranks. There's a massive upright fridge-freezer in the corner, a white-goods version of the Space Odyssey monolith, with a sort of recess in the door like a tiny shrine, housing an angled chrome lever. I give the mini-lever a tentative shove and win the Alaskan jackpot: a cascade of perfectly formed ice cubes clatters and skids across the terracotta floor tiles.

I wonder what all this says about Coombs and whether some measure of the inner man might be revealed by the contents of a fridge. This one is well-stocked, full of ready-made spaghetti sauces, cheeses, exciting pickles, thinly sliced ham, Continental meats and festive bags of ready-washed mixed salads and isotonic drinks.

I bite off a hunk of vintage Cheddar and filch a couple of the more immodestly proportioned Polish gherkins before allowing the heavy door to swing back on to its rubber seals.

There's a jaunty photo-calendar on the wall above, and curiously, the month of August features my old friend, Bibury bridge. It's not precisely the same photo as my jigsaw puzzle, but it is the same structure. Shot from thirty yards or so further downstream, crystal waters rush beneath those familiar buttery stone arches. The light is a little warmer in this shot, perhaps closer to late afternoon.

Did we run out of things to photograph in England, I wonder. We're such a dense population these days that the instant we find a patch of beauty or joy, we can't move for hamburgers, chips, clotted cream and jigsaw photographers urging us to get out of the bloody shot.

The days are filled with terse pencilled appointments, mostly to do with guzzling. Today, 18 August, for example, is: 'Lunch w. Terry/Sandy – Tosca's. Council Meet. 6.30, Drinks – Sour Grapes. Dinner w. Van Huis – Santorini.' It seems that Coombs is going Greek tonight. It strikes me that he might be better off talking to the Controller about a Weight Watcher's programme instead of that miserable bloody shopping mall and car park.

I wonder what's keeping Livia, so I trundle along the hallway and begin my ascent of the impressive staircase. There's no art on the way up, just framed photographs, shots of Coombs with his awful Bison-Branson grin, beefy arms draped across the sort of people my father would know and love: men in blazers or thornproof tweed with insincere smirks and comb-overs; their sleek, well-groomed wives.

I continue to climb, relying heavily on the banister, pausing from time to time to rest, and then the oddest thing: I find myself breathless on the third-floor landing with no memory of the last four steps, as though a cosmic film editor hacked a few seconds from my life. A time-stutter, is the only way I can describe it. A clear signal that my decline has begun. In a way, it's a relief, a timely reminder of my mortality. I can only assume that these episodes are going to get longer and more frequent until nothing remains of my conscious being. I decide not to mention it to Livia. She's had enough for one day.

Casa Coombs has no fewer than four floors and Livia has the uppermost garret. I climb, hauling away, hand over hand on the balustrade to relieve the strain on my quivering thighs and calves. Sure enough, at the fourth-floor landing I catch the sibilance of a power-shower from somewhere down the hall. At the same time I hear the subterranean rumble of an overtuned engine from outside. I peer out of a turret window and see Coombs cruising up the drive in his open-top MG.

Oh God.

I scuttle down the hallway and pound on the bathroom door.

'It's not locked.'

'Can I come in?'

'Be my guest.'

At any other time, I'd have been poleaxed by that invitation, a quivering blancmange of indecision. Now, I barge straight in. Livia is a nebulously pink outline through the frosted-glass cubicle. 'Ah . . . how are you feeling, Liv?'

'Better . . . more together.'

I slump on the fluffy pastel blue toilet-seat lid to catch my breath.

'We may have a bit of a problem.'

'I'm well aware of that. What's up?' I can tell by the staccato delivery that she's had a line of something, most likely the pure coke.

'We should go – now.'

'I'll finish my shower, if that's okay with you.'

'It's not okay. Coombs is back; I just saw his MG come up the drive.'

The power-shower hisses – the water snaps off.

'Shit, Mikey, why the fuck didn't you say so?' she barks from inside the glass box. 'What the hell is Coombs doing home now? He shouldn't be here. I check his diary every day; he's got a planning meeting with the council this afternoon; goes straight out on the piss afterwards. Always comes back late.'

We both freeze, straining our ears. I catch the faint sound of the front door slamming, three floors below, followed by heavy footfalls on the stairs.

'Go. Hide.'

'Where?'

The frosted-glass casement swings open. 'Get in, quick.'

I expect that there are plenty of good hiding places in this rambling house, so I wonder why Livia has chosen to play wet sardines like this. I'm not arguing, there's no time. I step into the cramped space and am forced to put my arms around Livia's warm slippery flesh. Renegade droplets pop and splatter on to my head from the faucet above. We're enveloped by steam, I can't see a thing, but I'm absolutely and utterly aware that Livia is naked: she has her arms loosely around my waist and I can feel her pointy breasts through the thin cotton of my shirt – a scenario that conforms to some of the more elaborate fantasies I've had since coming out of hospital. 'I'm keeping my eyes closed,' I promise, cravenly.

'You don't have to.'

'Really?'

'Don't be such a . . . a child,' she hisses.

All I can see is her sopping crown.

We hear Coombs stomping around a couple of floors below, followed by the unmistakable sounds of a bath being run.

Livia bundles me out of the cubicle and swiftly drapes herself in a thick white towel while I scrupulously inspect the carpet. 'Trust bloody Coombs. Usually, when he has a Thursday afternoon council meeting, they go off and get drunk somewhere, then on to dinner at the ratepayers' expense. He never comes home early on a Thursday,' she grumbles, before tip-toeing down the hall.

She reappears with articles of underwear, her mother's precious scarf (a diaphanous scrap of yellow shot through with red swirls) and a sandwich-bag bulging with white powder.

We wait until we hear the sound of a door slamming on the first floor, followed by the bellowing of a wounded hippo in a barely recognizable version of 'Blue Moon'.

'Right, let's go.'

'Go where?'

She puts a finger to her lips. 'Shhh!'

We stop short on the loose gravel at the end of Coombs's driveway. From the cover of the privet we can see that Bernard has returned, and, for reasons best known to himself, has decided to give the Volvo a polish now. We watch for a moment as he burnishes the paintwork in a compulsive, head-down, Amontillado-fuelled frenzy.

'Right: plan B,' mutters Livia, still robed in nothing more than the white towel as she drags me back up the drive. She flings her small armful of clothing at me and heads for Coombs's MG, where she sprawls across the passenger seat and delves expertly under the dashboard, into the bowels of the ignition system. Her towel rides up to reveal a thrilling pink curve, the gentle cosine of a buttock.

I stand there goggling, silk scarf round my neck, bagful of class-A drugs in one hand, Livia's random clothes in the other, trying not to look like someone who's never seen a girl's naked bum before.

It will be very bad if Bernard spots me now: I'm not sure how I can explain any of this.

Mercifully the engine grumbles to life. Livia reaches down and gives the accelerator a quick punch before emerging triumphant. 'Actually, it's lucky that Coombs did come home,' she announces, 'because now we're mobile again.' The motor roars as Livia slides into the driver's seat and gives the accelerator another rev. 'Climb aboard, Mikey.' She grins. I leap into the passenger side and we're away, careering up the drive.

'You still haven't told me where we're going!' I shriek.

'Come in, come in. Wonderful to see you both, and in one piece too,' announces a beaming Mr Truffles at the door to Roger's Cascades apartment.

'Is Roger back yet?'

'No, Roger's still *hors de combat*. He phoned first thing to say that he's been unavoidably detained . . . ah, with his lady friends. Everything's fine. He's filled us in on your ah . . . little adventure.' Mr T. grins. 'So I got straight on to AA Relay and had the Hillman towed back here.'

'Christ, the Hillman . . .' I'd forgotten all about the Hillman.

Thank God for Mr T. It seems that he's slowly beginning to rediscover some of that energy and initiative that once took him to the pinnacle of the restaurant world, along with his self-respect.

'Speaking of which,' says Livia, 'our own vehicle is a bit sort of borrowed-without-permission, is there any way we can get it off the street?'

'I'll open the garage. I daresay there's room for a small one,' says Truffles, smiling.

Livia must surely have a fair quantity of that cocaine still sloshing around her system, yet for the first time since I've known her, she seems relaxed and at peace. She's sitting upright in Roger's spare room, propped up on three pillows under an eiderdown, nursing a pint mug of cocoa. Pink and white mini-marshmallows bob cheerfully across the surface.

'Be sure to finish those marshmallows now,' advises Mrs Hodges, who appears to be something of a permanent fixture here these days. 'They're not at all healthy but are surprisingly good for the soul; marshmallows make everything better.'

Livia does as she's told. This is a Livia I've never seen before: she suddenly seems very tired and small and fragile. I sit quietly at her bedside. Mrs Hodges appears to notice me for the first time and reveals a seam of sensitivity that I would never have predicted: 'I should go and check on Mr T.; see whether he's burning the blueberry and ricotta scones.' She gives Livia's hand a little pat, almost swatting the mug from her grip, before hauling herself upright and thundering from the room.

'Well,' I say, clearing my throat, 'here we are, then.'

Livia finishes the remaining quarter-inch of cocoa, liz-arding a last white mini-marshmallow with a dexterous pink tongue. 'Thank you, Mikey. I think I'll go to sleep soon, if that's all right. I won't be away long.' The mug slowly descends and her eyelids flutter like a dying butterfly's wings. I take the vessel from her slack fingers, rising carefully so as not to disturb her. My left knee pops with a tiny pistol-cocking sound.

Her eyes flash open. 'Mikey, don't go just yet.'

'I'll stay here if you like and watch you sleep.'

'That would be nice,' she murmurs, fighting to stay awake. 'I want to talk to you about something first; explain what I'm doing here.'

'I don't suppose there have been many people you could trust in your life.'

Livia nods. 'It's lovely that your friends are so kind. But I'm running from, not running to. Do you see the difference?'

'I think so.'

Livia shakes her head. 'You heard my mum, she black-mailed Coombs to look after me. That's why he put a roof over my head for a while.'

'I know that.'

'When I got out of the young offenders institution a few months ago, I chose to come here and stay with Coombs.'

'You weren't to know what a bastard he was.'

'That's the thing, Mikey. I did know.' Livia takes her empty mug back from me and gives it a shake. 'Do you think you can get your hands on some alcohol in this house?'

'No. Yes, probably, but I don't think it would be a good idea. You should just get some rest now.'

'Not until I've told you.'

'Whatever it is can wait. It's been a rough day.'

She's smiling at me; it's one of those strange, regretful,

almost bitter smiles, as though she's just sucked a copper penny. 'I came here to set things straight.'

Livia hasn't slept for about a fortnight; she's taken a whole bunch of really bad drugs, followed by a bunch of, well, really good drugs, we hijacked an aircraft and her mum died. I think she's entitled to be a little off the plot tonight.

'I'm not with you, Livia.'

Livia places the empty mug on the bedside table. 'It was *me*.'

'It was you what? On the Grassy Knoll? You're not making much sense here.'

'Remember that first night up in the tree you asked me if I'd ever been here before? I lied.'

'I see,' I lie in return.

'I was here once before, a couple of years ago, when my mum first got ill and she went in to hospital for tests. I think Mum must have known what was coming because she signed some papers, making Coombs my guardian.'

'I don't . . . I still don't get it, Livia. Why lie about not being here before. I mean, Caversham's not exactly Monte Carlo or anything, but it's nothing to be ashamed of.'

Her face begins to wobble out of control. A fat tear carves a shiny track down her cheekbone. 'That's the point. I am ashamed, of what happened . . .'

I have to assume that this is delayed grief setting in. I'm not good at dealing with extremes of emotion; I never know what to do with my hands, for a start. My first instinct is to go and check on those ricotta scones. Fortunately there's a box of tissues on the side table; I whip out a couple and pass them to her. She gives me a grateful nod and snorts loudly.

'It was two years ago, in June. I was nervous when I arrived in a taxi from the station, I was only fifteen, didn't know much about anything. But Coombs was surprisingly nice and sympathetic; he can be, you know, when he wants something. After I unpacked, we had some white wine. He seemed sorry to hear about my mum, like he was an old friend. I was still a bit upset, so he brought out this packet of stuff and we snorted it and I felt better. I liked it; he gave me the rest to keep. I thought I was pretty smart and sophisticated in my white summer dress and my mum's silk scarf, I remember thinking things could be worse. We drank a lot more white wine. And some time that afternoon I passed out.'

I can see where this is going. 'Don't, Livia. I don't need to hear any more.'

Livia's on autopilot now. 'When I come to, I'm on my bed upstairs, he's fiddling with my dress. I've forgotten where I am, or who he is, I don't even know if any of this is really happening. I scream, fight like a wild thing and run to the window. Out there I see a young guy standing on the edge of a platform, like he's about to be hanged. I bang on the glass, this guy just stares right through me . . . then Coombs grabs me by the hair. As he pulls me away I can still see the guy. And then he's gone. I watch him fall.'

I take a deep breath. 'Christ, it was you.'

'It was me, Mikey.'

'I could have helped. I could have done something.'

Livia shrugs. 'You did help. Coombs let go of my hair. He was more interested in finding out what happened to you. You distracted Coombs long enough for me to get out of there. I'm half drunk and drugged up by the man who was supposed to be taking care of me. So I run, down the stairs, out of that house. I run in my white dress, in my bare feet and I run. I remember nothing until I get to Reading station. My soles are cut to ribbons and I've got no money but there's this woman on the platform, she's not paying attention, fussing with matching luggage and three screaming brats. I grab her handbag and I'm gone.' Livia takes a deep breath and searches my face for some kind of reaction.

I can only shake my head, overwhelmed by rage, sadness and a cacophony of questions.

'They find me at Newbury with the bitch's Mulberry bag and worse, Coombs's fucking baggie is still in the pocket of my dress. And guess what? It's about five grammes of grade-A coke. Shame, I did quite like that handbag. I am so done: a drunken, thieving, substance-abusing teen with an ex-junkie mum. Naturally, I get short shrift from Coombs's cop cronies with my side of the story.

'Later, I'm forced to watch while some cut-price, first-job solicitor comes to an arrangement with Coombs and the magistrate, and it dawns on me that I have absolutely no control over my life. I'm powerless. Coombs comes to court and sits there looking all sanctimonious and disappointed when I get a two-year custodial.'

Livia's eyes are closed now and her voice has become expressionless, robotic. She's so tired, she's almost speaking in her sleep. I don't want to torture her further, but there's something I must know. 'I don't understand why you came back. After all that, why did you return to Coombs, of all people?'

'I had no choice; it was part of the sentence. I only did eighteen months inside. Coombs was my legal guardian and even if my mum were alive and kicking, I'd still have to spend the next six months under his supervision; sort of a parole. Otherwise I go straight back into the Young Offenders.'

'But that doesn't make any sense.'

'Don't underestimate the influence Coombs has around here.'

'I don't mean that. I mean Coombs has already tried it on once, why would you stay? Why would you willingly risk that again?'

'It's okay. I learned a lot inside, I can take care of myself better these days. Besides, I wanted to.'

'Why?'

Livia's eyes suddenly flash open. 'Because I had nowhere else to go. Because I wanted to be near my mum. And because I wanted some kind of payback.'

'So, why didn't you do something straight away? Why hang about?'

Livia raises herself from the pillow for a moment, lost in thought, then props her elbows very gingerly at the edge of the mattress, as though any second a fire alarm might sound and she will take flight. 'Have you any idea how little real power you have in the world, Mikey?'

'Yes.'

'There's so little you can do without money or friends. I wanted to get back at him in some way, but in the end all I'm really capable of is physically damaging the bastard. I hadn't really worked out how to do it and get away with it. I mean, I could have hit him on the head with a golf club in his sleep, stabbed him in the shower or something, but I don't like innards and gore and don't especially want to spend the rest of my life back inside if I can help it.'

I'm beginning to feel a little prickle of premonition here. 'So . . .?'

She shrugs, unburdening herself easily, 'So, when you turned up with nothing to lose, I just sort of factored you into the plan. I suppose I imagined that if I helped you get your bloody DFC, I'd be able to convince you to do the dirty deed for me in the end.'

Even though I had seen it coming, I recoil, as though she's just flung scalding water in my face. 'And now? What do you think's going to happen now?'

Her head falls back on the pillow, she grins sheepishly. 'Now, I don't know. How do you feel about it all?'

I'm on my feet, the little wooden chair tipping slowly backwards. 'How do you imagine I feel? Fucking well exploited, manipulated. Used, if you really want to know.'

Livia shrugs. 'Okay, I can sympathize with that.'

'I thought I might be something more than your hired assassin. I'm well aware that I'm not exactly a pretty boy, but I really thought that there might be something.'

'There is something. You're right, you're not pretty, Mikey. But we trust each other and we like each other. That's a good basis for a relationship, the best, come to think of it.'

'You've just admitted that you set out to abuse my trust.'

'No. If you think about it; quite the opposite. I'm tired and can't think straight but I'm sure I've done a good thing – which, by the way, if you live to be twenty or whatever, probably nobody will ever do for you again – I've been utterly and completely honest with you.'

'So why do I feel betrayed?'

'Good. Multiply that feeling by about a hundred, add in a bit of exploitation, shock, terror and dismay, and you might – you might – have a little insight into how I felt when I came to and found Coombs's grubby fingers all over me.'

'This isn't about what Coombs or your mother did to you. I can't be held responsible for that.'

'This *is* about Coombs. Until you understand that you understand nothing. You don't see how much it cost me to be honest with you, Mikey. I'm not interested in using you or manipulating you any more. I'm too fond of you for that.'

'Are you?'

'I am.'

'So I don't have to kill or maim Coombs?'

'No,' she sighs, 'you don't have to kill Coombs. I've found other friends too, Mikey: these people here who have taken me in without question. I'm worried for them.'

'They can look after themselves, tonight.'

'Mrs Hodges can. I'm concerned about the rest.'

'Hush now,' I say, taking Livia's hand. I never imagined myself saying 'Hush now' to anyone, but she seems so vulnerable at this moment, it just sort of slipped out.

'I'm sorry, Mikey, but I just can't keep up with you. I'm so tired, but there are things to be done. The drugs. The people who own them are not going to be sitting around waiting for us to have a bit of a siesta. There's a ten-million quid bounty on us all. They're out hunting for us all, right now. And here I am, Lady Muck, flat out in bed.'

'They have no idea who we are. Let it go for tonight and stop worrying – we'll think of something.' I squeeze her hand. 'It's okay now. It can all wait until you've had a sleep. Everything can wait,' I croon. Mania recedes and Livia settles once more. Finally, her eyes clamp shut. She's gone, utterly exhausted, and I know she won't stir for an earthquake.

This morning, my life was simple: all I had to worry about was how to get a hundred kilograms of pure cocaine back to a powerful, ruthless cartel without anyone being maimed. Now I gaze at the girl who snores gently on the pillow and I understand her anger. She deserves better than this, she deserves some kind of justice. I wish I could be her Dark Knight or Caped Crusader, but the only thing I'm going to be changing into is a vegetable. I must clear my head somehow. I need air.

I slip downstairs and out of the door without alerting Mr T. or Mrs Hodges. It's lateish but still warm, and there's a soft breeze blowing off the water. I stick to the embankment and head away from the residential developments, up-river toward the neon glare of Friday-night Reading.

Twenty-Seven

'You are the wind beaneath my wiiiiiiings,' screeches a young female office worker with a voice like a condor scraping talons across a blackboard. The sliding doors of the riverside karaoke club are wide open, her audience spills out, boiling across the towpath, howling with boozy approbation, whooping it up like banshees with their plastic pint glasses. I nod and smile as I pick my way through the mayhem. Sweaty, grinning faces loom in and out, recoiling violently when they register that my flattened features are not, after all, a product of alcohol-adulterated senses but the genuine article.

'Hey, everyone. There's a chap here, got a nose like a cunt,' broadcasts a loud-mouthed teetering middle-manager, through sloppy, spittle-flecked lips. I'm shoved towards him by the jostling crowd, so close that I can smell the onion crisps and stale lager on his breath.

Handsome is as handsome does, I think, hoisting a knee with all my strength into his pin-striped nuts. 'Hey, everybody, there's a chap here with testicles like scrambled eggs.'

He drops; the crowd parts, eerily silent, like cinema curtains.

He can't have been all that popular, as I'm left unmolested.

The dying notes of Céline Dione's ballad punctuate my footsteps, then segue into the lively twang of a bouzouki. An opportunist restaurateur has strategically placed an array of bushes and potted plants out the back, asserting temporary territorial rights to the towpath: cheap plastic tables and chairs leak out from the rear of an unpromising blockish structure. A neon sign under the eaves proclaims, 'Santorini, home of the finest Aegean cuisine'. The setting may be a far cry from the Cyclades but the aroma from the kitchens seems authentic enough, along with the live bouzouki and clatter of plates.

I loiter by one of the plants, acknowledging the amorous young couple seated in the candlelight a few feet away. The young man nods uncertainly; it takes the edge off my rage. I smile in return. There's a tiny velvet box on the table between them; I assume that the young man has just proposed. I'm a gatecrasher, intruding on their happiness.

The couple clasp hands across the chequered cloth, and together, aim a plate at the concrete floor, enjoying the thrill of legitimate destruction.

'You've seen all the plans, permissions and projections, so are you gonna be filling your clogs with us or what, Mijnheer Van Huis?' I hear the familiar, over-loud, diphthong-slaughtering bellow. Even with a gigantic cheese plant obscuring my view, I know it's Coombs. I remember the reference to Santorini in his calendar.

The response is low and mildly guttural. I shimmy past the young couple's table and hunker behind a yucca.

'Mister Coombs, I own most of the key freeholds; I am already, by default, the majority partner in your endeavour. So, yes, I suppose you might say that I have indeed "filled my clogs".'

'Not sure we're speaking the same language, Mijnheer.

Last time I looked, my associate owned most of the riverside freeholds, which he will place in a corporate trust on Monday in exchange for a fifty-five per cent interest in the holding company. In return for my own small contribution, I hold fifteen-per cent of the stock. There's another five per cent to be spread about various other local councilors and officials. I'm offering you the remaining twenty-five. Ground-floor opportunity. Hurry, hurry, while stocks last.'

'You are most kind, Mister Coombs. My English is by no means perfect, but I believe I have made myself clear. Over the past twenty-four hours your associate, the Controller, has experienced something of a change of fortune. He has mislaid a rather valuable shipment and owes me a great deal of money. In the interim, he has signed over most of the free-hold deeds you mention by way of guarantee to me. A temporary difficulty for your associate, perhaps. Then again, perhaps not.'

'You are fucking joking?'

'We Dutch are not so like the Germans; we have a sense of humour quite similar to you British and find bodily functions vastly amusing. But alas, I never joke concerning my business.'

Coombs is crestfallen, silent.

'I am sorry, Mister Coombs, for putting this spanner up your pipe.'

I haven't had time to form a proper plan but I can't walk away now; Coombs is here and I'm compelled to confront him.

I rise from the foliage; he spots me instantly in the gaudy neon glow. I sense that I'm a welcome distraction.

'It's Mongo. Oy, you, Mongo, you lost or what?'

I need the man to drop his guard. It's the work of an instant to fall back into character; I relax my shoulders and release the drool-floodgates.

'Excuse me, Mijnheer, but I need a word with this moron. Oy, fuck-knuckle, where's that psycho-bitch? I want to see her, urgently.'

Coombs's companion has his back to me but he cranes his neck and I observe that he's a man in his early fifties with sandy-grey hair and piercing sapphire eyes. For some reason he reminds me of Roger.

'Get here, you.' Coombs waves me closer. 'Where's your tart, Mongo? You probably don't even understand this but that slag nicked my car today. She's a fucking degenerate as well as a tea-leaf.' He scans my slack face for signs of comprehension. 'That cooze Livia . . . is . . . a . . . car . . . thief and she's in big trouble. Comprendo, Mongo?'

I'm gazing down at the round-ended butter-knife on the pristine white tablecloth. I have a vivid fantasy where, when he says 'Mongo' again, I drive the tiny utensil into his right eye.

'Mongo, are you hearing me?'

Ah, sod it. I might just do it.

'She . . . nicked . . . my . . . car. Where . . . is . . . Livia . . . now?'

'Somewhere you can't find her, you bloody bully,' I snap.

The sandy-haired Dutchman snorts retsina.

Coombs stares at me like I grew another head. 'Oh, it speaks then? It's not a total retard?'

'It does, and it knows exactly what you did, Councillor.'

'You should be careful what you say in front of witnesses.'

'Livia told me everything.'

Coombs guffaws. 'Livia's a fucking fruit-loop. Jesus, a young girl with a criminal record for drugs and theft: lying her face off to a retard? I don't think so. Out of some misguided loyalty to her mum, I gave her a roof over her head. She pays me back by telling porkies and ripping off my motor.' Coombs directs this last to his companion, who raises

242

a sandy eyebrow, shaking his head: he couldn't be less interested.

'Oh, and by the way, Mongo, I consider Livia to have left my care now, no longer my responsibility, which means that it does not qualify as "borrowing". That bitch has stolen my car and you are most probably an accessory to the fact, so you've got serious legal problems too, even if you are brain-damaged.'

Coombs may be a powerful man, he may already own most of the real estate around here, but he's done a diabolical thing to someone I love and he's not immune to the consequences. Plus, I really object to being called Mongo.

'You're right, Coombs. I am brain-damaged, but it doesn't stop me thinking, only sleeping. You can sit here, smug as you like, but you'll always need to sleep. Think about this: one of these nights, Coombs, when you're on your own in the dark, I'm going to be there, waiting.'

It does the trick. Coombs sputters, hosing me with Greek brandy. 'You're actually threatening me, you disabled streak of piss?'

There's a commotion from the direction of young couple's table; laughter and broken crockery obliterate Coombs's profanities, which gives me the opportunity to turn on my heel and walk away with a bit of dignity for once.

As I head for the towpath, something glances painfully off the back of my head and shatters – a side plate, judging by the shards.

'Serves you bloody well right, Mongo,' bellows Coombs. I turn to find him grinning hugely in the candlelight like a rebarbative Jack O'Lantern.

My hands are trembling. And it troubles me. I thought I'd come to terms with my own imminent demise, so why am I so shocked? If my sands have all but run out, logically, what do I have left to fear? I know the answer: I've spent my entire life paralysed by a sort of constant low-level terror. Dread is hard-wired into my very being.

Coombs hoots, dismissing me with another sneer. Like all bullies, he thrives on other people's fear. Even so, I can't believe that he thinks he can just sling dinnerware at people and get away with it. I've made the error of judging him by the standards of normal people when in fact, he's a bloody lunatic. I've challenged him, and, before this is over, one or other of us is going to sustain some serious damage.

Well, that's just fine with me.

I reach down, grab something heavy from the abandoned table beside me and sling it as hard as I can at Coombs's grinning head. It turns out that filled pitta bread has almost no aerodynamic qualities whatsoever.

I reach again. My hands are still trembling, only now it's rage mixed with adrenalin. This time my fingers corral a solid beef kebab – half a dozen or so nice fatty chunks congealed on a hefty steel spike. I briefly heft the thing for weight and balance before throwing it overhand like a circus knife. To my astonishment the kebab stays true; somersaults through the air like a stiletto and implants itself beautifully, point-first, in Coombs's stocky pin-striped thigh just as he pours himself another slug of Metaxa.

The bottle drops from his fingers and he squeals like a stuck pig. 'Ow, Jesus Christ, Mongo . . . you lunatic. You've fucking stabbed me. That's actual bodily harm. You and your bitch are in serious shit, Michael Hough. This is another police matter: assault and battery, no, attempted murder in front of witnesses. You nicked my car and now you've pronged me with a kebab.'

For a moment I'm shocked by what I've done, but then I remind myself that I have nothing to lose. I am beyond fear.

'Somebody call an ambulance,' he bellows.

I stroll across as Coombs claws at the steel skewer stuck an inch deep in his thigh.

'You're not a vegetarian, are you, Coombs? It's beef.'

'Get away from me, you bloody mentalist,' he warns.

I lean closer and whisper, 'This isn't over yet. I know what you did, so you better remember to stay awake, because I never sleep.'

I'm gratified to see that for the first time Coombs looks genuinely alarmed. Mission number eight – sort of.

As I turn to leave, the Dutchman gives me a brief nod and a curious look. Not one of hostility though, far from it.

'Stop him,' yells Coombs. 'Make a citizen's arrest, somebody.'

I move through the shocked diners and treat the newly engaged couple to a reassuring smile. They're petrified. 'We . . . it was an accident,' the young man stammers. 'We just got a bit a carried away. I'm ever so sorry.'

'For what?'

'Smacking you on the head with that plate.'

Twenty-Eight

I'm back on the towpath in three quick strides and turn briskly towards The Cascades. I can't go back home now, that's for sure. I've just carried out an unprovoked assault on a local councillor; if Livia's story is anything to go by there's no point taking my chances with the law.

I'm desperate to get back to Livia. I'm on a clock. I want to spend my remaining time with her. Even if it's just to watch her snore.

I'm approaching the karaoke bar again. The business crowd hasn't thinned any in the past hour and I wonder if I can sneak past without being set upon.

'Hey, look everyone, it's the guy who nollered Harland!'

I can't run in any real sense of the word. At best, I can manage a sort of out-of-control totter, like a drunk tripping on a rug, propelled by his own momentum. Right now, I'm too weak even for that. I steel myself for a beating.

'Mikey, Mikey, Mikey, there you are. Thank God.' Hands emerge from the crowd; two big, rubber-sheathed, banana-fingered hands, followed by Mr T. as he squeezes himself through the mass. 'Where've you been? You might have told us where you were going.'

'I went for a walk, clear my head, Mr T.,' I explain, keeping a wary eye on the mob.

'Mikey, there's a big problem. Mrs H. hasn't been happy with Livia since she arrived. Not happy at all.'

'Oh God, what's she done?' Right now Livia needs all the friends she can get.

'A while ago, Deirdre – Mrs Hodges, that is – popped upstairs, just to look in on things. She was worried about her, you see, after that awful thing with her mum. Livia was in bed, but in a bad way: pale, sweating, shallow breathing and that. We couldn't wake her. So we checked her vital signs, pulse and blood-pressure: one-twenty beats per minute and fluttery. Palpitations. Blood pressure, one-ninety over one-ten. That's not good, not good at all. We took an executive decision and phoned for an ambulance. They arrived and carted her off, blathering about a myocardial infarction. You weren't there. Of course we've got no idea of parents or any other family. I hope we . . .' Mr T.'s face is white, features stretched between grief and guilt. 'We didn't know what else to do, Mikey.'

I'm gut-shot; at any rate, something strange and molten has happened to my stomach. I feel my knees beginning to buckle.

As I fall, in slow motion, I consider my relationship with this troubled girl. I'm pretty sure that a large part of the dynamic is based on my own imminent death. Over the past weeks I've tried to suppress a nasty little thought that keeps bubbling up in the muddy stream of my consciousness like a badly weighted Mafia corpse – the notion that the mercurial Livia only hangs with me precisely because I am so disposable. If you're not into commitment, I'm your guy – a quick, ugly, thrill. But I know what a myocardial infarction is, Bernard's younger brother died from one. It's serious – as a heart attack. The idea that Livia might go first, possibly even tonight, is a fundamental, life-altering, cosmic shift. No wonder my knees have given way.

Mr T. stands before me, flapping ineffectually, as though I'm some kind of duff soufflé, obstinately refusing to rise. He needs confirmation that he's done well; I need physical support. I kill two birds with one stone, clasping his shoulder while pulling myself upright, fighting for breath. 'You and Mrs Hodges did the right thing. I can't thank you enough for that.'

He swells visibly.

'I have to see her.'

'Of course you must see her. Come along.' Mr T. swivels to find that he has an audience. The lynch mob has first dibs on me.

'It's all right, Mr T., I'll deal with them,' I announce, releasing my grip on his shoulder. I finger the tiny butter-knife in my trouser pocket. I may be weak and floppy, but I have dispensed with fear.

'Are you okay?' asks an attractive blonde woman in her early thirties.

'What?'

'Oh, God, we must look like a mob. But the truth is we were all hoping to buy you a drink. But then we heard . . . God . . . how awful . . . your friend, taken to hospital. I'd like to help.'

'Why would you want to help?'

The woman considers this for a moment, puzzled. 'You're the one who kneed Harland in the nuts, which makes you a bit of a hero at Sedgewick Stainless Stationery Products.'

The crowd erupts, roaring at the name. Plastic glasses are raised in my direction.

'Harland's our general manager. He's gone home now. I'm Vanessa, by the way.'

'Mikey.' We shake hands. Hers is small-boned but firm, mine limpish and paper-skinned.

She smiles as she releases my hand. I notice that her gloss-red upper lip slants slightly higher to the right. It's quite nice.

'You must understand, Mikey, these people work eight hours a day at Sedgewick Stainless. At least seven and a half of them are spent fantasizing about kicking Gavin Harland's balls as hard as possible. And you just went and did it. You're a hero, you see. As a departmental manager, I'm not supposed to approve, but as a woman who has to work alongside that oaf I can't help but applaud.'

'Thank you, but I must go. Someone who means a great deal to me is ill. If you really want to help, you could get me a taxi.'

'No problem, consider it done,' she says, producing a small mobile phone, stabbing numbers.

Mr T. interjects, 'Mikey, I was thinking I could drive you.'

'Why?'

'We should get back to The Cascades, then I could run you to the Royal Berkshire in Roger's Hillman.'

Mr T. is diffident, evasive; something's not right.

'I have to get to Livia now.'

'I understand, Mikey, come back to The Cascades first. I'll take you and pick up Mrs Hodges. I promised I'd be back for her.'

'Surely Mrs Hodges can wait?'

'Ah.' Mr T.'s head drops.

'What is it?'

'Not long after the ambulance left, a bunch of louts arrived in a nasty-looking black people-carrier. A few bottles were thrown, walls sprayed, windows broken. We called the police, who turned up quite quickly for a change. At which point the yobs disappeared.'

'So?'

'The police interviewed Deirdre.'

'Oh God, she did the rant? The "them" thing?'

He nods.

'They didn't take her seriously, did they?'

Mr T. shrugs, unwilling to be disloyal. 'They took a statement and left. Soon as they turned the corner, the minibus reappeared.'

'And?'

'It just sat there, in the middle of the road, revving away. You know what Deirdre's like, she puts a lot of store in her taser and she's quite capable of looking after herself. She sent me down the towpath to tell you about Livia. But I don't like the way this feels. They don't seem like a bunch of louts on the lager, they weren't kids, this lot, more like bare-knuckle boxers. I don't know, Mikey, the police think Deirdre's a paranoid old time-waster, then they see me, an ex-homeless ex-alky . . . I'd really like you to come back and see what you think. Maybe we can get the authorities to take us seriously before something really bad happens tonight.'

'Where the hell is sodding Roger?'

'Still with his lady friends, so far as I know. I phoned the number he left. He said not to worry, and that he was dealing with everything, Mikey . . . but I don't see how . . .' Mr T. tails off. He doesn't want to be the one to voice it.

No doubt the minibus team belongs to the Controller: Ard-Corps most likely. I can't be sure if this is part of the Controller's ongoing programme of intimidation, or if he's already figured us for the drug-snatch. Either way, it sounds like he's playing for keeps tonight. I'm trapped in a conflict of loyalties: Livia needs me too.

Vanessa intervenes. 'Mikey, it seems to me that you are faced with two apparently equal imperatives. On my MBA course we were taught that one option always has the edge if you take the time to analyse it. For the optimal outcome, there is always one course of action which must be taken before the others. If you learn nothing else, you do learn to prioritize.'

I grit my teeth. 'Sorry, Mr T., but Livia, she . . .'

Mr T. nods philosophically.

'Good for you, Mikey. I admire you for that decision. So, perhaps I can help with your other problem?' Vanessa turns and addresses the throng like Boudicca. 'Sedgewick Stainless, listen up.' The suited drinkers roar and caper at the mention of their company name before settling into a more respectful silence. 'I know you're all enjoying yourselves tonight, and you're entitled to have a good few beers, but it seems a group of thugs are threatening an old people's residential community, a couple of hundred yards down the towpath from here.' She points in the direction of The Cascades. 'Does that bother anyone?'

A tubby guy in a tight brown suit steps forward. 'My nan's seventy-two and she can still kick her height.'

'That's very good to know, Marcus, and your point is?'

'Well, older people are not entirely useless and they, you know . . . they can still do things . . . and shouldn't be . . .' Clearly, Marcus is not destined for the fast-track at Sedgewick Stainless.

'Quite right, Marcus. The elderly have a right to enjoy full lives without being attacked in their own homes. Anyone else?'

A burly young go-getter steps forward; he wears a white shirt, beer-stained and unbuttoned from neck to navel. A red silk tie hangs loose across his chest like a halter. 'The way I look at it, Vanessa,' he volunteers, 'is that we can have a meeting and witter on about this for the next twenty minutes or a few of us could go down the road right now, sort out these bastards, quick-smart, and be back for a pint or seven before you know it. Set up on the bar waiting for us – on the company tab, of course.'

Vanessa beams at her corporate warrior. 'That's an excellent initiative, Douglas. I'll approve that.'

A small segment detaches itself from the crowd; a dozen well-built young men and one or two feisty young women congregate around Mr T.

'Come on then, Mr Tea-bags, show us where to go. Quickest duffed up, soonest mended,' pronounces Douglas.

'Go to it, Sedgewick Stainless. Make me proud.'

I must admit, I like this Vanessa.

She grins. 'Anyone can "manage", few can lead.'

'I don't think I'd ever be able to control people like you just did.'

'Michael?'

'Mikey.'

'Mikey, I pride myself on my ability to sort wheat from chaff. You're indisputably wheat.'

'I'm what?'

'Wheat. Charismatic wheat. You're a leader. I'd take you on like a shot at Sedgewick Stainless.'

'That's wonderful,' I say. I doubt if I'm cut out for the commercial arena, especially anything with a pension plan, although it does sound like I'd make an excellent breakfast cereal. 'Don't get me wrong, I'm very flattered, Vanessa. But to be honest I just want to go and see my friend in the hospital. It's a bit of a short-term goal, I admit, but really, that's all I want to do.'

With perfect timing the Corporate Cab pulls in at the top of the alley. I totter towards it.

Vanessa stares at me for a moment. 'You are for real, aren't you, Mikey?'

'So far as I can tell.'

'Good luck. And when you do get a chance to do some long-term thinking, just remember, a career in the office stationery industry is yours for the asking. Promise me you'll think about it.'

'I will. Thank you, Vanessa.'

I'm desperate to get to the hospital but Vanessa deserves something more than my ungrateful back. I turn.

'Vanessa, how do you make God laugh?'

She shrugs, almost invisible in the shadows of the alley.

'Tell him your plans.'

I hear police sirens approaching from all directions, underscored by the peal of Vanessa's laughter as I'm whisked away.

Twenty-Nine

There's a satellite broadcast van at the Addington Road entrance. Heavy-set blokes in half-mast jeans speedily unload electrical gear and an array of slim chrome film-lighting stands, which they wheel inside like so many anorexic emergencies. A young man in black jabbers urgently into a walkie-talkie.

I disentaxi and jog down the very same lime-green lino that I crawled along on my belly less than a fortnight ago.

Up ahead, I see a familiar figure waddling along the corridor. 'Aggie,' I shriek. 'Nurse Aggie.'

She's heard me but there's no pirouetting with Aggie. She slows and turns in a stately curve, like a supertanker. 'Nurse Koroma to you, boy . . .' Her mouth broadens in a vast embryonic grin until she registers my battered face. 'Jesus, Mikey, what the hell happened to you?'

'It's not me, Aggie, it's my friend. She's critically ill, admitted about half an hour ago. The ambulance people were talking about a myocardial infarction. I have to see her.'

Aggie sucks teeth. 'A friend? Not a chance, boy. A myocardial go straight to intensive. No visiting there, Mikey. Not till she stabilized and then only family. Not a chance in hell.'

'Aggie, I am her bloody family. There's no one else left.

Her mum died this morning, and I just found out that her so-called guardian tried to molest her. She's on her own. For Christ's sake, there must be something you can do.'

Aggie gazes at me for an age with a mixture of regret, suspicion and something else I can't read, fear possibly. I'm crushed; I think she's going to send me packing. Finally she speaks, but her voice is brusque and without its customary warmth. 'This Livia Knox?'

'It is.'

'I tried to warn you, Mikey.'

'Warn me?'

'I warned you to stay away from that girl.'

'Okay, Aggie, I fucked up. But I love her and I think she might be dying. I need to know what's going on.'

Aggie exhales explosively in frustration. With a sigh she waddles across to a wall-mounted phone and punches a button. 'Knox, Livia. No . . . not O-livia, Livia, with an L. Livia Knox. Intensive. Admitted . . .' she checks her watch, '. . . around ten, ten-thirty p.m. S'pected myocardial.' There's a pause. Aggie taps a white-shoed foot the size of a loaf. 'Uh, huh . . . uh huh . . . I see . . .' She keeps the blocky white phone to her ear, listening intently, hard black eyes never leaving my face. 'Uh . . . huh?'

Not daring to breathe I return her gaze, watching carefully for any sign of sympathy.

Nothing. No softening.

Which is why I'm certain that Livia's still alive when Aggie slams the phone back in its cradle.

'Thank fuck,' I exhale.

'All right, Mikey, it's not great but it's not so bad. Livia ain't gonna die tonight. One of these days soon, by the sounds of the way she been abusing her system, but most likely not tonight. She's been moved to cardiac care unit.'

Livia is still here, on this planet. I can breathe properly

again. I know they'll never let me see her but it's enough just to know that's she's not going to go tonight.

So I barely notice when Aggie grabs my shoulder, spins me round and frog-marches me back up the corridor like a truant schoolboy. We stop outside an examination room just long enough for her to flick across the 'occupied' slider, then she kicks open the door and thrusts me inside. 'Sit over there, boy, and keep quiet,' she orders, indicating the examination couch.

'Do I have to undress or anything?' I stammer.

'No, you don't have to goddamn undress. What are you thinking? Just shut up like I said, and listen.'

She paces the room, muttering to herself, 'Where the hell to begin. Where to begin, Aggie?'

'At the beginning, Aggie.'

'You smart-mouthing me?'

'No, I'm just a bit hysterical, right now.'

Aggie comes to a decision, halts, raises a hand to the low ceiling like an evangelist preacher and flicks the battery from the smoke detector with a carmine fingernail. She produces a battered gold packet of Benson & Hedges from one of the many pockets of her green nylon coat and lights up. I catch a whiff of sulphur.

'We not supposed to smoke inside. But this be an emergency.'

She looms over me, fag in fist, exhaling like Old Faithful. 'Why you mixed up with that girl, Mikey?'

'I don't know.'

'Shit.'

'What the hell, Aggie. I feel like I've been dying since I was born, suffocated by the radiators being turned up too high. Livia was like . . . I don't know, a wobbly tooth. You know it's going to be painful but you want to touch it all the same. She made me feel alive.'

'Your life been full of negative bullshit, I'll grant you that.' Aggie does something pursey with her mouth; disapproving and understanding at the same time. She takes another puff and exhales.

'Say something to me, Aggie. Tell me something worthwhile, or shut up and let me go. If Livia's definitely okay, there's something else I have to go and do.'

Aggie takes another drag. 'Mikey, it's like you grew up some years in just a week or two.'

'I sort of had a fight tonight: Livia's guardian, a man called Coombs. I think I hurt him. In the middle of all this mayhem, I was thinking about things and then suddenly, wham, I found I wasn't scared any more.'

'I know Coombs.' Aggie nods, spitting out a lungful of smoke.

'I've discarded fear, Aggie. I used to be terrified of everything. Now, I'm not scared at all.'

Aggie stares into my eyes, like she's scrutinizing my soul.

Thankfully, that gigantic mouth splits into a grin.

'Ah, you still scared. We always scared, Mikey; makes us human.'

'I'm beyond that. I'm fearless.'

Aggie exhales – a dragon breath. 'You think you conquered fear? For yourself?' She raises an eyebrow, nods. 'That's possible. I seen that a few times. But to conquer fear altogether? That's bullshit. Fear be a big chunk of love. It comes from the instinct to protect. You truly love someone, then you got fear for them. You never conquer fear. Not while you still a real person, you don't.'

'Maybe I'm not really human any more, Aggie.'

'Oh, yeah. You conquered fear for yourself. You go, be the warrior that you always were meant to be. But don't kid yourself. You came in just now and you were scared shitless, about your little girly – she lives, she dies. And you sit here and tell me you conquered fear.'

She's got me there.

'You're still a proper human being, Mikey. I can see that.'

'You win, Aggie. I'm scared for Livia. I admit it.'

'There's something you need to know about Livia Knox.'

Aggie ignites another B & H. She's taking her time. I get the impression that she's talking to herself as much as she's talking to me.

'They didn't come in so often, maybe once, twice a year. Mothers. Too young, too poor, too addicted. Whatever. But they didn't want what the Good Lord was about to bless them with. So, they'd ask the nurses here in a roundabout way if we knew of some place for their babies, where they'd be looked after, have a good life. Somewhere different to an orphanage. They didn't want that. You understand, Mikey?'

Aggie seems to be asking for my approval here. I nod.

'And there's these nice young couples coming here, taking fertility tests. We saw the results, knew who was never going to be able to have a child, Mikey. So, we put the two together. We thought we were doing a good thing. I know we were doing a good thing. We did the birth certificates too, all legal and proper.'

Aggie smokes hard, one eye seems to be blinking more than the other.

'But this one time, Jane Knox came in. A junkie lady. She was different though, she already decided not to keep her baby because she'd done a deal, for money: sold her child for cash to a middle-man – Coombs, the Wheeler-Dealer-Man. He never gave a shit about the good that we were doing. He gave a shit about the money though.'

'I know Coombs, I hate him.'

'Best you don't say too much about Coombs till you know what Coombs means.'

'Save it, Aggie. I already heard this nasty little story from the hearse's mouth, from Livia's own mum just before she died.'

'Shut up,' Aggie orders. 'You don't know nothing about nothing.'

She looms over me again. 'We never sold nobody. Never took no money. Ever. Not one penny. We tried to give them children a better life is all. We knew what was happening with Livia and we were going to let it happen, that's true. But we didn't sell Livia. In the end not even Coombs sold Livia. When them people found she had a heart murmur they said she was damaged goods. Didn't want her. So she went back to her mama, God help her.'

'Enough now. I don't want to hear any more. Go tell a priest or something.'

'Mikey, that ain't the end of the story. It didn't finish there. I heard that man Coombs found another child. A child *was* sold. No way was Coombs going to give that money back. This was big money and he already spent it. So, he found another child for the buyers. Not a baby, though . . . a healthy little boy, already eighteen months old . . .'

I already know how this story's going to end and I don't want to hear it. I brush her aside and totter for the door, fast as I can.

At the foot of the long, dismal green corridor I register Dr Darrow's angular features and bouffant hair. His head is illuminated by a halo of brilliant white light. I may be losing my mind, but to me, he resembles a saint.

I need to know how much time I have left and at the end of this corridor is the one man who even vaguely understands my condition.

I quickly realize that Darrow is merely backlit by a

powerful light. There's also a large grey camera pointing up into his face.

As I approach, a black-clad flunkess rushes to intercept me.

'Excuse me. We're filming. Can you go and wait somewhere else for a while?'

'Excuse me, I'm dying. Where would you suggest I go and wait?'

The young woman does a brief, passable impression of one of my Loh Hung carp. 'We're filming here,' she insists, as though that explains everything.

'I need to speak to Dr Darrow. He's my neurologist.'

The woman jabbers into her walkie-talkie.

'I'm sorry, you can't. But if you need to move along the corridor, you can pass now. Please hurry before we try for another take.'

I advance on the doctor but I only manage another ten yards up the corridor. This time, I'm obstructed by a fat film security guy with a goatee; much harder to intimidate, emotionally or physically. 'And where d'you think you're going, my friend?'

'I'm going to speak to Dr Darrow; I'm one of his patients. I'm not your friend, by the way.'

Goatee Bloke gives me a wry grin, barks into his walkie-talkie. 'Code Red. We've got one of Darrow's patients on the loose here.'

In seconds, I'm surrounded by a group of burly men in black T-shirts.

'OK, so calm down now,' orders Goatee Bloke.

'I am calm.'

'You're not calm. You should calm down.'

I'm shoved against the lime-green wall and pinned there by a dozen hot, meaty hands.

My nose is millimetres from the bubbling paint; I gaze at

it and find myself wanting to cry. Somebody did this job and took pride in it, even if they never intended their work to be so closely inspected: they've missed a few bits around the dados.

I stare down at my watch without blinking. The minute hand leaps almost all the way round the dial: forty-five seconds or so and I never even saw it move. Another time stutter.

'I'm calm,' I announce, raising my head. 'I'm calmly telling you that if you don't take your big sweaty paws off me right now I'm going to sue you for assault, unlawful restraint, and anything else I can think of.'

I'm released.

'You should take a chill-pill or something.'

'Well, maybe I will if you'd just let me access my doctor.'

Goatee Bloke smiles. 'Hey, we don't give a shit about Dr Darrow. We're only here to protect Chris Jenks.'

'Chris Jenks, who the hell is Chris Jenks?'

'TV chat-show host. Chirpy Cockney bloke, off *Hi Jenks*, you know? We're recording a segment for his next series.'

'I have no idea what you're talking about.'

'Chris Jenks is interviewing Dr Darrow right now for his show. So we're here to stop any of the patients from, you know, stabbing him or punching him in the face or something.'

'I see. Well, I'm unlikely to want to stab Chris whasis-name in the face or anything. I just want to talk to Dr Darrow.'

Just as Goatee Bloke is about to respond, Darrow strolls towards us, talking to camera: 'Primarily on this ward are the patients with organic neurological damage; some present behavioural symptoms, tics, disinhibition and so on, most are here for occasional treatment and will be back in the community within . . .'

'The Hazelnuts, yeah?' A pallid thirty-something with

thinning, spiky hair in a hoody-top shoves his microphone at Darrow's mouth.

Darrow stops dead, freezing or corpsing, or whatever they call it. 'I beg your pardon?'

'Hazelnuts. The thinner shells: nutty, but not all that nutty? Yeah?'

Darrow glazes over.

'Cut,' shouts the guy with the microphone. 'This is shit-house. Where's the sweary fighting? Where's all the tits?'

I wave at Darrow, enough to get his attention.

'I understood that you wanted an overview of the nation's mental health. That was my brief, Mr Jenks,' explains Darrow quietly.

Jenks cackles. 'Is that what they told ya? That's bollocks. That's not how we sell our programmes to the networks. What we want from you, Doc, are your half-wits, loopers and hazelnuts, fighting, trash-talking, tits-out, fucking and fisting each other. And then we say: "Goodness, look at the state of health care in Britain." Don't ya get it?'

'No, I'm not sure I do. This is a neurology ward, Mr Jenks.' Darrow seems drained and doesn't see me at all. Instead he stares down at the green lino floor, trying to figure out whether he's sold out or not.

'We need a fucking educational subject,' bawls Jenks. 'One of them who can't stop swearing, otherwise we're packing up. Hey, isn't there supposed to be a dog with two cocks somewhere near here?'

'Newbury,' advises a woman with a clipboard and a clipped tone. 'Labrador.'

'Right. There you are then. We're off.'

I wave madly.

Jenks stops in his tracks.

'Him. Yeah, the flat-faced nutter with the long hair,' orders Jenks. 'I want him . . .'

*

This is great.

I'm finally talking with Darrow. Quietly. Face to face, mano a mano, in one of the examination rooms.

'Hello, Michael,' says Darrow gently. 'How do you feel?'

'Fuck, tits, balls, toast.'

Darrow doesn't miss a beat. He stares straight into the lens. 'Michael has a fascinating and unique sleep disorder. More or less unprecedented because so far as we know Michael has now been without sleep of any kind for about as long as it's possible to be without sleep: twenty-odd days. Yet, this young man is still compos mentis.'

'Still mompos centis.' I wink at the camera.

'He does not have Tourette's syndrome.'

'Lying cunt,' I lie.

'He does not have Tourette's syndrome and, so far as we know, suprachiasmatic nucleus damage does not make one foul-mouthed, so you don't have to put up with him swearing like this.'

'Really? Oh, fuck? That's titting-well news to me. How the fuck would I know? Given that you never told me fuck-all about my arseing condition, Dr Darrow.'

'Enough, Michael.' Darrow rips off his radio mike and storms off-camera.

'Sensational,' bellows Jenks, as I chase my doctor. 'Both of you, congratulations. Fucking stunning TV.'

I trail Darrow along another long green hospital corridor and bring him to bay easily enough by a vending machine. He never wanted to escape, just change the venue.

'Mikey. I know I failed you.'

'You did.'

'Humiliated in front of sixteen million people seems like a fair payback.'

'We made some stunning TV though.'

'I wouldn't know, I don't watch much television.'

'So why agree to do something like that in the first place?'

'It's all about PR these days. It's about putting pressure on the right people. We need funding to make progress, to exist.'

'If it wasn't me being interviewed, it would have been one of your patients who didn't know any better; one of your hazelnuts. That's just shabby.'

'It was shabby. It's all shabby: that disgusting reptile referring to my patients as hazelnuts . . . everything. I'm so sorry I wrote you off so quickly in the first place, Mikey. That was shabby too. But your father wanted you home, he put pressure on us to get you home and really, we didn't . . . we don't have the funding or the time to do the research. We just don't. It might take years and millions to work out what's going on with you. We simply can't save you. You do understand that, don't you?'

Darrow drops a pound coin into the machine and selects a Mars Bar for me.

'It's okay. I understand that. I haven't come here to harm you or anything.'

'So, why do you need to talk to me at all? Like this?'

'I don't know. I know that time is running out for me. I'm like Frankenstein's Monster, I return to my creator to ask why. Why am I still here and still able to question my existence?'

'You're right to ask, Mikey. But I didn't create you. You should be dead, dying, or at least psychotic by now. If I did have the funding, I'd have you in a glass box under intense scrutiny right now. Have you slept at all since you left this hospital?'

'Not a wink.'

'Jesus.'

'I don't even get tired any more. I did at first, but I don't any more.'

'Have you experienced anything like sleep: a nap, a doze, since you came out of the coma?'

'No. Not even once.'

'Episodes? Anything unusual?'

'I got tasered. I didn't lose consciousness, but since then there's been a few tiny stutters.'

'Stutters. An articulation problem?'

'No. Stutters in my reality.'

'What stutters? How do they work?'

'It's like watching a film when it jumps a frame or two.'

'When these stutters happen, do you get the sense that time has passed?'

'Yeah . . . maybe . . . definitely. My watch jumped.'

Darrow grins broadly. He pulls my head towards his and whispers. 'Michael. I won't pin my reputation on this. If you live to be a hundred you can never say I said this.'

'What?'

'These stutters, I think they're moments of nano-sleep. It's possible that your brain is beginning to find its own way to shut down from time to time.'

'How?'

'Don't ask me how, Michael. Massive areas of the brain and its workings are still largely terra incognita to us. You can't quote me on this, I can't be optimistic, but it may be that your brain is finding a way to sustain higher function, for a little while at least.'

'So, you're saying I might have a chance?'

'It's not a reprieve, Michael.'

'Well, what is it then?'

'I don't know.' Darrow tips his head noncommittally. 'But don't make any long-term plans.'

Thirty

'That's him. Arrest him.'

I spin.

Coombs is emerging from A&E at the distant end of the long green corridor. I'm not surprised to see that his wheel-chair is propelled by Wenner and Davis.

Urged on by Coombs's bellowing, the ungainly coppers leave him behind and charge towards me. I'm a gazelle by contrast.

I give old Darrow's hand a valedictory squeeze and hobble round the corner, retreating up the passage towards Jenks's twitchy entourage. They're all smiles now that Darrow and I have given them good TV.

'Hi there. I've just run into a couple of friends of mine who are desperate for Chris Jenks's autograph.'

'Happy to do it, mate.' Goatee Bloke beams.

'They're actually some of Darrow's out-patients, but very nice people.'

Goatee Bloke nods uncertainly.

'Provided you don't challenge them, they're pretty calm. Although there is a slight chance that they might try to arrest you.'

Goatee Bloke's brow furrows.

'They have vivid, authority-figure cop-fantasies. Sorry,

you've just gotta work around that. I wouldn't say Chris Jenks is in any real danger though.'

Goatee Bloke gives me a look.

I leave him to it.

'The Tank Engine,' I bark.

The cabbie doesn't ask for an address. 'That place won't be kicking off for an hour or so yet,' he informs me.

'I expect.'

'Going early-doors are you? Looking for some nice young dolly-bird to cop off with? Go ugly early, son. That's my advice. The ugly ones are always grateful.' He catches sight of my face in the rear-view mirror. 'Oh, hang on, you might want to think about a prozzer, with a boat-race like that.'

I maintain a dignified silence.

There's no red rope or pulsing neon yet and it's too early for the hooded, denim-clad crowds. Without sound, light and energy, the place seems tawdry, threadbare and a little eerie. A couple of under-age girls in white heels and micro-skirts loiter unsteadily over by the bus shelter, killing time over a sodden bag of chips. The front door of the club is locked so I punch the intercom and wait.

'Piss off.' Eugene's voice crackles out from the little speaker.

The girls cackle drunkenly.

I hold down the button. 'It's Michael Hough,' I announce.

In moments I'm rewarded by the sound of heavy footsteps from inside. The door is flung open and Eugene reaches out across the threshold. He grabs the top of my head with his gigantic mitt, tweezing finger and thumb into the dents of my temples, like a bowling ball. The girls giggle nervously, uncertain whether they're witnessing a VIP or an RIP.

I'm steered inside, manhandled upstairs by my skull, and shoved before the Controller.

The man is working overtime tonight; he stands, surrounded by the waist-high landscape, manipulating at least four fast-movers around the tracks. They hiss past one another at the junctions, missing by a whisker. It ought to be laughable but, oddly, it's not. It's a breath-taking exhibition of split-second timing and skill applied to the nerdiest of pursuits; like watching high-speed, synchronized stamp-collecting. I'm utterly absorbed. Eventually, though, the Controller relinquishes the complicated slider control panel, passing it to Eugene in exchange for a hand towel. Eugene does his best to keep the speeding engines from colliding but he lacks the knack. Large droplets of sweat quickly form around his baldy head, the tip of tongue appears at the corner of his mouth, his brow furrows with concentration as near misses occur with increasing frequency.

The Controller dabs at his forehead with the hand towel before giving me brief nod. 'Entropy, Michael, any idea what it means?'

'It's a complicated notion, and there's actually more than one definition depending on context.'

The Controller looks a bit miffed. 'A simple yes or no will suffice.'

'Yes, then.'

The Controller continues regardless, 'Entropy, Michael, is the inevitable tendency of any structure, society or system to deteriorate.'

'I knew that. In terms of physics it's also a measure of the amount of thermal energy not available to do work.'

'That is very annoying,' he says.

'I think it can be,' I agree, 'if you're an engineer trying to work within limited thermal tolerances—'

'I'm trying to explain my place in the scheme of things.

Given that our world in microcosm, or indeed, macrocosm, has a tendency to deteriorate or deconstruct, then there must and should be a force exerted to prevent it from doing so. A necessary force applied without fear or favour: that which brings order from chaos and clarity to the universe. Surely even you, Michael, can see that?'

The Controller grabs another control panel from a nearby hillock and fingers the slider. In response a long black locomotive emerges from its branch-line shed, like a mamba. The sinister engine slithers out from the siding and strikes, broadsiding one of Eugene's beleaguered chuffers with astonishing violence. There's chaos as the remaining engines inevitably pile-in at speed. A shrapnel of tiny brass wheels and locomotive parts pings across the miniature landscape. The message is clear and unequivocal.

'Balls,' I say.

'You're not entitled to say nothing,' advises Eugene, obviously sulking from his cack-handed performance.

'That's a double negative,' I point out reasonably.

He jabs me twice, quick blows in the upper arm. There's no spare flesh to cushion the blows, so they hurt like hell.

'That's a double-dead-arm,' explains Eugene.

'You still want to fuck about?' says the Controller, as I rub to diffuse the pain. 'Michael, human beings are a competitive species, not especially cooperative by nature. Someone has to enforce teamwork, otherwise you end up with mayhem. It's why all societies gravitate to strong leaders. I am one of those: I control, and by so doing bring order to chaos. I cannot have runaway trains in my sphere of influence. Runaway trains are bad for the network. I want that understood, firstly.'

'Understood.'

The Controller gives me a thin smile. 'Good. Now, I believe we have something more immediate to discuss?'

'A small private aircraft, which you, ah . . . don't actually control any more.'

'That's one way of putting it,' concedes the Controller.

'The thing is: I know where it is.'

I was expecting more of a reaction here: a kind of one-billion-pennies-dropping kind of thing. But it doesn't happen. The Controller is very, well, controlled. 'Good,' he says blandly, 'I thought you might.' He grins and rubs his hands as though I'd just announced crumpets for tea. 'Excellent. If someone has to have my Cessna other than me, Michael, I'm glad it's you. The disappearance of my aircraft gave me palpitations for a while, and, in the past forty-eight hours, has unquestionably caused me a great deal of financial inconvenience. So I'm relieved to know you've got it; I think you know how to look after things, I feel better for knowing that.'

'I didn't say I have it. I said, I know where it is.'

'What are you after, Michael? What are your terms?'

It's all going rather better than I expected here, I feel that genuine progress is being made.

'I'd like to discuss the property development you've got going with Coombs.'

The Controller gives me a respectful nod. 'You want a slice? Very shrewd. I'm impressed. How come you know so much about my business?'

'Coombs told me. My girlfriend has been . . . residing with him.'

'Well, Coombs should learn to keep his yap shut, but no matter.' The Controller's dead shark eyes find mine. He tries on an affable grin; his features don't much like the fit.

I'm about to give the Controller my non-negotiable ultimatum when he raises an index finger, allowing it to hover before his lips as though an idea has just occurred to him.

'One tiny thing before we continue. When you stole my

plane we went looking for you from the air, as I'm sure you know.'

'I didn't steal your plane.'

'No, of course. After whoever it was stole my plane we carried out a pretty extensive search from the air, but obviously we didn't find anything.'

'Obviously.'

'Like looking for a needle in a haystack really.'

'I imagine it would have been.'

'Back at the airfield we had a bit of squint around the surrounding area. Not too far away we found an old car parked off the road under some trees, a Hillman Hunter, as it happens.' He cocks his head quizzically.

My stomach tightens. 'Joyriders. Or a breakdown.' I shrug. 'Surely you don't think the thieves would be that . . .'

'A breakdown? Yeah, that'd be it,' he agrees. 'At any rate the AA people arrived and towed it away pretty quick-smart.'

I wait for the perplexed expression to disappear. It does, to be replaced by a smirk. 'On the off-chance we followed the tow-truck. You'll never guess where it ended up.'

I respond with my best poker face.

'The Cascades. Bit of a coincidence that, wouldn't you say?' The Controller sucks his teeth, then laughs: a series of harsh barks. 'There was me, sweating like a rapist in church, thinking I'd been stitched up by the Dutchman or the Turks. I've gotta tell you, Mikey, you and your pensioner had me going there for a while.'

Eugene nods. 'You did too.'

The Controller shakes his head, scarcely believing his own conclusion. 'You and some dozy, superannuated airman just waltz into my airfield and swipe a hundred kilos of uncut cocaine from under our noses – all this strife for a fucking chunk of old tin.'

The fruity baritone descends to a deadly basso serioso.

271

'Mikey, I warned you the first time we met that I'm very protective of my property. That product is very dear to me, and,
whilst you don't appear to be concerned about your own
well-being, you should know that my crew is already round
The Cascades as we speak, with instructions to determine the
precise whereabouts of my shipment. The gloves are off: if
your pensioner mates don't give it up, then my lads have been
instructed to do some serious damage; torch the lot if necessary. Every last one of them.' The Controller folds the hand
towel with geometric precision. 'So, that doesn't leave you
much to bargain with, now does it?'

I stare at the track for a while, marvelling at the detail,
thoughts spinning like those little brass wheels. The Controller's in no hurry to break the silence. He is, after all, the
Controller. He enjoys this.

'All right.' I sigh. 'This was never about some old codger's
lump of scrap-iron. You know that.'

His left eyebrow climbs a couple of millimetres. 'Now
we're getting somewhere. I'm listening.'

I exhale slowly, a man pushed to the edge. 'The truth is,
Coombs stitched me up, stitched us both up, in fact.'

'Is that so?'

'The medal thing was just a blind, a pantomime. A good
one though, to make you keep your eye on the codgers while
the real prize, the cocaine, was spirited away right under your
nose. This whole thing was only ever about the shipment.'

The Controller nods. 'The break-in, the trade-off in the
swimming pool?'

'Theatre.'

'I thought so.'

'The Vester . . .?'

'Just another patsy.'

'The girl?'

'Window dressing.'

'Very good, Michael.'

'They were all stooges, Controller.'

'All of them?'

'Well, except me, of course, and Coombs.'

'Coombs. Why am I not surprised?'

'Coombs knew when and where your shipment arrived. He paid me to steal it: I get five per cent for my trouble, Coombs gets the rest. You blame the silly old buggers at The Cascades. Neat.'

The Controller tweezes his temples. For a moment I think he's going to have a seizure, but he manages to retain an outward calm. 'I've kept that consignment sitting on the tarmac for two weeks now, waiting to release it at best price, holding on until demand is high and supply low. The problem is, the Dutchman is not a patient man. He's been pressing for payment. Push him too far and I've got a war on my hands. Two days ago that consignment was pre-sold to my distributors. They pay me cash on delivery, I pay the Dutchman. That's how it works. Except, of course, none of that's going to happen now because my product's gone walkabout.'

'You had to sign over your freeholds to keep the Dutchman sweet.'

The Controller attempts to mask shock. 'If you don't mind me asking, how the fuck would you know about that?'

'You've been had, Controller. Coombs and the Dutchman had a cosy little meeting tonight to carve up your chunk of the property pie. I invited myself along.'

'You had a sit-down with the Dutchman?'

'More a stand-around-and-throw-things-about. There was a bit of unpleasantness – with Coombs.'

'I heard a whisper.' The Controller nods. 'They say Coombs got himself perforated by some nutter tonight. You?'

I smile modestly. 'Lucky for him someone called the cops.'

The Controller grimaces. 'I take my hat off to you, Michael.'

I look the man full in the eye. 'You get the Coombs info gratis, because the bastard ripped me off. But I am the only person who knows where your shipment is. And that *is* going to cost you. Your thugs can knock every pensioner in the Thames Valley into the middle of next week for all I care, but they'll be wasting their time.'

'You have been busy, haven't you, Michael?'

'I don't have time to mess about. I'm sick: the Royal Berkshire washed their hands of me a fortnight ago. The NHS doesn't have the cash to treat me or even figure out what's wrong. In theory I should already be dead, I'm on borrowed time. There are people in the States who can help, specialists with equipment and medication to keep me alive. I need cash, fast; I don't care what it takes to get it.'

'Some kind of chromosome disorder, yeah, like Downs syndrome? I can see it in your . . . you know.' The Controller indicates his face.

'This thing is a sleep disorder. It's not connected to the way I look. My face is the least of my problems, thank you.'

'Jesus, you poor bastard.'

The Controller prowls his network for a while, considering, fiddling with engines. Finally he turns to me. 'I appreciate your bollocks, Michael. You walking in here, telling me all this shows a lot of bottom. I like that too. I sympathize with your predicament. So, what's it going to cost to reclaim my product? Tonight.'

'The deal I had with Coombs, before he reneged, was for five per cent. I'll settle for that. Cash, naturally.'

A twitch of irritation creases the Controller's brow. 'You forget, you're standing in my club. There are no witnesses here. I could have you topped right now. Easy as breathing.'

I shrug. 'Without the cash I'm dead anyway. Without the

consignment, you forfeit those freeholds. You're left with nothing.'

'Fair point. Shall we say two point five per cent?'

'Two point five per cent of ten million is quarter of a million quid. That ought to do it, even with stateside prices . . .'

'Woah, back up a second there, my friend. Ten million? Where did that come from?'

'I've consulted an expert who has been able to value the cargo quite precisely.'

'Street price. Ten's about right, street price. The wholesale value is under half that. I pre-sold to my distributors for five. I'm paying the Dutchman four. I stand to make about a million. Less, after expenses.'

'My heart bleeds.'

'I'll give you an egg, Michael. Don't ask me to kill the chicken.'

'Okay. Let's not quibble. I agree to a value of five million. What's two-point-five per cent of five million?'

'One hundred and twenty-five large.' The answer trips off his tongue. He's quick on the maths, I'll give him that.

'Deal?'

'Deal. I want it in cash. In a briefcase. And, of course, I require an assurance that I'll be permitted to walk out of here intact.'

'On my honour, Michael.'

'Just in case, I think I ought to point out that if I don't return within the next two hours with some money, my associate has instructions to destroy your product; incinerate it to the very last gram.'

The Controller nods briskly at Eugene. 'Pull the lads off The Cascades right now. They're to stop molesting the old folk and get busy with anyone that owes us. Get 'em grafting. They're to call in all my loans and any debts above five K. "Sorry, I'm a bit short right now" is not an acceptable excuse, from anyone. "Sorry, you will be a bit short, when we cut your legs off at the knees." is the response. I want the cash here within the hour. In a briefcase.'

'With a matching wallet, and a Parker pen,' I add.

'Any special colour?' asks Eugene.

'Ox-blood, I think.'

'Just get it bloody done, Eugene,' barks the Controller. Eugene scuttles away, muttering.

Alone, the Controller and I embark on an eyeballing contest.

He blinks first. 'I certainly underrated you, Michael. For that, I apologize. But one thing you did was unforgiveable: chopping the head off my horse. That was a mistake.'

'I'm sorry. It wasn't part of the plan. Should never have happened.'

'I was very upset.'

'If it's any consolation, my associate performed the decapitation.'

'This associate of yours has a lot to answer for.'

'More of a trainee really. School leaver. Not very bright. Does what I tell him but occasionally oversteps the mark. I'm sorry.'

'That was the first horse I ever rode. It has sentimental value. Did I mention, I was one of nine kids?'

'First time we met.'

'Nine kids, piss-poor family, and the ugliest, youngest and smallest was me. So how did I end up here, with all of this? Not by being a nice guy, I can tell you.'

I decide not to remind him of the fact that he's just been forced to sign over a sizeable chunk of his precious assets because of me.

'I climbed the ladder fast by stamping on my opponents' fingers, then pulling up the ladder. Kick a man when he's down, that's my way. It's the best time to do it, so he won't get up and trouble you again.'

'I'll try to remember that.'

The Controller is blathering now, more to himself than me.

'With nine siblings you don't get a lot of time with your mum. But this one day, I can't for the life of me remember why, it was just her and me. She took me up to the fairground by the river. I think the idea was to look around, soak up the atmosphere of the place. But I was a whiney little toe-rag and I wanted to ride the carousel. Wouldn't shut up till I got my ride. Of course, she gave in, eventually. That's what mums do. She even had a little go herself. I don't remember what it cost, not much, but it was housekeeping. She shouldn't have spent it. So it had to be our secret. Maybe she did the exact same thing with all the kids. I'll never know and I don't care. It was our secret and I never grassed. I think my mum was the only person I ever really loved. After that, whenever we saw a horse she always gave me a little wink or a smile. Sharing a secret with my mum like that was almost better than the ride. It made me feel special. Not an easy thing to do in a family of that size. You know, I still miss her, Mikey.'

I'm out of my depth here. All I can do is keep nodding, fingers crossed, hoping that the headless bloody horse isn't going to be a deal-breaker.

'After she passed away, I tracked it down. Wasn't difficult, given that the exact same funfair pitches up by the river, year after year, without fail – same old crappy rides mostly, same bunch of scruffy gyppos ripping you off. And there's my magical carousel, looking a bit worse for wear, but it's unmistakably the one. I see this gum-snapping greaser and make him a generous offer for the horse. I even promise to have another one made to replace it. Cocky little arse-wipe turns me down flat. That's the trouble with those people, no sentiment. No class.'

The Controller shakes his head. I'm prepared to swear that those dead eyes are actually moist.

'So what happened?'

'I had that pikey-fucking-merry-go-round burned to the ground. After my little horse was extracted, naturally. That painted piece of lumber, Michael, connects me to my dear old mum, a memento of great sentimental value. I wish you hadn't chopped its fucking head off.'

'It was sort of amputated, with a hacksaw.'

'That does not make me feel any better.'

The Controller reaches for the multi-slider control panel. A bright red train leaps into life from a siding and chunters round the track towards us. There's a curious metal armature projecting from one of the cars like a crochet hook; behind the armature is a tiny net.

'You ever hear of a gentleman named Ronald Biggs?'

'The Great Train Robber?'

'That's the one. Got away with two point six mill. Doesn't sound like all that much now, but that was a right result back in sixty-three.' The Controller brings the red train to a halt over a little bridge where there's a cluster of tiny figures and a couple of Matchbox Land Rovers. 'Bridego Bridge, Ledburn. My little tribute,' he says proudly.

'That'd be Ronnie Smalls then?' I point to the lead figure.

The Controller fails to crack a smile. 'What you're looking at there is a perfect replica of a mail train, the TPO or Travelling Post Office. They used to pick up the mail bags at high speed and sort the letters on the go. Saved a lot of time. You want to see how they did it?'

He doesn't wait for a response, which is just as well. The red train shoots away again. Further up, to one side of the track, is a little metal pole, like an old cast-iron street lamp with a tiny leather satchel suspended from it. As the mail train passes, its metal armature hooks the satchel and whisks it away. The engine powers around the track without slowing.

'That hook device is called a traducer arm. Simple, but nifty,' chuckles the Controller. 'I have one of the very last TPO-franked envelopes in my collection, as it happens.'

'Wow,' I say, and I mean it. The Controller has managed to elevate dull to a whole new dimension by combining scale-modelling with train-spotting *and* stamp-collecting in one mind-numbing package.

I'm saved by Eugene, who appears at the top of the stairs, having cranked up the sound system below. He breezes in to a thumping back-beat, like a force of nature. The effect is amplified by the one-to-one-fifty scale when he slams a heavy brown briefcase down on top of the rolling green hills of Berkshire.

The Controller nods. 'Open it, Michael. It's all yours.'

It's a combination-lock case. Helpfully, the numbers are set to zero. I flip the shiny brass toggles and push back the lid. There's a serious chunk of cash inside. Randomly bundled notes, to be sure, but to the untrained eye it resembles a hundred grand.

The Controller hovers expectantly. 'Well? What do you say? You want to count it?'

'Nah. I trust you.'

It's not funny and wasn't meant to be, but it's the cue for good-natured chuckles all round.

'You're free to take the cash and good luck to you. After you give me the location of my product, that is.' The Controller taps his teeth expectantly with an engine coupler.

I enjoy a nanosecond of control over somebody else for a change, aware that this is a turning point in my life, or what's left of it.

I consider the words of the great Miguel: 'You cannot begin to live unless you take yourself to the edge.' The real wonder of the phrase is that its meaning is capable of almost infinite application and relevance, like some gnomic aphorism from a WACO whacko. It means something; it means nothing.

Even so, I prefer to believe that Miguel is more than just some skinny-dipper with a death-wish. When you put your mortality on the line on a daily basis for the loose change of gringo tourists, I reckon you do end up knowing a thing or two about life, whether you like it or not.

I've taken myself to the brink by coming here tonight. I'm about to dive. And if I've learned anything it's that you can't pull out in the middle of a dive, even if the tide's on the turn and things are changing on the way down. You're still going to hit the water. Mostly you emerge, sometimes you don't. The dive's the thing; the ability to commit unreservedly to an action with an uncertain outcome. Now, that's what makes Miguel great.

'Pond's Farm, Wallingford. The big barn. That's where your shipment is . . . minus a gram or two.'

There. I've said it.

'The place is owned by a pair of ancient, doddery spinsters. Completely barking. Haven't a clue what's sitting in their barn. It's the perfect hiding place.'

I reach for the case. The Controller intercepts my hand and pumps it. His palm is clammy and cold, but I'm happy to shake; a simple gesture, marking the end of my mission.

He seems reluctant to release me. I wrench my hand away. The Controller tightens his grip.

In a flurry of violent motion Eugene wraps salami digits around my neck, dragging me backwards; at the same time he shoves a chair under me with his other hand. He presses down hard on my shoulders while the Controller uses a roll of thick black industrial duct tape to bind me to the seat.

'Controller, I've told you where your cocaine is. I've been straight with you.' I'm disappointed to hear the whining note in my voice. Fatalism lends a certain immunity to fear, but not, it seems, self-pity.

'Shut up, Michael, Mikey, whatever you call yourself.'

'Either is fine.'

'Now, we're all going on a little trip. The bad news, Michael, is that you'll be going by mail.' With that the Controller reaches under the trestle for a small metal carton. He raises the lid; nestling in a bed of foam rubber is a small greenish-brown object. He dangles it before my eyes. It's a grenade. Not one of those big pineappley, cross-hatched things you see in all the war comics though. This one is smooth, like an outsized olive. For some reason it looks far more deadly. There's a metal ring attached to the pin. He inserts a finger and tugs. The pin slides out about halfway.

The Controller shuffles along the edge of the trestle table until he reaches the little mailbag pole. He tapes the grenade firmly round the pole, making sure that the ring dangles over the side of the track, precisely where the little leather satchel was hanging a few minutes ago.

He looks back down the track. 'Sorted.' He grins.

Eugene cracks open a couple of bottles of brandy and begins to empty the contents over the miniature landscape.

The Controller twists the top off a bottle of Grey Goose vodka and offers me a shot.

I shake my head; he splashes some around the floor and empties the remainder over Bridego Bridge. 'There you go, Ronnie, have a little drink on me.'

Of course I knew they'd never let me go. I've done what I set out to do: Roger and the rest are safe from retribution, even the Pond twins, who should have no trouble convincing the Controller of their insanity. I ought to be content with that. But I'm not. Miguel was absolutely right. I've never felt more alive. And now some survival mechanism has kicked in, which compels me to make one final plea.

'You've won, Controller. You get your drugs back, you get your plane back, you get everything. Keep the money.'

'I can keep the hundred grand?'

'Keep it.'

'Thank you, Mikey. I really appreciate that. Good news, we can keep the money, Eugene.'

Eugene grimaces. 'Took the boys a hell of a lot of work to pull all that cash together in a short time.' I'm not sure he really understands irony.

'You don't want to do this, Controller. I haven't lied to you; I'm dying anyway, so what's the point?'

'The point is that you have come here tonight and taken me for a fucking idiot. You've come into my club and taken the piss.'

'I came here and told you where your cocaine is.'

'You did, but you reckoned you were doing a deal. You've inconvenienced me and you've inconvenienced Eugene.'

'You have too. And the lads,' confirms Eugene.

'You think you're entitled to negotiate with me, after what you've done?'

'But you can get it all back now. All the freeholds, every-thing.'

'The Dutchman can keep them. They're mortgaged up to the hilt anyway, like the club. And I think you and Coombs have pretty well screwed up the property deal. No, I'm better off keeping the drugs, the plane and this nice chunk of cash. Start over in Spain, me and Eugene, living the *vida coca*. Although the trains in Spain stay mainly on the plain, there's some very nice single gauge over there. And I've always fancied doing the Costa Blanca run, maybe the Limón Express down to Benidorm.'

'But I told you the truth.'

'I believe you.'

'I told you about Coombs.'

'I believe that too. And trust me, Coombs will have his day.'

'Surely that's worth something?'

'It is, Michael. That's why I'm making this much less painful than it could be. My enemy's enemy is my friend and all that.'

'Couldn't you just let me go? It's not like I've got much time left anyway.'

'You may be at death's door, but I'm holding it open for you and shoving you through – for my horse's head, for screwing up my deal, for stress, inconvenience and your general disrespect. And I'm afraid I do need you here, Michael. Leastways, I need your unidentified body, in the nasty electrical fire we're about to have – all this loose wiring up here. Gives me a bit of a head start, see.'

The Controller's fingers flicker across the multi-slider. The mail train leaps into life, picks up speed, and glides away up the track in an anti-clockwise direction.

I assess the complex network laid out before me: it's awesome, accounting for most of the square footage up here on the first floor, but no railway network is ever going to be expansive enough for the unwilling commuter at Grenade Central.

'In case you were wondering,' advises the Controller, 'it takes about seven minutes for the mail train to make a full circuit. It's non-stop, Michael, and I don't expect you'll be getting much interference from Ronnie and the lads tonight.'

'Your shipment will be ashes by the time you get there,' I say.

'I'll take that chance. You see, I don't believe that you ever had an associate.'

Apart from the location, it's the only thing I've told him which isn't absolute bollocks.

'I'll tell you anything,' I wail.

'You've already told me everything I need to know,' whispers the Controller.

'I lied about the location,' I gibber.

'I don't believe you. Adios, Michael.'

The fear has returned with a vengeance. I'm screaming now, but no one will ever hear over the bass beat of the empty club below.

Thirty-One

I grind my hips, savagely gyrating from side to side like a demented hula-dancer. Although I detect an almost imperceptible slackening in the tape, it's nowhere near enough to pull myself clear. I don't have the strength to continue squirming; I'm reduced to watching, hypnotized, as that bloody red engine emerges from the last tunnel at shocking speed, armature outstretched, like the hand of doom poised to snatch away the dangling pin. A few hours ago I thought I'd made my peace, come to terms with it all; I imagined I'd left fear behind for good, but this is something else: this is true horror. I grit my teeth, anticipating the explosion.

Suddenly there's silence. The world turns blacker than the Earl of Hell's riding boots.

'Michael?' an urgent hiss. 'You are Michael Howguh, yes?' The speaker expectorates consonants like phlegm.

'No.'

'Ach, sheiss.'

'My name is Hough.'

'Not Howguh?'

'My name's Hough – Huff. Can you get me out of here, please? Those maniacs were about to blow me up.'

'That is not good, Huff, but we have instructions to remove Michael Howguh. There is only limited time available to us within this temporary blackout opportunity.' A second, deeper voice, same sing-song cadence

'For Christ's sake, please just get me unstuck before the power comes back on.'

There's a whispered conference, which sounds like a minor flu epidemic.

'We think this is very bad for you, Huff, and we are full of regretment, but we are unable to assist. Our time is limited, we must find Michael Howguh.'

'I *am* Michael Howguh, for Christ's sake.'

'Please to describe yourself.'

'Thick black hair, long . . .'

'Yah, and the face? Like the cake slice?'

'No. I . . . my face is a bit unusual but I wouldn't . . .'

'Possibly could you describe it like the underside of a steam iron, would you suggest?'

'No, I would not bloody suggest, but my name is Michael Hough, spelled H.o.u.g.h.,' I bellow. 'It's me you came for, isn't it?'

Another whispered conference.

'You are Michael Howguh?'

'I'm Michael Howguh.'

'You should have informed us of this earlier, Michael Howguh. We are here to aid your escape.'

'Well, for Christ's sake, take the sodding grenade off the track.'

Another pause.

'And get this sticky tape off me.'

Silence.

'Uh . . . our English is maybe not so good. Explain your exact predicament please, Michael Howguh.'

My saviours are a couple of astonishingly effective blond body-builders in matching black leather jackets and grey

T-shirts; I discover this as we descend the stairs and step over the recumbent forms of two very large doormen and the even larger form of Eugene. There's no sign of the Controller though.

The Dutchmen form a flying wedge and drag me by the wrist swiftly through the mêlée outside, straight-arming any eager clubbers, male or female, unwise enough to get in their way. For a wild minute I feel like the President of the United States.

One of the giants bundles me into the back of a tiny bright red Vauxhall Corsa – by flicking me with his forefinger, I think. He somehow folds himself into the passenger seat. Despite the mayhem his partner at the wheel is in no hurry. 'Michael Howguh, you must belt yourself in please. I cannot proceed until my dashboard warning system confirms that all persons within the vehicle are secure.'

With the Aryan features and phlegmy consonants it wouldn't take a Wenner or Davis to deduce that these two are connected to Coombs's Dutch associate. I've stepped straight out of the frying pan into a Dutch oven. If I tried to run I wouldn't get five yards, so I simply tap the driver on his meaty shoulder before complying with the seatbelt mandate. 'Let's just get this over with,' I sigh. 'I don't expect you to let me go but I'll make all our lives easy and tell you exactly where the shipment is right now.'

The driver shifts his gaze in the rear-view mirror from me to the road, indicates, and pulls away from the kerb in a sedate textbook manoeuvre. 'That will not be necessary,' he advises. 'You must relax now until we arrive at our destination. We may be some time.'

His passenger turns with an affable smile. 'Michael How-guh, you should count yourself lucky that your train was delayed tonight. Typical of your English railways, yah?'

'You are fortunate that it was not a more reliable European

Express,' chuckles his partner. 'What is it that you British say? You must be well chuffed.'

Our suspension begins to rock alarmingly as my companions chuckle at their Hollandaise micro-witticisms.

'Where are you taking me?'

'You must not concern yourself with that detail, Michael Howguh.'

'Who sent you and how did you know I'd be at the Tank Engine?'

'We observed you arriving at the establishment. The individual without hair was forcing you inside.'

'Ah yes, the gentleman with a head like an upside down ice-cream scoop,' adds the driver.

'Nein, nein, not scoop. His head was long and narrow, I believe,' objects his partner.

'Yah, for certain, scoop, I believe, is correct.'

'Nein, not a scoop, too shallow for that exact shape.'

For some reason the driver seems to have taken serious umbrage at this mild criticism of his simile. I'm worried that the silver-back gorillas might start duffing each other up in the cramped confines of the vehicle over an ice-cream scoop. Having just survived being blown to kingdom come by the skin of my teeth, I have no desire to be caught in a lethal crossfire of steroidal punchy limbs.

'You don't remember Bartel Harring's Deep Scoop cone . . . in Roermond?'

'Oh, yah, I do. The Special Vanilla?'

'Yah, exactly. Bartel Harring's Deep Scoop Special Vanilla. You remember Mijnheer Harring's special ice-cream scoop for the Deep Scoop Special Vanilla cone? Narrow, but somewhat unusually deep?'

The passenger sucks his teeth for a moment, lost in some deep visualization process.

'Oh, yah. Now I see it. Yah, Mijnheer Harring's Deep

Scoop for Special Vanilla is somewhat correct. I always had double scoop.'

'So, you see it now? Upside down, yah?'

'Yah, yah. Upside down, certainly. I see it now. I sit corrected. The gentleman's head somewhat resembled that shape. The gentleman I had to hit three times with the Rotterdam sandbag.'

Violence averted, I breathe a sigh of relief. These two have obviously known each other for many years but I notice that not once have they referred to each other by name. I'm impressed by their professionalism, although mildly concerned by their obsession with kitchenware.

'You work for the Dutchman, I assume?'

'You have many questions, Michael Howguh.'

'I do. So how about answering one?'

'All these questions will be answered in time, Michael Howguh,' intones the passenger. 'Or not,' he adds with impeccable logic.

'Try not to concern yourself, Michael Howguh,' advises my driver. 'We have no instructions to inflict unnecessary pain at this time.'

It's an epic drive through the night-time countryside, and even though I'm expecting to be tortured, maimed or killed at the end of it, I can hardly wait to get there. The Netherland Neanderthals play a version of car-cricket which is just so fucking wrong, evil and pointless it has me screeching from the back seat.

'How the fuck can you keep on batting when you haven't decided which colour car is supposed to be a wicket?'

'Blue vehicle. Extra single,' intones the passenger.

'Green vehicle. Another five runs for the Dutch,' replies our driver. An impossible-to-confirm vehicle shrieks past. But then, of course, they're almost all impossible to confirm in the brief flare of jousting headlights.

'Red car, passing.'

'Thank you so much, good old chap.' The driver grins, flashing white.

'We're all supposed to agree on the rules before we start; you can't just keep on batting for ever. It's not how the game is played,' I fume.

'I think you may be a horrible sport, Michael Howguh. You are in danger of conceding another witkit and maybe having your bails knocked off if you are not so pretty careful.'

'Silver car, thirteen runs, plus one extra leg over to us for arguing with the referee.'

'For Christ's sake.'

'Ah, foul language. Another silly-fuck-off-point from the English team.'

'. . . Who are now minus thirty-seven runs . . .' announces the blond passenger. 'We may have to give you another witkit, Micahel Howguh, unless you cheer up.'

A 'witkit' is a painful cuff around the head from one of those ham fists so I'm loathe to argue too emphatically, but I'm buggered if they're going to have it all their own way. As luck would have it, a rare, bright orange Beetle overtakes us. 'Orange car,' I shriek, 'clean bowled, ha, ha, ha. Middle stump. You're both out in fact, like a couple of sad, stupid, overgrown childish Dutch bastards. Take the long walk, boys.'

My companions exchange a long-suffering look instead.

'Orange, Michael Howguh? Orange for Dutchmen is never bad. Orange is our very special national colour. Orange is always lucky for us. Thank you for pointing out this vehicle, but we are sorry to inform you, Michael Howguh, that while we follow behind this orange automobile, it signifies, from now on, extra double-plus runs for the Netherlands dream-team . . .'

At times, I really do miss the ability to sleep.

The Corsa finally turns in to an open gate. We trundle down a rutted track towards a house. A couple of the ground-floor lights are on and I know that in one of those rooms I'm shortly to face Coombs's buddy – the Dutchman, Mijnheer Van Huis.

Of course I'm going to sing like a canary. I can only hope that Van Huis, the Controller and various minions, all arrive at Pond's Farm at the same time and end up shooting one another dead.

The Corsa skids across the track and I get one of those sudden orientation clunks – like when you turn a corner and recognize the landmarks of a familiar place approached from an unfamiliar direction. My heart sinks.

Pond's Farm.

A figure emerges from the front door, silhouetted and unnaturally elongated in the porch light, and flags down our car. Whoever it is, I'm fresh out of ideas and luck; I've nothing left to bargain with. My instinct is to hunker down behind this comforting wall of muscle and black leather, but the passenger turns, flicks open the rear door, prods me out with a bratwurst finger.

'Go, Michael Howguh, we are sorry but you cannot spend all night taking it easy, playing vehicle-cricket with us. The time has come for you to take responsibility for your actions.'

Being shoved out of the Corsa by these big boys is more or less the equivalent of a bug being chased across a wind-screen by a vegetarian – we don't want to hurt you, but if you hang around, you might regret it.

'Bye, guys,' I say, as I step in farmyard cack up to my ankles. I balance on one leg while I pull my house-brick loafer from the muck, which reluctantly releases it with an amphibious objection. 'Thanks for . . . well, you know . . . thanks anyway.'

'Farewell, Michael Howguh. It was nice knowing you. You made us laugh a great deal, although you are a rotten sport. To be clear, the score is: Netherlands – 8,763 runs, not out. England – minus 83 runs for six witkits.'

(This is simply not true: for the record, the Dutchmen were all out for 37 early on, when we were overtaken by a lurid pink Metro – which they chose to ignore. The English batsman then put in a steady performance and declared at a respectable 1,862, despite having to endure half a dozen 'witkits'.)

'The result is very much contested,' I point out.

I give the hot bonnet of the Corsa a manly pat. I'm beginning to crumble as I watch the dangerously front-loaded vehicle reverse away through the mud. I know they weren't exactly on my side, but somehow I felt safe in the car with those two giants.

Now I have to face reality: the Dutchman has found us. I've been saved from the Controller, only so that the Van Huis can get his licks in first: a salutary lesson to anyone who messes with a drug cartel. No point running, as usual. I hobble uneasily to the porchlight and my fate.

'You, the one with the long hair . . .'

Thirty-Two

The guernsey-clad figure at the threshold gesticulates impatiently. 'Come here and make yourself useful.'

It's one of the Pond sisters, the one with the eyes, or the complexion. Right now, she's the one with the gun: a double-barrelled shotgun, which she waves in my face.

'Where's Roger?'

'Gone,' she snaps.

This is not good.

'Gone where?'

'You're to keep quiet and make yourself useful. Get over here and milk a cow, you pointless waste of skin.'

'What do you mean, "gone"? What's happened? What have you done with Roger?'

'Don't worry about Roger. You'll see him soon enough.' She smirks, and motions for me to follow. She strides across to one of the smaller barns where a squat three-legged stool lurks in the shadowy muck of the forecourt.

'Sit,' she barks.

I've underestimated these two. Somehow they've done a deal of their own. It looks like they've sold us all out, including Roger. And now Mijnheer Van Huis has decided to have a little farmyard fun before I'm dragged off to the compost heap. But that reckless, fearless mood is upon me again; if

I'm going to go tonight after all, it'll be with dignity, on my own two feet. I spin round the sinister farmyard, bellowing. 'Come on out, Van Huis, wherever you're hiding. I'm not playing bloody milkmaid for your amusement. I'm tired and I've had enough. You may as well get this over with now.'

'What's wrong with you, boy?' hisses the twin.

'Where are they? In the barn, waiting with the power tools?'

'Who?'

'The cartel.'

'There's only Cacafuego and Santisima Trinidad in there.'

'Eh . . .?'

'Milk cows. We named them after old Spanish ships of the line, can't remember why now.'

'Where's Van Huis?'

The woman compresses thin, bloodless lips, enjoying this.

After my experience at the Tank Engine tonight I'm pretty well prepared for physical violence. But I have to admit, I'm not equipped for these exquisitely subtle mind-games.

'Is it Coombs then?'

'Barry Coombs?'

'Yeah. Coombs.'

'Don't be so stupid. There's no bloody Coombs in there, nor ever will be. We may be late with our subs, but that does not give Coombs the right to worry our cattle.'

'They found you, didn't they? And you sold us out. At least tell me what's going on. Georgia?'

'Georgina. I'm the one with the complexion, as if you couldn't tell. And you'll find out soon enough. You've caused enough trouble tonight,' she hisses. 'In the meantime you can just bloody well stop there and think about what a bloody nuisance you've been.'

She strides into the black maw of the barn, reappearing moments later leading a stately brown and white cow on a length of frayed green twine. The shotgun is still cradled comfortably in her other hand. 'Now, make yourself useful,' she orders, looping the twine around the legs of the stool. 'Sit,' she repeats, jabbing my ribcage with the twin-barrels by way of punctuation.

I squat, folding my long spindly legs on either side of me, like a dead spider.

Georgina fetches a zinc bucket from somewhere nearby and positions it beneath the bloated pink washing-up-glove arrangement dangling from the cow-creature.

'Take one of the teats, the pink things, between thumb and forefinger and pull, with a sliding motion. Don't yank, pull and slide, gently.'

For a moment nothing happens, then the beast lets off catastrophically. I leap a good couple of inches off the stool at the sound. 'Jesus, did I break something? Is that supposed to happen?'

Georgina cackles like a bonfire of November leaves. 'Cacafuego,' the woman shrieks. 'It means shit-fire. Now I remember why we called her that.' Clearly this is the most amusing incident on the farm for at least a century, since the twins hit adolescence. The old horror clutches her chest and almost drops the weapon.

Finally she regains her composure and levels the twin barrels at my face. 'I'm going inside for a while now, young man. Stay here and milk. If you try to escape, I'll hunt you down and shoot your head off like a runt-puppy. Do I make myself clear?'

'You should just let me go,' I mutter, 'it wouldn't cost you anything.'

'Wouldn't it? Shows what you know,' she responds grimly.

I never much liked these two ghastly old waxworks

anyway, so I'm not surprised to find they've cut their own deal.

I've nothing better to do so I begin milking and quickly discover a little rhythm, which I believe Cacafugeo enjoys, judging by the frequency and scale of her farts and the syncopated jets of pristine white milk, that sputter into the zinc bucket at her feet.

Sun inches over the horizon; light infuses the farmyard, filling crannies with liquid bronze. What was a black midden now teems with life. From empty my bucket is almost overflowing.

I've had another time-stutter.

No one came leaping out of the barn to hack me into slices with machetes, attach pliers to my nipples or rip my fingernails out. On the whole it's been a good couple of hours.

'You can stop doing that, young man. They're here.'

I peer up. A distant flash of mechanical blue light aquatints orange sky.

Police.

Georgina quickly retreats to one of the other barns.

The approaching vehicle rumbles up the drive and I see that I'm mistaken, it's an ambulance lurching towards the house, carving fresh creases in the corduroy track. An ambulance is worse: most likely Coombs, with Wenner and Davis in tow, come to see his mate the Dutchman get his revenge. Maybe it's Eugene, fresh from casualty with the Controller and his Ard-Corps lot. Could be any of them.

Either way I'm past caring now. These time-stutters are becoming longer and more intense; my mind is faltering. I've entered psychosis-phase, my death-dive.

So, fuck off, the lot of you.

*

I keep my hands to the teats, head down, like Bernard buffing the Volvo. Nothing bad can happen when you're busy like this.

Something warm and dry brushes my neck. I squint up into the rising sun.

'There's a sight for sore eyes,' chuckles Roger, removing his hand.

I don't particularly want to speak to the man but I don't see why I should make this easy for him. 'Your horrible girl friends have betrayed us, Roger. Or maybe you already know that?'

Roger seems amused.

I nod in the direction of the ambulance. 'I put Coombs in hospital tonight, along with one of the Controller's men, so I've a pretty good idea what the ambulance is doing here and who's inside. I'm not stupid, Roger. The twins have done some kind of a deal. Or maybe you have?'

'What on earth would give you that idea?'

'I found out that the cocaine belongs to a Dutchman; a couple of his bruisers brought me here tonight. Then Georgina threatened to shoot my head off if I tried to escape.'

'That was a wee bit excessive, I admit. But they don't get out much, I'm afraid. I did ask them to keep you here, Michael.'

'So, what am I supposed to think? While you've been God-knows-where, the rest of us have been through hell over the past twelve hours. It might interest you to know that Livia's in intensive care, fighting for her life. Mr T. and Mrs Hodges have spent the night fighting for your home. In the meantime, I've been assaulted by Coombs, a bunch of drunken office workers, a TV crew, and the Controller's gorilla. And for what? So you and those mad old witches can sell us out to the highest bidder?'

Roger considers this.

Cacafuego farts. I pull on one of her teats.

'I think you should stop milking now; she's empty, you know.'

'I put my life on the line for you tonight. Literally.'

'You're hysterical, dear boy. You should calm down and come inside.'

'Oh, shut up. Everything else in my life is corrupted and rotten. Milking's the only thing I have left, the only thing I can't mess up. I'm doing this for Livia now, and no one else.'

Roger beams. 'You must take her a nice big glass then, dear boy.'

I glare up again. 'I told you, Livia's very sick; in the cardiac care unit.' I squeeze, releasing a pitiful dribble; Roger is right, the beast is pretty well milked out.

He stoops and gently pats the top of my head. 'You're a remarkable young man in many ways, Michael, although occasionally prone to self-pity and histrionics. Livia's here, in the back of the ambulance, and in quite good shape, all things considered. Let's go and see her, find out if your magic's working.'

'I'm not going anywhere near that ambulance.'

Roger turns away, cups hands around his mouth and bellows, 'Nurse Koroma . . .'

Aggie's unmistakable bulk detaches itself from the driver's compartment of the distant vehicle. She waves impatiently. I'm not entirely reassured by her presence; the jury's still out on her dubious past, but I can't squat on this ridiculous stool for ever. Besides, Cacafuego is dry and my knees are beginning to cramp.

'Get your ass over here, boy,' she yells. 'You think we got all day to be sitting around? Livia's be waiting for you.'

Cacafuego jerks at her twine, startled by the din.

I squint up at Roger.

'You're not the only one who's been busy tonight,

298

Michael. We were all hoping to surprise you, but you really are such a cynical mistrustful fellow, you know. I don't imagine Christmas can have been any fun at your house.'

'It wasn't.'

'You're also a very elusive fellow. I would have expected to find you pacing the corridors of the Royal Berkshire after I heard about Livia.'

'I had to leave. They told me Livia was going to be okay.'

'Well, the local constabulary were beginning to exhibit an unhealthy amount of interest in her – to the point where we felt it necessary to spirit her away in a borrowed ambulance. No doubt you'll remember to thank Nurse Koroma for that particular favour.'

I focus on the distant ambulance. Mr T. emerges from the passenger side, equipped with what appear to be a couple of outsized baseball-catcher's mitts. I can see his grin from here.

'Ah, yes. And Mr T., who, as you so forcefully pointed out, has spent the night battling for my home. I found him in A&E alongside the wonderful Mrs Hodges. D'you know, Mikey, I'm beginning to believe that they may be something of an item.'

Roger gives me a gentle shove. 'Go on. Go and tell Livia how hard you've been working for her.'

'Holy cow,' I yell, giving my beast a valedictory slap on the rump. 'Take over for me?'

'Ah, I don't . . .'

'Pretend it's Georgia or Georgina.'

'Now you're just being vulgar . . .'

Aggie gives me a cautious look, it's intended to be disapproving, but she can't sustain it. 'You get here,' she orders, spreading powerful arms. She's like one of those sci-fi tractor beams; I'm powerless to resist. The breath is squeezed out of me. 'You really been through it, Mikey.' I can feel Aggie's huge body begin to spasm through the nylon uniform. For a moment I wonder if it's another infarction, until I realize she's sobbing. 'I'm gonna miss you, boy,' she chunters, before pushing me away.

There's something I've been meaning to do for days now. I reach down into my trouser pocket. 'Aggie, I want you to have this. To remind you of me.' My own bottom lip is trembling now as I hand over the precious object. 'It's amber. If you look closely you can see a tiny creature inside, a mayfly. They don't . . . they don't live for very long.'

Aggie holds the lump up to the dawn light. 'Ah, but I reckon they live a beautiful life, Mikey. They gets to fly.'

I rub my eyes. Mission four. Better late than never.

The twins appear out of nowhere, thin-lipped as always. 'I'm sorry I doubted you,' I say. 'I thought you'd sold us out. After all, you did have a gun and . . .'

'Huh, shows what you know,' says the one with the dog's arse mouth. With that, they turn and trudge back towards the lower field.

I step over to Mr T., who waits patiently by the cab. I was right about the hands – they're gigantic, swathed in layers of fresh bandages. 'We did good tonight, Michael. I'd like to shake your hand, but . . .'

I direct my gaze at his outsized, freshly bandaged mitts. 'The Cascades?'

Mr T. shrugs. 'A small petrol bomb which required extinguishing; minor singe, nothing of consequence, nothing a little antibiotic and few painkillers can't put right.'

His face has a pink parboiled appearance and his eyebrows have entirely disappeared.

'Christ. What happened?'

Mr T. grins, raising his arms like a heavyweight. 'It was a rout, Mikey: a glorious victory for the Cascadian forces and our gallant Sedgewick Stainless allies. One moment all punches, brickbats and Molotovs flying; next, thugs running in disarray, retreating to the safety of their minibus. Then gone, just like that, back to whichever black hellhole they emerged from. You should have seen Deirdre, laying about her, taser in one hand, cricket bat in the other. She was an Amazon, Mikey, a veritable Valkyrie. You'd have been amazed.'

No I wouldn't.

'I'm sorry, Mr T. I should have been there . . .'

'No, Michael, you did what you had to do. You did the right thing; that's all anyone can expect.'

'Yeah, just like you done the right thing, Mr T.,' Aggie interjects caustically, 'losing them lunch-hooks in some dumb rukkus. Mr T.'s fingers be like deep-fried pork scratchin's, Mikey. Nothing under them bandages but cracklin' now.'

'They're just a little well done, is all,' protests Mr T. 'Poetic justice, some might say.'

I don't ask him to elaborate: there are too many things I don't understand right now.

Besides, Livia's waiting.

I clatter up the aluminium step to find her wrapped in a blanket, sitting up on a truckle bed. The interior is silent and oddly monochrome under muted cabin lights. Livia seems fragile, removed, almost other-worldly, her face pale and waxy, framed by that thick dark hair. She holds an oxygen mask to her nose and mouth. I take a tentative step and reach out for her hand, imagining that my own life-force will leak into her and the world will enjoy colour once more.

She smiles weakly and removes the mask.

'Fuck, this is good stuff.'

'What?'

She absorbs another lungful. 'Nitrous oxide. They used to call it laughing gas. It's a bit like skunk only doesn't give you the munchies. Here, have a bang.' She offers me the mask.

'You have got to be kidding. You were at death's door tonight, probably because of your stupid drug habit, and here you are, fresh out of intensive care, off your face again.'

'This stuff's good for you. It's medicinal. If you don't want it, give me the mask back. I need another blast. Stat.'

'Livia, you've got a chronic condition.'

'Oh, bollocks, Mikey. I fainted; Mr T. and Mrs H. panicked. I've been overdoing the stimulants, too much adulterated crap. So I had a few palpitations, fibrillations or whatever. I've got beta-blockers. End of story.' She sits up, swinging herself round so her feet are on the floor.

'Do you have a death wish or something?'

'Do you?'

I was really looking forward to seeing her; I can't believe how quickly she's managing to piss me off.

'The opposite, I think.'

'Shit. Sorry, Mikey, sorry, sorry, sorry. I keep saying awful things to you. I don't mean to.' Tears form across her lower lashes. She offers me the mask. 'Go on, please have a turn.' I snatch and inhale. I'm not impressed. On the other hand, my knees suddenly feel like someone pulled the pins out.

I drop the mask and sit heavily on the truckle beside her. Livia grins, her face much larger than I remember.

'Michael, I've just had a near-death experience, I'm entitled to live a little,' she whispers. Her lips are fuller than I remember, too; her breath is a bit cheesy. A tongue flickers into my mouth, exploring. This is something I've been fanta-sizing about ever since I met her in Coombs's garden. I want to keep kissing. The blanket falls away; under the thin cotton of her hospital gown I can feel the hard points of her breasts pushing against me. My own heart yammers against my chest like a canary.

Something clicks in my head; I remember who I am.

'This is wrong.' I pull away, shaking her off.

'What the fuck, Mikey?'

'It's wrong, very wrong.'

'How can it be wrong?'

'Ask Aggie, she knows.'

I'm gratified to find that Livia takes me seriously enough to switch off the nitrous oxide.

'What *are* you talking about?'

'Who was your father, Livia?'

'Darth Vader. How the fuck do I know?'

'It was Coombs.'

'Don't be such an idiot. My mum hated Coombs.'

'She slept with him, she said as much, Livia.'

'He's not my father. I'm as sure of it as I'm sure of anything. He had me put away, for Christ's sake.'

We both know how flimsy an argument this is. Neither of us is keen to give the precarious logic a final shove.

'Livia, Coombs may have been my father.'

True to form, Livia defaults to vaudeville.

'Agh, you're a Coombs, Michael Coombs . . .' Livia clutches her chest and slides off the truckle.

'I'm serious.'

Livia sprawls on the floor, motionless.

'I was the baby sold in place of you, Livia. To the Houghs.'

No response.

'Coombs pulled me out of a hat at the last minute, when the Houghs decided they didn't want you; that you weren't good enough for them.'

'So what, Mikey?'

'So it was a really lucky break for the Houghs, if you ask me.'

She rises from the floor like a banshee, grabs me round the neck and bites down on my left ear. I feel her soft warm flesh through the gaping gown. 'You fucker, Mikey. My mum never told me who my dad was. But she sure as hell told me who he wasn't. She hated Coombs, trust me on this, Mikey. He's not my father, I know it. I feel it. He's not your father either. Who's to say that Coombs didn't just bribe some other random, anonymous, desperate single mother?'

'Mothers don't just hand over their own kids.'

'For Christ's sake, Michael, grow up.'

I'm not sure which is more depressing: that I was discount-retailed by my natural mother, or that I may be Coombs's natural son.

'Anyway, you don't look anything like him.'

Roger coughs discreetly before stepping into the cabin. We break apart like guilty schoolkids.

'It's time we were going.'

'Going where?'

'Ah, of course, I didn't quite finish, did I? The truth is, you were right, Michael. I did make a deal.'

Thirty-Three

'So you made a deal with the Dutchman.'

Roger strokes his upper lip. 'After you both shot off like mad things yesterday, I had another little poke around the Cessna and discovered Dutch registration papers and a logbook. I decided to give the owner a call, see if we couldn't sort this out like civilized human beings.'

'Mijnheer Van Huis.'

Roger nods. 'Technically the Cessna is owned by a ceramics company based just outside Delft – Vliegerskruis Porcelyne BV, but I gave the gratifyingly fluent receptionist a brief, sanitized version of our predicament. Within minutes I was patched through to your friend Van Huis on his portable transceiver. He's been over here on business.'

'He's no friend of mine.'

'He seems to like you; not two hours ago he described you as a feisty young man. I understand you broke bread together last night.'

'We broke plates.'

'I expect that's why he likes you: you're good for business, if you happen to be in porcelain.'

'He's in drugs, Roger.'

'That's as may be. Yet he appears to possess a moral compass; an honourable man.'

'He's a crook. You can't trust any of these people, not with millions in drugs at stake. They're animals.'

'He came across as perfectly civilized and rather charming. Of course, the real clincher for me was the name of his company.'

'Fligsfrigtwigs?'

'Vliegerkruis, the Flying Cross, Michael. Turns out that Van Huis senior flew Spits for Prince Bernhard's 322 Squadron. A flight commander, shot down twice over France, wounded three times, awarded the Vliegerkruis in forty-five. Set up the porcelain business just after the war. Sadly, Flight Lieutenant Van Huis handed in his mess tins in eighty-one. Since then, young Dickie has managed the firm.

'Once our respective credentials had been established we got on like a Fokker on fire. He was very understanding of our DFC quest; somewhat miffed with the Controller for having pilfered the item in the first place. And also for blithely assuming ownership of the Cessna, which I understand was not part of their deal. To cut a long story short, I agreed to return all his property forthwith, no recriminations, no questions asked.'

I'm somewhat miffed myself that Roger has sat on his arse, drinking whisky and stuffing himself with cake and still achieved more with one brief phone call than I did over the course of the worst, most terrifying twenty-four hours of my life. And I'm not entirely happy with the way Livia has gone all starey and wide-eyed in his presence. I want to punish him.

'Well, that's a wonderful, heart-warming story. But the truth is that you've done a deal with the Devil when you didn't have to. I already had the situation under control.'

Roger allows himself a half smile. 'The Devil? I've said it before but you young people do tend to see the world in black and white. Morally, we are all flawed in some way, you know.

The quicker you accept that fact, the happier you'll be, take my word for it. Compromise is the true essence of negotiation – it enables us to do business with people we don't entirely endorse. Sometimes you see, it's possible to salvage something good from an otherwise bleak and morally ambiguous set of circumstances. It's what we mean when we say that clouds sometimes have a silver lining. Forgive me, Mikey, but I understand that when Dickie's men caught up with you tonight, the situation did not appear to be especially well under control.'

'Oh God, tell me,' says Livia, all ears suddenly, sensing a good story.

Roger skims a hand across her shoulder, gives it a squeeze. 'You're safe, Livia. That's all you need to know. Aggie must return the ambulance. Tempus fugit, and so must I. The girls have towed the Cessna to the lower paddock with their tractors, I've done a pre-flight and there's suffient fuel on board for the trip despite the mangled wing.' Roger winks at Livia as he backs out of the rear doors. 'I hope you'll both accompany me. But the choice is yours.'

Livia jumps to her feet and gropes for her overnight bag on the shelf above. 'Where to, Squadron Leader?'

'This little aircraft is going home. Netherlands. Delft. Dickie Van Huis flew back on a commercial flight last night and will be there to meet us in person.'

'Is there a first-class section? I don't mix well with the hoi polloi.'

'Only a first-class pilot,' chuckles Roger, rubbing his hands. He's looking forward to this. 'Mikey?'

'What?'

'You're coming of course?'

'I hadn't really . . .'

'What?' Livia's face collapses like a burst balloon.

I'm a wanted criminal now. Everyone wants a piece

of me, especially the Controller and Coombs. I can't stay in Reading.

'Of course I'm coming. I've got fifteen quid to blow, without receipts.'

The twins approach. I can already hear the tension in their voices before I make out the words.

'I bloody knew it.'

'I bloody knew it too.'

'We should have cracked him in the . . .'

'Goolagongs.'

'I was going to say skull.'

'Either would have suited me.'

'I concur.'

They appear at the rear doors to offer a breathless report.

'Company.'

'Three-vehicle convoy approaching: couple of saloons and a black people carrier.'

Georgina points a gnarled finger at me. 'The little twerp must have dropped . . .'

'. . . his guts,' finishes Georgia.

'Spilled his guts,' clarifies her sister. 'Dropped us in it.'

'I think I know what I mean,' insists Georgia primly.

Roger unbuttons his tweed jacket; the closest I've ever seen him come to alarm. 'Is that true, Michael, did you let anything slip tonight?'

'Not exactly . . .'

'Michael, what did you do?' prompts Livia.

'You broke under questioning, didn't you?'

'I was doing a deal as a matter of fact,' I protest. 'How come my deal's automatically the crappy one?' I already know the answer.

'Oh, Michael.' The unkindest cut from Livia.

'And how was I supposed to know I was going to be rescued? Anyway, they took their bloody time about it.'

'Those men weren't there for your benefit, Michael,' he says tersely. 'Van Huis is a downy old bird, he doesn't take anything at face value. In truth he wasn't entirely convinced that the Controller had mislaid his shipment at all. His chaps were keeping an eye on the club for evidence of double-dealing and skullduggery. It was only after they'd made one of their regular wireless telephonic reports to young Dickie that he recognized you from their description, understood that you might be about to bugger things up, and decided to send in the cavalry. It's fortunate you have such a distinctive appearance.' He sighs. 'I suppose we must make the best of things.'

He turns to address the twins at the rear doors, 'Ladies, start up your tractor engines; delay them if you can.'

'Everyone, hang on to your asses,' bellows Aggie from the front seat as she fires up the ambulance.

The harridans disappear, scrambling for their John Deeres.

Roger reaches for a loose strap as we lurch away.

'Michael, on active service, it's axiomatic that one never releases critical information for at least twelve hours after capture.'

I grab one of the guard rails to steady myself. 'It's just as well I'm not on active service then, isn't it? Seeing as how I'm not very active.'

We lurch downhill, quickly picking up speed, the open rear doors thumping and clanging against the sides. The three of us bounce off each other in the back, like pinballs. From time to time Roger grabs me and bawls recriminations in my ear, most of which are masked by the racket, but 'Poltroon', 'Cad', 'Hound' and 'Fifth Columnist' are definitely among them. Livia declines to mediate on my behalf; she has no idea what I went through to protect them all.

'What happened to all the "remarkable young man" stuff?' I yell.

'You're remarkable all right. Remarkably stupid,' he bellows.

In the paddock the Cessna is waiting, its mangled wing tip giving it an asymmetrical, wounded appearance.

Livia leaps, unassisted, out of the back of the ambulance, treating Roger and I to another heart-constricting flash of flesh, and hoists herself into the aircraft like a gymnast. I climb into the passenger seat and carefully buckle up. I don't want a repetition of my last flight.

Roger boards from the far side and begins pulling levers and pressing buttons.

The propeller starts first time with a nice aggressive roar.

I crane my neck through the perspex side window to watch as Aggie guns the ambulance back up the slope towards the approaching convoy. At the last moment she pulls off some kind of handbrake manoeuvre, slewing the vehicle sideways across the path, effectively blocking the narrow entrance to our temporary runway.

We trundle down the long paddock. From my window I can see that one of the vehicles has managed to slip past Aggie's makeshift barricade by negotiating the treacherous pools of green slime surrounding the field. It's the people carrier.

We're heavily laden for a small aircraft: three passengers and a hundred Ks of luggage means we're failing to pick up speed despite the open throttle. The carrier swerves past a couple of trees before biting into the firmer ground. With improved traction it easily overhauls us, then slows and keeps pace at our wing. Through the windscreen I can see the Controller bellowing orders from the passenger seat, his face tight with fury. Now the side door slides open to reveal a bunch of shiny black-jacketed Ard-Corps operatives, fizzing with malice, like a nest of blowflies. A short, ugly gun barrel is pointed in my direction; I duck instinctively. When I pop my head up again the weapon has disappeared; presumably the Controller has figured out that the misuse of firearms could jeopardize cargo as well as passengers.

Instead, the operatives emerge one by one and gingerly cling to the side of the vehicle. The carrier inches towards our wing. Being a seasoned wheel-strut traveller myself I see what they're up to. They're going to try to weigh us down. My pizza buddy is in there, and I recognize the guy who offered to give me a flying lesson on the toe-end of his boot. He's the first to take a shot: the undamaged wing tip is comparatively steady, about level with his chest. He grips it with both hands and springs away from his vehicle, boosting himself up on to the wing. Our tiny aircraft wobbles alarmingly as he kicks his legs to give himself additional momentum. I quickly lose sight of him, since the wing is fixed above our cockpit. I assume that the man is slithering about up there on his belly. I crane my neck to see thick, powerful fingers curling over the leading edge. He's done it; fixed himself to our aircraft like a giant remora. The carrier creeps towards us again. Now that they know how easily it can be achieved, the remaining Ard-Corp men are all champing at the bit, anxious for their chance to play Harrison Ford.

'Bad idea, bastard,' screeches Livia from her little window behind me. 'Turn, Roger, before they weigh us down. Shake him off.'

'Can't swerve too sharply at this speed, old girl. Might end up upsetting the whole ruddy applecart.' I don't know whether it is courage or something else, but Roger appears preternaturally calm. He tracks the carrier's progress from the corner of his eye as two of the larger Ard-Corp men prepare themselves for their leap. Roger waits a beat before giving one of the rudder pedals the smallest tap; we veer away at the exact moment the big boys commit themselves. They hit the dust at thirty miles an hour behind us.

Slowly but surely we build speed, escaping gravity's grip like a spatula from a stale glue pot. Our unwanted passenger must understand that he's now alone and unlikely to be making any new friends. I see his fingers grudgingly unclench. He's whipped off the wing faster than a magician's tablecloth and falls away behind us, bumping heavily across the paddock below like a bouncing bomb.

I slide back the perspex and recline in my seat, luxuriating in the joy of escape, the sense of relief. I have all of three seconds before Roger starts giving me orders. 'Michael, this is not a joyride. You see what's in front of us?'

'Sky.'

'Right, well, from a line directly intersecting us you are now responsible for the entire area of sky to the left of the cockpit. I want to see your head swivelling constantly from here until we land. I don't expect company, but as you know, these people have access to light aircraft, so we can't be too careful.'

'Okay, all clear in front. Zero bandits at this time.'

'Livia, you are responsible for what happens behind us. Likewise, I require you to keep a constant vigil.'

Livia gazes out of her window. 'Reporting blue all round with occasional white-fluffy-type structures in between, Roger.'

Roger sighs. 'When you fly unfriendly skies, your life is at stake. You watch the heavens or you die. You scan three hundred and sixty degrees, up and down. And you do it from the moment you take off till the moment you touch down. Why do you think we pilots wore silk scarves? To show off? To look dashing for the ladies?' He doesn't wait for a glib answer. 'The scarf was not an affectation. It was essential lubrication for the neck, for all that constant twisting and turning. We are not out of the woods until we land. My eyes are not what they used to be; I'm relying on the two of you now. Keep them peeled.'

'Roger, Roger.'

Someone had to say it, sooner or later.

Livia rummages in her overnight bag and produces her mum's silk scarf, which she wraps around my neck. 'So you can look dashing for the ladies, Mikey.'

I doubt if I resemble an ace with all these swirls, more a big queen I expect, nevertheless I'm flattered to have this precious thing adorning me.

Roger pincers the steering yoke between steady fingers.

For a while there's a silence in the cockpit as we contemplate the upturned blue bowl of sky before us.

Roger breaks the silence. 'You know, back in nineteen forty, keeping an eye out and not getting shot down was almost better for the war effort than being an ace, given that the entire Battle of Britain was a question of attrition . . .'

'Absolutely . . .' breathes Livia. 'But you did shoot some Krauts down, too?'

There's a small black dot in my quadrant which I probably ought to mention, but I don't want to be considered an hysteric on top of everything else today, and I don't want to annoy Roger in the middle of one of his interminable fighter-pilot stories. I decide to wait and see if it's an eagle or an albatross.

'I did. Six, in fact, but only because I absolutely had to. You have to remember that fully armed a Spit or even a Hurricane has only fifteen-seconds worth of armament, which must be delivered through a deflection shot, rather like a hosepipe . . .' From a state of tight-lipped efficiency, Roger has become genial, almost garrulous. He's in his element now.

The black dot has now become a rather large and rather

313

red blob. The blob metamorphoses into a biplane which settles into a position slightly below my window, the pilot clearly visible. I'm delighted to see that he wears a leather helmet and a flowing silk scarf like mine. It's like we've travelled back in time to a more innocent age. He waves at me. This is all rather jolly. Weird things happen to people when they're in boats, trains or planes. Perfect strangers are compelled to wave at each other for no other reason other than to say: hey, look at me, I'm in a boat, or a train or a plane.

I wave back.

'The trick was maintaining a height advantage . . .'

Something smashes through my side window, showering me with shards of perspex.

Livia screams, a high-pitched peal of terror.

Actually, it might have been me. I can't be sure.

Roger slams the yoke sideways and puts us into a sharp bank.

'What the hell was that, Mikey?'

'Some bloke in an old-fashioned aeroplane; he waved at me.'

Roger is silent, concentrating instead on a complex sequence of manoeuvres involving yoke, pedals and throttle. I can only swallow repeatedly until he levels the aircraft.

Roger glances accusingly at the small entry hole through my passenger window, then the larger exit hole though his own side window by way of reply.

The red biplane shoots past the cockpit at an angle some way above us. My stomach is compressed through the top of my skull as Roger hauls back on the control yoke, clawing for height.

'Idiot,' grumbles Roger.

He kicks hard on the right pedal. The Cessna skids through the sky. We have a second to observe the biplane as it flashes past us in the opposite direction.

'Pitts Special,' announces Roger grimly. 'I think he took a shot at us. What the hell were you doing, letting him creep up on us like that?'

Roger banks hard.

'Roger, I really think we should—' From the back seat Livia projectile vomits across my shoulder. Hospital food. It wasn't exactly haute cuisine when it started life and now quickly fills the cramped space with a stinking hogo of unwashed socks pickled in vinegar. I flick a pale, half-digested mushroom off my thigh and concentrate on overcoming my own gag reflex.

'The man's a pro,' pronounces Roger, waggling the control yoke. 'Stunt pilot, probably.'

'Ah, well, not a professional killer, at least.'

'Worse. An excellent pilot with a highly manoeuvrable weapons platform. He's here to turn us back or force us down. We're over the Channel now, if he shoots us down they know they can always salvage the packages.'

'You're the fighter pilot, outfly him!'

'His plane easily outmanoeuvres this thing, even if I didn't have the wing damage.'

By way of confirmation the biplane levels with us, more or less wing tip to wing tip. The pilot repeatedly stabs his thumb over his shoulder, an unequivocal gesture for us to turn back. To reinforce the order he produces a machine pistol and aims at our propeller.

'Dive, Roger,' someone pipes in an hysterical contralto.

I think that might have been me again.

Roger slams the aircraft almost perpendicular; the biplane banks and follows us down. The view ahead becomes a spinning patchwork of browns and greens which instantly morphs into a rotating disc of sludge brown.

I'm engaged in a swift, vicious tug of war with my own oesophagus. There's a yell from behind me. The wind yips through my broken window and I'm vaguely conscious of having pebble-dashed Livia as we hit the bottom of a high-speed curve. I'm thrown back into my seat as we begin climbing.

'I'm going to attempt an Immelman,' bellows Roger over the shriek of the engines. 'It's basically a ruddy great somersault with a twist. I don't expect it'll work, but it's all I've got.'

We crash through the cloud cover; sun rays briefly explode into the cockpit before my stomach informs me that we're doing another horrible upside downy twisty thing, then we're back in shadow and into another dive. I've lost sight of the biplane. I'm not even sure which way is up until Roger levels off, bleeding speed.

'He's about quarter of a mile ahead of us,' announces Roger to no one in particular. 'Overshot on my turn.' A little tut. 'Not nearly as good as he thinks he is.' Roger takes his eyes off the sky for a moment. 'Listen to me now. Here's the thing. I can't keep him off us for ever. The odds are that he will down us eventually. But there is precedent for a victory in this situation, albeit only once or twice that I know of, and an absolute long shot at that.'

'What are our options?' says Livia.

'We could turn back, land at Wallingford Airfield or Pond's Farm, take our chances.'

'No.' Livia and I say it at the same time.

Roger nods slowly. 'As I said, it is possible to beat these odds but only if you're prepared to risk everything. And I mean everything.' He turns in his seat to address us both. 'I'm an old man, I've had my fun, I've had a very good life.'

I shrug. 'I should be dead in any case,' I say.

We turn to Livia. 'Fuck it,' she announces, 'I've got a heart murmur.' She gives me a 'don't start' kind of look. 'Truth is, I probably won't see thirty anyhow.'

Roger nods. 'Good. Then it's settled.'

He tweaks the yoke, lining us up against the fast expanding black dot in our cockpit window, setting up for a head-on collision.

Our opponent holds all the cards, he has no need to play high-speed 'chicken' like this. But of course Roger is banking on hubris, and possibly, an innate sense of chivalry.

Roger has read his man right. Instead of manoeuvring, the stunt pilot duly steers his own aircraft directly towards us at speed. It's a modern-day joust.

I almost feel sorry for the other pilot. I imagine he's a decent enough sort of man, who enjoys life, prancing around in Rayban Aviators, hefty leather jacket, silk scarf; he zooms around in his crate, does tricks, supplements his income with the occasional crafty duty-free flight. Sometimes, he's a bit naughtier. He's fallen into Roger's grey area. Today, he's been given automatic weapons and an unambiguous brief. I'm sure he's a good pilot but he's not a ruthless one. And he has a life, which he probably values. Loves, even.

We, on the other hand, have nothing to lose.

So, what does happen when an unstoppable force meets an immovable object? We'll never know. Because at the very last moment the stunt pilot decides not to be an unstoppable force. He breaks left.

Which is what does for him.

Our slightly serrated but sturdy metal wing tip slices through the wood and composite resin laminate of his tail like a Ginzu knife, amputating it, sending his fragile craft into an instant and irrecoverable spin. We watch as a tiny figure leaps from the open cockpit. The pilot tumbles towards the unforgiving glum waters of the English Channel two thousand feet below. At last a perfectly round yellow canopy pops and blooms like some kind of exotic mushroom.

Roger is silent the rest of the way and so are we.

Thirty-Four

'Roger, you old bastard. At last, here you are in the flesh.'

Roger is his usual undemonstrative self. The Dutchman releases him from a bear-hug and regards his battered aircraft.

'*Godverdomme*, Roger. My Cessna has been through the wars, no?'

'Indeed it has, Dickie, but your cargo is intact.'

The Dutchman snaps his fingers, sending a host of overall-wearing operatives swarming. Van Huis smiles fondly as his employees set up a chain and begin to unload the distinctive green plastic bricks.

Livia and I stand on the airfield, stinking like wet dogs.

'Ah, and here is my friend, Mongo.'

I bare my teeth. I'm in no mood for laboured humour from any buddy of Coombs.

'I'm sorry. I understand, Michael Howguh, that you may still be smarting from your recent loss at cricket,' he says, deftly reminding me of my debt to him.

'I'm fine, thanks. Your guys were very . . . well, they were very professional.'

The Dutchman grins. 'I'm pleased to hear you say this, Michael. They are two of my finest young men. Always the right level of service, I feel.'

'I don't know, they were very nice to me but I think they might have been quite unpleasant to certain people.'

'Of course, we offer violence where violence is due. But we are quite selective in this respect. My people are given a great deal of . . . ah . . . latitude in this area. They are chosen for their dispassionate outlook. When they come to us for interview, Mongo, our candidates are given a small tame mouse to hold in their right hands. They are subjected to the most stressful questions we can devise, including many insulting references to their mothers. If the mouse survives, we generally take them on staff – the people, not the mice. This is the best way we know to identify the most resolute individuals. But then, we do get through a great many pet mice.'

Roger chuckles. I have no idea whether I should be taking this man seriously or not.

'So, you see, Mongo, you were never in any real danger from my men.'

'Stop calling me Mongo.'

'Ach, my friend, you just murdered the mouse,' announces Van Huis with a frown. 'I have been observing your hands, Michael. You failed. In the local community, my interview technique has become so well known that any kind of failure is known as "*muis-moorden*" or "murdering the mouse".'

'How proud you must be.'

He produces a couple of booklets from his jacket pocket, one green, the other blue.

'Roger, these are for your dear ones, as promised. In the short time I was only able to get one American passport, the other is the closest I could find. Still, they must go now. Then you and I will talk.'

Roger flips open the green booklet. A Mexican passport in the name of Miguel Hernandes. Inside is a thick sheaf of

American dollars. He hands it all to me. The guy in the picture is actually a few years older than I am and has a proper, fully featured face, long dark hair and the same complexion.

The American passport is for Livia: her name is Dorothy Ettie Mortimor Dalrymple; the photo looks like she might have done at fourteen if she had a big round sweaty white face, then swallowed a wasp.

Roger takes my head in his hands and kisses me on the forehead.

'Michael . . . Miguel. With these passports, you can go anywhere you like, and be anything you like, for however long you've got. You've earned it, you deserve it.'

He grips Livia and repeats the valediction.

A black limousine pulls up beside us.

We climb inside, still foul and stinking of old vomit. Livia is enveloped in the folds of Roger's old tweed jacket. I let her go first on the off-chance that she might flash her wonderful bum at me again.

We settle back into forgiving seats, smearing greasy vomit across the beige calf-skin upholstery.

'Where to, Dorothy Ettie?'

'Good question, Michael. What d'you reckon?'

'I do have one idea . . .'

Epilogue

Circus Circus, Las Vegas

*Up there he cannot be judged by appearance. Neither ugly,
nor beautiful, a thin black pencil line in the air. He tiptoes to
the edge of the board,* en pointe *almost, arms outstretched
like a sleepwalker. Then explodes in a blur of motion, a kind
of human pyrotechnic, whirling, spinning, fizzing as gravity
takes hold.*

*Below, the high-rollers, men who have trained themselves
to reveal nothing, are often moved to inhale sharply and with
approval.*

*He is what they would like to be: a man who can stand
on the edge and risk it all. The consummate gambler.*

He has nothing to fear, nothing to lose.

Not even his trunks.

*For this Miguel, like all true Miguels, wears a one-piece
black leotard which remains just so when he hits the surface
of the three-metre-wide tub below.*

*The Circus Circus regulars are inclined to appreciate
Miguel in any case, since most of them owe him a small fortune and he is lax about pressing his claims.*

*Naturally, Miguel has advantages at the table: a face like
the Nullarbor Desert, which reveals nothing to the casual*

traveller, an aggressive fearlessness, a certain notoriety. And let's not forget the beautiful, unnerving, slightly enigmatic figure always at his shoulder.

Usually, I wear a loose, white silk dress and make sure to bend low across the table when I help Miguel scoop his winnings.

Fuck, men are so easily put off their game.

Typically, perversely, Miguel and I prosper and flourish here in the desert.

I'd like to have spent more time in Europe, but with a wad of hard cash and a Mex passport in hand, Miguel insisted on the first available flight to Acapulco, where we hooked up with the Clavadista.

Amazingly, Miguel does have an aptitude and might have stayed for ever. But of course, we're on borrowed time.

Mine, as it turns out.

Michael's time-stutters have increased in both length and frequency. It seems Doc Darrow was right: these are periods of nano-sleep. Miguel's brain is repairing itself. He's sleeping – not as you and I know it, but parts of his brain are briefly but effectively shutting down from time to time and regenerating, doing whatever it is that sleep does. This is good news for Miguel, though he refuses to accept it, conflicting as it does with his philosophy of fatalism and utter fearlessness. Besides, he's not around to observe himself when he suddenly switches off and starts drooling like a moron for thirty or forty seconds at a stretch.

As for me, I know that the arrhythmia will close my account before I'm twenty-five – they made that abundantly clear during my stay at the Royal Berkshire. Miguel just thinks I'm doing too much toot. All the stuff I'm shoving up my hooter isn't helping of course, no question of that, but I *like to keep pace with Miguel. And fuck it. This is the life I chose. And I did choose it. That's the point.*

So are we happy?

That depends on how you classify happiness.

Some people think it's a state.

Nevada is a state.

Happy is a moment. It's a kiss. A desert dawn; a line of grade-A coke. It's three aces; eight squares of English chocolate; a novel with a plot. It's Roger writing to tell me that he came into a little money and opened the DFC – the Delectable Food Co-operative (the Drug Financed Café just between friends): Mr T. with his useless, blackened claws in the kitchen, bellowing recipes and orders at Mrs H. at the stove, Roger out front, schmoozing the clientele. It's the news that Gerry is thriving in his new role as founder and chairman of the Society for the Prevention of Cruelty to Plants (soon to be the Royal Society for the Prevention of Cruelty to Plants, now that Prince Charles has expressed a keen interest in becoming its patron). By all accounts the organization is extremely well funded by the legacies of dotty old ladies who want to ensure that their rose bushes remain in good hands. It sounds like a scam, but it could actually be for real. Probably a bit of both, knowing Gerry.

Happy is knowing that Coombs sits night after night barricaded in that house, terrified of reprisals, overdosing on caffeine pills, too frightened to sleep.

Happy is a cloud with a silver lining.

At a pinch you might describe us as content. Miguel and I kiss and touch passionately and often, but we're tentative when it comes to the squelchy stuff: in case he explodes my heart; in case he's screwing his great-aunt or second cousin twice removed.

But, as he says to the kids who flock to his matinee

performances: You cannot begin to live unless you take your-self to the edge. So I live in hope.

And in Las Vegas.

Which is a fucking great town for those who never sleep.